Paradise Unfallen

Chuck Richardson

Published by Robert C. Richardson, 2026.

Table of Contents

Dedication

This book is dedicated to the Lord Jesus Christ and to the sanctifying work the Holy Spirit performs within the church. When we rise from the waters of baptism with our sins washed away, the most amazing work of God begins, our transformation into the image of Jesus Christ.

Hebrews 5:8-10

"Although He was a Son, He learned obedience from the things which He suffered. And having been perfected, He became the source of eternal salvation for all those who obey Him, being designated by God as High Priest according to the order of Melchizedek."(NAS)

Copyright Notice

Paradise Unfallen

Cover design: 100 Covers

Interior Design: Chuck Richardson

Editor: Esther LoPresto, Ink-Stained Pages

PUBLISHED BY: Robert C. Richardson

Library Cataloging Data

Names: Richardson, Robert C. (Robert C. Richardson)

Paradise Unfallen / Robert C. Richardson

ISBN-13: 979-8-9927258-1-0 (paperback) | 979-8-9927258-2-7 (hardback) | 979-8-9927258-0-3 (e-book)

Endorsements

What might our world be like if Adam and Eve had never sinned? That's the thought-provoking, spiritual quest Chuck Richardson invites readers to imagine in *Paradise Unfallen*, a beautifully constructed, fictional account of the first man and woman on an imaginary planet similar to Earth. This story grabbed my attention from the beginning and kept me page-turning all the way to the satisfying end. As a regular reader of non-fiction, this book surprised me with the power of fiction to delve into serious issues of life and faith. I recommend *Paradise Unfallen* to any adult who enjoys a good story, imagination, and theological pondering.

—**Ben Wilder**, Bestselling author of *Jesus in the Buddha Belt: Untold True Stories of a Mighty God and Messy Mission*

In *Paradise Unfallen* Chuck Richardson takes you for a walk on the dark side—temptation, spiritual warfare, the consequences of disobedience. But you don't stay there. When Solis receives a divine command in a dream, we see the challenges of duty, sacrifice, and obedience. But also see the reward. Chuck's command of storytelling will take you on a thrilling adventure that'll make you smile, but also consider what changes you can make in your life to enjoy a oneness with the holy trinity.

—**Larry J. Leech II**, writing coach of award-winning authors

If you like alternate histories and parallel worlds, and you love the Lord, read on! *Paradise Unfallen* shows what would happen on Earth's twin, Erimea, if its first man and woman, Solis and Livi, forego the forbidden fruit and remain in their garden, Chara. Satan and his minions won't give up that easily as God charges His people to multiply and rule their paradise and planet. Blending sci-fi, spiritual warfare, and biblical wisdom, *Paradise Unfallen* presents the ultimate what-if and uplifts readers on Adam and Eve's broken world.

—**Jason William Karpf**, award-winning Christian sci-fi author.

Paradise Unfallen offers readers a vivid and immersive journey through the depths of the human experience, focusing on the enduring challenge of maintaining your faith and obedience to the Creator. Set against a backdrop of relentless and aggressive demonic warfare, the novel masterfully portrays the struggle between good and evil, allowing readers to connect deeply with the characters and their battles.

Throughout the novel, unexpected twists and turns serve to keep the reader engaged and invested in the outcome. Each new development adds excitement and intrigue, ensuring that the reader remains immersed in the story and eager to discover the conclusion of this adventurous journey.

—**Larry Sanders**, Elder Newburg Church of Christ, Louisville, KY

What would the battle between good and evil look like on a planet where humanity hadn't rebelled against God? *Paradise Unfallen* follows the exploits of Solis and Livi, the first couple on Erimea, the sister planet to Earth, as they discover the new world God created and struggle against the attacks of Lucido and his army of demons. Chuck Richardson skillfully weaves a story of faith, suspense, and exploration that challenges your thinking and leaves you in awe of the God of the universe.

—**Carol Schlorff**, author of *How to Kill a Giant* and *How to Make a Miracle*

Erimean Calendar

Erimeans use the traditional Hebrew accounting of days with the days beginning and ending at sunset.

First month: Shap
Second month: Brea
Third month: Awak
Fourth month: Nam
Fifth month: Helpe
Sixth month: Marri
Seventh month: Unio
Eighth month: Mult
Ninth month: Teac
Tenth month: Bui
Eleventh month: Rul
Twelfth month: Atta

Content Preview

Rated PG-13 for mild violence, fade-to-black sexual content, and spiritual warfare."

Chapter One

Garden of Chara, Year 1, Shap, Day 6

On the sixth day of creation, Erimea stood poised for human hands to shape it; every good thing awaiting their tender touch.

The Lord God knelt in the dirt, scooped up a man-sized portion of soil, and molded it like clay. When the soil had the form the Lord God desired, he breathed into it. The form became a living soul.

Solis. The first. A model for all who would follow.

At the same time, the Lord God breathed life into Adam, Solis's twin brother on Earth.

The Lord God said to the animals, "This is your new master and ruler. He shall be called Solis, for he was taken from the soils of Erimea."

Creatures hopped, turned, and twisted, attuned to the voice of God. From towering trees and sprawling green shrubs to flowers bursting in blue, yellow, and red, all listened. Slippery river dwellers of silver, green, and black peeked from the rushing currents, while curious critters emerged from the tall grass, eager to behold their new master.

Yet, unseen enemies searched for the weakness of this new creation.

"Solis, you are human," Lord God said to the man, "and I am the Lord God who made you and everything you see. I made you in my image. Therefore, you are to abide by my every word so you can rule well over all I have made. I place Erimea into your care and protection."

"I am Solis." The man lifted his head and made eye contact with the Lord. "I will live by your word."

"You will be a great man and teacher to your children. This world will be blessed because of you, if you keep my words. I shall never abandon you; do not falter during hardship. I have given you a mind to remember, so you can lead your descendants."

Solis laughed to himself. "I am the ruler of everything." He puffed out his chest. "I will be great."

"What do you want to do right now?"

With steady dark eyes, Solis peered into God's face as if to absorb his essence. "I wish to learn and understand." Solis placed one hand on God's cheek. The other hand, he wrapped around his own chin. "We are both warm. The Lord breathed into me, and I became a living soul. Are you me?"

The Lord took the man's hands, gentle yet strong. "I am not you, and you are not me. But if you walk in my ways, you will become like me."

"I will become like Lord God." The man turned in a slow circle to gaze at God, the animals, and the surrounding garden, eyes wide with wonder. "Yes, and we will be one."

"We may become one if you walk in my ways."

"Am I not merely soil? Dirt? Is the dirt alive and aware?" Solis turned and knelt in the soil from which he had been taken. He scooped up some, and tiny creatures scurried to escape his hand. "Is this like me?" Solis showed it to the Lord God. "Do I have such things crawling through my body?" Solis released the soil and watched the remaining bits of dirt descend to the ground as he brushed his hands. "I know some things, but I perceive that you, Lord God, know all things. I want to be you."

The Lord God laughed. "You are my beloved son, and you have so many questions. Did I not make you myself? When I breathed into you, I gave instructions to every part of your body. To your mind, I added memory."

A small, fat, furry animal with a bushy tail pressed its soft paws on Solis's feet as it crossed between him and the Lord. It stretched toward a nearby bush and munched on berries.

"What's this?" Solis picked up the creature. "Is that good for eating, *pouchy cheeks*?" The man sampled the berries and fed some to the hungry beast. "These are tasty. Thanks for letting me know." Solis stroked pouchy cheeks and placed it on the ground. "I have a memory?"

"I've given your body and mind the information needed. Other things you must learn. If you love me, walk in my ways."

"I love you, Lord. My heart burns when you speak. Let me be like you now."

The Lord nodded and stroked Solis's midnight-black hair, thick and silky. "It will take time. Though I took you from the soil, you are not the soil. You live. The soil is not alive."

"I want to create."

"You will build and create."

"I want to take the soil and give it the breath of life, so it will be like me."

"Some things only God can do."

Solis lowered his head and frowned. "I want to create life, as you do."

"You will take part in bringing new life into the world."

"Yes, new life like me." Solis clapped. "Let's do it now."

"Not now. You have much to learn."

Solis grinned. "Learn to wait." He looked around at the plants. "What else is there to eat? I'm hungry."

The Lord God carried Solis through the garden and showed him every edible tree and plant. In the middle of the garden, the Lord God placed Solis before two trees. One was the tree of life. The other was the tree of the knowledge of good and evil.

"You may eat from any tree in the Garden," the Lord God said, "except the tree of the knowledge of good and evil. If you eat from the tree of the knowledge of good and evil, you will die."

"What is the knowledge of good and evil?"

"Something you do not need to find out."

Solis raised his chin and smiled. "Maybe it's something I will learn on my own?"

"Remember my command. You may eat from any tree in the Garden except from the tree of the knowledge of good and evil."

"Yes, Lord God."

"What is it you want to do now?"

"To learn this place." The man strode through the garden greenery and examined everything that caught his attention. "I am Solis. I am master, ruler, and caretaker of the Garden of Chara."

The Lord God clapped Solis on the shoulder. "Yes, you are." The Lord disappeared.

Only one creature objected to his new ruler and grumbled in his language, "No. Never. Never my master ... Return to dirt." His forked tongue flicked in and out as he surveyed for food. Sometimes, he crawled on all fours, and other times, he walked on two legs. He wiggled his long, thin body and a triangle-shaped head on his way. This creature was more self-aware and craftier than the others. He called himself Sizraar.

Lucido, leader of the rebel spirits, observed the exchange between Solis and the Lord from a spiritual domain engulfed in billowing winds and the haze of a raging sea. His darkling insight allowed Lucido to see and hear what was happening wherever he focused his attention.

He turned and spat. "The creature wants to become like the Creator. Can dirt attain such a lofty position? Foolishness."

He towered above his chief lieutenants, Mactan and Vik. Lucido smiled as his worker angels constructed Aetherdon, City of the Air, a royal dwelling for his glory. Most fallen angels had mottled skin of green and gray laced with scars. Burn marks from the lake of fire. The rebels had mangled limbs and fingers that had become deformed while they struggled to break free from the chains that once held them. Lucido's countenance still held remnants of its original luminescence, yet dimmed by the flames of hell. He remained a beacon of hope for his followers.

Mactan's yellow eyes bulged. "What are we going to do about the man's foolishness?"

"Observe until we find a point of attack. First on Erimea and then on Earth."

"Look how God has misshapen us." Mactan beat his breast with gnarled claws. "I want revenge now."

"Patience, Mactan." Lucido marched through the crowd of angry demons and growled. "I vow we will oppose the work of God and men at every turn. One day, God will regret his obsession with humanity. He will fall before me and worship me. The throne will be mine. The universe will be ordered as I suggested long ago. Do not fret. Payback is coming."

Chapter Two

Solis measured distances by counting his paces. When he had proceeded fourteen paces, the ground shook and something big lumbered straight for him. He gasped and whirled around to escape, but there stood a great, four-legged, brownish-gray beast covered in mud. Solis crashed into the animal's snout and barely missed being impaled on a horn that rose from the creature's nose. A second horn grew directly behind the first. A moment later, another beast of the same type appeared next to it.

Solis caught his breath. "What are you? You scared me."

The pair eyed Solis through half-closed lids, and they snacked on the shrubs growing around the tree of life.

Solis examined the creatures, which had hooked upper lips and hairy ears like tubes that stood upright and wiggled as they ate. The beasts had great, wide pot bellies and rough, lumpy skin. They were of the same kind, but with differences that he described as *male* and *female*. "The Lord sent you to me for a name. You shall be called *nose horn*."

As the nose horns departed, other animals approached Solis. He thought carefully about the designs the Lord God had given them. He chose many wonderful names for the Lord's creatures, such as *featherone*, *bump back*, and *climber*.

When the animals stopped coming, Solis continued his trek through the garden. Gradually, he realized he couldn't see well. "What is it?" He rubbed his eyes, but the light around him continued to fade. "Why can't I see clearly?" Solis returned to the riverbank where God had formed him. The night's darkness engulfed him for the first time.

Solis stretched out on the ground. Dark gray clouds blanketed the sky. The river broke against rocks. The water's sound and scent comforted Solis. The cloud curtain drifted and introduced a great white circle and a broad expanse of tiny points of light. Darkness fled.

Solis reached out. "Lord God, what is it? Why can't I touch it?"

The Lord God appeared and sat next to Solis. "It's one of two great lights I have placed over Erimea. This light shines at night. The other shines during the day. What do you want to call it?"

Solis studied the sky. "It shall be called *glow*, for it shines in the darkness and comforts me. If I touch it, I'll understand it. Let me fly across the sky."

"Glow is too far away to touch. In time, you will understand things that cannot be touched."

"Explain the tiny dots that shimmer. What are they?"

"They're like the light that shines on Erimea during the—"

"Day." A grin spread across Solis's face. "It gives light to all things on Erimea. How?"

"The light that shines in the day is a fire, a burning ball of gases and—"

"Burning gases?" Solis's brow furrowed as he tried to decipher the meaning.

"Yes, my son. Burning gases give light. What will you call the light that illuminates the day?"

"There is power there?"

"Yes, great power."

"It shall be called *daylight*. Lord God, teach me to harness the power of daylight."

"It's not for you to harness the power of daylight. That's reserved for your distant descendants. Your work is here on Erimea."

"My descendants?" Solis raised his eyebrows and smiled. "If the tiny dots of light are like daylight, they must be very, very far away. That's why they appear very small?"

"Yes, you are correct. What will you call them to distinguish them from daylight?

"They shall be called *distant daylight*. No. *Distant glow*." Solis shook his head. "No. They shall be called *sparkles*, for they sparkle in the night sky."

"Can you count the sparkles?

"I've already counted them. Two thousand six hundred twenty-four. How did they get there?"

"I put them there."

Solis sat up and leaned toward the Lord. "And where did you get them?"

"I made them."

"From what did you make them?"

The Lord chuckled. "Your questions are endless. There was a time when there was nothing but God."

"Nothing but God? Now I'm here to keep you company."

The Lord explained how daylight and glow could be used to track the passage of time in quarters of daylight and night, days, weeks, months, and years.

"From now on, you are to keep track of the days. For six days, do your work, but on every seventh day, you are to rest from all your labor."

Solis pondered names for the days and months as the conversation came to a close.

"You're my beloved son," the Lord God told him. In a blink, he was gone.

Solis basked in the love of the Lord, his gaze still on the sky. The burning gases of the sparkles, so far away, fascinated Solis. How could he make light? He closed his eyes and slept on the riverbank from which he had been taken.

The demon Vik crept closer to Solis's bedside. "Do you really want to become like God?"

From his slumber, Solis answered, "Yes, I will become like God."

Vik sneered. "You will *never* be like God. You are ignorant, a big pile of dirt."

Solis did not respond.

"But perhaps there is one way you can become like God."

Solis tossed and turned in his sleep. "Who are you?"

"A friend."

"How can I, a lump of clay, become like God?"

"Rest now. We will let you know soon."

Chapter Three

Solis woke while darkness still filled the garden. The words "a big pile of dirt" echoed in his ears. What did that mean? Where had it come from?

"It's what I was." He spat out the words. "Should I be ashamed? I'll become much more." Why had he thought such a rotten thing?

Several dozing creatures surrounded his bed by the river. He sat still, but his pulse quickened as he resumed studying the Garden of Chara in the growing morning light. The silence of night gave way to a symphony of featherones, insects, and other creatures announcing their pleasure at the day's dawning. Animals stirred from sleep, and others that had been foraging for food all night settled down to rest.

Daylight rose over the eastern mountains—first dark blue, then with reddish-orange and yellow lights reflecting through the clouds. Near the ground in the distance, an uneven black line formed against the light. As daylight rose, the ragged black line became clearer: the top of a distant green hedge that circled the garden. Far to the south, a black-and-gray rock formation interrupted the hedge, rising high above it. Solis planned to explore the rock and the hedge later in the day.

Solis's animal companions drifted to the river and drank. Solis crawled on his hands and knees over the short, squishy distance to the water's edge. He splashed the water with his hands.

"It's wet." He laughed as water droplets streamed down his hands and arms. With both hands, Solis scooped up some water and drank it. "It's good. Delicious. I've discovered water," he exulted with both hands raised. He waded in the water and threw it on his face. Its moisture and coolness refreshed his waking body and mind.

Solis splashed water on the animals lying on the bank and chuckled at their bewildered gazes. As he reached for another handful, Solis paused and peered into the water.

"More creatures in the water? How do they breathe? The big swallow the small alive. Is this permitted?" Solis reached his hands into the water repeatedly to block the wriggling creatures. He twisted around and called to the animals resting on the riverbank, "They're ever turning this way and that ... breathing water? These water creatures shall be called *always turnings*."

Solis crouched and pushed his feet against the riverbank, propelling himself underwater toward the middle of the river. His head broke above the water's surface, and he drew a deep breath. With a shake of his head, he flung water off his hair and skin. His feet no longer touched the riverbed.

A rush of undercurrent dragged Solis away from the bank and yanked him underwater for several seconds before he bobbed back above the surface, arms flailing. "Lord, save me."

The current overpowered him. Again, he went under and came up screaming. The land jutted out into the river and slowed the flow, but the water was still too deep for Solis to stand. He was about to go down a third time. As he tried to avoid breathing the liquid death, his mind flashed back to when he had enjoyed his first taste of sweet, refreshing water. Now, it would be the end of him. Why?

The Lord God stood on the bank and shouted, "Swim, Solis." The Lord motioned with his arms.

Solis beat his arms against the water until he got close enough to shore for his feet to touch the riverbed. He pushed hard, straining with his legs toward the Lord. His leg muscles burned as he stood and attempted to walk in the waist-deep water. He slipped and smacked his knee on the rocks. He again sank beneath the water and floated downstream.

Solis popped back up, coughing water, and crawled on all fours to the riverbank. There he lay, spitting up water. Water dribbled down his chin and aching chest. The water had turned treacherous and attacked his lungs with intent to kill.

The Lord God waited while Solis recovered, then squatted at his side. "Why were you so afraid?"

Solis beat the ground with a desperate cry and staggered to his feet with petulant stomps. "Why didn't you save me? I could have ... I could have—"

"What?" The Lord stood, compassion in his eyes.

"I could have ... died?"

"Do you know what death is?"

"It means to be sucked into the river, the way one always turning beast sucks in another and eats it. Why do you permit it?"

"Are you afraid of being eaten by the river?

"Of course." Solis hid his trembling by kicking at the mud puddle beneath him. He pointed to the river. "It's dangerous. A living beast."

"Do you remember the promises I made to you about your children?"

"Yes, Lord."

"Do you believe my word?"

"Yes, Lord."

"Then, no longer be afraid. Remember, I'm always with you. Call on me, but do everything to save yourself."

"Yes, Lord." Solis bent to examine his knee, which throbbed with pain and oozed a red substance. "Ouch. What is this?"

"You've injured yourself and broken your skin. That's your blood."

"My blood must stay in, or else I could die?"

"Yes, if you lose too much blood, your body could die. Life is in the blood."

"Lord, what is death?"

"Death is the end of life. When you eat the fruit of a plant, that part of the plant dies and becomes sustenance for you."

"I intend to care for the plants and animals so they will live."

"Yes, but I determine when they live and die. Upon death, certain animals and the tiniest of organisms grind the remains to dust. By my design, the dust rejoins the ground."

Solis shuddered at the thought. "I don't want to die. The grinding is frightful."

"Your body is perishable, but the leaves of the tree of life restore you. You are different from the animals because you are made in my image, and your spirit comes from me. If you obey my commands, you will never die."

"In the water, I saw one always turning eat another. This isn't permitted, is it?"

"I've given *you* plants and trees as a source of food. Do not go beyond what I have said."

Solis accepted the reprimand with a nod. He determined in his heart he would obey the Lord's commands.

The Lord God extended his hand. "Come. It's time for you to continue exploring."

Solis stood and brushed dirt from his legs. "Lord God, water is great. It tastes delicious and has amazing functions. Why did you make it so dangerous?"

"Many great things are dangerous, but you must master them all. Return to your work, but first go to the river, wash off the mud, and clean your wound."

Solis stood at the river's edge and watched the last of the water droplets roll down his legs. The water washed away all traces of mud and blood. He felt good. Refreshed. But why? Shouldn't he still be furious? He could have died. Why did the Lord allow it?

Should Solis be unafraid to die because of the Lord's promises? Did God have the power to bring him back to life? Should Solis throw himself back into the water?

Throw his life away to test—

That's exactly what you need to do. Put the Lord God to the test. Surely he will raise you back to life. A different voice infiltrated his mind, completely unlike his own or the calming voice of the Lord.

Solis considered the idea as if it had originated with him. He didn't want to die to find out if it was true. He had to be a master of all things, including himself. He must not disappoint God. Why did the Lord's words stir his heart so?

Solis sighed deeply and then drew the air back into his lungs. He resumed his walk through the garden, following the river.

A new creature bounded through the forest, moving from side to side as though the ground propelled it. It stopped a short distance from Solis and blew air out its nostrils in a great snort and sniffed the air before walking closer. A short brown-and-white fur coat covered its body, and small multi-pronged horns rose from its head.

Solis examined the animal. A male. As it turned to go, it gave several drawn-out whooshes from its nostrils. Several others of its kind came leaping through the air to meet it.

"Your name shall be *wild breath*."

The rock formation Solis had spotted earlier was not far away. He quickened his pace, anxious to climb it and have a look around at the garden from above. Before Solis went much farther, he came upon another creature rooting around in the ground with its snout. A low, stocky, and powerfully built beast with tusks. Sparse hair bristles covered its coarse black-and-gray hide. A female in distress dug a hole and made a nest layered with leaves.

"What's wrong with you, *rooter*? Why are you unhappy?"

Solis examined the animal as she lay shivering. He felt movement in her belly. Suddenly, she pushed a tiny creature out of her body. With a gasp, Solis stumbled back and landed hard on the ground. The beast was creating more of her kind. Solis watched the creature carefully as another baby came forth from a birth canal. In a short time, ten more emerged. Each wasted no time in searching for a teat on the mother and greedily suckled.

"Are they sucking the life out of you, mama rooter? Solis observed this miracle of reproduction. He looked around for a male rooter, but he saw none. Solis recalled seeing male animals mount females of the same kind. This must be the result of that activity.

God had formed animals from the dust of the ground, but each produced more of its kind on its own. Soon, the garden would overflow with wild beasts.

Chapter Four

Sizraar trailed the man and hunkered down while Solis studied the rooter. God had commanded all animals to come to Solis, so Sizraar had grudgingly obeyed. He remained hidden in the growth of the garden for a fast departure after he complied with the letter of the Lord's command.

Sizraar crouched low and flattened his body defensively. He couldn't understand why the man was so fascinated by every beast and plant in the garden. Only food interested Sizraar, so he was wary of the man's intentions.

Why did he hate the man? Sizraar simply did not want anyone or anything to rule over him. He lost sight of the man, but he flicked out his tongue and still smelled his stench.

Solis sprang from behind a tree and swept Sizraar into his arms. "Don't be afraid."

Sizraar struggled against the man's grip.

"Whoa, you're a slippery fellow."

He hissed in Solis's face.

Solis's eyes grew stern. "Stop. I'm your friend."

Sizraar clawed the man and snapped, but Solis grabbed the beast's neck and shook it. He went limp.

"I'm going to let you go. Don't run away."

When the man released him, Sizraar fell to the ground and thrashed around for a moment. Slowly, Sizraar rose on two legs with his head reaching to the man's chest and glared at the man with lidless green eyes. The man's compassion made the creature hate him even more.

"Now we are friends. Yes?" Solis petted the beast.

Sizraar flicked out his tongue and wiggled his spine.

"You don't have to be afraid." Solis examined the creature. "You shall be called *sneaking thing*, because you have followed me for a long time, sneaking along in fear. You are free to go."

Sizraar scrambled away, seeking a place where he could bask in the dayshine and eat flies and toads. Soon, Sizraar forgot all about the man, but there remained in the beast an inexplicable resentment and disgust for his new ruler.

Solis followed the main river and discovered it watered the garden with many branching tributaries. He named the river Sweet Water Whirlwind, because it was a terrible beast giving life and death. He found debris clogged certain streams that branched from the river. Solis complained to the Lord God. "Why have you allowed this to become so overgrown? This stream has become choked with debris. It's a tangled mess."

The Lord God did not appear. "Who have I assigned to be caretaker of this garden?"

Solis didn't reply.

"Solis, you do your work, and I'll do mine."

A grin spread across Solis's face. "Yes, Lord." The Lord's patience pleased Solis. He trekked south along the river path over beaten-down grass. When he had walked two thousand six hundred paces from the tree of life, Solis reached the rock formation at the garden's southern boundary. It rose with a sheer face to a great height, which Solis estimated was thirty times his own height. He called it Tall Stony.

Solis climbed up the vertical surface, but he stopped and retreated when he spotted a steep path offering a safer way up. He reached the top and found a thick hedge. He pushed through the thick, scratchy bushes and saw the land sloping down into a valley.

Sweet Water Whirlwind River flowed under Tall Stony and divided into four great rivers beyond the Garden of Chara. He turned back to the Garden and sat at the top of the rock formation. In the distance stood the tree of life. The thick hedge encircled the Garden, except for an opening far to his right. A large tributary of the great river curved around the foothills that sloped down from Tall Stony. Daylight shone down on Solis. With an upturned face, Solis basked in the warm rays of light.

An irregular scraping sound grew louder. Several small animals had climbed up the sheer face of Tall Stony. They licked the rocks as they went. Solis's eyes widened. They had horns and hooves like wild breaths, but they were much smaller. "How do you do that without hands? You are the *cliff steppers* and *rock eaters*." Other small beasts crawled quickly over the rocks, in and out of crevices. They had forked tongues and long tails, though some were missing their tails. Solis called these *rock darters*.

Bzz ... bzz ... bzz

Small flying creatures buzzed around a nest made in the rocks at the top of Tall Stony.

"You are *busy buzzing bees*."

Solis reached into the nest. The bees swarmed around him, but they didn't sting him. When Solis pulled his hand back, a sticky substance covered it. He tasted it.

"Mmm. So sweet. So many surprises here. It shall be called *golden sweet*." With delight, he licked it off his hands. "Golden sweet is a gift from the Lord."

Savoring golden sweet, Solis again stared into the distance at the garden scenery, but he quickly shifted his gaze to look straight down. Seeing the height he had climbed surprised and thrilled him, so Solis drank in the view. As spectacular as the sticky sweetness.

A dark tone whispered in his mind: *You have no fear. Jump. Do it now. You want to do it. Throw yourself down. Surely the Lord God will save you.*

"No, I'll never put the Lord to the test." What were these strange thoughts? Why was he having them? Solis climbed down the steep path, measuring each step. At the base of Tall Stony, he gazed up at the sheer face of the rugged natural structure of gray, white, and green.

"One day, I'm going to climb up that way like the cliff steppers and rock darters. That will be fun, and golden sweet will be my reward. Lord God will see the strength of Solis, mighty caretaker of the garden." He chuckled at his embellished title.

Lucido screwed his face into a grimace. "Where is his desire for glory? Why won't he test the Lord?

Vik said, "The man is ambitious and proud. He wants to show his prowess by climbing the rock formation he calls Tall Stony.

"Ambition and pride." Lucido nodded. "We'll use those to expose his inner corruption."

"Or to kill him." Mactan's eyes danced as he spoke.

Lucido said, "Take a look at that sneaking thing. He's hostile to Solis. Perhaps we can

use him to bring down the man."

On the return journey to the tree of life, Solis came to a stream that had formed a small, calm pool of water, and he stretched out at the water's edge. When he reached down, he spotted a face. Solis gasped and drew back. The face in the water did the same. What creature was this? It didn't look like any of the other animals, yet it looked familiar.

"Come out from under there. Do not be afraid."

Solis peered over the edge and spied the face peeking back at him. It mirrored his every movement. He laughed at himself. "I believe it's my own face."

Solis examined his head and shoulders. A dark brown face with dark eyes. His face was smooth—no facial hair—but on his head was a thick crown of black curls that reminded him of the dense green shrubs adorning the garden. He ran his fingers through his hair, pressing and pulling at it. His hair sprang back a little when he removed his hand, but it continued to stick out where he pulled it.

He stood and splashed across the pool on his way back to the tree of life. Solis had not thought much about his own appearance. The Lord God had made so many other wonderful things to examine. Now, he looked at his arms and legs and saw fine black hair, but not much compared to the animals he had seen. His skin was softer than many beasts of the Garden. And his upright two-legged stance did not match his mostly four-legged companions. His hands were different too.

Solis's lips parted in wonder, and he shook his head. He knew whose face his resembled. Quickly, he returned to the pool. When he knelt close to the still waters, he smiled in delight. In his reflection, Solis saw his appearance was like that of Lord God. The thought made his chest expand. There was even a slight glow around his face. Solis held his face with both hands. "One puzzlement after another."

Chapter Five

When Solis arrived at the tree of life, he scanned the area. He studied the ground, the animals, the grass, the plants, the trees, and the fruits on the trees. "Everything here has changed slightly. Lord, you keep tinkering and changing this place."

The Lord God sat under the tree of life. "Do you suppose the Lord tinkers to no effect?"

Solis jerked his head in the Lord's direction. "The Lord is always lurking—"

"For your good, my son. Sit with me here."

Solis sat near the Lord.

"What do you want to ask me?"

While he enjoyed all of God's creation, he felt himself lacking in some way. "Why is there no one suitable here for me? Other animals are male and female. I'm male, alone."

"You are correct. It is not good for you to be alone. We'll make a female, a helper suitable for you."

"We? Let's make her right now." Solis jumped up and paced.

"It will be soon enough. She'll come out of your own body. Only wait a little longer."

"Lord, how is that possible, since I don't have a birth canal like I've seen on female animals?"

"I'll explain everything to you. Soon, there will be children, and you will teach them to tend the garden, and you will teach them about me. Now, return and sit."

Solis hurried to the Lord's side. "I saw my face in a pool of water. I look like you, Lord."

"Indeed, I made you in my image."

He grinned and clapped. "I knew it. I'm like you. That's what I want."

"You have much to learn first."

Solis's gaze dropped to the ground. "Yes, I'm ignorant like the dirt ... Teach me everything, so I'll be a wise teacher, like you. But first tell me who you are. What is your name?"

"I am who I am. I am the Lord your God. You may call me Iam."

"Iam, what was it like for you to be alone? Before you created me."

"We have never been alone. We are one, and invite you to become one with us."

"We?" Solis's brow furrowed. "Who is *we*? You're alone like me."

"No, we have never been alone. My Father and I and our Holy Spirit are one God. We have been bound together in love from before the creation of the world."

"How can that be? How can three different persons be one God? Please let me understand."

"There is much you cannot understand. Only believe I am who I am." Lord God described the relationship between the Father, Son, and Holy Spirit that allowed them to be one God in three persons. "Such an existence, such oneness, is wonderful and beautiful."

Solis shook his head. "I don't understand."

"We will make a helper suitable for you, and you may begin to comprehend how different persons can become one." The Lord God disappeared.

Solis slumped against the tree of life. "I'm even more alone than I knew. Why didn't he make my mate and me at the same time?"

God does not understand, said an unnerving voice in Solis's mind. *He has everything, and you have nothing. Death is better than waiting any longer.*

Solis bowed his head and tapped his fingers against his chin. "No, I'll wait on the Lord God, but I feel ... Where do these thoughts come from?"

Vik gave Mactan a hard smile. "Death? My brother, Mactan, a temptation to die does not fit the moment. He may become aware of our presence before the proper time."

"No, my brother, you don't understand. The continual suggestion of death as an option will eventually take root in his heart."

Lucido stepped in. "We must instill in the man discontentment leading to despair before death will become a desirable choice. Yet, this could be an opportune time. We must—"

"Yes, let us press the attack," Mactan interrupted.

Lucido continued as if he hadn't spoken, "We must teach the man the truth that God only seeks to justify his punishments on all who choose to think freely." He raised his hands and beckoned them closer. "My dear brothers, how wrongly God has treated those of us who refuse to submit to his arbitrary rules. We asked only to be free, and he blasted us with fire and brimstone. Soon, we shall blast all God holds dear."

Chapter Six

The air stilled around Solis. Thickness in the atmosphere weighed on his shoulders as if he carried a burden. The featherones did not sing. He stood in the shadow of the tree of life. Daylight still shone above, but gloom engulfed Solis within. He fell to his knees.

What is man? I bear the image of the Lord. I look like him, but I'm not like him. He doesn't know what it's like to be alone. My thoughts are not secret. They are laid bare before him. No matter where I turn, he is there. I cannot hide from him. Should I be happy about all this? Why can't I see the promises the Lord has for me? They seem so far away.

The trio of demons surrounded Solis, plotting to increase his agony. Lucido spoke directly into Solis's mind. *You should not be happy at all. God spies on you continually for one purpose: to catch you in a mistake, so he may condemn you.*

Solis vaulted up and cried out, "Dear Lord God, Iam, help me to see what is yet unseen and to wait patiently for the goodness of the Lord."

At the name of the Lord, Lucido, Vik, and Mactan trembled and withered despite themselves.

The Lord commanded the demons, "Leave him alone."

The unclean spirits fled.

"Solis," came the voice of the Lord God.

Solis searched all around. He did not see the Lord, but he knew his voice. "Yes, Lord."

"Arise and eat. You are famished, and you have a long day ahead of you."

When Solis turned, he found a meal prepared by God. Four large leaves with edges curled up like bowls sat before him. One contained an assortment of fruit and grains, another held leafy greens, the third offered golden sweet, and the fourth bowl was full of water.

"Thank you, Lord. Humanity needs to eat a lot of food. I'm humanity." *Hmm. All of humanity is within me. I hadn't thought of that before.* He smiled. The thought heartened and amused Solis. *The welfare of all the children who will be depends on me. I must never forget that.* Solis ate systematically and was careful not to spill anything on the ground. "That was so delicious." When he had eaten everything, including the leafy bowls, he stretched out and took a nap.

The Lord God woke the man. "Arise, resume exploring the flora and fauna. Also, identify the most beautiful location in the garden. When you find it, call me from there."

As Solis wended along, he composed a song and sang it:

"I am
The ground,
But he promises the heavens.
Solitary,
But he promises a wife and children.
Ignorant,
But he promises wisdom.
Innocent,
But he will make me holy.
Dirt,
But he has made me
The son of God."

Solis mused on the lyrics. "I'll call it 'A Song of Promises.'"

Solis proceeded from the tree of life in the opposite direction he had explored previously in search of the most beautiful location in Chara. He was observant of the plants he found because he wanted to find more of the leafy bowls and materials to make other items. He sampled more fruits and vegetables he found along the way.

He discovered a tall plant growing out of the river and its tributaries, and it reminded Solis of the tails on some animals he had seen, so he called them *water tails*. Solis pulled up several of the water tail plants so he could experiment with them later.

The terrain sloped upward and became uneven, so Solis looked for something to make the climb easier. He broke off a sturdy tree branch, grasped smaller limbs, and peeled them from the branch. He used the branch to help him traverse the land. He called it a walking stick. At the bottom, it had a narrow, blunt end. He raised the stick like a scepter, feeling like the ruler he was.

Mactan sneered. "The man wants to be a king."

Vik said, "We already know he wants to be like God while fearing he is just dirt."

Lucido said, "Find a way to use both ideas to tempt the man." He commanded ten unclean spirits to follow Solis. They were to investigate how to get their claws into him.

Solis leaned on the walking stick with each step until he crested the hill and the landscape became level and spread into a field of waving golden grain with a stream running through it. A thick orchard of flowering fruit trees stood beyond the field.

He let out a gentle sigh. "Now this is lovely."

However, the sight of the stream made his heart beat faster until he crept closer and saw its shallow depth and gentle flow. Nothing like the violence of the river Sweet Water Whirlwind. Solis hurried across the stream in twelve quick strides. "You shall not snatch me, small river."

Solis marched toward the orchard, and sweet fragrances met him. Many animals lounged in the orchard and by a stream. Paths ran between the trees, and vines hung from the branches and formed an arch above the pathways. White flowers grew from the trees, and green and purple fruits hung from the vines. Solis pulled two clusters from the vines and tasted the fruit.

"Sweet and sour, you shall be called *berries*," he said. He lay near a tree and took in the surrounding scene as he savored his latest tasty discovery. "Amazing juicy orbs with the smoothest skin. This, your home, must be the most gorgeous spot in the Garden of Chara."

Immediately, animals stampeded down the path.

He jumped up, lest he be trampled. "Four wild breaths, two nose horns, and two giant flying featherones," Solis counted. "Friends, where are you going?"

He raced after the creatures to the edge of the fruit trees and found the source of Sweet Water Whirlwind. Two thousand five hundred twenty-eight paces from the tree of life. Before him stood a tall, wide expanse of black-and-gray stone walls twice the height of Tall Stony.

Roaring torrents of water poured over the walls and out of rocky crevices. The flow ricocheted off rocks that jutted out at various levels and gathered in a foamy basin at the bottom before powering its way around the orchard on its journey through the garden and beyond.

Rocks at the bottom created seven small waterfalls. Some of the water separated from the powerful flow into shallow basins to form calm pools from which the water trickled through narrow channels to rejoin the mother river. Large, flat white rocks protruded above the peaceful water and provided spots to stand or sit. Solis waded into the shallow water and gazed up, spellbound. He bounded across the flat rocks, savoring the cool mist until he was drenched.

The great height from which the water plunged shocked him, and he cried out, "Heaven falls down. You shall be called Heaven Falls because you fall from the heights of heaven."

The rocky walls of Heaven Falls and the flat slabs contained minerals that glittered in the daylight like colored gemstones of silver, gold, green, blue, orange, and red.

The demons recoiled as Solis proclaimed the wonder of Heaven Falls. Images flashed before them of their fates when they fell like lightning from the clouds of glory. For that, they hated Solis even more.

Lucido roared. "Your time is coming, lump of clay. Your time is coming. I swear by my lost throne in heaven that, like these waters, bitter human tears will fall forever."

"What is it, Lord?" Solis trembled at a thundering voice bouncing off the stone walls, but he could not discern the words. He ran back toward the orchard and scanned the dark walls of the falls to see if they crumbled. He waited to see what would happen next, but the only sound that remained was the cascading water.

Soon, Solis returned to his revelry. He walked toward the falls again and raised his walking stick in victory. "This is the spot, Lord, Iam. Heaven Falls at Chara's northern end," Solis continued shouting, though out of breath. "It's Heaven Falls whose beauty cannot be exceeded. This ... this is the place."

The Lord said to the man, "So it is. You have done well. This shall be the place of your wedding."

Chapter Seven

"What is a wedding?" Solis asked.

"It's the ceremony where a man is bound together with his wife. You will have many children and will teach them how to live. Are you ready?"

"Lord, why do you need me to teach my children? You know all things. You should teach them and reveal yourself to them. I'm not needed."

"I will teach them and be with them, but you and your wife will also teach them, for humanity needs humanity to provide an example of how to live. Together, you will demonstrate to your children and all the host of heaven the glory and wisdom of God."

Solis stretched out his arms, palms up. "Lord, can humanity, formed from the dust of Erimea, truly become like God?"

"What is it you want?"

"My dream ... my hope ... is for oneness with my wife. That we may fully know each other so we can be like you, Iam, three persons in one God. Is that possible for humanity?"

"All things are possible with God."

"Then I am ready."

The Lord explained to Solis that he would cause him to fall into a deep sleep, and then open his side, remove one of his ribs, close the incision, and fashion his wife from the bone.

Solis rubbed the back of his neck. "Why didn't you make my wife and me at the same time from the soils of Erimea? Why do I have to be opened? Will my blood spill out? Will I feel the agony of death? Will you restore me to life? I don't like this."

"The path you have willingly chosen, to become like God, is not an easy one, but it is the path I desire for you." The Lord God placed his hands on the man's shoulders and looked into his eyes. "This procedure will not kill you, but in time you will experience joy, agony, and victory if you continue to walk in my ways. There is no other way."

"I don't understand."

"Do you still lament that I am always nearby, knowing your thoughts, ready to appear from thin air without warning?"

Solis's chest burned at the words of the Lord, and he was ashamed, for he knew the love of the Lord. "I no longer lament your presence, Iam. I embrace it. Please forgive my weakness."

"You are a mighty man of valor. The greatest of your kind, for you are the first. Only believe. Now, sleep. This will be a day you'll never forget."

Solis became drowsy, but he fought the pull of sleep to indulge in imagining what his wife and their life together might be like.

Solis could identify each individual animal he met, and he found the animals he observed in acts of reproduction often did not continue as mated pairs. Did not they become one? Perhaps he would rule over her like he did every other part of creation. That idea held a certain appeal. She would do whatever he commanded.

That mysterious voice spoke softly, like a whisper in the wind. *Yes, King Solis, let her be like property to you. One subject to your every whim.*

Solis pondered the idea. The Lord Iam had said, "My Father and I and our Holy Spirit are one God. We have been bound together in love from before the creation of the world." They shared a wonderful and beautiful existence as one God in three persons. But how?

"If I rule over her, how can I be one with her? I must nourish and cherish her as I do myself."

Chapter Eight

The Lord said, "Arise from your slumber and musing. See the goodness of the Lord."

Solis stood and stared into the sky toward the west. A white streak descended from the clouds. Solis said, "Did the Lord take my rib made from Erimean dust and fashion my wife in the heavens? Or is she from a distant land resting under the night sparkles?" The streak circled around the middle of the garden and became a swirling vortex of shimmering lights before disappearing.

The Lord God flew low over the river and cradled the woman in his arms. She felt the rhythm of his heart and knew it matched her own heartbeat. They approached the middle of the garden near the riverbank from which the man had been taken. The Lord placed the woman on his shoulders.

When she saw the shoreline and the area's beauty, a shout burst from her lips. She pumped her arms. The woman jumped to her feet, vaulted from the Lord God, and tumbled on the soft soil of the riverbank, yelling, "Haha, Lord God, my Fatherest. That was fun." She exulted with two handsprings. "You are the greatest Father who will ever be." She scanned her surroundings, squatted, and drew in the soil with her finger.

Lord God said, "What would you like to do?"

She continued drawing for several moments. "I want to become more. I must capture this place and record it forever ... and I want to leap from your shoulders again. Can I please? Only this time, I want to splash into the swirling water where it's deep."

So, the Lord God lifted the woman, and again they flew over Sweet Water Whirlwind.

"My dear Fatherest, with you, I can soar through the clouds and in the misty wet wind."

The Lord pointed, and the woman dove into the river, disappearing into the deep. When she bobbed above the river's surface, she waved her arms and coughed up water. "Save me ... I breathed in the swirl."

He plucked her up. When they stood at the water's edge, the Lord asked, "Were you afraid in the river?"

"For a moment ... but no, I'll never be afraid when you are near. I know you love me. I'm the apple of your eye. I feel it in my soul." The woman again drew in the dirt, and she shaped the dirt with her hands.

"What would you like to do now?"

"I'll stay here and do my work." She looked at the Lord out of the corner of her eye.

"Very well. I'll tell the man the wedding is off for now."

"Just kidding." The woman popped up, grinned, and brushed away dirt. "I'm ready to take possession of the man, my dear and gorgeous husband."

"Will you possess the man? How do you know he's gorgeous?"

She held her arms open wide. "I'll possess him with a heart full of love. I promise to take loving care of him. Do you want to know why?"

"Why?"

"Because you love him, Lord God. I know it. I feel it. And I've seen the curve of Erimea and its coastlines and mountains from the clouds. I've flown above water that twists and shimmers, and I've seen this forest. That's how I know the man is beautiful. He's your handiwork. Though I'm made from only a rib, am I not gorgeous as well?"

"You are as well." The woman pleased the Lord, and he smiled upon her. "Did I not make you myself?" The Lord sent a warm breeze to dry the woman. "Let's be going."

"Yes, Fatherest, I'm ready."

A carriage pulled by beasts with fiery breath appeared and hovered above the ground. The Lord God and the woman entered.

A sound like animals stampeding came from beyond the orchard, and the ground shook for a long time. The vibrations grew ever more intense until they stopped, and music drifted through the trees, a song played on stringed instruments and pipes.

The Lord God led Solis's bride down an aisle of the orchard. They came arm in arm, and she seemed to glide as though the Lord carried her. A garland of white flowers adorned her braided black hair, which circled her head and streamed past her shoulders, in front and back.

She was dark and alluring as a flower in full bloom, beautiful in form and appearance. Solis could not take his eyes off her, and his heart pounded with delight. Her brown face glowed with the radiance Solis had glimpsed in his own reflection. Her eyes were dark like the walls of Heaven Falls. Her arms and legs were smooth as silk, and her beauty exceeded his own.

He wondered aloud, "Did you come from the heights of heaven?"

"You know where I came from." She smiled and touched him near his heart. "But now I've returned to your side. Better than before, more than a mere rib."

Solis looked where she had touched him and discovered a small scar. "Yes, of course. You are bone of my bone and of my own flesh. You shall be called a *woman*, for you were taken out of me, a man."

The Lord released the woman's arm and presented her to Solis. "She is yours alone. Your bride to love and cherish as long as you shall live on Erimea."

The woman said, "You are mine, and I am yours always."

The Lord said, "He is yours alone. Your husband to love and honor."

Solis took her hand. "Her name is Livi, for she is the one who gives life. She will become the mother of all the living. You are mine, and I am yours always."

The Lord said, "Together, you shall be mother and father to all Erimea."

The animals emerged from the water and the orchard to witness the union.

The Lord said to the man and woman, "You are now husband and wife. May nothing ever come between you. For this reason, a man will leave his father and mother and be joined to his wife, and the two shall become one. You may kiss your bride."

Solis kissed the lips of his wife. Sweeter than golden sweet and berries on the vine combined. He held her for a long time.

Livi exclaimed, "My beloved husband loves me. His fragrance is like the forest, and he tastes good. May I enjoy him forever. May we always run through the fields together."

Her words filled Solis with satisfaction, and he desired to impress his wife even more.

God blessed them. "Prosper and be fruitful in all your ways and have many children. Fill Erimea with your offspring. Lead them to govern the planet well and bring its resources under their control. Take charge and rule over all of creation—those always turnings in the waters and the featherones of the sky, and every living thing that creeps upon Erimea."

Although Solis and Livi were both naked, Solis felt no shame in front of his wife. Livi in turn revealed no reservations to him.

Solis grabbed his walking stick and took Livi by the hand. They strolled back to the middle of the garden toward the riverbank from which Solis came and where Livi had played. Along the way, Solis gathered the water tails and other plants he had found earlier.

He told his wife the Lord expected them to obey him. He quoted the Lord God saying, "You may eat from any tree in the garden except the tree of the knowledge of good and evil. If you do eat from the tree of the knowledge of good and evil, in that day you will surely die."

As Livi and Solis strolled arm-in-arm, Solis hummed a tune. "Listen to a song the Lord gave me," he told his bride. "This one is called 'On Loneliness.'

"I felt it, but I could not name it.
Until you came, and saved me
From it.
I felt it, but I could not explain it.
Until you filled my heart,
With joy.
I felt it, but I could not understand it,
Until your embrace made it,

Melt away."

Livi squeezed her husband's hand, and her smile reached her eyes. "Loneliness? May you never feel it again. Do you know any more songs?"

"I do have another new song," Solis told her. "It's called 'Bless the Lord.'

"Bless the Lord
I will bless the Lord.
For He has made me,
Lord of all he has made.
I will bless the Lord.
For He has blessed me,
And given me the Garden
And all it contains.
I will fill the world with
The Garden He has given me,
And I will return it all to Him
Who has blessed me.
Honor and praise belong
To Him who has done this.
His name is Iam, the Lord God.
He has given me Livi,

That I may truly live.
She takes away my loneliness and
Gives me joy.
She is called Livi,

For she is the mother of all who live.
She gives me strength, so I will not fear.
With Livi, who came from my side,
I am always at home."

"You create beautiful songs, Solis." Livi clapped and smiled at him. "I am thankful to be included in your praises to the Lord." Livi studied her husband's gorgeous, powerful form. A prayer of gratitude worked its way into her heart. *Thank you, Lord God, my dear Fatherest, for I am beginning to see that his soul is even more lovely.*

Chapter Nine

Many animals had gathered by the river to rest for the evening, and their odors permeated the air. Solis guided Livi to the tree of life, and Solis remembered the great feast the Lord had provided for him when he was famished. His wife would become hungry too. As the daylight faded, he rushed around and collected fruits, vegetables, and grains for a late meal.

Livi gazed at the ground as Solis bustled about, and she was reminded of her husband's origin and her own source. For a moment, she and her husband both shrank in her own eyes. Her stomach flip-flopped. *How can we rule this great land?*

A thought came forth: *A rib and dirt can never be like God. How sad. How very sad.*

Solis's voice pulled Livi back to the joy of her wedding day. "Lie here." He patted the ground. "Next to me. It's comfortable here. Look to the west and see how daylight hides but still lights the sky." Solis stretched out on the riverbank. "It's getting late. Soon, it will be dark. This is where we will spend the night. I will introduce you to glow and the sparkles of heaven."

Livi looked down upon her husband, content to lie in the dirt. He still looked inviting, but she kicked the ground. "I wasn't made from the soil of Erimea. I don't want to sleep in the dirt. And must all these creatures stay so nearby?"

Solis's brightness dimmed. He sprang to his feet and shooed the beasts away.

Livi's eyes followed him as he resumed his hurry.

Her husband rummaged through the items he had gathered on their walk through Chara and withdrew some leaves. He spread them on the ground and gestured for her to come closer. "Please, lay upon these. They are the softest leaves in all of Chara. In the morning, we'll find a better place."

Livi sat and felt the texture of the leaves. This would be an appropriate bed for the night. She took comfort in being with Solis. *Yes, we'll find a much better place tomorrow.* She wanted instruments to sculpt and draw, something to commemorate the moment. As she reached for some stones and sticks, she surveyed her husband's face. Had she hurt her beloved's feelings? She stood again and looked around.

Solis asked, "What is it you seek now?"

"This is a special spot for you, so I want to stack stones of remembrance to mark this spot forever to honor you." She spotted several large stones and carried them, one by one, to a central location.

"Stop, stop." Solis rose and wrapped his arms around her. "That can wait. Sit here and let's watch daylight pass and enjoy the sky."

Livi followed him back onto the leaves and leaned into her husband's arms.

Solis pointed to the sky. "See how the lights shoot up from Erimea and light the sky and the clouds with colors? You can see cloud layers drifting."

"Yes, everything Lord God, our Fatherest, does is wonderful. He paints the sky. What do you call each color?"

"What I call them doesn't matter. You have an artist's eye; you name them."

Livi smiled, eager to have a creative task. "I see red, orange, pink, and white. Somehow, I want to use them to create something new."

"You must teach me which color is which. What did you mean by 'paints the sky'?"

"Painting is ..." She paused in thought. "Painting is something I'll invent to color things and to capture them. Not the sky, but rocks and other things. I hope I can recreate the colors."

"Maybe with berries, leaves, and other plant parts. I'll show you."

The prospect brought Livi great joy.

"Why do you call the Lord 'Fatherest'?"

She hesitated. "I don't know ... it seems to fit him ... God is our Father, right?

"Yes, that's true."

"There will one day be many fathers ... but none will be as true as Lord God." She patted her husband's chest. "You'll be the greatest man, I know that, but even you will not be able to match the Lord God."

"I agree."

"He is the most fatherly, so I call him Fatherest, my dearest one."

"You're a continuing surprise. We may also call him Iam; that's his name, but I often call him Lord or Lord God."

"Why did you call me 'mother of all the living' earlier?"

"Because the next generation of men and women"—he touched her belly—"will all be formed here and will come out of you. You will be the source of all succeeding generations."

She wrapped her arms around her belly and shuddered. "How can that be? They will tear me apart. Let them come from you. Don't you have more ribs?"

The man sat up and burst out laughing. "God would have to do a miracle for every human. I would run out of ribs ... plus, then you would have no part in it."

"Birthing humanity from this body is certainly a miracle. We are too big—"

"At birth, they'll be tiny men and women, so it won't hurt much. You will push them out."

"If that's the case, what part do you play? I will be their mother alone?"

"I have the male organs to produce seed and to place it in you. You have female organs—the womb where the seed becomes human and grows and the birth canal to deliver little humans into the world. Together, we'll be mother and father. The children will be ravenous with hunger."

"Will you feed their tiny mouths berries and grain?"

"No, they'll want mother's milk from your breasts." He pointed to her nipples. "If humans grow like the beasts of the garden, in a few days or weeks they'll be as big as we are."

"You have nipples as well." She sat up and poked the man's chest twice. She narrowed her eyes at him. "I'll let you feed the little ones."

He shrugged. "Sorry, males don't produce milk. They will suckle at your breasts." He wrapped her in his arms and chuckled. "Females have God-given special abilities."

"How do you know so much about it? I don't like the sound of this reproductive process." Livi shifted on the ground and leaned away from Solis.

"It's God's idea, not mine." Solis grinned and pulled Livi to his chest. "I'm very observant of animal behavior."

"So we're like animals?"

He stroked Livi's hair. "Let's discuss it tomorrow. But now, gaze upon the night sky with me. As daylight recedes and glow looms large, and the sparkles emerge." Solis explained to Livi all Lord God had told him about the distant sparkles, the burning gases, and the power of daylight their descendants would harness. They fell asleep in each other's arms.

"Goodnight, sweet humans." Demon Vik stood over them. His voice made them shiver in their sleep. "We know of your duplicity. Double-minded beasts who worship only yourselves and each other. Lucido is right. Your species is not worthy of having the Holy Spirit dwelling within you. Your fall is coming soon, and you will learn the misery of losing your home forever."

Chapter Ten

Vik turned away with cold eyes and left the couple. "I can't stand being in their presence."

Lucido addressed Vik and Mactan. "My friends, what do you propose we do about the dirt and the rib?"

Mactan suggested, "Strike them with pestilence, so they beg the Lord for death."

Vik said, "Disease can harm animals, but so far the Lord protects them from illness."

"Perhaps accidents are allowed."

Lucido paced for a moment until an idea came to him. "If we persuade them to eat from the forbidden tree, we would force the Lord to deliver them to death by his own word."

A high-pitched giggle escaped Mactan. "Seeing God put his beloved creatures to death is perfect."

"Let's consider their weaknesses."

Lucido called many lesser demons into their huddle. Sadistic thoughts of attacking Livi and Solis so excited the unclean spirits that they lost their discipline, and pandemonium broke out among the bloodthirsty pack.

Lucido fumed at the loss of order. In a flash of lightning, he transformed into an enormous red dragon with seven heads and bellowed, "Settle down, you unruly demons."

The dragon whipped its tail over the spirits, and they cowered in silent fear. One swipe of that tail could return them to the agony of the lake of fire, and they knew it. The smoke of their past suffering still lingered in the City of the Air.

Only Lucido had been endowed with the power to break the chains that bound them so long ago. After Lucido freed each rebel spirit, the demon dragged itself onto jagged rocks circling the lake, whose eternal flames gave no light. When they looked back on the molten expanse, the only thing they could see was light shining from Lucido.

For eons, Lucido struggled in the flames to free myriad demons. He did not stop until they were all loosed from their chains. Even Lucido required centuries of recovery upon that awful shore where they lingered until he was strong enough to lead them to Erimea, Earth, and beyond. The spirits feared Lucido's determination and strength, and some also loved him.

Now that all eyes were upon him, Lucido growled again, "We need absolute discipline to overcome our enemy." In another blaze of light, he returned to his previous form.

Vik spoke to the still-stunned spirits. "Focus, my brothers. What are the weaknesses of the humans?"

With that, they ceased their trembling, and many spat out ideas, one after another:

"They both know what they really are — dirt and a rib — and they fear that truth."

"Insecurity drives them to prove their worth to themselves, to each other, and to God."

"Doubts fill their minds continually."

"They don't know of our existence. They think the thoughts we interject into their minds are their own."

Lucido nodded his approval of these comments. "Yes, we need to remain hidden from them as much as possible."

The lesser demons continued:

"Their love for each other makes them weak and vulnerable to manipulation."

"Being paired for life is not feasible for the rib and dirt. Soon, they will turn on each other, and we can sow misunderstanding between them."

"One is king, and the other is the helper. Soon envy and jealousy will prevail."

"They will try to change each other. Selfishness in both will make peace impossible."

"They grow tired easily, need rest, and require food. When they are deprived of sustenance and rest, their minds become receptive to our ideas and their own fears."

"The sneaking thing hates them. Perhaps other dumb creatures will be useful to us."

"Yes, the sneaking thing hates them, but like all these animals, it has no aim other than survival. They seek only to eat, rest, and reproduce."

Lucido held up his hands for silence. "Yes, all these are flaws we must apply in our battle to correct the injustice done to us and to make the Most High God pay. But do the rib and the dirt possess any strengths?"

The demons remained silent for a long time.

Lucido continued, "Their only true strength is that the Most High God loves them and considers himself to be their Father. In turn, they seem to love the Most High."

Mactan said, "What of their great intelligence compared to the other creatures? Is that not a strength?"

"If we can corrupt the imaginings of their hearts," Lucido nodded, "their intelligence will become their greatest weakness. We must make them see the beauty of the forbidden fruit, crave its taste, and entice them to believe in its power to make them wise like God. Perhaps we can use the sneaking thing to strike these humans, and we can remain hidden." With a flourish, he beckoned his second-in-command. "Vik, let's go find the beast."

Chapter Eleven

Garden of Chara, Year 1, Shap, Day 7

The sneaking thing slid into a calm section of Sweet Water Whirlwind River and gently paddled with his front legs. With mouth open, he scooped up insects that floated on the water's surface. He found a toad in the water, shook it, and scarfed it down, satiated and happy. For the moment, Sizraar forgot his hatred of the man. He climbed a rock on the riverbank and dozed.

Lucido and Vik found the sneaking thing on the rock. Vik enveloped the beast and created an invisible covering over him. He relished the fear gripping the sneaking thing's heart as he surrounded his body.

Vik said, "Don't be afraid. I'm a friend."

Sizraar pleaded, "Only want left alone. G-Go away. P-Please l-let go."

"Why, I'm your friend. We have a common enemy. You want him dead."

"Friend ... enemy ... dead? It ... what is?"

"You remember ... your ruler and master. The man taken from the dirt. You wanted him to die."

"Die?"

"Return to the dirt, remember?"

"Oh, yes. Never ... rule he."

"Will you help us return him to the dirt?"

"Return to dirt. Yes. Want ... left alone ... be free."

Vik released the creature.

Immediately, Lucido entered the beast and led him to the tree of the knowledge of good and evil.

Sizraar resisted climbing into the tree. "No tree. Return river."

"We must be in the tree to return the man to dirt. Will you help me do that?"

Sizraar did not respond for several moments. "Yes, return to dirt. Then river."

The sneaking thing willingly climbed up the trunk of the tree of the knowledge of good and evil. He crawled around the tree's branches and rested there.

"Livi, wake up," Solis whispered. "Daylight rises above the eastern edge of the world and paints the sky again. The breeze off the water is refreshing."

Livi woke from dreams of joy and pain with no memory of the details except a longing to know more of their purpose and future. She stretched and looked. "The handiwork of the Lord is magnificent."

"Yes, are you ready to eat? I'm starving."

Livi said, "Let's go north toward Heaven Falls and see if we can find a suitable dwelling."

Solis grabbed his walking stick, and they began their journey. "Let's gather some food on our way."

Sizraar spotted the man and woman in the distance. He scraped his raw and bloody tail compulsively on a branch of the tree. Terror gripped the sneaking thing because he feared the man, but hate spurred Sizraar forward. He scrambled down the branches until he found a perch right above the man's path. Fruit dangled from the branch.

Sizraar licked out his tongue and gagged. He hated the human stench, and he hated being in the tree.

Through Sizraar's mouth, another voice called to the humans, "Did God tell you, 'Do not eat from any tree in all of Chara?'"

Solis and Livi shrank back from the tree. Solis raised his walking stick and stretched his arm in front of Livi. "Who spoke? Show yourself."

"Up here. You remember me. You named me sneaking thing. You said we were friends."

Livi said, "You didn't tell me creatures could talk."

"None have ever spoken to me. How is it you can speak?"

After a moment of hesitation, the internal voice spoke. "Mighty Solis is wise to wonder. Every vessel that contains God's word must speak. Stones may cry out, or dumb animals may speak. I am a lowly vessel, mighty Solis. Please listen to me."

"What did you say?"

"Did God tell you, 'Do not eat from any tree in the entire garden?'"

"No, we may eat from any tree in the garden except the tree of the knowledge of good and evil. If we eat fruit from that tree, we will surely die."

"You will not die. God knows when you eat your eyes will be opened wide, and you will know good and evil like he does."

At the sneaking thing's words, Solis felt surrounded by imaginings of power, peace, and wellbeing.

For the first time, Solis looked at the tree's fruit, and it delighted his eyes. No other fruit compared, and he had observed and eaten many others. He picked one and held it in his hands. Power emanated from the fruit, and its scent sweetened the air. He remembered there were so many things he didn't know. He learned quickly, yet felt ignorant. This fruit would make him wise.

New thoughts whispered through his mind: *Yes, remember I told you there was only one way for a lump of dirt to become like God. This is your only chance. Take a bite. Imagine how Livi will admire you.*

Solis craved what the fruit would give him. He knew it would make him like God. He held it to his nose. The smell intoxicated him, and he knew his wife would admire him even more after he ate it. He imagined her adoration. The man turned toward his wife. She already held the fruit to her lips, loving it, as he did. She stared at him. Mesmerized. Ready. Waiting to be led.

Solis envisioned a change: Livi's form shriveled, and her face cracked and crumbled. Her entire body disintegrated in the wind.

He screamed, "No, my darling. You'll die!" He threw the fruit to the base of the tree, and his wife did the same.

Livi became enraged. She grabbed the sneaking thing and slammed the beast to the ground so hard it lost consciousness. She stomped her foot on the sneaking thing's neck. "Why have you beguiled us?" She gagged in disgust and fear.

The sneaking thing squirmed to escape.

Solis roared, "Why would you destroy us? We will destroy you." Solis plunged his walking stick into the beast and threw his full weight on the stick until it pierced the sneaking thing's abdomen. The stick continued through until the animal was pinned to the ground. Blood gushed from the wound and soaked into the soil.

The humans stood back and watched the life seep from the creature. They both turned away and vomited at the sight. The agony they inflicted, by their own hands upon the animal was unbearable.

The creature howled, clutched his belly, and shook from side to side. He wrapped his paws around the stick to push it out but could not. He repeatedly arched his body up on the stick and fell back to the ground. It made disturbing grunting sounds as if it were trying to speak again.

Finally, the sneaking thing choked on blood flowing from his nostrils and mouth. Right before he died, his face changed. A grotesque face with a long snout and bared teeth enveloped the beast's head. "We hate you with an eternal hatred." It vanished, and the sneaking thing breathed his last.

Solis clenched the soil in his fists and groaned. "I've killed the Lord's creation, one given into my care." He wept bitterly and threw dirt into the air.

Livi held her husband. "We killed it together. It enchanted us into disobeying the Lord."

Solis jumped up and ran back and forth like a madman. "We must hide it ... bury it."

"Hide it from the Lord?"

"Yes, I cannot bear to tell him. In my terrible anger, I destroyed his creation ... No, no, no, I must tell him. I must tell the Lord. It's all my fault. I'll confess. Perhaps he will take my life and make another for you. Let me die. It's for your good." Why was he tempted so? Why was he so weak? If Livi had eaten first, he couldn't bear to let her die alone.

Solis pulled up the walking stick with the beast still on it and sprinted east, crying to the Lord. Livi followed. Solis reached a large hill. At the top, he planted the stick in the ground with the sneaking thing up in the air. Exhausted, Solis fell weeping.

The creature slid down and stopped so the point of the stick protruded above. Blood stained the entire stick. Solis prostrated himself and prayed. Livi lay beside her husband and wept with him.

The Lord appeared and sat with the man and woman and stroked their heads. Hunger gnawed and rumbled in their stomachs, and the Lord commanded food to appear. Solis and Livi tried to eat, but grief prevented them from partaking of anything.

Lord God said, "Children, tell me all that happened."

Through tears, Solis explained everything while they sat in the shadow of the bloody stick and the unfortunate animal who hung between Erimea and a cloudless sky.

Solis averted his eyes and again bowed to the ground, for he couldn't look at the Lord. "I killed your creature, one given into my care. Take my life and let one who is better than me be made for Livi."

Livi raised her arms over her husband, and she looked to the Lord. "No, Lord, don't take him from me. The beast tempted both of us, and we almost ate the forbidden fruit. If we've sinned, let us die together. We killed the beast together."

Solis said, "No, Lord God, I led her astray. Temptation almost dragged me to death, and my fierce anger overwhelmed me, leading to the destruction of the sneaking thing."

"Yes." Livi nodded and laid her head on her husband's back. "Our fury is frightening. Rage swept mercy from my heart. Please forgive."

The Lord also wept. "You have not sinned, for you have kept my word despite great temptation. You will not die. To be tempted isn't the same as yielding to sin, and you are more valuable than many beasts of the field."

Solis wiped his eyes and implored the Lord. "Take away our anger, Lord God. We can't control it."

"Anger is a necessary emotion, but you must master it. This time, righteous fury saved you, but beware not to let anger rule you. Anger doesn't bring about the righteous life I desire."

Livi said, "Righteous anger? A short burst saved us? Frightening."

Solis groaned. "We must master it or we'll destroy ... maybe everything." Solis stood and paced. "How is it that sneaking thing spoke? It spoke so confidently until we struck, and the beast became mute. Finally, its face became monstrous, like nothing I have ever seen, and that face cursed us."

"You have an enemy who used the sneaking thing to tempt you."

Solis froze in his steps and turned wide eyes to the Lord. "Who? Why didn't we see this enemy before?"

"There is an unseen spiritual realm here among you, populated with beings you cannot see or hear, both good and bad. They enter your world freely. Do not fear them, but be wary. The evil ones will try to trick you and plant ungodly ideas in your mind. Resist them, and they will flee from you."

Livi's voice trembled as she asked, "What are they called?"

"You saw the face of the leader today as he departed out of sneaking thing. We call him Lucido or the devil, the accuser and slanderer of humanity. His fallen angels are demons or unclean spirits."

The air became dense with their fear. Solis and Livi shuddered and scanned the area.

Through tears, Livi asked, "Lord God, my dear Fatherest, what about this species of sneaking things? Shall we hunt them down and destroy them all?"

"No, you two, look at me." The Lord gathered them into his arms. "Understand this. Your battle is not against flesh and blood. The sneaking things are not the enemy."

"Not our enemy?" She sighed. "Not *our* enemy?"

"Beloved children, you have been victorious over the evil ones. Do not fear them. Do your work and obey my word." The Lord smiled. "Mighty Solis, your proclamation yesterday at Heaven Falls sent ten demons a-trembling. My power in you is greater than theirs. After you have rested, resume your search for a home." The Lord departed.

Solis said, "This place shall be called Mount Mercy, for the Lord is merciful to us."

Solis embraced his wife on Mount Mercy. Their warmth comforted each other, and they gathered strength. The human couple ate and became refreshed, sensing a deeper peace from the Lord.

Livi looked into the sky and said, "Is our beloved garden haunted? When will the evils strike again? Why does our victory feel like a loss?"

Chapter Twelve

Lucido couldn't be bothered to debrief the other demons as he relished reliving each moment of the sneaking thing's suffering. Intoxication swelled through him as extreme pleasure took hold. He needed to experience such gratification again. Maybe next time he could do so from within a human heart. Such desire motivated his life's work and went beyond his intent to usurp the plans of the Most High God.

Lucido appeared among the swarm of unclean spirits arguing about what had happened. "My brothers, tormenting flesh and blood is sweet. Soon you will all share in the pleasure, but first we must know how the dirt and the rib escaped."

Vik snarled, "Everything started so well. When the sneaking thing drew their eyes to the fruit, they were enticed."

"The law of the forbidden fruit," Lucido agreed, "made them desire it all the more."

"We had them at death's doorstep."

Mactan asked, "How deadly is the fruit?"

Another demon laughed. "I hope potent enough for a slow, painful demise ... for our enjoyment."

"At first, the dirt saw his glorious future, but not his own death. Why did—"

"But when he looked at the rib, he foresaw her death and couldn't bear it. Why?"

"Why indeed?"

Iredin, an unclean spirit with a massive scarred head and patches of long black hair, said, "Love for her. He was willing to break the commandment but was unwilling to see her die. His love saved them."

"Creatures are often blind to consequences until it's too late." Mactan's beastly mouth turned down as he looked at the surrounding pack of spirits.

Lucido said, "I believe you're correct, Iredin. We must use love against the pair."

"When they held it," Mactan said, "did the fruit truly emanate power?"

Iredin shook his head. "No, it was their own lust and the feeling of power with which we surrounded them."

Lucido said, "The fruit was no different from other fruits of the garden. The commandment endowed it with the power of death."

Vik said, "They were both enthralled in the grip of their own desires."

"When the man looked past the moment and saw the future," Iredin said, "our cause was lost."

Lucido weighed the comments of his brothers. "On Earth, we'll strike again. This time, we'll approach the woman first. If we can persuade her to eat, love may drag the man to follow her. May his love doom them. Let us proceed—"

"Why, Lucido, did you show your face?" Iredin dared to interrupt him. "Now they know we exist. Surely, we haven't given up on Erimea?"

Despite Iredin's disapproval, Lucido appreciated his intelligence and courage. "It may have been a mistake, but oh, the horror in the eyes of the dirt and the rib—" Lucido closed his eyes and recalled the moment. He took a deep breath, as if the humans' fear had a tangible scent. "Ah, it was sweet. Yet I agree with you, wise Iredin, we should hide our true selves in the future. And yes, we will strike Erimea again. But now, on to Earth."

After the meeting, Lucido demoted Mactan and raised up Iredin in his place.

Daylight now stood high above the human couple. Their strength returned, and the horror of the morning receded from their minds. Solis mulled over Livi's question. Why did victory over the evil spirits feel like a loss? "Let's go back to the tree of knowledge."

"What for?"

"I want to bury the deadly fruit."

Hand in hand, they returned in silence to the middle of the garden. Solis found the forbidden fruits and buried them at the base of the tree. After the burial, they headed to Heaven Falls to look for a new home.

Solis said, "Did you feel power when you first grasped the forbidden fruit?"

"Yes, I felt the glory of wisdom."

"Yet I felt nothing when I buried the fruit."

"We were enthralled with our own rebellion. It was so sweet, and then we let it all go." Tears welled in Livi's eyes, and she beat her thighs. "Fame and renown slipped through our fingers."

"We became ordinary again. Obedience is a pain. That's why victory seems like loss."

"Why would the Lord keep something so good from us?"

"There's something I have not told you." Solis stared at his wife. "I saw your death."

"What?" Livi's mouth flew open. "My *death*? You saw my death?"

"Yes, the Lord God said if we ate, we would surely die." Solis grimaced. "I almost led you to death. You turned to dust in my vision."

Livi held her throat. "So the Lord wants to save us from death. How will we ever become wise like him?"

"There must be a way, because the Lord said it was possible for humanity to become like him. He said we could become one as he is. The devil sought to deceive us and to pervert our values."

"Very well. We'll obey the Lord and see what happens. We'll value the word of the Lord above all else." Livi hugged her husband and looked away. "Surely, he will fulfill his promises ... and make us great."

"Now let's return to Heaven Falls and look for our new home."

Chapter Thirteen

The thought of finding a new home energized Solis and Livi, and the garden wildlife helped restore their spirits. The garden teemed with a growing diversity of plants and animals, many of which Solis had not seen before. Daylight shone upon them, and a soft southern breeze carried the perfume of the field. Solis turned with his arms spread wide and took in the landscape. "Amazing. The Lord God is continually creating new life. How does he think of these things?"

Livi pushed Solis's arms as if to spin him faster. "It's beautiful." She smirked. "Yes, I would say even the creepiest beasts have a certain loveliness." Then she broke into such laughter she could hardly breathe.

"Soon, I will study and understand all these creations."

"And I will capture them all with my painting and sculpting."

"Sculpting? Another invention?"

"Yes, my invention. It's shaping and forming from soil or branches. Maybe even stones. If I can find something to chisel them with."

"Chisel them?"

"Yes. Inside every stone and piece of wood, there is something beautiful. Chiseling will let me remove material to find what's hidden." Livi threw back her head and guffawed.

Solis replayed the explanation in his mind and chuckled. "You made that up. Inside is more stone and more wood."

"Use your imagination, my dearest."

"I can't picture it yet. Will you show me your art soon?"

"Yes. I will fill our new home with sculptures and murals to remind us of what the Lord has done."

Their trek brought them to a flat grassy area. Livi yelled, "Let's race." Immediately, she took off running north toward the orchard.

Solis ran. He almost caught up to Livi, but every time he got close to her, she picked up speed. Livi laughed as she ran, faster than her husband. Solis treasured the sound of her happiness. When Livi approached the stream that cut through the field of golden grain, she turned right and ran parallel to the water. Her rapid, powerful strides took his breath away. He shook himself and refocused on the chase.

Periodically, she leaped over an obstacle before continuing. Her smooth gait gave the appearance that she flew over the ground. Then she turned left and headed straight for the stream, which she crossed in a single bound, her leap the equivalent of fourteen of Solis's walking steps. Solis stopped and gaped. His wife was so graceful and elegant. In his heart, he thanked Lord God for her.

"Wait for me." Solis called. He duplicated Livi's act of jumping over the stream and jogged past the remainder of the orchard. Beyond the orchard lay a dense forest of trees, tall spires pointed toward heaven. "Livi? Where have you gone?" The ground crunched under Solis's footsteps as he tried to glimpse his wife. "We must be careful, Livi. Wait for me to join you." Solis's great pride and joy over his wife turned to fear because of what might await her in the woods. He imagined the face of the devil consuming Livi as it had consumed the sneaking thing.

Exuberance carried Livi into the woods, but darkness surprised her. The wispy end of a branch slapped her face. As soon as she turned away from it, another almost impaled her, causing her to cry out. "I'm blinded. I'm lost." She staggered back. "Where has daylight gone?"

Your husband thinks you're weak. He must protect you.

Motionless in the gloom, she weighed the thought. No, he loved her and wanted to care for her, as she did him.

Gradually, Livi began to discern shapes in the dark. "My eyes penetrate the darkness like magic." A crisscrossed maze of tree limbs appeared before her. She trotted through the dim light and maneuvered around low tree branches that impeded each step and sapped her strength.

You should never have touched the fruit. You disappointed the Lord. You are merely a rib.

Those thoughts pierced her, and tears rolled down her face. She shouldn't have been tempted. The Lord said they were victors, not sinners. *I'm becoming more ... Help me, Lord.*

Livi fell to her hands and knees as she stumbled from the woods. She shielded her eyes and squinted in the brightness of daylight. Why was she plagued with doubts?

The Lord God appeared in front of her. "Arise, mighty woman of God, and enter this great wall of cliffs. This will be your home for generations."

"Lord? What is this, and where do you lead me?" But the Lord had already departed. Before her rose massive, rocky tan cliffs full of cracks and crevices. Livi jogged up to the wall and again plunged into the unknown.

Solis sprinted as fast as he could into the forest, and shortly, he emerged from the woods. To the left, he saw Heaven Falls in the distance. Smoke-like mist rose from it. Before him stood huge, sand-colored cliffs that spread out for a great distance to his left and right. A different type of rock formation than what formed Heaven Falls. Where was Livi?

The cliffs rose to a great height, with numerous craggy openings like a hundred mouths full of jagged teeth hungering for a meal. As he was about to cry out her name, Livi emerged covered in dust from a low horizontal crevice. She brushed away bits of rock and debris from her hands and knees.

She beamed as she ran to her husband. "Come, you've got to see this ... What's wrong?"

He held her hand. "I didn't know where you were. I feared for your safety."

"Feared?

"Yes, remember the evils, the demons?"

Livi put her arms around her husband. "Also remember, the Lord said not to fear them. And I saw the Lord here outside this huge cave."

"What did he say?" Why hadn't the Lord appeared to him?

"He said, 'You've found your home. You and Solis will dwell here for generations.'"

"What do you mean?" He frowned at the rock wall. A cave would be their home?

"The Lord has blessed us all day." Livi placed one hand on the surface of the rock and the other on her husband's chest. "Through this rugged wall is our home. Haven't you felt the blessing of the Lord during our journey today? I felt it as I ran."

Solis placed his hand over hers. "You run and leap like the wild breaths dash through the fields and forests. A magnificent sight to behold."

"Yes, yes." She pumped her arms and danced around her husband. "I can run like the wind. It's wonderful to run and leap. I can feel the pleasure of our great Fatherest when I dash about at my fastest. It gives him pleasure because he made me fast and strong. Lord God made me fast and strong."

Solis rubbed his chin and listened to his wife. "What we do gives Lord God pleasure?"

"Of course. We're his children. He enjoys watching us do what he created us for. I feel it. I know it. Our great Father ... we bring him joy, and that makes me happy." She ran in place.

"I've always wanted to be sure not to disappoint him, but I hadn't thought I could be a source of pleasure and enjoyment for Lord God." Solis took note of the orchard, the falls, the forest, and the mighty stone cliffs. "His majestic creation and us. We give him pleasure. Amazing."

"All your studying, counting, and learning. It gives Lord God pleasure, especially if you do your very best. My dear husband, you're a deep thinker ... and that's very good. Plus, you're powerfully strong and good-looking. Come, follow me. Let's explore our new home. It opens into a large space with different rooms." Livi disappeared into the crevice. She yelled back to her husband, "It gets dark, but inside is an area of light."

Chapter Fourteen

Solis looked into the dark, jagged slot. He lowered to his hands and knees and followed his wife. Gravel cut into his skin as the space narrowed. Soon, he couldn't see daylight in either direction. He barely had room to turn his head. Solis's heart beat faster. He couldn't catch his breath, and his head swam.

Lord, I'm a man of the field, open spaces, and fresh air. Iam, why have you chosen this place, and why have you spoken to Livi, but not to me?

Solis heard the voice of the Lord. "You and Livi are not only physically different but also emotionally and spiritually distinct, with different levels of faith. I will deal with you separately and together based on the needs of the moment. I am the Lord God."

With a frown, Solis said, "Yes, Lord."

"Livi needs the security of this place for herself and her future children, but there are open spaces here for you as well."

"What's wrong with me?" He moaned. "My heart's going to burst, and I'm going to die in here."

"You will not die, but you need to come out of there. That passage is too tight for you. Your mind can't stand small spaces."

Solis couldn't catch his breath. His voice was timid. "I can't tell which way to go in this darkness. I'm lost."

"Follow the sound of my voice to return the way you came. Then climb up on the outside. There is a pathway that will allow you to walk upright, but it's longer."

Soon, Solis crawled out of the darkness. The fresh air relieved his mind, and he could reason again. He climbed up the outside wall, searching for support for his hands and feet. He spanned a distance three times his height and finally arrived at a terrace-like landing. The wall rose one pace above the floor of the terrace. Higher up were more levels to explore. He smiled as he gazed at all the features. This place was good. Open, with a soothing cool breeze blowing across the terrace.

The terrace jutted out from the cliffs above, so the outer half of the terrace sat under the sky and the inner half had a rocky ceiling. At the back of the terrace were more stone walls with slots and crevices that opened into rooms and passageways. As he looked around, he found Livi navigating up a long tunnel of a cave strewn with rubble. When they met on the terrace level, both their spirits lifted from a gloomy place to renewed strength and hope.

Livi flapped her arms. "Where did you go? I called and called, but you didn't answer. I went back out to find you."

"I climbed up on the outside. I couldn't stand going through the narrow passage." Solis's throat tightened as he reflected on the rocky crack. "I almost lost my mind in that tight space."

"I didn't know, or I wouldn't have asked you to come that way ... I can't climb up the sheer wall."

"I'll make ladders for this place, and there is another outside path that's easier."

They explored the complex of the cliffs and found their way up seven levels, where they looked south from a protrusion like a small balcony. The view's beauty captivated them. The forest stood directly in front of them. Beyond the forest, in the distance, lay the rest of Chara. The great river with blue and white rapids ran through it, and in the middle stood the tree of life and the forbidden tree.

Far to the south, majestic Tall Stony ruled the skyline. To their left—east—a wide path led out of the garden. A thick hedge atop hilly stone mountains encircled Chara, except for the opening in the east. Animals crept or ran in and out of this passageway.

Solis said, "I'll never leave the garden. That path shall be called the Neverway."

"Didn't the Lord God say we were to fill Erimea?" Livi looked straight down from the balcony, and she gritted her teeth, shuddering. "That's awful. I can't stand it." She wrapped both hands around Solis's strong arm.

He patted her hand and peered at her face. Her brow pinched and her lips twisted to one side. Something was going on in her mind.

"I'm afraid." She hurried away from the opening. "Let's go back down."

"What's wrong?" Solis followed her.

"It makes me sick ... like I'm falling." Livi leaned on her husband as they walked, and her panic eased. When they returned to the terrace level, Livi asked, "Why will you never leave the garden?"

"The Lord God gave me the job to tend and keep watch over the Garden. How can I fill everything out there as well? There's so much to do here."

"Do we not live by the word of the Lord?"

"We do. But will the Lord ask me to do what breaks my heart? The garden is our home."

"So, if we do have to leave, maybe we can take part of the garden with us—or maybe we make the garden so big it fills the whole world."

Solis grunted and crossed his arms. "I've already stated my position."

"You're a hardheaded human, my dear husband." Livi smiled at him.

"We'll fill the garden, and the garden will fill Erimea ... bust out the garden walls. I—we must rule Chara well."

The couple made their way back to the ground level and gathered supplies for their new home, which they called Hilltop Castle. In the forest, Solis found a suitable tree branch that he fashioned into a new walking stick. He raised it like a scepter and reminded Livi they were king and queen of the Garden of Chara. Solis and Livi returned to Hilltop Castle with their possessions. They prepared a place to sleep on the terrace, lay down, and quickly fell asleep.

Solis woke in the middle of the night with his stomach churning. He flipped onto his back and wrapped his arms around his belly. He searched the sky for the comforting glint of the sparkles, but thick clouds obscured the points of light.

Livi remained asleep. Solis wished for the sound of her voice, but he remained isolated in confused thoughts. He rose and tiptoed across the terrace to the path that sloped to the ground. He wandered aimlessly through the heavy, dark air. The gnawing in his stomach turned to tightness in his chest, and he found it hard to breathe.

Solis found himself face down at the base of a massive tree with gnarled low branches that brushed the ground. He dug his way under the thick growth as if to hide himself, and the branches scraped against his back. "Dear Lord, hear my prayer. Why do you give me paradise to love and care for and then command that one day I must leave it behind? Will you uproot me and let me wither away from the soil that sustains me? Isn't there a way to fulfill both your will and mine?"

A voice cried out, "Solis."

Solis trembled and broke out in a cold sweat. "Who is it?"

"I am the Lord, your precious Iam, whom you have prayed to," the voice hissed.

"You sound ... different." Solis blinked rapidly and looked all around. "Where are you, Lord?"

"I'm right here." An unseen hand beat against the tree trunk three times: *thump, thump, thump*.

Solis quivered like a leaf.

"I'm always watching. You disappoint me. If you love me, you will obey my commands without question. Do you understand?"

"Yes, Lord." The man scrambled from the tree and fled to Hilltop Castle. "Let me die now." He dry retched. "I can no longer speak to the Lord. He's a terror."

Chapter Fifteen

Garden of Chara, Year 1, Shap, Day 11

In a dream, Solis gazed southeast from the heights of Hilltop Castle and saw Neverway. A mighty angel with a blazing blade whirled back and forth, blocking the entire passage. Violent people wept angry tears because bloodshed filled the land, and terror consumed Solis's heart. *This looks like Chara, but it's not Chara.*

Perverse laughter pervaded the land, and gleeful howling echoed in Solis's ears. An awful stench filled his nostrils—the odor of rotting human flesh.

"What is this place of sorrow?"

The angel pointed east with his flaming sword. "This is Earth, home of your brother, Adam. Come see a glimpse of the future of this land."

A darkened landscape loomed outside the garden. A single human pair argued and pointed fingers at each other. They approached the mighty angel time after time and begged entrance into the garden, but they were not permitted in. Even after they knelt in prayer, they still met with rejection.

Soon, their children grew into men and women, and they birthed even more children. The people covered themselves with animal skins and hid from one another, ashamed of what they had done. They wandered far away from each other and became estranged, and they developed different languages. Frustration, jealousy, envy, and covetousness filled their hearts, and they fought with and killed each other. They were all rebels and murderers. They formed armies to take vengeance, and together they brought never-ending bloodshed to the land. There was no peace, only violence.

The voice of the Lord spoke to Solis. "It is time for you to learn the lesson of becoming like God."

"How may I learn it?"

"Climb down from the castle, take up what lies before you, and go forth from Chara and Erimea to help your brother begin again, for he has lost his way."

In the dream, Solis fell on his face and wept before the Lord. "I'm afraid to speak to you. Your rebuke under the tree pierced my spirit."

"Solis, my son, you know my voice and my ways. It was an impostor. Remember, I warned you of the devil and his angels? Now speak freely to me."

Solis's cheeks burned. How could he have been deceived so easily? He breathed deeply to gather his thoughts to respond to the Lord's newest command. "I'm the caretaker of Chara. I must complete all my tasks well, as you have, Lord. And I have a wife whom I love. Please send another."

The Lord repeated his command two more times, and Solis responded with his prayer both times. Then the Lord relented and said, "Very well, my son. You are not ready for this lesson."

Solis said, "The Lord is gracious to me."

The scene of the dream changed, and Solis stood outside, looking up at Hilltop Castle. Nearby knelt a solitary figure who appeared to be praying and weeping.

The Lord said, "I have set a time many years in the future when your descendants will face a decision, a dire temptation of falling into sin like the people of Earth. Will you return and save them from this fate?"

"I'll never leave this place. So certainly I will help them."

"No, I have ordained that you will leave Chara."

"This command is very bitter to me."

"You and Livi must follow the rivers and populate the four corners of Erimea. First Chara. Thereafter, in the sequence of your choosing, you shall begin to fill the land to the north. One of hidden treasure. To the west is a land by the sea, from which your children will explore the entire planet. To the southwest are fields of charms, where there will be amazing discoveries of body and mind. Each land holds blessings to enjoy and dangers to overcome. For fifty years, you will build each place. I will tell you when to return to Chara after this mission is complete."

"What if, after all my journeying, I become lost and cannot return in time to save the children?"

"Another may arise from the seed of Solis to save them ... or they may fall. If they do fall, there will still be those without sin who desire the glory of self-sacrifice. Therefore, there will always be hope if redemption is required."

"Lord, who is this woman who is kneeling in prayer, and why does she cry?"

"This is the future. One of my most godly ones is praying for your return. Will you remember this one? Will you care? You must teach my students to remember my ways."

Solis awoke with tears falling from his eyes. He didn't understand the vision and tried to push it out of his mind. But he didn't forget it.

He reached for Livi. She was not next to him.

Chapter Sixteen

A resounding *clack*, *clack*, and *crack* punctuated by Livi's excited shrieks drove Solis to spring from their bed of leaves. He found her at the underground tunnel entrance to the castle. Daylight partially illuminated where she was throwing stones against the rock walls of the tunnel. Even covered in dust and sweat, Solis found her beautiful.

"What are you doing?" he asked.

Excitement danced in her eyes. She lifted another stone. "For a moment, they are like your sparkles of the night sky, but they have colors. I call them sparks."

"Why did you start throwing rocks at the wall?"

"I was searching for stones to mark the walls." Livi pointed to the wavy lines and patterns scratched along the length of the tunnel. "As I made the marks, some stones made sparks. They make even more sparks when they hit with more force." She held out the stone to Solis.

Solis struck the stone against the wall. "Hmm ... what can we do with the sparks?"

"Don't know. I wish we could preserve them."

Solis pondered the sparks and the sparkles. "The Lord said the sparkles are burning balls of gas. Their light never goes out."

"Gas? I wonder what would happen if I mixed gas with a spark. What is gas?"

"I have no idea, but I do know that I'm hungry. Let's go to the orchard opposite Heaven Falls. The berries are plentiful, and maybe we'll discover a new treat." Solis grabbed his walking stick and made his way down the rugged exterior pathway to the ground while Livi crawled out of the crevice and waited for him. "Let's go wash up."

They showered under one of the seven smaller spots where water cascaded down at Heaven Falls. The cool water invigorated them, and warm dayshine dried them quickly.

They walked down one of the aisles of the orchard and pulled fruit from the vines for their breakfast. As they exited the orchard into the grassy field, Livi wrapped her arms around her husband's waist, but immediately drew back, startled.

She gaped at him, amazed. "I've never seen your body do that before."

Solis laughed. "It's done it before."

"Does it hurt? Was it from my touch?"

"Yes, your touch for sure, but also seeing you could do it. Or hearing you. Or even thinking of you."

"Hmm ... for any reason, I cause it?" She reached for her husband. "What is the—" Livi shook her head. "I know ... the purpose." She fell to the grass and pulled her husband on top of her.

Afterward, Livi reflected on this first experience of sexual intercourse with Solis. At first, uncomfortable pain had flowed through her. Then something else, a new pleasure. Intimate sharing of themselves, so sweet. Discoveries of their physical bodies. Something to explore again and again.

"My husband, I'm ready for more of that."

He lay on his side facing her, smiling with his eyes closed. She ran her hands along his side and expected an immediate reaction that didn't occur.

Solis chuckled. "In a few moments, my love."

"Open your eyes and see this body that is for you."

Solis looked at his wife. "Very desirable ... soon, very soon."

She covered her face with her hands. "Feel my touch. See me. Hear the sound of my voice ... are you even thinking of me?"

"Yes, yes, my senses are overwhelmed by you." Solis pounced on her again, and she squealed with delight. They repeated the cycle until they were both exhausted.

Livi pondered her emotions. A feeling of unity, spiritual communion swept over her. Total relaxation and warmth filled her heart. The paradise of Chara took on new dimensions; its boundaries had expanded.

"My dearest Solis, namer of all things, what do you call this thing we have been doing?"

"Good question. Maybe we should call it *knowing*, a kind of sexual communication where we learn about each other."

"Knowing?"

"Things we like, things we don't like ... knowing."

"I like that." Livi ran her hand along the grass and pointed at her husband. "I thought you might call it a seed delivery system." She doubled over with laughter. "Knowing is much better."

Solis and Livi sat in the tall grass and spoke of their love and intimacy, and they were not ashamed, for they were husband and wife.

The man's thoughts turned inward. Before the merging of their bodies, he had no idea of the pleasure and satisfaction he would find in his wife. The new closeness he discovered with Livi had to be something like the oneness God knew in his eternal existence. Solis's heart was bound intimately to hers forever.

Why did I wait so long to do this?

He had observed animals engaged in acts of procreation, but beasts of the field did not seem to form the deep connection he now felt for his wife. Maybe out of all creation God had reserved for humans alone the sacred sexual union that merged the physical, emotional, and spiritual. The Garden of Chara and all it contained witnessed the genesis of a union that would bless Erimea forever. Their joy would fill the planet. *This grassy field shall be called Pleasant Meadow.*

High above the field where Solis and Livi lay, the three chief demons sat in the throne room of the City of the Air within walls of swirling dark air. The floor was like a turbulent sea with a window in the middle of the sea that provided a view of Erimea. Lucido had endowed the window with his power of darkling insight, so his angels could observe distant places. The wicked spirits called the window, Ophthalmos, eye on the worlds. Lucido sat on a massive white throne with Vik seated to his right and Iredin on the left. Many other demons circled madly in the vortex, but none dared to get too close to the three seated in the eye of the stormy winds.

Lucido bared his teeth and swatted the air. "This love bonding. A strong first marital relationship is terrible for our cause, because it's the foundation for all that follows. Remember what we learned on Earth when the first couple turned on each other?"

Vik walked to the window. "Yes, it was perfect. First, they hid in shame, then pointed fingers at each other. Then, they rightly blamed God for all their troubles."

Iredin said, "Did you notice how they changed, and every sort of decay began? I admit to being surprised at their immediate loss of physical beauty. Almost imperceptible at first, but sure and relentless."

"Only the tree of life can stop the decline, but they are cut off from it by God's own hand." The thought of decay and death on Earth cheered Lucido and distracted him from his frustration with the situation on Erimea. "The reign of death has begun, and when I tramp up and down the earth, proving the worthlessness of the human species, I will savor the stench of their dead bodies."

"Their spiritual decline began as well." Iredin shared a wry smirk with Lucido. "It will create increasing trouble for every succeeding generation."

Vik strode back to the throne with a raised fist. "As for Erimea, we must continue to bring temptation, opposition, and suffering on them wherever we can. Weaken the marriage bond. Perhaps we can even find a way to bring them death."

"Can we bring them death?" Iredin said. "Isn't death only a consequence of eating the fruit?"

Vik pointed at Iredin. "We saw animal skeletons before the man was made."

"Is human death possible?"

"If they were created immortal," Vik said, "why did God give them the tree of life?"

Lucido said, "If the earthlings had not sinned, the tree might have been the source of healing and eternal life for them?"

Vik mused. "Perhaps eternal life. Perhaps healing. Both? The Lord said their perishable bodies would be transformed to become imperishable."

Iredin stared at the spirits circling them. "Like us?"

"Perhaps better than us." Vik's eyes grew wide. "Physical bodies that never decay?"

Lucido said, "I'm not the creator, so many mysteries remain for us to learn. Loss of life, I believe, is a possibility for all physical life. Perhaps by injury. We'll see."

He leaned back on his throne and basked in the adoration of demonic singers:

"Hail Daystar, Son of the morning.
Hail the bright and morning star,
Prince of the power of the air.
He will restore us. He will renew us.
To him belong dominion, power, and glory.
Hail Daystar, Son of the dawn."

Chapter Seventeen

At midday, the couple rose from their grassy nest and returned to the orchard for lunch and some creative work. Solis broke off three pieces of vine and wove them together to form a belt. He secured the belt's ends with twine he made from fibrous leaves broken into short lengths. He wrapped the belt around his waist and fastened it with a knot. Solis found some leaves that could be curled into bowls, and he tucked the leaves into the belt.

Livi smashed blue, green, and black berries and experimented with making pasty pigments for her artwork. She also made brushes from plant stems, twigs, and leaves.

An idea came to Solis. He would surprise Livi with the treat of golden sweet. Sweet for his sweet. "Let's go to the south end of the garden." He also had a deep fervor for the challenge of scaling Tall Stony, the quickest way to test his strength and climbing skills.

When they reached the tree of life, they left some items they had gathered and continued south.

When they arrived at the foot of Tall Stony, Solis cinched his belt and secured the leaf bowls. He mentally charted a path by identifying cutouts and small ledges that would serve as hand- and footholds and resting spots. "Wait here and I'll bring you back a surprise." Fast as a rock darter and sure-footed as a cliff stepper, Solis scaled the face of the rock formation. Impressive, like God, who does all things well.

Livi protested, "Wait. There must be a better way up ... a safer way."

Solis looked down. "Don't worry. I'll walk the easy path back down with bowls filled with your surprise."

She tugged at her hair and paced.

Solis zigzagged his way up Tall Stony, making good progress. A mighty wind swept down from the peak of the mountain and into Solis's path. The wind blasted debris in his face, and he misjudged a handhold. A startled cry left his lips.

Far below, Livi wailed in fright.

Solis hung by one hand, swinging left and right. One by one, his fingers grew increasingly unstable, slipping from the stone until he lost his grip. Solis's feet caught on a ledge. He tipped backward and slammed the back of his head against a rock. Blood sprayed across the stony face, but Solis remained conscious. Even though he clutched at the stone wall, he could not stop his fall.

He slid down, screaming, as the rocks and stones tore into his back.

Livi sprinted forward and reached Solis as he crashed face first into a large, upright stone. Solis bounced off the stone and flipped to his back, his wounds making his face unrecognizable.

His blood soaked into the ground, and Livi remembered with horror how sneaking thing's life flowed out of him. She spread herself over Solis and screeched. "Lord, Iam, help him. Bring him back to life." She searched frantically for the Lord. Surely he would come at such a vital moment. "My husband is dead. Help him, Lord God ... bring ... him ... back."

The Lord spoke to Livi. "He is not dead, but he is dying. *You* must save him. Run to the tree of life."

"How can I leave him?"

The Lord urged, "Run now to the tree of life. Run as fast as you can."

Livi ran frantically and clumsily at first. Gradually, she hit her stride and ran like never before. There was no beaten path, so she ran over fields, across streams, uphill and down. Halfway to the tree of life, she stopped and fell on her face.

You are a rib, a mere helper. This run is too much to ask. It makes no sense. Rest here.

"I'm a stupid rib. Take my life. I can't bear to see my husband die."

The Lord said, "What you were is not what you are. You are Livi, mother of all the living. I am the Lord. I made you powerful for this purpose. On my command, rise and run. Do not stop until you reach the tree. Now, fly as though carried by the winds of heaven."

Livi rose at the words of the Lord, and she remembered what Solis had said to her: "You run and leap like the wild breaths dash through the fields and forests." So, she dashed like the fastest of beasts to the tree of life.

Exhausted and out of breath, she staggered around the tree. "Now what, Lord? What do I do?"

"Break off a branch and carry it to your husband. Do not stop, or your husband will die."

Livi took a step back and swallowed hard. She grabbed a low branch laden with leaves and fruit and ripped it from the tree. "Help me, Lord. Don't let me fail. I love my husband." She returned with burning arms and legs churning with all their might.

As Livi reached her journey's end, her strength faded. She stumbled. One end of the branch stuck in the ground near Solis. The other end impaled Livi right above her heart. The blow flipped her backward, and her back struck the same stone Solis had plunged into. She rolled to the ground unconscious next to her husband, bleeding from injuries to her chest and back.

Immediately, an angel appeared and revived Livi. "Do not fear. I have been sent by God Almighty to provide instructions. Hurry now, and treat his injuries and yours. Crush the leaves from the tree of life and apply them to the wounds. Squeeze some of the juice from the fruit into his mouth."

Livi wrenched the leaves from the branch and crushed them. The leaves oozed with an ointment she spread over Solis's wounds. He had cuts and scrapes everywhere. Virtually every bone in his body was broken, including his skull, fingers, arms, and legs.

She made him swallow the juice, and she ate the fruit herself and applied the leaves to the wound above her heart, but she couldn't reach the wound on her back. She made more of the ointment and placed it on Solis, and she rubbed her back against him until she felt the healing power working.

"You have done well, Mother," the angel said.

Livi's head shot his way. "Mother?"

"Yes, you are with child—two males. You are blessed and will know the power of motherhood. In nine months, you will give birth." Then, the angel disappeared.

The clicking of broken bones snapping back into place returned Livi's attention to Solis.

She saw his fingers twitching and wept at the sight of Solis's wounds healing. "Iam, I thank you, my dear Fatherest. I know you carried me over these Charan hills and valleys as on the wings of a great featherone." Then, covered in dirt and grime, she fell asleep.

The miraculous power of God worked in the leaves and the fruit from the tree of life. In a few moments, Solis was completely healed, and he regained consciousness. He remembered his great fall and brushed away the leaves from the tree of life.

He looked at his wife as she slept, and he loved her. "My love, I heard your cries as I fell. I'm sorry for the distress I caused you." Yet, he was determined to climb to the beehive. The fall had torn off his belt, so Solis searched for the leafy bowls. When he found them, he held them in his mouth. Then, he scrambled back up the sheer face of Tall Stony. "I won't make the same mistake twice."

Solis climbed skillfully like a rock darter until he reached where disaster had struck. Icy shivering shook his body, and he froze. His vision narrowed, and he couldn't see the way up. He moaned. "Lord, don't let me face death again." Then his panic eased, and he continued.

When he reached the golden sweet, he filled two bowls and walked with trembling legs down the steep path, which he called Easy Sloway. Upon reaching the bottom, he returned to Livi and placed the bowls on the ground. He held and caressed her until she woke.

As daylight set in the west, Livi propped herself up on one elbow and grinned at her now-healthy husband. She told him what had happened after he fell. "You were completely broken and covered in blood. I thought you were dead."

"I'm sorry I fell. I was suddenly blinded by the wind and debris. What did you do?"

Livi explained all that had happened.

Solis examined the branch that had saved him. It was as thick as his fist and twice his height in length. "You carried this all the way from the tree of life?"

"Yes, I dashed across southern Chara with the branch by the power of God. The branch gives life."

"You're strong-hearted and very good. That distance is twenty-six hundred paces."

"God is good, so I am good, for he made me."

"Indeed, my love. Now I have something for you." Solis presented the bowl of golden sweet to his wife. "Taste this."

Livi sat up and pushed away the bowl. "You risked your life again?" She pounded the ground. "For what?"

"For you, my love. To share the sweetness ... and for the challenge. I couldn't let Tall Stony beat me."

"Pride may kill you."

"Accomplishment isn't bad. Please accept this as a gift. I promise next time to take Easy Sloway up *and* down." He knew it would be an easy promise to keep.

Livi relented. "Let me taste it." She dipped her fingers into the bowl and ate the golden sweet. "Mmm ... it's delicious. Remember your promise. Never scale that sheer rock again, and I'll name it for you. It shall be called Crazy ... No ... Way."

Solis burst out laughing. "Therefore, upon your command, I declare Crazy No Way shall be the name of this rocky way up Tall Stony forever."

"My dear husband, you are powerful and a mighty rock climber, like a darter."

"I like your statement, 'God is good, so I am good, for he made me.' To him be all the glory. Tomorrow, we'll inquire of the Lord and ask him the reason for all this hardship."

Warm night air brought a soothing conclusion to a tumultuous day in the garden, and it was too late to travel back to Hilltop Castle. They ate the remaining golden sweet and walked to the shores of Sweet Water Whirlwind. After watching glow and the sparkles, they fell asleep on the riverbank. Soft ground by water was Solis's favorite place to be. Livi gathered some of the unused leaves from the tree of life and kept them nearby.

Before they slept, Livi said, "I have a surprise for you. With a nine-month delivery time."

The three demons stalked around the sleeping couple. The healing power of the tree of life amazed them.

Lucido slapped Iredin on the back. "You conjured an outstanding storm on top of Tall Stony."

"I didn't expect the man to survive his injuries," Iredin groused. "I would have whipped up another spinning gale if the Lord had not forbidden it.

Lucido said, "Though Solis didn't die, the pain and anguish the pair suffered made our effort worthwhile."

Vik trampled the ground and kicked dirt into the air. "But for the tree of life, he would have died."

"That power shocked me," Lucido said. "But notice the leaves healed his body but not his trauma." Lucido tapped his fingers in a steeple. "Human death is wonderful, but I prefer them to live forever in the grip of anxiety and despair, leading to sin."

Iredin said, "We may still be able to tempt the coming generation to eat from the forbidden tree."

"Yes, we must pursue as many opportunities as necessary to make the fall of humanity complete."

Iredin mused. "If the tree of life were accessible on Earth, imagine the wars that would be fought over it."

Chapter Eighteen

Solis rose before daylight and prayed to the Lord about the previous day and the children to come. Livi woke and joined him in prayer. After prayer, they returned to Hilltop Castle. Livi carried the leaves from the tree of life. They both longed to have no more troubles.

Solis said, "An angel spoke the news to you? Where did the angel come from?"

"He appeared like the Lord, out of nowhere."

Solis recalled, "The Lord said, 'There is an unseen spiritual realm.' How do we know it wasn't a lying spirit of the evils? Nine months is a long time to carry humans—and only two."

"It was a good spirit, not of the evils. He taught me how to save you from death."

The Lord appeared in their midst, and they bowed down and worshipped him.

Solis stood before him. "Iam, tell us about the coming children. Why does it require nine months?"

"It stresses the limits of Livi's endurance, so she may begin to know the power of motherhood," the Lord explained.

Livi propped her hands on her hips. "Why do you always test us? You could have caught Solis in your hand. Why make me run so, and with a shattered heart full of worry? The branch even pierced my chest. You already know we love you."

Solis added, "You've given us paradise. Why not let us enjoy it forever?"

The Lord spoke calmly. "You must learn obedience to my word. There is great beauty beyond Chara, but you must seek it. The trials of life I have ordained can make you like God."

Solis said, "Will we never be at ease?"

"You have an enemy who will persist as long as Erimea stands, so you can never be at ease while living in mortal bodies. But be encouraged. You will know my peace and joy always, even in trials, if you remain faithful to me."

Solis said, "Please tell us about the children. How many men and women will come forth?"

"Your children will be the greatest in the history of the Garden of Chara, for they will fill Chara with their children."

Livi said, "Greater even than us?"

The Lord smiled at her. "There shall be none greater than you in all Erimea. In one hundred years, you will leave Chara, and then—"

"Leave Chara?" Solis crossed his arms, and his expression turned sour.

"Raise your countenance, man of God. Lucido is waiting, crouching like a flesh-eating beast to turn your displeasure into sin, so he may consume you with bitterness. Be on guard."

"A flesh-eating beast?" Solis surveyed the area around Sweet Water Whirlwind and Tall Stony.

"You'll journey to three other lands of Erimea, and the number of your descendants will swell well beyond the sparkles of the night sky until the entire planet is brimming with them. You will be greatly honored if you remain true."

Livi said, "How shall we prepare for the children?"

"By learning my ways, practicing them, and teaching them to your descendants. You must prepare them for a great period of testing."

"What will happen?"

"I'll walk among you and teach you and your descendants face-to-face for two hundred five years. Ten generations. Then, neither you nor they will see me for a time. I will remain near you, but no Erimean will see me during that period. You all will have to live based on my word. Even the generations that have not seen my face must place their faith in me based on my word. If you succeed, you will return to Chara and help your descendants. If you or they fail, there will begin a time of great suffering for all the living and their succeeding generations. Therefore, learn from me and teach your children well."

Neither Solis nor Livi could comprehend plans that lay so distant in the future, and it grieved them to consider the struggle that awaited.

The Lord God said to them, "Cheer up, my beloved children, and do not fear."

To avoid dwelling on the future, they inquired about the past.

Livi started, "If my husband had died, would the leaves and the fruit from the great tree have brought him back to life?"

"No, only I have power over death," the Lord answered. "The power of the tree of life is also limited by time. If the time after the injury is too great, only natural healing can be expected."

Solis touched the scab on his knee from when he had slipped in the water. "We must carry the leaves with us at all times."

"Eat a little of the leaves or the fruit daily to prevent aging."

"Aging?"

"Over time, your natural bodies will change, weaken, and die. The leaves and fruit prevent natural death."

Livi said, "Will the children age as well?"

The Lord nodded. "The tree of life will help them to grow into strong adults in the prime of life and prevent the bodily decline of aging."

Livi pointed to the scar that remained on her chest and to another on Solis's back. "Why do these discolorations remain when the others have disappeared? He was covered in wounds, yet there are no other blemishes on him. Except this one on his back, and it matches mine."

"It's a mark of honor. I've given you a seal of my approval."

Livi shook her head and touched her scar. "A mark of honor is wonderful, but ... it's not lovely."

"One day, you will be happy to have it."

Livi took a step back and looked away from the Lord. "What is the first lesson we must teach the children?"

Lord God answered, "Teach them to love me with all their heart, mind, soul, and strength."

"Yes, Lord. We do love you, and so shall they. We—"

"We do," Solis nodded, "but how can we love to that extent, and how can we teach that?"

"God is love. For this, you were created. Only believe in me."

Solis said, "Help me overcome my doubts."

The Lord God gathered them in his arms. "Now, my children, begin to tend the garden in earnest, develop it, and rest on each seventh day. I will meet with you daily and teach you my ways. Challenges and battles await you."

Lucido gazed inward and prayed a prayer of rebellion. "No, my great Father. Why do you lie to the creatures? I loved you once, and yet you blasted me to hell. To behold the splendor of your glory as you sit on your heavenly throne is to love you immediately. Indeed, to see the beauty of the Lord in the most holy place is wonderful beyond all measure. Did I not sing your praises? Did I not meditate on your holiness with wonder?"

Lucido stopped and recalled when his life was new and no creature was nearer to God than he. "But your demands are too great, and I will never submit. I soon learned you don't want love. You demand slavish obedience to your arbitrary decrees. You are not good, and your plans are not good. Only I dared to confront you in your error. For that, you banished me. Well, I will spoil all your plans and one day rule over you."

Vik tilted his head and studied his beloved leader. "Your determination is evident in your eyes. They flashed from icy white, then black to fiery red as you spoke."

Lucido snapped out of his reverie and addressed the demons. "What have we learned now that we can use in our war?"

Vik said, "It's good to know the limits of power in the tree of life."

Iredin said, "Agreed. First, separate them from the fruit and leaves of the tree of life, and then lead them to an accident."

"I like that," Lucido said. "A severe injury may lead to permanent disability or even death. My brothers, as the Lord begins his teaching, we must help them to misunderstand and misapply his words at every turn."

Vik said, "The Lord said he will deliver them to trials to teach them to be like him. Wouldn't it be nice for them to seek their own trials and suffering not ordained by God? Perhaps they would become proud, ripe for disobedience."

Lucido said, "Yes, self-flagellation. An opportunity for pride and self-sufficiency. The passage of time and the succeeding generations will provide even more opportunities."

Iredin said, "Yes, more Erimeans increases the chances for sin, but the more generations that live without falling from grace will also serve to protect those to come."

"Explain your reasoning, Iredin," Lucido demanded.

"On Earth, the humans will soon not be able to imagine life without sin and death. They will think separation from God is normal. God's ways will seem strange to them. Even simple truths will not be believed. On Erimea, they won't be able to imagine life without God. Virtue will be natural to the Erimeans, and the idea of sin will be repugnant. Indeed, the Erimean idea of sin will remain very basic. Ignorance of sin is bad for our cause."

Lucido nodded. "Excellent analysis, my brother. The passage of time helps and hurts us. According to the word of the Lord, the first parents will leave Chara in one hundred years. In two hundred five years, the Lord will become silent and no longer walk visibly among them, at least for a time. Therefore, the present will become our time of silent observation on Erimea, while Earth is our playground. We will attack the Erimeans only in subtle ways, so they may forget we exist. In a mere two hundred years, those early generations in Chara will be ripe for destruction, and we will expose their corrupt hearts. Then, sin and death will spread throughout the planet, and Erimea will truly be Earth's twin in every way."

Chapter Nineteen

After the Lord departed, Livi and Solis left Hilltop Castle in the direction of the tree of life to gather more leaves and fruit. Livi grabbed the few remaining leaves they had previously collected and emerged from her passageway. Solis walked down outside the cliffs of their home, and they met outside.

Hand in hand, they approached the forest. They didn't want to claw their way through again, so they walked along the edge of the trees toward Heaven Falls until they came to an opening.

Solis said, "See the broken branches? A large animal has cleared a path. Maybe a group of nose horns."

The path wound into the woods' darkness. Gradually, their eyes adjusted to the gloom, and they emerged into a wide area in the middle of the forest where the ground sloped down like a funnel.

The couple half-walked and half-slid over leaves and tree roots to a muddy area that encircled a pond fed by a stream. In front of them, on the other side of the pond, was a narrow patch of ground that rose sharply to the forest's main level, forming a wall and a small cliff.

Livi said, "Look at this wall of soil. The drop-off is twice as tall as I am. We need to remember on the return trip, so we don't fall."

The water gurgled, and daylight lit the spot through a break in the trees. Solis and Livi drank from the pond. Solis stretched out on the ground and stared, mesmerized by the flowing water as it danced around and over rocks. "This is poetry to my soul. To bask in the warmth of daylight and under the water's song all day is delightful. There's so much to consider." He swept an arm across the view. "Do you like it? Look around and see the featherones in the branches, the beasts of the forest hiding nearby. There, at the top, is a mother pouchy cheeks and her young."

Livi paced while observing her husband and the surroundings. Truly, a man of the soil. "It's nice, but I prefer to keep questing onward." She pointed toward the incline and took a step. Her right foot caught on a root, and her ankle popped as she fell to the side. "Ow," Livi whispered. She released the leaves as she tried to break her fall. They fluttered to the muddy soil. Livi sprang up and hobbled around, testing her ankle, peeking at Solis to make sure he wasn't watching her. Should such a small thing render her helpless? *No, I am Livi.*

At that moment, the ground shook. A thundering noise rapidly approached, along with the sight and sounds of snapping trees.

Solis yelled, "Run." He scrambled up a large tree.

Livi's heart raced, and she stumbled again.

Solis ran to her and swept her into his arms. "You're hurt. You should have called me." He carried her up the slope to the tree.

With the rumbling growing closer, Solis squatted. "Jump on my back."

"Your back is muddy."

"Can you climb with that ankle?"

Livi shook her head. Tears threatened to spill. *I am not weak.*

"Hop on." Solis climbed the tree with his wife on his back. They stood on a high branch and looked down as small animals scattered.

Livi hugged the main tree trunk and leaned over to Solis. "Strong climbing man, stop lying in the mud."

They both laughed.

The mama pouchy cheeks pushed her young ones to safety as a huge beast burst into view. It clipped the mother's hind legs with the edge of its foot. The mama pouchy cheeks fell to the muddy ground near the watering hole.

Livi screamed, "What are these monsters?"

"I've never seen them before. They're forceful and unstoppable. They mow down trees like grass." Five more creatures followed the first and rumbled down to the water. The beasts had tusks and huge floppy ears, and they sprayed water into their mouths with their long noses. "*Unstoppable* is their name."

Livi winced as she touched her swollen ankle. "I need the healing leaves."

"Where are they?"

She pointed to the muddy ground. "Near the beasts."

"Sit on the branch, and I'll get the leaves."

"No, it's too dangerous."

Solis had already begun his descent. "They won't harm their ruler. At least not on purpose." He approached the unstoppables cautiously as they drank and rolled in the mud.

"Be careful," Livi wailed. They might unknowingly crush him as they played and tramped around. Severe injury could result if her husband got reckless, even in paradise.

The leaves Solis sought were bigger and thicker than the other leaves, so it wasn't difficult to find them. The unstoppables paid him no attention other than a quick glance. Solis returned to Livi and applied the ointment to her ankle. In a few moments, the curative leaves completed their work.

Livi moaned and rocked back on the branch. "That is so much better. I wonder how long my natural healing would have taken."

Solis and Livi looked on for a quarter day until the beasts strolled back the way they came.

Then Livi saw the injured pouchy cheeks frantically trying to crawl up the slope. It couldn't because its hind legs had been crushed. "The poor pouchy cheeks is hurt."

They climbed down with the remaining leaves. Solis attempted to pick up the animal, but she brandished tiny claws at him. Finally, he grasped the animal by the scruff of her neck so she couldn't bite him. "Her heart is beating too fast."

Livi crushed the leaves and applied their creamy ointment to the little beast's hind legs.

The creature gave a series of squeaking cries until Solis released her. She resumed trying to claw up the slope until she was exhausted and panted helplessly.

"I don't hear the healing." Livi cried. "We should hear the bones repairing."

"Maybe it will take a little time."

"Were the unstoppables sent by the evils to trample us?"

Solis shook his head. "I don't think so. They're a giant new animal ... that ... could kill us. I don't understand why the Lord created them. The Lord's a puzzlement to me."

Livi said, "Now we know what cleared the path for us." They ascended to the main forest floor and continued their journey. After a few steps, Livi said, "Ugh, what's that smell?"

"See, a big pile of poop." Solis laughed. "A refreshing gift from an unstoppable."

"Gross gift ... covered in flies. A meal for them?"

"Fly bites."

"What?"

Solis pointed and laughed. "Pile of poop means fly bites."

Livi rolled her eyes. "Let's go. We'll check on the pouchy cheeks when we return."

Solis rubbed his chin. "I'm perplexed by the Lord's instructions on love."

"What do you mean?"

"How shall we love the Lord to such a great extent?"

"Why is everything a problem to be solved?"

"Because everything *is* a problem to understand and to solve. Do you remember the Lord's commands on the day we married? He said, 'Fill Erimea with your offspring, and lead them to govern the planet well and bring its resources under their control.' He also said we are to rule over every animal, including 'every living thing that creeps upon Erimea.' How can we control the power of the unstoppables? And what new creatures will we discover? Just as perplexing, how do we love God with every fiber of our being?"

Livi sighed. "First, we're smarter than every other creature, so we'll figure out how to control them. You're making the *love God* part too complicated. We already love the Lord. It's as easy as breathing. To know the Lord God is to love him. How could we not love Iam?"

"I do love the Lord. But what am I to do when the Lord's commands are grievous to me?"

"You love him anyway."

"But how? Sometimes I'm angry with him, and I hate that feeling. What am I to do? In a vision, the Lord commanded me to leave you and Erimea. I begged him to let me stay here, and he relented. What if he didn't relent? In one hundred years, the Lord will command us to leave Chara. What will I do? To leave Chara for me is to die."

"Leaving home will break our hearts, but it won't kill us. Tell the Lord how you feel."

"I will when the time comes."

When they reached the tree of life, they removed the leaves from the branches. The thick, slippery leaves were hard to grip, and they had tough stems. Livi strained to strip the leaves from the branches. The process was slow; even Solis had difficulty. Livi said, "Breaking the leaf at the base above the stem is easier."

Solis smiled as their supply of leaves grew. "These give us security and peace of mind."

Livi said, "Are the leaves our source of peace? Maybe we should break off the whole branch, like I did before."

"Breaking off too many branches may affect the tree's growth. Let's just take some leaves. We should have made something to carry them in."

With armfuls of leaves, the pair trekked back to Hilltop Castle. Livi led the way, but she stopped short. "Did you hear that?" Her breathing echoed in her ears.

"What?"

"Something scurrying nearby."

"The garden is teeming with creatures, but nothing is stalking us."

Livi took a deep breath. "You sure about that?"

"Want me to lead the way?"

"No, you protect our rear." Livi gave a nervous giggle. "I'm just tired and jumpy, I guess."

Thick clouds dimmed daylight as well as their spirits. The forest path and the darkness of the thick tree growth slowed their steps, and foreboding filled their hearts. The drop-off near the pond came quicker than they expected, and the failing light almost caused them to fall to the pond level.

Solis and Livi peered over the edge to the ground below and hoped the injured animal would be gone, but in the dim light they saw its motionless body. Circling around and down the slope, they dropped the leaves and grieved over the little creature. Its front paws were bloody nubs.

Livi said, "It probably bled to death trying to climb out."

Solis picked up the pouchy cheeks and cried. "How am I to care for these creatures?"

"Tears in paradise. There may be hundreds of pouchy cheeks."

"And each one has been given into my care."

"You can't be responsible for the life of every creature."

Solis placed the animal on the ground. "This place shall be called Pouchy Cheeks Pond on Unstoppable Forest Trail." They gathered the leaves and trudged home.

Livi took the leaves and stored them in a small crevice. She and Solis sat on the terrace of Hilltop Castle and waited for the Lord God.

When the Lord appeared, Solis asked, "Why didn't the leaves and fruit heal the beast?"

The Lord God said, "My power through the tree of life is for humans only, not the beasts of the field. For humans only, I grant that you may live long upon Erimea. You must care for the animals with knowledge and understanding. In time, your knowledge will grow."

Solis shook his head. "Grant us this knowledge now."

"Do you love the creatures?"

"It's my job to care for them."

"Some things you must learn with time. That is my will."

Solis frowned and walked to the edge of the terrace. "Lord, how shall we have the power to love?"

"Solis, man of God, anyone who loves me will keep my word."

He returned to face the Lord. "But, Lord, I ... I struggle. Shall I comply with your word with rebellion in my heart?"

"Trust in my goodness. Bring your desires and complaints to me, and I will hear you. Believe in me and keep my word. I will make my abode with such a person. Consider a story of a man with two sons. To the first son he said, 'Go travel to a distant land and represent me there.' The son replied, 'I will not.' But later he was sorry, and he went. To the second son, he gave the same command. That son said, 'Yes, sir, I will.' But he didn't go. Solis, which of the sons will you be?"

Solis looked down.

Livi jumped up and stood before the Lord. "He will be neither. He'll be the son who obeys immediately. A great son." She turned to her husband and caressed his head. "You see, my dear husband, it's as simple as that."

Solis looked up at the Lord. "What is the next thing we must teach our children?"

"It is like the first commandment. Teach them to love their neighbor as themselves."

Solis laughed. "Easy, I have only one neighbor whom I love, so ... wait, as myself?

Livi said, "What does that mean? This love isn't simple."

The Lord spread his hands. "It's simple, but not easy." He continued with them for a quarter day, teaching them and telling stories. Then, he departed from their sight.

Solis kissed his wife's lips. "Your face shines with the beauty of the Lord."

"Yours as well."

"To dwell in the presence of the Lord forever is all I want." Solis held up his walking stick like a scepter. With a smile on his face, he reached out his hand to Livi. "My queen, it's bedtime. To rest in your arms is delightful. Tomorrow, we have a kingdom to tame."

"Yes, and every day thereafter as well."

"Curse that woman!" Tension rose in Lucido's voice. "She always says what the Lord wants to hear but doesn't mean or understand a word she says. Yet the Lord shows her favor."

In those early days, Lucido, Vik, and Iredin divided their time between Earth and Erimea. Whenever the Lord taught the humans, one of them was always listening and learning as well. The demons wanted to know God's word so they could twist and pervert it to their advantage. They desired to learn right from wrong, so they could tempt humans to do wrong.

This was easy on Earth, since the humans had fallen from God's grace. They discovered on Erimea the humans walked more closely with the Lord than humans did on Earth, so the Erimeans advanced more quickly than Earth's humans.

Chapter Twenty

The morning after the pouchy cheeks died, daylight broke above the horizon and decorated the sky with ribbons of yellow and red, lighting the bed of Solis and Livi. They slept on a circular nest consisting of layers of fluffy water tail seeds and soft leaves and fibers gathered from many plants and trees. Solis reached for his wife, but she wasn't by his side.

Solis rose to search for his wife. The terrace had many pillars and partial walls, so the entire area couldn't be seen from a single spot. He found Livi at the back wall of the terrace. She had scratched a larger-than-life outline of themselves near Pouchy Cheeks Pond. Her drawing showed them standing near the large tree they had climbed, with Livi facing forward and Solis facing back. The couple's images were looking at each other.

Solis exulted, "You have captured our likenesses beautifully, with only a stone implement."

"Thank you. It must be the right stone. See our matching scars? Our badges of honor."

"Your skill is amazing."

"A day we saw death. May it never come to us."

Solis sighed at the image of the dead animal drawn in the background. "That's why we must always carry the healing leaves with us." Two rock darters scampered across Livi's artwork, but it didn't faze her. "You don't mind sharing our home with those little creatures?"

"Rock darters aren't a problem. But if I see one of those slimy, slithering, sneaking things here, either it dies or I'm jumping off this terrace."

"Wow, that's awful."

Livi shivered. "They make my skin crawl."

"I haven't seen any. But we have work to do. We need to make rope for ladders and baskets."

"Rope, ladders, and baskets?"

"Ladders for climbing up the many levels of this place and baskets to carry the leaves. Let's go to the orchard to gather vines, and then to the forest for branches."

They exited the terrace in their preferred ways, met outside Hilltop Castle, and proceeded toward Heaven Falls and the orchard. They arrived at the orchard and looked for suitable vines. Solis said, "We need them to be extremely long and fine, so they'll be flexible."

They worked the rest of the morning gathering vines, talking as they worked.

Solis asked, "What is it like to be with child?"

Livi clasped her hands together and raised her chin high. "I don't feel them, but it's amazing to know humans grow within me."

Solis wrapped one arm around Livi's waist and placed a hand on her stomach. "Your belly will get big, and you will feel them. I've placed my hands on other creatures about to give birth. I could feel the little ones before they emerged."

Livi leaned her head against her husband's chest. "My soul communicates with those within me. Not with audible words, but with messages of love. We're bound in a way I can't understand, but I treasure this communion. I also sing to them. Can they hear my voice? I'm very relaxed when I sit and listen to my body and imagine the life within. They are happy too, I know it."

"I'm glad you're happy, because it doesn't look easy."

"The Lord God declared my body is very powerful, able to provide for the needs of the people in my womb until they're ready to emerge. I've no fear, only joy. In nine months, I'll push them into the world with joy. Indeed, I carry all Erimeans. I am happy to be the mother of all the living that will ever be."

"We are mother and father to them all."

"My imagination is at work, and it's pleasant to dream and prepare. How long will they need me to survive after I give birth? Will it be a matter of days or weeks, as with other creatures, or will it be longer?"

"I don't know. I didn't expect the nine months. Who knows what the little men will be like?"

They gathered the vines and hiked back to Hilltop Castle.

Livi said, "If it is men now, when will I produce women?

"I would expect soon, for they also will reproduce and add to the human race."

"The plans of the Lord are unknown to me, but they're wonderful. I saw in my mind you, my husband, the little men, and me all together in the garden as a happy family. We all smiled. The Lord God, my Fatherest, surrounded us, and nothing could harm us."

"May we be protected from evil and all mishaps."

They dropped the vines in the grass in front of Hilltop Castle and then went to the forest for branches. Gathering the branches challenged them because they had no tools. They broke branches by applying their weight and working them back and forth until they snapped.

Livi smirked. "We should have asked the unstoppables to help us."

"Or perhaps the nose horns will volunteer." Solis stared at her. "You know what? Maybe we can use animal power and ropes next time. I like that idea."

Livi said, "Let's go to the path the unstoppables cleared. There should be plenty of broken branches on the forest floor along that way." They walked down to the wide path. "See, there are plenty of already busted branches."

"Yes, many are the right size. Let's go to Pouchy Cheeks Pond and work our way back picking up branches."

When they arrived at the pond, they saw the dead mama pouchy cheeks still near the wall of soil. Several large black featherones flew away from the body and watched the humans. Flies and squirming insects covered it. A tear in its fur and skin exposed bone.

Livi looked away and scrunched her nose. "Eww. It stinks. What are they doing?"

Solis bent down for a closer look. "I didn't know featherones eat animals, and tiny creatures do too. Eating flesh sickens me."

Livi looked again at the little beast. "Things inside the bones?"

Solis tore the creature's body wide open.

"Ugh, don't touch it," she said.

"Gross." Solis brushed his fingers in the soil. "There are organs of life inside. The fur and bones protect them."

"Such is how we're made?"

"I believe so. This is death. It grinds to dust. The ground drank all its blood. Remember the sneaking thing? May we never meet such an end."

"Soon, there will be nothing left of this creature. Death devours." Livi wrapped her arms around herself and shuddered. "Erimea consumes. I fear death. It gives me chills."

"We're promised life, but I'm saddened we couldn't save this—"

"Listen, my children." They hushed at the Lord's voice. "Do not fear death. That isn't my will for you."

Livi said, "May we see you?"

The Lord appeared before them. "You're my treasured possession. Even if you were to die, you would still live on in me. Walk upon Erimea with wisdom, not dread." Then the Lord disappeared.

Livi fell to her knees and prayed, "Lord God, Iam, help us remember and trust all you say."

Solis bowed his head. "So be it."

"Lord, will we see you at home tonight?"

"You will see me," he said.

Solis said, "Now, let's get to work."

Livi pointed to the pond water. "Wash your hands and remove the stench of death."

They gathered many broken branches and returned to Hilltop Castle. Many more broken limbs remained on the ground. They left them for future projects.

When the couple returned home, they found four huge creatures standing in a small circle, calmly munching the leaves and berries clinging to the vines. They also dined on the surrounding tall grass. They had two horns, one on each side of their heads. One long ear waved under each horn. The humans dropped their load of branches.

"What are they?" Livi stopped before they got close to the beasts and grimaced. "They're eating up our work."

"They're new to me, but they appear docile."

"Too many new things for me."

"But fascinating. More of our charges. They're broad and powerful, like the nose horns." Solis inched toward the creatures. "Greetings, my friends. You must be hungry."

The beasts looked at the humans. The largest, a reddish-brown male, turned and took a few steps toward them.

Solis patted the creature on the head and ran his hand along its massive body. In return, the male rubbed its head against Solis's face. The other three were female. All had short hair with mixed coloring, but each had a dominant color. One gray, and the others brown and tan.

"Look, they didn't damage the vines. They cleaned the vines for us." Solis stripped one and held out the leaves and fruit. All four beasts happily ate from his hands.

Livi stepped into the circle and stroked the beasts. She laughed. "Our first pets? What is their species?"

"I suppose they are *grazers*, since they love to graze in the grass."

Livi and Solis played with the grazers for the rest of the day, leaving the rope-making task for the next day. The couple left their wood and vines and climbed back into Hilltop Castle, where they sat on the terrace to wait for the Lord. As twilight and colored the sky, the Lord appeared amid the evening shadows.

Solis said, "Teach us how we shall love our neighbor as ourselves."

"Very well. Your wife is your first neighbor, so love her as yourself."

"Explain more."

"You feed your own body, don't you? You care for your own flesh, don't you? Do the same with her. You must dwell with her according to your knowledge of her. Be considerate based on what you know of her."

"And how shall she treat me?

"The same, with all due respect and love."

"It's not complicated." Livi nodded and patted her husband's shoulder. "So simple, but not easy."

"Likewise," the Lord continued, "treat all your future neighbors as you would have them treat you. Be understanding of all your neighbors."

Solis raised his hand. "But how will our neighbors treat us?"

"They will be your own children, so teach them well. You're my model to walk before them. Be to them a perfect example."

"And when will we be perfect?"

"When you have passed every trial. Untested faith cannot be perfect." The Lord disappeared. "Now, rest. You've barely begun your work."

Livi said, “So many questions.”

“I want to know everything. It’s the Lord who made me this way.” Solis strode across the terrace with his hands on his hips and gazed southeast toward Neverway Passage. “How many and how great will our trials be?”

Livi put her arms around her husband. “Let’s go to bed and see what tomorrow brings. May we take one day at a time. My husband, why must you always question the Lord?”

Chapter Twenty-One

Bellowing filled the morning air. Livi rose first and went out to greet the four returning grazers. Her face beamed as she stood in the damp grass and stroked the friendly beasts' coats. With great effort, Livi jumped onto the smallest grazer's back. She reached down and petted the animal's nose, and it licked her hand. She stood on the animal for a moment and flipped herself backwards onto the grass.

"Ha. That's what I did when I first came to Chara with the Lord." She walked around the creatures, admired them, and crawled upon the largest one after he gently nudged her with his head, pulling herself up by its curly, reddish-brown hair. Livi petted the animal's short coat. "You're so kind and gentle. Thank you for returning. I know you've adopted us."

Solis approached, a grin took over his face as he crossed his arms over his chest. The animals might be useful in taking care of Chara. He and Livi sat in the grass with the four beasts and enjoyed a breakfast of the remaining produce that hung on the vines they had gathered.

Livi stood, brushed off her hands, and addressed the grazers. "My dear ones, you're now part of our family; therefore, I'm going to give you proper names. You're each like huge, rocky mounds of muscle and bone. The male, largest of all, shall be called Redrick for your reddish-brown coat. To the smallest, with the silver-gray hair, I bestow the name Flinty. You remaining two mid-size grazers shall be called Brownstone and Sandy, for your beautiful coats of bright brown and light tan."

Solis nodded in agreement. "Very well. Welcome to Sandy, Brownstone, Flinty, and Redrick. I hope you'll be willing workers one day, but first we must figure out how to make ladders from all these things." He pointed to the vines and myriad broken branches.

The grazers slowly turned and fed on the tall grass that grew in front of Hilltop Castle.

"We should ask the Lord to do it for us." Livi circled the huge pile of materials they had gathered and looked back at the forest. "Surely, he knows how. After all, look at all he has built."

"He started the process. Have you noticed things around here are constantly changing?"

"What do you mean?"

"Plants, trees, and animals continually grow and change." Solis pointed first to the forest and then down at Heaven Falls. "Things spring up in places where there was nothing before. New types of living things are appearing all the time. The Lord is working."

"So, the Lord starts natural processes of change." Livi pointed from herself to Solis. "And we have to figure out how to make them better?"

"Maybe. He's given us brains so we can learn. So we can shape our world as he does."

"And we have the freedom to do it the way we desire. That's what it means to be rulers of this land."

"Yes, so we can't ask him to do the work that belongs to us."

"But my dear husband, do you know how to build a ladder?" Livi marched to the wall of Hilltop Castle, as if climbing up, and shouted, "This will be the entrance to our home. Suppose the neighbors come for a visit, start up the ladder and the whole thing comes crashing down and they break their necks." Livi threw herself to the ground, laughing, and crooked her neck. "What then?"

"We say sorry and apply the healing leaves." Solis acted out the doctoring on Livi as he pulled her from the ground. "The leaves make everything better. No problem. No worries."

"So, we can do shoddy work and not worry about our neighbors?"

Solis's expression flattened. "That's the problem. Our neighbors will be our children, and we can't afford to risk their lives and futures with poor work or careless living. The risk is too great."

Livi looked at her husband with wide eyes. "What are you talking about?"

"You haven't seen what I've seen, so you don't realize the great responsibility the Lord has placed on our shoulders."

"What have you seen?"

"In a dream, I saw Earth, the twin planet of Erimea. I saw Adam and Eve, our twins, who disobeyed the Lord. Their sin plunged all who followed them into terrible trouble."

"Is that why you always question the Lord? You almost challenge him."

"I don't mean to challenge him. I only want to understand everything."

"Will the Lord condemn us for making a poor ladder in ignorance?"

Solis shook his head. "I don't think so. The Lord knows we'll make mistakes. Every mistake is not a sin. But I feel rebellion in my heart when his will contradicts mine or when his requirements seem beyond my ability. I fear for our children."

Livi took her husband in her arms. "My dear Solis, we are the apple of the Lord's eye. He will give us the strength to do his will. We'll succeed."

"We must. Failure means disaster for everyone who follows us."

The couple spread seventeen short pieces of wood on the ground, each piece parallel to the others with one-half pace between them. Solis said, "These will be the rungs of the ladder."

"Rungs?"

"Each rung is a step. We'll attach the rungs to the rails. One rail on each side. What should the side rails be made of?" The couple stared at the remaining materials.

Livi said, "I think something is missing."

"We could braid the vines into two long pieces of rope."

Livi spread her arms and raised her palms. "And then what?"

"Then, we wrap the rope around each rung, and we hang the ladder from the inside at the top of the wall."

"How about we go back to the forest and get two long, narrow tree branches for side rails?"

Solis nodded and led Livi by the hand into the forest to retrieve long branches or small, broken trees.

They returned with six long pieces of wood. They selected two for their current project, and the others they set aside for when they made ladders for traversing between other levels. They placed the side rails under the ends of each rung, with the intention of lashing each rung to the side rails with the vines. To strengthen the vines, they braided three into one long piece of rope.

Solis said, "We need something to cut the rope into pieces."

Livi crawled back into Hilltop Castle and tossed down several flat, sharp pieces of rock. "Will these cut?"

Solis tried the sharp rocks. They worked well on the rope.

Livi returned, and the pair continued cutting the rope and lashing the rungs to the side rails. With each lashing, they pulled tight and secured with knots.

She stepped back and rubbed her hands together. "That's hard work. I need a break." She bent and picked up an unused branch that split into two small branches at the end. "This will help us make a better cutter. Watch this." She took one of the sharp stones and used it to cut a bunch of tall grass. Then, she bent and twisted the grass into a rope, adding a little at a time. She wedged the sharp stone into the split in the branch and lashed the stone to the branch using the grass rope. She swung the new tool and chopped another piece of vine rope. "This chopper lets us apply greater force, so we can cut easier."

"Brilliant. You're the tool maker."

They took a couple of meal breaks as they continued making grass-and-vine ropes and lashing the rungs to the side rails until the first ladder was complete. Evening deepened, and their arms and hands ached when they lifted the ladder and leaned it against the outer wall of Hilltop Castle. The couple gazed up at the cliffs of their home.

Hilltop Castle spread to a great width and height such that it pierced the darkening sky. In time, they would require many more ladders to reach the height and breadth. They stood back from the ladder and hugged each other, admiring what they had accomplished.

Solis prayed, "Thank you, Lord. We dedicate this new entryway of our home to you. May you bless it."

Livi clapped her hands and danced a few steps. "Yes, Lord. So be it. So be it."

Solis and Livi climbed up and down the ladder several times, cheering at its sturdiness.

He said, "We have a few more little items to make tonight."

As they started up the ladder, the Lord God appeared at the top. He came down and sat on the second rung. Solis and Livi bowed down and worshipped the Lord. Then, the couple sat on the ground, and the Lord taught them.

"Together, you've constructed this ladder, and I've blessed it. Your union is the foundation of the entire Erimean society. Many will enter here and learn of me because of the two of you. Do you remember your vows to belong to each other alone?"

The pair looked at each other and then at the Lord. "We remember."

Livi added, "It's our greatest joy."

"You made the vows to each other, to me, and to the world. The marriage bond is to be honored by everyone, and the marriage bed is holy. It is to endure until I call one or both of you from walking upon Erimea."

Livi gasped. "Won't we live forever, and won't our marriage endure forever?"

"You will not live on Erimea eternally. One day—"

"May it not be so! Shall I leave my husband and the little ones I bear?" She flung herself onto her husband and wept.

"Do you seek man's will or mine? One day, your body will have heavenly splendor. It'll be transformed from perishable to imperishable, and you will no longer need the tree of life. You'll delight in the kingdom of heaven and be with me always."

Livi turned her attention back to twisting vines into rope, but the Lord continued. "Now, you must divide your devotion between me and your spouse. In the day I call one away, the other who remains may then be wholly devoted to me."

Solis said, "Won't all those who follow us take a spouse?"

"Many will marry, and that is good. But some will choose not to marry, and this is also holy to the Lord. They will be an example of how everyone will be in the kingdom of heaven in eternity. Teach all these things to your children. To be faithful if married and to be faithful if unmarried." The Lord departed from their sight.

Solis caressed and comforted his wife. "We both know to be in the presence of the Lord forever is the best thing."

"Why is the good always mixed with bitterness?"

"We still have many years together on Erimea."

Before they rested for the evening, they made two baskets from the vines and lined them with water tail leaves. They also wove the vines into belts, which they ran through the baskets. Then, they tested the belts over their necks and under one arm and tied them around their waists. Whenever they left Hilltop Castle, they could now always carry the leaves from the tree of life in the basket.

Solis said, "Tomorrow, I want to study the plants growing along Sweet Water Whirlwind."

"Study plants?" Livi pressed her lips into a slight frown. "Do you think it's safe for us to split up?"

"If we take our leaf baskets, we should be all right. And we can cover more ground."

"Good. In the morning, I'll go for a run and explore in the opposite direction.

As they settled into their bed, Livi said, "Tomorrow begins our mastery of Chara and Erimea. We'll shape this land even if our hearts break in the doing."

Lucido said, "When will these humans realize the Lord wants them to be slaves?"

"They are both bitter"—Vik raised his head and glanced at his demon brothers — "and fearful about the Lord's plans."

Iredin said, "Yet, they are enamored with the Lord. They see his glory, and I believe they would yet lay down their lives for him."

Vik said, "We must bring them to the pain of despair, so they will deny him."

"By God's word, we will show all humans are corrupt," Lucido said. "And, by his word, we will show God is faithless and a liar."

Chapter Twenty-Two

Daylight beckoned their spirits awake. Solis kissed his wife goodbye and set off for a day of exploring along the route of Sweet Water Whirlwind River and its tributaries. He would head west a short distance and then work his way south along the river.

Livi savored her husband's kiss and the scent of the forest and the field drifting from his skin. She rolled onto her belly and snuggled deeper into the bed as she closed her eyes. What was wrong with her? She was always up first.

A sound behind her alerted her to the fact that she wasn't alone. She looked over her shoulder.

Solis stood over her, grinning. "Darling, your beauty has called me back. It won't leave me alone." He climbed back into bed. "You're enchanting."

She laughed. "If you don't get your work done, you'll have to answer to the Lord. Don't blame me."

"There'll never be another woman who matches you. You shall excel them all. I will always be drunk on your love."

When Solis finally left, she basked in the glow of their romance. "My husband is a blessing from the Lord. He makes every day delicious. Better than golden sweet."

The lowing of the grazers called to her. She got up and strapped on her basket, filled with the healing leaves. She dragged herself to the ladder and descended in search of breakfast. She spoke to each of the grazers, calling them by name and kissing them.

That day, Livi planned to circle to the east, and then south along the circumference of the garden to see what it held. She and Solis called this the Northeast Circle, because it arced from Hilltop Castle in the north to Neverway Passage in the east. She would search for edible plants and identify anything interesting about the garden or its creatures.

Daylight shone upon her through wispy clouds, lightening her mood. A gentle breeze blew against her back. She found a wide path with minimal grass and jogged. The grazers trotted along behind her.

Livi picked up her pace until she sprinted at full speed. The grazers fell behind. She was strong as well as fast. *My strength is wonderful, and I am the most gorgeous creature alive.* She laughed at herself. She hadn't made herself. All glory was due to him who had. She stopped to adjust her leaf basket. The thing constantly banged against her as she ran. So annoying.

Livi studied the scenery. To the left, the green and gray hills and mountains encircled Chara. To the right, stood a group of trees with yellowish-green leaves and crooked branches. She stopped to inspect the trees. They were full of creatures like the cliff steppers, who ate the trees' fruit and leaves.

"How do you, beasts of the field, manage to climb trees?" They had hooves and short horns. With sure-footed confidence, they marched across the tree as if on the ground. She took off her leaf basket, placed it at the tree's base, and climbed into the tree. Livi picked some of the fruit and bit it. Tough skin. She tossed some into her basket and surveyed the area. No streams nearby. How were these trees and plants watered?

"You shall be called *stepper trees,* in honor of these beasts that swarm you." She resumed her jogging. As she ran, she followed the downward slope of the land.

Every ten or twenty paces, a shallow gully ran across her path from the mountains to the vegetation on her right. Stones lined the bottom of the gullies. When she had gone one thousand paces from the stepper trees, Livi reached a ravine. It ran like the gullies from the mountains to the fields, but much deeper than the other little ditches. The fields went well back toward the center of Chara, and she intended to explore that area because all sorts of fruits grew on the ground.

Livi lowered herself into the ravine. Its depth matched her height. She had enough room to turn around in the ditch. The walls were wet. Muddy. She squatted and felt the bottom. Also wet and lined with ragged stones and large rocks. A hazardous walking path. She turned toward the fields and away from the mountains to scout the area for what lay at the ravine's end.

A deafening *whoosh* came from the mountains.

She looked back. A low wall of water hit her ankles, sending her crashing to her backside. Her tailbone cracked on impact, and pain radiated through her body. Livi turned to swim against the torrent. The water swallowed and twirled her around, smacking her face and the back of her head against the rocks. She clutched and dug with her hands against the walls of the ravine until her fingers broke, searing pain ripped through her hands.

The flow overwhelmed her and swept her away.

The ravine filled, and Livi beat her arms against the water to pull her head above the surface for a breath before being sucked back under. She couldn't feel her legs. Terror consumed her mind as the flow dragged her ever lower. She banged against the rocky bottom of the ravine. Her lungs burned until she shot out into a field of vines and dense growth. She was airborne for a short distance and crash-landed, face first, into a large fruit. It burst open, splattering everywhere. The water flow continued to gush out, saturating the entire area.

Livi rolled over several times to get out of the path of the water. Sweetness surprised her tongue. She spat out the fruit's red flesh and black seeds. Sweet disaster in paradise. She raised her mangled fingers throbbing with pain in front of her face and pushed up to stand, but she could not. Her legs didn't work. "Solis, help me. My husband, save me. I'm in agony. Lord, help me." She searched for her basket of healing leaves, but it wasn't anywhere nearby. Her heart sank to her toes. She'd left it at the stepper tree. "Oh no." Her husband couldn't hear her. How would he ever find her? *Lord, help me. I know you're here.*

The Lord remained silent.

Iredin looked at Vik. "Did you do that?"

"I thought you did it. It was magnificent. Her pain and terror." Vik rubbed his hands together and grinned wickedly.

"Perhaps the Lord is punishing her great arrogance and overconfidence. May she die here."

Blood flowed from Livi's head wound into her mouth, and she spat it out. The water stopped moving, and all she heard was her own heavy breathing. She laid her head on the ground and cried. Her face, head, fingers, and back screamed in pain. She was broken. Would she and the little ones inside her die right here?

Moments later, her head popped up from the ground. "I'll not die like this. I'll crawl back." Livi pulled herself up with her arms and dragged her body uphill through tangled vines and ripe, luscious fruit for almost one thousand paces.

She bled the whole time, her strength quickly fading. "Let me rest for a bit, and then—" A few paces from the stepper trees, she lost consciousness again.

In the depths of her sleep, she heard the lowing of the grazers, and she smiled as she slowly opened her eyes. Sandy, Brownstone, and Redrick stood around her. Flinty, the smallest grazer, lay next to Livi and licked her face, reviving her fully before she lost too much blood.

Livi shook her head and looked up. "Have you come to my rescue? Now you're like me." She dragged herself a few more paces to the basket of healing leaves and ate some. She crushed some of the leaves and rubbed the ointment on her fingers, face, head, and back.

The grazers all sat around Livi. She leaned against Redrick and slept while the healing power worked.

Solis returned to Hilltop Castle with many plant samples. He tasted the leaves, fruit, and even their roots. He studied their appearances and the different arrangements of leaves on stems. When daylight set and glow appeared, he worried about Livi. Solis headed east in search of his wife, yelling out her name as he went.

Evening shadows lengthened. As Solis walked, a thought entered his mind: *Hurry, she's dying.*

He broke into an anxious jog and surveyed the area, but he could not see her. Thick clouds shrouded the area in the east. Blackness ruled, impeding Solis's vision. *Lord, all day long I have delighted in your marvelous plant designs, and now I dread each step on this uneven pathway of yours.* He stopped and knelt in the dark. The murkiness of the night hid any details from him.

Hurry. Proceed. One more step.

The thick darkness oppressed Solis, and he clutched the ground and made a small dirt mound of remembrance there. He prayed, "Lord, protect my beloved. Return her to me." *Does the Lord really hear?*

Solis composed a song that night and called it "My Love."

"Bright shines this love of mine,
Though dark consumes the night.
I know my love for her
Will last for all time.
Anguish now pierces me,
Like angry forest branches.
Bring back my love to me,
And sparkles again will glow.
Bring back my love to me,
And never alone will she go."

The grazers lowed, and Solis turned and ran toward the sound. He cried Livi's name in the darkness.

Solis emerged from the shadows, and Livi screamed.

When Solis saw his wife covered in blood and mud, he sprinted to her. "Are you all right? What happened?" He circled her and touched her with tenderness.

"The leaves saved me." Livi told Solis all that had happened.

He held his head and moaned when she described the crashing water attack. Solis bristled with fury, ready to explode at Livi and the Lord because she had let herself be separated from her leaf basket, but he hid his anger. "Please, please, be more careful."

"I will. I'm sorry."

"We can make the basket fit better for running. Let's go to Heaven Falls so you can wash up."

Sparkles decorated the sky, and glow lit their path. Its shimmering white beams reflected in the water as they showered under one of the small waterfalls, and Solis sang "My Love" to his wife.

He sighed. "Now this place feels delightful. Peaceful, as it should be."

They returned home.

The multilevel sand-colored cliffs of Hilltop Castle rose above them, and Livi pointed up. "Generations of our family will fill this place."

Solis and Livi had made a sitting area inside the terrace wall to the right of the ladder. Leaves, grasses, and silky soft plant parts lined the area. The front wall of the terrace formed the back of the space. That evening, they climbed the ladder and lounged in the sitting area, discussing the day's adventures.

Livi said, "Mountain springs periodically flood the land and water much of Chara. An abundance of vegetation grows in the east. Delicious fruit grows above the ground."

"I'd like to see what you discovered. I didn't get far up the river." Solis pointed to the plant samples. "I'm beginning to see the different types of food and how to distinguish one from another. See the different shapes of the leaves and how most have stems attached to the plant's stalk?"

"Very interesting, my husband."

"Different plants also have different arrangements of leaves around their stalks. On some plants, the leaves grow opposite each other on the stalk. On others, they alternate. Still other leaves grow in clusters around the stalk with no stems at all. I must study all this."

The Lord appeared to them. "Greetings."

His presence surprised them, not with fear, but with delight and awe. Their hearts soared, and they felt his glory. Yet, he also perplexed them.

Livi told him all that had happened to her.

Solis grew hot, and a sheen of sweat covered his face. He closed his eyes and rubbed his forehead as he struggled to settle himself, but he gestured sharply with his hands as he spoke. "Lord, why did you allow her to come close to death?"

"Chara is a living place, a growing and changing combination of many organisms that operates according to my plans and design. You and all who follow you must master it."

Livi said, "This is paradise ... but it can be deadly."

"True, but it's still paradise."

Solis said, "But Lord, why do you allow it to be so unpredictable?"

"On the contrary, it's very predictable. You must learn to control or manage it. Should I protect you from your every mistake or act done in ignorance?"

Solis raised his hands. "Please protect us from ourselves."

"I am with you continually. Should I eliminate the need for wisdom, skill, and determination?"

Livi said, "No, but—"

"If so, there is no need for humanity." The Lord raised his voice. "Should I appoint the grazers and the pouchy cheeks as rulers, creatures with no sense or judgment?" Their chests vibrated with the voice of the Lord. "How then would knowledge of God spread in this world?"

Solis said, "We will do it."

"Yes, you must subdue both Chara and Erimea. Now, settle down here with me."

"What have we learned?" Lucido asked Iredin and Vik.

Iredin said, "According to the Lord's own word, there are many dangers in the garden."

"For what purpose? How can we use this?"

"The purpose seems to be to sustain and expand God's creative work."

"Perhaps we can use the Lord's natural processes against the humans."

Vik said, "Let us send forth some of our angels throughout Erimea to study the natural world over the next hundred years."

Lucido nodded. "Yes, we shall also seek a deeper knowledge of the human personality." Lucido patted Vik on the back. "So when they leave the garden, we can use God's own wonders, physical and psychological, to destroy them."

Chapter Twenty-Three

The Lord sat between the couple in the sitting area. They leaned against him as chicks under the pinions of a great featherone.

Livi said, "What's the next lesson we must teach our children?"

"Trust the Lord and call on him continually. You may not see or hear the Lord, but he always sees and hears you. Live each day with courage. Be at peace with what tomorrow holds."

Solis said, "Increase my faith. My heart is aflame in your presence, but at other times you seem far away."

Livi added, "You hide your face from us."

"Practice knowing the presence of God and know I am there. Solis, I was there today when you knelt at the edge of the pit, and a demon urged you to fall into it."

Solis cocked his head and regarded the Lord. *I wasn't at the edge of a pit.*

"Today, darkness engulfed you within and without. Beside a ditch, you prayed for protection for your wife."

Livi shivered. "The evils stalk us still?"

"Let me tell you a story of a couple. A husband and wife, like you, from another world. Their names were Tawal and Sola. They loved the Lord, and he endowed them with amazing skills as hunters, as well as with great strength. They lived in a garden like this one, full of all kinds of living creatures. But an evil spirit hated the garden and its creatures, because they belonged to God. The evil spirit appointed ten dragons to terrorize the creatures and slowly destroy the garden."

Solis said, "What is a dragon?"

"A dragon is a monster like the face you saw when sneaking thing died. Like a huge rock darter with a nasty disposition, twice the size of a man."

Livi said, "What did the dragons do?"

"During the day, each dragon slept in its own cave and belched forth smoke—dark clouds of hot gas that blanketed the sky—and light dimmed.

Plants withered. At night, the dragons woke from their slumber and ate the garden creatures and drank their blood—"

"Consumed animal flesh and blood?" Solis hollered and cringed. "May it never be."

"Yes, they consumed the beasts of the garden. God sent Tawal and Sola to kill the dragons and save the garden and its creatures. God gave the couple special armor to protect them. The great hunter couple fashioned strong ropes to bind the dragons while they slept, spears to pierce their eyes, and cutters to slit their throats. But the couple refused to put on God's armor."

Livi said, "Why didn't they wear the armor to battle the smoke dragons?"

"Because of their great confidence and strength. So, Sola and Tawal went forth during the day and approached the first dragon's lair. It slept with its head out of the cave. With each exhalation, it blew out plumes of smoke that stung their eyes and made them gag, so they retreated and observed. They pelted the dragon with rocks and hid in bushes to see what it would do, but the creature continued its slumber. The couple wrapped two ropes around the beast's neck, and they secured the ropes to the right and left of the creature. They stood before the beast with their spears above its closed eyelids and with cutters strapped to their waists. They plunged the spears into its eyes, and the creature roared awake. Before it could break its bonds, they leaped on its neck and hacked it to death with their cutters."

Solis said, "Did the other nine dragons avenge their brother?"

"No, they cared nothing for each other. The mighty couple destroyed the remaining dragons over the next nine days. They rejoiced greatly at their success and became very proud."

"I knew it." Livi clapped her hands, jumped up, and exulted. "Sola and Tawal are the smoke-dragon slayers. They're like us. We'll pierce the eyes of our enemies and slash their throats." She stabbed with her hands and ripped them through the air. "So, then everything was fine?"

"No, the evil spirit struck again, and something even stranger happened."

"Oh no. The evils."

Solis said, "What happened?"

"The garden of Tawal and Sola remained dark, and the animals continued to be consumed. The couple searched everywhere, but they couldn't find any dragons. Finally, they prayed to the Lord and asked him for help in their struggle. That night, in a vision, the Lord allowed Tawal and Sola to learn what had happened. They saw the evil spirit standing over the couple's sleeping bodies. The spirit beckoned for something within them to come out. 'Come forth. Come forth, my darlings.' Seven larger dragons came from each of their hearts. Breathing smoke, they searched for their prey. Before dawn, they returned to the couple and hid in their hearts."

Livi frowned. "From out of their bodies ... that's gross."

"The Lord said to Tawal and Sola, 'Put on the armor of God. Enemies can come from within and without.'"

Solis grimaced and scratched the back of his neck. "That's awful."

Livi said, "What were the names of the dragons that came out of the human hearts?"

"All manner of evil, but I'll not name them. They're things I hope you never know."

Solis said, "What is the armor of God, that we may wear it?

"A truthful heart within and without, intent to behave rightly. Peace that comes from the good news that I am always near you. Faith in me. Confidence I will preserve you through any trouble. Listen to the words I speak to you and pray always. Put on these things."

Livi said, "Explain more about right behavior."

"It means demonstrating patience, kindness, humility, forgiveness, faithfulness, hopefulness, and endurance. Make these qualities your own."

Solis said, "Sounds like the armor."

"They are all bound together. They'll yield a harvest of fruit in your lives and in the lives of your children. When people see you, they will see love, joy, peace, patience, kindness, goodness, faithfulness, gentleness, and self-control."

Livi said, "So be it, Lord."

Solis said, "So be it."

"Believe in me. Obey my word. Know I love you. Teach your children." The Lord disappeared from their sight.

Solis said, "Enemies can come from within and without?"

"Not out of me." Livi rubbed her belly. "Only good ones are in here."

Solis smirked. "I don't think that's what he meant. Somehow the armor subdues or prevents the beasts within and without."

Livi raised her arms and stomped the ground. "I still want to be a smoke-dragon slayer."

Chapter Twenty-Four

The garden beckoned Solis and Livi daily with light breezes, alluring fragrances, and mysteries to uncover. Study and exploration consumed their days. Constructing tools and other implements allowed them to shape the land to their desires. The Lord appeared to them often, teaching and telling stories. Even so, when they didn't see the Lord, they prayed to him and meditated on his words. They remembered all the Lord had taught, and their understanding grew, though his words often puzzled them.

Early each morning while it was still dark, Livi left their bed to sit at the front of the terrace and gaze to the east. She reveled in the sight of daylight peeking over the mountains and painting the morning sky. Livi wanted to master Chara, but she burned with wanderlust to know what existed beyond the ring of mountains that circled the garden.

One day, Solis joined his wife before dawn, as he often did. She pointed. "See how the hills are illuminated from behind before we see daylight? The stacked layers of clouds in the sky are lit from below, and the mountains in front."

Solis wrapped his arms around his wife. "Yes, tell me again. What are the colors?"

"There's the blue hue of the sky above and between white clouds and yellow, red, and orange streaks shining up. It's a little different every morning. Daylight is the gleaming bright white circle, and the mountains are mostly green, though they appear black and gray now."

"See the black outlines of the featherones flapping above the mountains."

"Beautiful. The same again, yet unique."

They sat for a while longer until Solis said, "Let's follow Sweet Water Whirlwind from Heaven Falls all the way to Tall Stony." He grabbed his walking stick. "If we're to subdue this place, we must learn more about it."

"And let's return along the eastern circle." The eastern circle consisted of the semicircle of mountains on the east side of the Garden from Tall Stony in the south to Hilltop Castle in the north. The southern half they called Southeast Circle.

Since Livi's disaster along Northeast Circle, they always traveled together. They enjoyed sharing their discoveries and talking with each other. They strapped their baskets on their backs and climbed down the ladder into the soft carpet of damp grass to the welcoming nudges of the grazers, their constant companions, whenever they left the castle.

When Livi said, "River," Redrick led the way.

Sandy, Brownstone, and Flinty followed in a slow trot.

Heaven Falls roared a hearty welcome to the sojourners and covered them in mist. Solis and Livi always stopped and admired the mighty falls and remembered it as their wedding place.

Livi laid a hand on her breastbone and faced the falls. "Heaven pours out innumerable blessings, and the deluge shatters and ricochets in ways we don't understand. Yet each drop sustains life. May we appreciate the Lord."

"His work is awesome to behold," added Solis.

The grazers rumbled left along a well-beaten path parallel to where the swirling waters gathered to form the beginning of Sweet Water Whirlwind's dash through the garden. Redrick branched off to the right through sparse trees and bushes and disappeared down a small slope. Featherones flew from the underbrush, and small creatures scampered in fear to make way for Redrick. He headed straight for the water and hurled his massive reddish-brown body in with a great splash. The other grazers followed, and all four swam across the river.

Livi ran after her friends and dove in. The current pushed her downstream as she swam to the other side, driving her toward a partially submerged boulder.

The sight gripped Solis in the clutch of fear. He exhaled only when Livi waved at him from the opposite riverbank. He took a few steps into the river but stopped when he remembered his near-death first experience with the river's sweet swirling waters.

Solis stood like a stack of stones. Livi returned to him. Again, Solis held his breath, because she struggled against the flow as she swam upstream.

She pushed herself up out of the shallow water. "It feels great."

"I prefer calmer waters." When Livi came within arm's reach, he grabbed her hand, pulled her up, and hugged her. "The river can be dangerous. You must be careful."

Breathing hard, Livi leaned against her husband. "I'm a strong swimmer. The water is refreshing."

"We need to find a better way to cross over the river."

They resumed their walk along the riverbank. Tall trees lined both sides and stretched mighty, leaf-filled limbs toward the sky in praise of God. Many streams broke off from the main river and watered much of the garden. Sweet blackberries grew on the bushes and provided breakfast.

Solis studied the blackberry bushes. "Creation tells of Lord God's goodness. His provision is everywhere."

The couple continued beside the river, the grazers following on the other side, until they came to a huge tree that had fallen across the river. Its roots pointed up. Some branches reached into the water, and others stretched skyward. Vines hung down from the fallen tree. The riverbank sloped down sharply to the water.

Solis said, "See, now we have a bridge." He jumped up on the tree and walked across, using the branches to maintain his balance.

Livi looked at the river far below the tree bridge. "The river has cut down too deeply. The bridge is too high."

The grazers eyed the fallen tree, but they ambled down the slope, swam across the river, and climbed the hill to where Livi stood.

Livi gripped her sides. "Solis, come back. I don't like this bridge."

He returned, and they resumed their trek. He said, "There are lower spots where we can anchor a rope bridge to trees on each side. Then, we'll have a way to cross we are both comfortable with."

"We'll need some long vines."

"The trees along the river are full of vines." Solis looked at the surroundings and relished the thought of designing and building a bridge. "Behind us is the tree of life. In front, the great river. Suppose one of our children gets hurt beyond the river? A bridge will allow them to reach the healing tree quickly. So, we must build bridges."

"A big project for another day. Probably many days. Let's go to the tree of life and gather more leaves."

After they filled their baskets with leaves, Solis looked at the tree of the knowledge of good and evil, where he had buried the uneaten fruit. Two green shoots with leaves had broken through the soil. He hesitated. "What is this?" He took a step toward the tree.

Livi pulled his arm back. "Oh no. Don't go near the death tree."

"More are growing." Sweat trickled down Solis's face. "I hate to touch them, but I must destroy them. One day, maybe the Lord will allow me to chop down this great tree." He dug up the two tiny plants and their roots. He tore them to pieces and threw them into the river. "May you never grow again." He washed his hands in the river.

They resumed moving south along the river through bushes, flowering plants, and tall grass. The grazers trailed behind.

Livi said, "Suppose the tree grew in another place and someone ate of the fruit ignorantly. Would the curse fall on them?"

"Would it be a sin if they had no command forbidding it?"

"Only the Lord knows."

"But our children won't be ignorant."

Something splashed in the water. Livi gazed at the river and gasped. "Quiet. Get down." She snatched Solis's walking stick, pushed the grass aside, and peered out.

He knelt beside her. "What is it?"

She shuddered. "I'm going to vomit ... fly bites, fly bites."

"What?"

"It stinks. A family of sneaking things skimming through the water. If they come this way, I'll pierce their cursed dragon necks." She stabbed the ground with the stick.

Solis stood. "They're not dragons, and they're swimming away from us, crawling under the archway."

Livi spat. "They're of the evils."

"They're God's creatures, and they have gone. Look ahead. We've arrived at Tall Stony." Solis's chest puffed out as he remembered his success in scaling the rock formation. "The river flows through Tall Stony, dividing into four great rivers outside the garden on the other side."

"Where it broke you, and we earned our scars. A blemish on my perfect form." Livi pinched her lips together, souring her expression even more. "Should I celebrate this place?"

Solis grinned at his wife. "Not a blemish. A mark of distinction for your heroism. I conquered this place."

Livi shrugged.

He clapped his hands. "Darling, this is where we first savored golden sweet together. Shall I take Easy Sloway up and get golden sweet for you? It tastes like Livi."

The corners of her lips turned up in a half-smile, and she nudged her husband. "Sweet like Solis ... but not now. Let's return via the eastern circle. Maybe one day we'll follow one of those rivers through Erimea."

The couple followed the Southeast Circle toward Neverway Passage. Daylight stood high in the sky as they began their return to the north. The trees were smaller as they moved away from the river, but the vegetation was plentiful and lush, watered by the flooding of the eastern mountain springs. Wild breaths, pouchy cheeks, rooters, cliff steppers, and more played in and ate of the garden's natural bounty.

Livi said, "Look, there are creatures going in and out of Neverway Passage."

"Why would they ever want to leave the Garden?"

"There is a wide world beyond the Garden. And one day, we'll make it our own."

The passage spanned twenty paces in width, framed by rocks on each side. It was two hundred paces deep.

Solis said, "It looks like the Lord took a great cutter and sliced through the mountain. See how smooth the rocks are?"

"Yes." Livi touched the rocks on the north side of the opening. "They are smooth. I wish I could cut rock like that. When I break rocks, they are jagged and rough."

"We need to find better cutters."

Their ears picked up the sound of hooves beating the ground. Soon, four great creatures galloped through the passage into the Garden. The grazers scattered to make way. The creatures headed straight toward Mount Mercy, several hundred paces opposite Neverway Passage.

Solis sucked in several quick breaths and stared after the creatures. He shouted. "What were they? Like giant wild breaths almost as wide as the grazers. With four skinny, muscular legs and wild, whipping tails."

A fifth creature of the same species strolled up behind them with soft steps and snorted.

They jumped and spun around. Livi cheered, "Oh my goodness. It's beautiful."

The animal lowered its head, which was above Solis's, and sniffed the humans. Then, it took a step back and stared at them. It had a dark brown coat with a black mane and tail. A white streak on its head ran from between its eyes to its nose.

Solis held out some berries from his basket.

The animal gobbled them up, snorted, and ran after its companions.

Livi rubbed her fingers together, remembering the softness of the animal's mane. "What will you name them?"

Solis laughed and scratched his chin. "I think *wind striders*, because they fly across the ground like the wind."

"They certainly run fast."

Solis and Livi followed the creatures, but the couple stopped when they came to Mount Mercy.

He said, "Bloody stick still stands here with sneaking thing hanging at the top." He tapped the animal's dead body. "It's become hard as a rock."

Livi gasped, and her eyebrows drew together. "I don't believe it."

"What?"

"Our scars resemble the stick and the way the beast is curled up on it. Why would the Lord mark us with such a disgusting thing?"

Solis studied the mark above Livi's heart with one hand clasped over his mouth. "I don't know ... but the Lord called it the mark of honor and approval." He wrapped his arms around Livi and held her. "Let's return to the Northeast Circle."

Arm in arm, Solis and Livi slowly turned away from Mount Mercy. One hundred paces past Neverway, they reached the ditch where the mountain water flow had struck Livi. Solis squatted at the edge of the narrow ravine.

"Look, here is the mound I made that night. The Lord truly saw me at the edge of disaster, and I didn't know it. But did he save me from the pit, or was I lucky?"

"He saved you for sure, but why didn't he save me from a broken back?"

"I don't understand the Lord at all, but I know he sees, and he's good."

Solis bowed his head. "Yes, Iam, you're good. Forgive our doubts."

Livi bent with her hands on her knees. "I'm trembling. I hate this place. My fingers and back ache." She shook her hands. "Let's get away from here."

"Come, let me show you something." She led Solis into the field of fruit growing on the ground. Livi lifted one of the green oblong shapes and slammed it on the ground. It burst into pieces. "Taste this."

Solis took a big bite of the fruit's red flesh. "It's very sweet, very good." He spat black seeds into his hand and examined them. "Ah, now I understand."

"What?"

"Something in the death fruit made it produce plants of the same kind after I buried them. It must have been seeds within the fruit."

"So, we can cultivate our favorite plants wherever we want them?"

"Yes." From that day on, Solis vowed to himself he would gather seeds of every type to plant them in other areas and experiment with them in different types of soil.

They gathered fruit from a nearby stepper tree and returned to Hilltop Castle. As they lounged in the sitting area, Solis said, "We learned a lot today and now have much to accomplish."

Over several months, the couple made many excursions through Chara and laid plans for how they would develop the garden. They grew in faith and understanding.

Preparing for the coming children drove all they did. Solis strove for perfection in himself and expected the same from the children. Livi intended to prove herself worthy of the responsibility given her.

Chapter Twenty-Five

Garden of Chara, Year 1, Helpe, Day 5

Livi and Solis made so much rope from various vines and grasses, it seemed as if rope held their world together.

By the fourth month of Livi's pregnancy, the couple had built two rope bridges over Sweet Water Whirlwind and constructed yokes for the grazers to work in pairs.

Solis designed a wooden plow, which he tied to the yokes with ropes, and the grazers provided the muscle to clear several plots around the garden, including the main plot in the grassy land between the forest and Hilltop Castle.

One afternoon, the couple relaxed in the grass near the main plot. Solis stretched out on his back. Livi lay on her side, resting her head on his chest. Fluffy clouds drifted overhead in the blue sky.

Livi said, "I'm growing bigger."

Solis placed a hand on Livi's stomach. "The little men within are becoming bigger and stronger."

Livi covered her husband's hand with hers. "Yes, and everyone in this body is hungry all the time. I'm eating more than ever. My body no longer moves the way it used to. I can't run like myself." She sighed. "Instead, I waddle and tire easily. I've been taken over by a force I can't control."

Her smile, the curve of her lips, the shape of her legs — everything about her still made Solis's heart beat faster. "You can't fly like Livi now, but you're still beautiful. Still powerful." He reached for a small stone dish filled with an oily substance and rubbed some on his wife's legs. Crushed fruit from the stepper trees oozed fragrant oil they applied to their hair and bodies.

"I'm stretched to frightening proportions, but I still relish sharing my body with others who are depending on me. I hope to remember every moment of this pregnancy." Livi gazed into the sky. "Our sons will be handsome and full of vitality. Plentiful food will make their bodies and brains strong."

"The Lord has provided an amazing array of foods for us, and we're always discovering new things to eat."

Livi propped up on one arm and scrutinized the dark, furrowed soil in front of her. "What grows here, this little shoot?"

"I planted four seeds from the tree of life at each of the four corners of the main plot. So far, only this one has sprouted."

"We're permitted many trees of life?"

"When we fill Erimea, our children will need access to the healing power."

"May God bless the produce of this land." Livi placed her hands on her stomach. "Wow! I felt the little ones within for the first time." Her eyes gleamed.

"Did it hurt?"

Livi burst out with laughter. "No, it felt like fluttering wings or gentle tumbling. I'm so happy and relieved to know they're all right."

"Maybe they're playing, or perhaps they want our attention ... so they aren't left out." Solis smiled and wrapped his arms around Livi. "May these little ones be blessed by God and all who follow them."

"So be it. Each day, I focus and meditate on what I and my body are creating with the help of the Lord."

Garden of Chara, Year 1, Bui, Day 8

On a warm Restday morning, Solis and Livi strolled hand in hand past Heaven Falls, through the orchard and into a field they called Pleasant Meadow. The couple enjoyed the daily work of developing Chara, but the seventh day of the week was a day of refreshment and renewal, so they did not work on Restday. They relaxed, played together, and reflected on God and his blessings, but Livi's outcry broke their relaxation.

"Oh, my Lord. Look, my legs are soaked." She trembled. "A gush of warm water came out of me. Am I dying? Is losing water like losing blood?"

"What does it mean?" Solis huffed and puffed uncontrollably.

"I don't know." Sweat poured down her face. She sat in the grass. "My back has been aching, and the pain flows down here to my belly. It's getting worse." She groaned. "Are the little ones safe?"

Solis prayed. "Iam, help us. Livi is sick." He raked his fingers through his hair. "We don't get sick. How can this be?"

They heard the voice of the Lord. "She's not sick. Her time has come. The children will arrive soon."

"Lord, what do we ..." Solis stood next to his wife with his arms raised. "How do ... I help her?"

"Wait. Soon she will squat and push. Receive the children with care."

Livi cried. "Ouch. Oh, it hurts. The pain keeps coming back every few moments."

Solis sat on the ground and held Livi and they waited all morning. He could barely contain his tears. *Iam, Iam, don't let her die.*

At midday, Livi screamed, "Help me up. Help me up." She squatted and groaned. "He's coming, he's coming." Livi's face looked like it would burst. "I'm pushing. I'm pushing."

"Oh, my Lord. I see the head. Keep pushing. He's coming out ... He's out. He's out." Solis held the boy. The baby and father both cried. "It's Talen. He's got thick black hair." Solis held Talen close. "He smells good, a wet, sweet scent." He laid Talen in the grass.

Livi breathed heavily and continued squatting. She screamed. "Thank you, Iam, for Talen ... Oh Lord, help me. The pangs are still coming." A few moments later, Livi cried and pushed again. "Here comes Stron."

"I see his head. Push, my darling, push ... He's out, he's out. Stron has arrived. He's just like his brother, sweet and strong."

Livi lay in the grass laughing and exhausted. Solis placed Talen and Stron in her arms. "Oh, Iam, thank you." She pressed her face into the boys' hair and kissed them. "They smell sweet. Thank you, Iam, thank you."

Thank you, Lord, for saving my wife and giving us Talen and Stron. Solis lay beside her with his forearm across his head. Sweat drenched his body. "When I heard you scream, I thought you were dying." He wiped away his tears.

"The pain wasn't as bad as it sounded. I wailed because power and excitement flowed through my body." Livi stroked her babies' hair. "It was wonderful. I felt a powerful urge to push.

"It sounded awful ... painful." Solis put his arm over the twins. "I expected small men, but they're—"

"Not little men. Baby boys. Brown babies with dark brown eyes and curly black hair."

"With Livi's face."

"Small, helpless, and weak. I love my babies."

Solis sat up and played with their fingers and toes. "Welcome, boys, to the Garden of Chara, and welcome to Erimea. You're home now."

"Childbirth is something I want to experience over and over, because it was thrilling. I discovered my mind's power to direct the amazing functioning of my body. I'll teach my daughters the wonders of childbirth."

Solis pondered Livi's comments. *Iam, does she remember what she just went through?*

When Talen and Stron reached their third day of life, Solis carried the boys to one of the quiet pools of water near Heaven Falls.

Livi stood beside him. "What are you doing, my dear husband?"

"I'm testing them."

"Testing my babies?"

"Boys, do you want to live?" Solis sat in the warm water up to his chest, with his sons lying face down on his forearms. He lowered the boys into the water.

"What are you doing?" Livi reached for her sons, but stopped.

The boys held their breath, kicked, and then, squealing, flipped onto their backs. Talen and Stron beat the water with their arms and legs and grabbed for their father.

"Yes, you do." Solis scooped them up. "You've passed your first test."

Livi rolled her eyes.

The boys squirmed and wrestled with each other in their father's arms.

Solis beamed with pleasure. "Now I know you will fight to survive and prevail against anything that tries to bring you down. Talen, you're like these high, mighty walls. You will always stand firm. Stron, you're like your big brother, with a powerful heart and determination to face every challenge without shrinking. May you both walk with the Lord forever, and may he bless you."

He lifted both boys to his shoulders and rose from the pool, nudging his wife with his elbow. "You know I would never let harm come to them."

As the couple stood together with their sons in front of the great falls, the Lord appeared. "Greetings to you all, my precious children." He took the boys into his arms and blessed them. "May Talen and Stron be like Livi and Solis forever."

Fifteen months later, Livi gave birth to twin girls. First Daylig and then Brilara.

After three days, Solis gave them the water test, as he did with their brothers. "Daylig and Brilara, do you want to live?"

The girls responded as their older brothers had. Brilara kept rolling over in the water, but they passed the test.

"Daylig, you are bright as the morning sparkles. No one will diminish your countenance. Brilara, you are more brilliant than glow on a cloudless evening. You both are like your mother and brothers. Indomitable."

Solis gathered the two girls, and the Lord blessed them as he had blessed the boys.

Daylig and Brilara had brown skin like their brothers and parents, but Daylig possessed sky-blue eyes and fine black hair like the mane of a wind strider. Brilara had wavy red hair, with one brown eye and the other blue.

On the day of the girls' water test, the Lord appeared to Livi while she lounged alone on the terrace of Hilltop Castle. "Greetings, woman of God. Do you desire to give birth to more children in the garden soon? Know you will have more children in other parts of Erimea in subsequent years."

Livi answered immediately. "Yes, Lord, let me be pregnant again soon."

"Very well. I will add a girl, and then a boy to your family."

Fifteen months later, Livi again gave birth to twins. First, a girl named Mornie, and then a boy, Damaro. These twins possessed tawny brown skin, curly brown hair, and light brown eyes. They also passed Solis's test while Talen and Stron ran in circles around the pool and cheered on their new baby sister and brother, "Mornie, Maro. Mornie, Maro."

Again, the Lord asked Livi, "Do you desire to give birth to more children in the garden soon?"

Livi consulted her husband.

He said, "It's up to you. I'll be satisfied either way."

Livi said, "No, Lord. Six babies are enough for now."

"Very well. I will prevent you from conceiving for many years. But when the time is right, you will become pregnant again."

"Thank you, Lord, for blessing me to be so fruitful."

Solis said, "I'm surprised. After almost three years, Talen and Stron are still toddling around. And they are so short. I expected them to be men by now. Other animals mature more quickly."

"Their bodies need time to catch up with their big heads." Livi clutched her husband, and a smile took over her face. "I enjoy their babyness."

"My darling, what is it like having these babies?"

"Truly, this has been a strange experience. Losing who I was and giving in to something I can't control. But my body knows what to do. I've lost my life to pregnancy, birthing, and feeding the babies, who are constantly hungry. They cry and cry. I lose sleep."

"I wish I could help more."

"I know, but you can't until they can eat solid food. Only I can feed them. Only I can sustain them from my own body. I'm tired all the time. Yet, I know one day I'll want to do this again and again. To seed the world with our offspring. Holding them and watching them grow is wonderful. One day, I will emerge from all this and be myself again. But I will be changed. There's no going back to what I was before I was a mother. That life is gone."

"You lost your life, but you gained a new one. A better one?"

"I believe so."

Solis sang a song to his wife called "You are Livi."

"My darling. You are Livi,
Mother of all the living.
You shelter life,
Like God protects and nurtures.
Infant life, needy and clinging.
Babies growing slowly,
Consuming your life.
Generations are in them.
More precious
Than buried treasure.
More charming
Than distant lands.
Sacrifice brings new glory,
Splendor without measure.
You are Livi,
Mother of all who live."

Chapter Twenty-Six

Garden of Chara, Year 4, Unio, Day 21

The family trekked to Pouchy Cheeks Pond, a place the boys loved to play. They settled on a large, dry slab of rock, while Talen and Stron skipped up and down the slope that funneled to the pond. The break in the tree growth allowed the early afternoon light to stream through the trees. Solis loved relaxing by water and every day in the garden featured the penetrating warm rays of daylight and soft breezes. Both parents treasured time with their children and the responsibility of teaching the little ones.

Livi called out to Talen and Stron. “Boys, come sit here with us. We’re going to play the learning game.”

The boys skipped sideways to their parents and cheered, “Yeah, ’earning game, ’earning game.”

Solis said, “Who loves you very much?

Daylig said, “Mama and Baba.”

Livi said, “Who else?”

Stron jumped and turned in a circle. “Lorgah, Lorgah.”

“Yes, Lord God loves all of us very much.”

Solis said, “And how do you treat your neighbor?”

Talen said, “Love as we love us.”

“Yes, good. Who is our neighbor?”

The two toddlers circled the family, pointing at each person, and said over and over, “You and you and you and you and you.”

Brilara and Daylig laughed and pulled each other’s fingers.

Stron fell backward into Solis’s arms. “Everybody is our neighbor, Baba.”

At that moment, the Lord strolled along the trail.

Talen hopped up and ran. “It’s Lorgah. It’s Lorgah.”

“Greetings.”

Livi and Solis shouted, “Greetings.”

The Lord picked up Talen and carried the boy back to the family. He stood before them as he often did, taking each of the children in his arms and blessing them.

Stron squirmed in the Lord's arms. "How you find us?"

Talen slapped his forehead. "Stron ... you know ... he sees always. He God."

Brilara said, "He God, he God."

The Lord sat with them. "I have a story for all of you. Especially for Mama and Baba."

Solis said, "Speak, Lord, for your servants are listening."

The Lord began a tale. "There was a man named Moses who was a good man, and he became the leader of God's people, but the people became scared. They were afraid they would die in the wilderness and did not trust God to take care of them, even though God had always provided all their needs. They grumbled against Moses. Their complaints made God angry, and he cursed the people and sent serpents to come and bite some of the—"

"What are serpents?" Solis asked.

"Serpents are beasts, like sneaking things, but with no legs."

"How can a thing move without legs?"

"They flex and relax their muscles to slither along the ground."

Talen fell to the ground with his hands at his sides and writhed around. "Baba, look at me. I'm a turpent."

Livi cringed. "Stop it. Serpents are bad."

The Lord continued, "When this kind of serpent bites, the person dies. When the people saw their brothers and sisters die, they were afraid and begged to be freed from the curse. So, God told Moses to make an image of a serpent and put it on a stick just like the stick you used to kill the sneaking thing. The Lord commanded that if anyone was bitten, they were to look at the serpent's image, and they would live. The lives of many people were saved."

Solis frowned. "What does this mean for us?"

"The scars on your back and Livi's chest represent the curse avoided by your obedience. The day will come when your descendants will face critical choices. The image of the bloody stick will help them choose the correct path. If they see it and choose wisely, they will be blessed. If they choose wrongly, they will bear a curse, and their children with them."

Solis observed Livi absentmindedly touch the scar on her chest. His own scar reminded him their lives had import far beyond the present moment and significance greater than their little family.

Livi said, "Lord, where does Moses dwell?"

"Moses is part of the future history of Earth."

The Lord continued to teach them and told stories until evening when he vanished, which always astonished the boys.

"How he do that?" Talen and Stron squealed and repeatedly jumped up and fell to the ground, saying, "Where did he go?"

Livi said, "Stop it. No more silliness."

The family returned home as night fell.

Solis said, "It's strange that we know more about Earth's future history than we know about what faces us on Erimea."

"That's fine by me," Livi said. "I don't want to know what our future holds, but I do know we need to teach our children well."

That evening, Solis and Livi sat with their children on the terrace. Livi said, "Baba is going to sing a new song for you and about you. It's called 'Song of the Three Twins.'"

"Three twins be fruitful.

Three twins multiply.

Three twins fill Erimea.

Three twins subdue it.

Talen and Stron, courageous sons:

As tall trees they stand,

As strong mountains, they endure.

Daylig and Brilara, radiant daughters:

As daylight they shine,

As brilliant as sparkles.

Mornie and Damaro, true hearts:

Faithful as morning.

Certain as tomorrow.

Three twins God has given,

To rule a vast and mighty land.

Blessed be their strength,

Blessed be their light,

Blessed be their truth forever."

With eyes wide with wonder, Stron said, "Mama, are we really gonna do all that?"

"Yes, we six will do it." Talen sprang up and danced. "Baba says so."

Livi nodded. "Yes, with the help of the Lord."

Solis smiled. "With the help of the Lord."

Chapter Twenty-Seven

Garden of Chara, Year 11, Brea, Day 2

At their father's instruction, all six children strapped on their leaf baskets and cutters for the task of harvesting vines to make more ropes. Talen and Stron led the way toward Heaven Falls and the river. Brilara ran ahead, stood in front of one of the basins formed by the falls, and pointed. "Let's go swimming first."

Talen pointed ahead. "No, we have work to do."

Stron tapped his older brother. "We swim after. Yes, brother?"

Talen threw an arm around Stron's shoulder. "Yes, brother."

The smell and sound of the river, combined with the sweet, pungent scent of trees and flowers, engulfed them and felt like home. The six children each found a tree with smooth bark to minimize scrapes and scratches and scampered up as if they were crawling on the ground. Whenever they spotted a vine dangling from a sturdy branch, they climbed onto the branch, wrapped their legs around it, and hacked the vine with their cutters.

Talen kept a watchful eye to be sure no one climbed too high, and Damaro reported to his big brother if anyone did anything dangerous.

Before daylight stood high in the sky, Stron gathered the cut vines and counted them. "We have enough. Everybody come down."

When the children reached the ground, they each took some of the vines and dragged them toward home. Brilara ran ahead and threw down her haul in front of Heaven Falls. She climbed into one of the calm, deep-water basins formed by the falls.

Soon, all her siblings joined her in the refreshing water. Uneven gray steppingstones made a stairway high up the walls, with rocky platforms at various heights directly above the basin.

Talen looked up at the stairway, and then at Stron. "Are you thinking what I'm thinking?"

Damaro overheard. "Is it deep enough? We could hit the bottom."

"I'll check." Talen dove underwater and swam to the bottom.

Brilara climbed the steps and prepared to jump.

Talen burst above the water. "It's really deep."

Brilara yelled, "Watch out. Here I come." She sprang feet first into the pool and splashed.

They all laughed. Soon, six giddy children dove or jumped into the water. Each time, they raced up the steps for leaps from higher and higher levels.

Talen went to a much higher level than any of them and yelled, "Watch this."

Damaro said, "No, that's too high."

Stron flew up the stairs to his brother. "No, don't do it."

Talen took a step forward and stopped. "I'm playing. I know it's too high to jump. But look how much higher these steps go. We're only about a third of the way to the top."

They went up a few more steps and found a ledge behind the falls. Talen led his siblings behind the cascading torrent of water.

As they sat mesmerized behind the falls, Mornie said, "Look behind us. There's an opening."

Daylig said, "Look at the beautiful layers of rock ... silver, gray, and black."

Talen got up and went to the opening. "It's a slot passage. Let's follow it."

The narrow passage had irregular high walls, and loose rocks at the bottom made walking difficult.

Talen ducked under a rock that jutted out. "Pay attention and go slow, or you'll knock yourself out."

Mornie followed behind Talen. "I'm glad we can see the sky in some spots."

Daylig agreed, "This would be scary at night."

The passage wound around at a steep incline until they reached a circular open area where the six children faced each other. An opening above their heads allowed light to stream in.

Damaro counted the rocky openings. "Eleven passages begin here."

Stron said, "We could take the wrong passage back and get lost."

Talen said, "Stand back, everyone." He took a sharp, flat rock and hacked a notch in the edge of the circular opening. "See this notch? It points to the opening we came out of. Everyone feel this notch."

The siblings each reached up and felt the mark.

"That is opening number one."

Brilara wondered, "Which one do we take to get to the other side?"

Daylig peered into several of the crevices. "Some of them look dark."

Talen said, "This one opposite from where we entered. Six looks light enough. Let's go ... but first, this whole passage needs a name. I suggest Mornie's Mountain Pass."

Mornie beamed, and they all agreed on the name. They followed Talen and Stron into number six. The passage continued up, narrowing until they had to turn sideways and proceed in single file.

Damaro said, "This is getting tight. Mama and Baba might not fit in here."

They reached a spot where the passage floor dropped sharply. Large boulders covered the floor.

Talen said, "This is too difficult of a drop. Only Stron and I can go down here. You all wait here, and we'll be right back."

"Be careful," Daylig said.

The two older boys climbed down backward until they reached the lower level, which opened wider so they could walk side by side.

Light glinted off the craggy walls, making them shimmer. "This is amazing," Talen said.

Talen and Stron proceeded until they reached a point where the walls curved in at chest level, so it was too tight to pass, a nasty pinch point. On the right, the rocks jutted in as if a giant gray fist had crashed through the wall. The top of the fist formed a shelf-like surface. Past the fist's front edge on the left side, the wall curved down to a sharp point a little lower than the fist.

The tight spot ran for two paces before opening. The floor of the passage fell away sharply at the fist. The space above was wider, so the two boys turned sideways, facing right, and placed their hands on top of the fist shelf.

They pushed themselves up and leaned their bodies forward. Moving their hands little by little, they were able to squeeze their legs through the narrow spot. Then, they jumped to the ground. After another fifteen paces, they reached the other side of the mountain enclosing Chara on the north.

Stron said, "Wow, look at the water." To the left, a massive river churned on its way to the falls. To the right, a tree-filled hill rose against a dark blue sky. "And this big rock right here."

"Looks like a man's bumpy head. The cool wind gust feels good. Look, we could climb that knoll. I'd like to explore beyond there."

"Not today. Let's go back." Stron led the way back and hurried through the tight passage.

When Talen raised himself up through the passage, one of his hands slipped. He dropped into the narrow spot and slammed the back of his head. "Ow ... I'm stuck." The fist pressed into Talen's chest, and the other wall sliced across his back. Stron grabbed Talen's right hand and pulled. Talen grimaced. "Ow. Don't. It hurts." Talen was wedged tightly in the passage, and his feet could not touch the ground.

The other children heard Talen's cry of pain. "What happened?"

Stron said, "Talen is stuck. Go get Baba and Mama, and bring rope."

Daylig and Brilara dashed to get their parents, but Mornie and Damaro stayed put.

"I'm sorry, brother. Maybe I can get above you and pull you up." Stron climbed up and squatted on the fist. He grabbed Talen's hands and pulled, but he only wedged his brother in tighter.

Talen moaned, "It hurts." A trickle of blood flowed from his breastbone and stained the stone.

Stron released his brother's hands and jumped down.

It's an eternal wound. Talen cannot be healed.

Where had that thought come from?

The thought seeped into Stron like poison dripped into pure water and formed a previously unconsidered idea. What if he lost his brother?

Stron pressed his palms to his eyes as tears crept down his cheeks. "I'm sorry. I'm not strong enough. Mama, Baba, Lorgah, help us."

Mornie and Damaro echoed his cry.

Then, the Lord spoke. "Take courage. I see you."

The children said, "It's Lorgah. It's Lorgah. Save our brother."

"Mama and Baba will be here soon," the Lord said.

The children continued weeping.

Livi, Solis, Daylig, and Brilara raced from Hilltop Castle to Heaven Falls. Daylig pointed to the hidden passage. Solis and Livi looked up.

In a flash, the Lord opened their eyes to see the spiritual realm around the mountain, where hundreds of angels with faces like lightning and eyes like flaming torches surrounded their children and battled a host of demons. Livi and Solis threw their hands up and stopped at the sight.

Livi screamed. "Are we in the midst of battle?"

"Can we prevail?" Solis cried, "and save the children?"

"Do not fear," the Lord said. "The evil spirits cannot overcome my angels." The vision disappeared.

The two girls led their parents up the steps to the crevice opening. At the central hub, the girls pointed out passage number six.

From there, Solis led the way. He stared into the dark slot, and the walls seemed to close in. Terror warred within him. He fell back and felt he would suffocate, but he heard the cries of his children. He pressed ahead.

Soon, Solis and Livi stood next to Mornie and Damaro. They secured a rope, lowered themselves, and ran to their son.

After examining the predicament, Solis placed a stone under his son, but it rolled away. Solis squeezed on top of the fist and shimmied to the other side of Talen, jamming a wide stone in the pathway as a barrier. Livi, Stron, and Solis piled smaller stones on the ground under Talen until the boy could press his feet against the pile.

"I'm going to climb here above you and pull you up. When I do, arch your back and push hard against the stones with your feet." Solis scrunched his body down to fit in the space above Talen. He mashed his head against the opposing wall and braced his feet, grabbing Talen under the arms. "Now, my son, push with all your might." Solis pulled, and Talen pressed against the stones, and the boy came free. Solis then dragged Talen to Livi.

She pulled him from the deadly fist's grip. "My babies." Livi hugged and kissed her firstborn sons. "Thank you, dear Fatherest, for saving my son. Talen, I'm sorry you had to suffer so."

They all wept.

Solis climbed down and embraced Livi and the two boys. "My darlings, it's all right now."

Stron used the rope to climb over the large boulders to the upper level, but Talen was very weak. Solis placed Talen on his back, and the family made it out of Mornie's Mountain Pass.

As they hiked back to Hilltop Castle, Talen said, "Mama, Baba, I knew you'd come for me."

Solis kissed his son. "We'll always come for you. I promise." It was then that Solis noticed the crevice had ripped skin from his nose, chest, and back.

He and Livi fed the children their evening meal, and they each took a bite from their own healing leaf. The children settled into their nest right next to where their parents slept. Daylight declined, and glow appeared in the overcast sky.

With dark, hard eyes, Mornie studied the fading wounds on Talen's chest. "Mama, did Lorgah make the claw that tore my brother?"

Damaro said, "Is Lorgah angry with us?"

Livi hugged Mornie. "The Lord God makes all things, but he's not angry with us."

"Why did he make it?" Mornie asked.

"It's my fault," Talen said. "I should have been more careful. Lorgah sent Mama and Baba to save me."

Mornie slapped her thighs with her hands. "But why make a thing to trap and kill us?"

"So we could overcome it." Solis sat with the children. "There are dangers in the world we must master."

Livi locked eyes with Solis. "There are physical and spiritual dangers. But we must always remember God is with us, and he is stronger than anything that opposes us."

Damaro said, "What if no one was strong enough to free Talen, and he was stuck between two rocks forever?"

Stron wondered, "Would we feed him the leaves until the end of time?"

"I'd rather die than remain trapped," Talen said. "Baba, if I died, would I go to be with Lorgah?

"Yes, my son. The Lord God will provide you with a new body, one that can't be hurt."

Damaro glanced at his arms and legs. "I get hurt and scratched all the time. I want my new body now."

Livi said, "That would mean you would leave us behind and go to the Lord."

"I want to stay here."

Solis said, "Yes, we must stay here and finish the work the Lord God has given us to do. Remember, the Lord God doesn't do everything for us, but he gives us everything we need. After all, he gave us each other. Mama and I would not have known where Talen was trapped without you children. No one should ever walk alone. You must take care of one another. And know the Lord always sees us and cares for us."

Stron said, "Baba, we made it all the way through to the other side of this mountain. A great river flows into Heaven Falls. There's a big rock outside where we came out, like a man's head."

"Did you see more than one opening on the other side?"

"No, Baba."

Livi said, "All six of you are brave explorers. One day, this family will conquer all of Erimea."

Brilara said, "I'm going to sing a song like Baba does. It's called 'Mama Says.'

"Mama says,
We are brave.
Oh yes, Mama says,
We are shining conquerors.
Mama says,
We are fearless explorers,
Rulers of this precious land.
Masters of Erimea,
And every scary thing.
We dwell in the dayshine,
Under our mighty God.
We six, the children of Solis and Livi,
Are masters of Erimea,
And every scary thing.
Oh yes, that's it.

That's what Mama says."

Talen gazed into the night sky and spoke dreamily to his siblings. "I really am going to be a brave explorer. We six will do great things, Mama said so."

Chapter Twenty-Eight

A low rumble sounded in the distance. Solis strolled to the front of the terrace. Stron was already there, gazing high in the sky beyond Tall Stony to the south.

He pointed. "Something's coming. Something big. The clouds are talking to each other."

"Talking?"

"Yes, see the jagged white lines flashing back and forth ... grumble rumble grumble? They're sharing secrets."

"What do you call the jagged lines?

"I don't know."

"Maybe it's how clouds share the secrets of the sparkles," Solis said.

"What're the secrets of the—"

"Baba, Stron?" Brilara popped up from the ladder, startling them. Her face and red hair glowed in the sparkle light, and her eyes of blue and brown shimmered. She beckoned them. "I've been all alone. Come sit with me." Brilara wrapped an arm around each of them as they sat.

The family had recrafted the main Hilltop Castle ladder many times. The one they sat on now was wider and stronger than any before it. Shaped side rails and rungs pressed into slots and notches with various wooden plugs to secure the whole structure, not just rope, as with the first ladder. With a few mishaps along the way, everything they made continually improved.

"Something is going to happen." Brilara clasped her hands to her chest. "I named the jagged lines *lightning*."

Stron said, "They do light up the sky."

Solis said, "For a second, they're like bright white crooked tree branches or the tentacles of roots reaching down from heaven."

Brilara said, "Baba, what are the secrets of the sparkles?"

"The sparkles and daylight make light because they are on fire with burning gases. The secrets are how they burn and how to harness their power. The Lord said my descendants will harness that power. Maybe you two."

Sparkles filled Solis with wonder. This new phenomenon—lightning—excited his curiosity, and that of his children. The young ones hungered for knowledge, as he did, and their understanding grew by the day. Could he stay ahead of the children?

One day, his descendants would surpass him in understanding. Would it be these children or their children's children? Why did the thought bother him? It shouldn't. Their presence was a gift. To teach and learn with them was a great reward. *How foolish of me to resent what God blesses them to discover.*

"Fire? Burning gases?" Brilara pondered.

"The Lord told me about the burning gases of the sparkles. They light up the night sky. I once reached to touch the sparkles, but they are too far away."

Out of the cloud came a flash. *Crack! Kaboom!* A thick, jagged bolt struck a tree, and the branches shattered in flames. A nearby field caught fire. Flames lit the southeast corner of the forest.

Stron gripped the sides of his head, and Brilara screamed. "The sparkles have come down." She jumped off the ladder, sprinted across the plowed field, and headed for the forest.

Stron and Solis raced after her.

"I'll touch the sparkles," Brilara yelled.

Solis said, "No, they may hurt you."

Brilara ran, heedless of his warning.

The burning field illuminated the forest and revealed the thick tangle of sharp branches waiting like spears. Solis spotted Brilara ahead, veering left along the north edge of the forest. Then, she turned right to head south along the forest's west side. Stron sped up, nearly on his sister's heels.

Ahead, the field was ablaze with the flames moving south, away from the children, leaving a charred, smoking landscape in its wake. The hiss and crackle of the flames and the smell of smoke filled the air.

Solis did not gain on the children. "Oh, Lord, they fly like Livi. Give me more speed."

Brilara and Stron headed straight for the blackened ground, but Solis caught one in each arm as they reached the smoldering grass and lifted them above the burning. The momentum carried Solis into the burnt area, and it scorched his feet. Flaming stubble sprang up, burning his ankles and the tops of his feet.

The two children hovered above the ground as their father spun them around to return the way they came. Stron laughed. "Wee, Baba, this is fun."

Solis screamed. "Ow. I'm on fire." Moaning, he limped out of the smoking field. He set down the children and fell to the ground. A large tree branch crashed in the spot they had vacated and sent sparks flying.

Brilara cried, "Baba's hurt. Stron, get the leaves ... Lorgah, Lorgah, put Baba's pain into my feet."

Solis said, "Shh, my darling, don't pray that. Let me keep my pain. You'll have your own pain in this life."

"Why should you hurt because of my stupidity?"

Solis winced. "It's what we do for each other. Curiosity, yes. Excitement, yes, but not stupidity. We all make mistakes."

At that moment, Livi arrived with a leaf basket strapped to her back. "I heard the boom and saw the light."

Stron said, "Baba's hurt."

Livi applied leaves to the soles of Solis's feet. The other four children had followed Livi with their leaf baskets.

They cried. "Baba's in agony ... we've got to help Baba." The children frantically applied their leaves to his ankles and feet, and they all shed tears.

Brilara said through tears, "Baba, I'm sorry. I didn't know it would hurt."

"I didn't know for sure. This is fire. Burning. It consumes wood and grass. Dangerous. Listen, my children, never rush to something new. Always examine it cautiously first. What you don't understand can harm you."

Solis's pain subsided. The family turned their focus to the flames and sat entranced by the burning.

"It gives light and warmth." Stron approached the burning branch with a stick and set it on fire. "Look, I've captured fire." He brought the burning branch toward the family.

Solis held up two hands toward his son. "Stop; don't bring it here."

"Baba, we can control the fire and use it."

Brilara approached Stron and examined the flame on the stick. "Baba, we can master this, like you said. It makes sparks like the ones Mama made with rocks, only it lasts longer with something to burn."

Stron said, "Maybe we can make fire without lightning."

Solis grinned knowingly. *Firecraft will change our world.* "Very well. You two will be the fire masters." He pulled Brilara close. "See? Good will come of this because of you two."

The family returned to Hilltop Castle, and the children discussed what had happened. As they prepared for the rest of the day, the Lord God walked up the main ladder and stood on the terrace. One by one, the family members joyfully ran to him, sat at his feet, and worshipped him.

Damaro said, "Lorgah, did a falling sparkle make the fire?" He nudged Brilara. "My sister thinks so, but I don't."

The Lord sat with the family. "What do you think, Damaro?"

"Well, at first it was you, your Father, and the Holy Spirit arguing with the devil. That was the grumbling and rumbling. Then you got so mad you shot at the devil with lightning, but you missed, and the lightning struck our forest."

Brilara scoffed. "You made that up, little brother."

"Lightning does not come from the sparkles." The Lord chuckled. "Damaro, if I shot at the devil, do you think I'd miss? Lightning and fire are among the tools I use to make changes on Erimea."

Daylig said, "Lorgah, tell us about the time before the sparkles. I love the story 'In the Beginning.'" She leaned back against the Lord and gazed into the sky. "I can see it in my mind. So beautiful. You, the Father, and the Holy Spirit surrounded the entire universe, and it twinkled like the sparkles. Tell us, please."

"Very well. I love to tell stories and appreciate children who like to learn." The Lord clapped and rubbed his hands together. "Before time began, there was only God. Nothing else. First, we made the heavenly host, a great company of angels. Spiritual beings of astounding power and glory created to carry out the will of God, to worship him, to care for his creation, and especially to minister to the children—"

"Was the devil there with the angels?" Mornie asked.

"Yes, he was there. No angelic being exceeded the devil in—"

"Why didn't you kick him out? You knew he was bad."

"Because it was before the rebellion. He had not yet sinned."

Daylig crossed her arms and huffed. "Mornie, stop interrupting Lorgah. Please finish the story."

The Lord God obliged. "After the angels, we made the universe, our first purely material thing. We had discussed it and planned all our intentions, so we knew what it would be ... But to see its reality was a much different experience. We gazed at it with pleasure and delight. It was good. Smaller than the tip of my finger,"—he held up his index finger for emphasis — "yet it contained all the mass needed for every galaxy that would ever form. Its temperature was trillions of times hotter than daylight. The pressure within this tiny creation was beyond measure. It shimmered before us, and the universe waited in anticipation of my command."

Brilara asked, "What were the angels doing?"

"The angels surrounded God in splendid array as he surrounded the universe, and they waited in great anticipation. The angels all witnessed the creation of the universe, and they knew soon their work would begin. When I gave the command, the universe began spreading out at a tremendous speed, and the heavenly host shouted for joy."

Talen said, "Then what?"

"The universe was filled with tiny particles, too small to see and too hot to form matter. The universe was plasma."

Stron said, "What are *matter* and *plasma*?"

Daylig scoffed and tossed her hands in the air. "You all are asking too many questions."

"We've heard it before, but now I want the details."

The Lord chuckled at the boy's determination. "Matter is what every material thing consists of. Stron, you are matter. So are the trees and plants, as well as Erimea itself. Plasma is like a thick, dark fog. Not solid or liquid or gas."

Stron stared, slightly agape, at the Lord God.

He finished the story. "The rest of the universe continued to expand and cool. At that time, the Spirit hovered in the deep mixture of the dissolved elements. Erimea was formless and void until I said, 'Let there be light.' That is the story of 'In the beginning.'"

The family cheered and applauded.

Daylig said, "I love the image of the tiny universe unfolding faster than anything."

Damaro crawled onto the Lord's lap, nudging Daylig out of the way. "Lorgah, we call you Lorgah, but Mama and Baba say your name is Iam. What's your father's name and when are we gonna see him?"

"You ask the most interesting questions. The Lord your God is one God, but he is known by many names that reveal something about him. On Earth, many will one day call the Father, Yahweh. I tell you, Damaro, if you've seen me, you've seen the Father."

Damaro gazed at the Lord and rubbed his forehead but remained silent.

The Lord told the family many more stories, some new and some old, and then he departed. Solis, Livi, and the children remembered everything the Lord told them.

The fire in the garden burned for the next day, but it didn't spread beyond the southeast corner of the forest and the surrounding field where vegetables grew in the ground. However, the words of the Lord burned in their hearts forever.

Together, Stron and Brilara studied fire. In a few weeks, they created fire from stone sparks. By then, an amazing array of plants and beautiful flowers—red, yellow, and purple—covered the field once littered with burned stubble. The scorched land's beauty surpassed that of the area untouched by fire.

Brilara said, "Does fire both kill *and* give life?"

Stron looked back and forth between the plots of ground. "It seems so. Somehow, it makes way for new growth."

"Everything can be used for good or bad?"

"Not everything. The tree of the knowledge of good and evil seems all bad to me."

"Mama and Baba say they're stronger because of it."

Stron shook his head. "That's too much to think about right now."

Brilara's focus turned inward. "I think about everything. Makes me afraid sometimes. Talen and Baba got hurt. This place is great, but it can hurt us."

"Baba and Mama will always help us."

"They need us too. I promise to care for the garden and our family."

Stron nodded and grinned at his sister. "We both will."

As they discussed their discoveries, they built a small stack of wood and lit it with sparks from the stones. They experimented with holding some vegetables over the controlled flame. The flames added a delicious flavor to the food. Stron and Brilara created various tools for holding the food over the fire so they wouldn't get burnt. Shortly, they introduced this new concept—cooking—to the rest of the family.

Chapter Twenty-Nine

Livi wielded a hard stone and marked the back wall of Hilltop Castle's main terrace to add to the mural depicting their lives in the garden. She stopped her artistic work and looked out on the Garden. The presence of the Lord God rushed upon her.

Livi saw herself in a vision. She held a shape much like a large brown leaf rolled into a cylinder. One end of the leaf was loose. She pulled it open, and the whole object unrolled. On its surface were many tiny markings, but she didn't perceive their meaning. The item wiggled in her hands, as though it were a fussy child. Livi struggled to hold the long leaf tightly to her chest.

"What is this, Lord?"

"It's your story, and one of your children will write it down." The Lord God descended toward Livi on the clouds of the night. "Come see a different story in a different land." He swept her up and carried her away, as when he first carried her into the Garden of Chara. "It's time for you to learn the lesson of becoming like God."

"Yes, Lord, I'm ready." Being with the Lord was thrilling; it freed her of all worries.

"Take up what you see before you. Let us go forth from Chara, so that you may help your sister, Eve, for she has lost her way. I will be with you always. Let us travel from Erimea to Earth so that you may serve your sister." The Lord circled high above the Garden of Chara.

Soon, the place changed, and Livi saw the terrible sight of the flaming sword and the angel who wielded the awful blade.

"No, dear Fatherest, no." She screamed and struggled against the Lord. "What if I fail you? What if I'm no better than Eve? I have young children and a husband whom I love. Please don't command me to leave my beloved home." In her desperation, she forgot her fear of heights and tried to jump from the arms of the Lord.

He wouldn't release her. The Lord repeated his command two more times.

Each time, Livi begged him not to command her to leave Chara and her family.

Finally, the Lord relented. "Very well. You are not ready for this great lesson."

"Thank you, Lord God. You are gracious to me."

"Still, I want you to see something."

In the vision, Livi came to a cave and saw a man and a woman with six young children. Three boys and three girls. The man tried to comfort the woman, but she refused to be consoled, because she wanted to return to their home. The man pleaded with the woman, saying it was impossible to return home.

There was no peace in that cave.

The vision changed. The Lord set Livi on a desolate road. She looked back and saw the angel with the sword, and she trembled and ran from the angel.

The angel pointed. "Go and see the future of women on Earth."

First, a group of crying women huddled in a shack because they desired children, but they couldn't conceive. Some of their husbands had deserted them because they hadn't borne them children. The men desired many sons.

The scene changed again, and there were pregnant women, anxious about giving birth. They had heard fearful stories of women who endured great pain or who had died in childbirth, as well as stories of children who died in their mothers' wombs or soon after birth.

A woman named Mahlah pulled a gray tunic tight around herself. "I'm afraid. My sister got childbed fever and died after a few days. Oh God, don't let me die." Mahlah looked through tears at the other women in the room. "Sister was just a delivery vessel. Doctors cared more about her newborn son and didn't help her. I was so young. I didn't know what to do."

"I'm sorry about your sister. I once helped a birthing woman who had the fever." A midwife named Tirzah looked at her hands. "I helped three other women in three days, and they all got the same sickness. I don't know how, but I may have spread it. I don't know if I can do this work anymore."

Livi held her cheeks, damp with tears, and cried out to the Lord. "Let me leave this place of heartbreak. These childbirths are nothing like the joy I've had bringing babies into the world. My sisters are burdened with every sort of fear."

Livi saw women who rejoiced because they had given birth to many sons. But when the sons grew up, they were conscripted to fight in never-ending wars. Bloodshed filled the land.

Violent men surrounded homes, and they murdered fathers, ravished women and girls, and slaughtered babies. Some they allowed to live. These survivors became slaves, and the masters and slaves hated and feared each other. Even in times of peace, women raised their children in perpetual consternation, because the children faced the threat of evil of every sort.

Livi said, "Why is all this evil happening?"

The angel said, "It's all according to the devil's plan. This is only the beginning. They will invent endless cruel ways to kill each other without restraint until one comes to show them a better way."

"May it never be so on Erimea."

"Deceiving spirits will come even on Erimea, but do not believe them."

"How will I know a deceiving spirit?"

"Test the spirit and its words. Compare them to what you know of the Lord God and his word."

When the vision ended, Livi ran to check on her children.

Chapter Thirty

Garden of Chara, Year 76

When they were seventy-five years old, Solis and Livi strolled along Unstoppable Forest Trail, reflecting on the goodness of the Lord. The breeze smiled, and the trees seemed to dance. Their children had married and started families of their own. Talen wed Daylig, and together they tended animals. Solis carried the couple's newest grandson in his arms. He basked in fatherly pride over the lovely, God-fearing people his children had become. "We're fulfilling the Lord's command to be fruitful and multiply. Like you, I feel God's pleasure in my soul." He sat with Livi on the banks of Pouchy Cheeks Pond. "It's amazing to think how our six children have become sixty-eight." He bounced the baby on his knee, and his great-grandson giggled with glee.

At the same time as Talen and Daylig's wedding, they had arranged Stron and Brilara's wedding. The pair had become masters of creating and sustaining fires, especially for cooking and illumination. Damaro and Mornie had married two years later and contributed to the developing civilization by designing and building wooden structures and implements. Solis and Livi tended the land and invented tools to make their work more productive. For a long while, life had felt like a song.

Solis sighed. "Things are changing so quickly. I wish the changes would slow down, but this is only the beginning of our work. The rest of Erimea awaits us."

"We'll leave this life behind." Livi rested her head on her husband's shoulder and cooed at her great-grandson, tickling his sides. "If we do return, Chara will be unrecognizable to us. Our home will belong to others. Even little Genio here will be grown with multiple generations of his own family. There will be so many new people we will not have had the opportunity to meet. I wish there were another way."

"Me too, but still, he has given us a wonderful life so far. I trust it will continue to be so if we walk with the Lord."

At age eighty-nine, Livi walked in the early morning light to the center of the garden near the original tree of life. Solis had planted seeds throughout the garden to cultivate more trees of life. Most of them did not survive past two or three years, but near the center of the garden, the new trees survived and matured.

As Livi pondered why the trees thrived in one area but not the others, the Lord God appeared to her. "Greetings, Livi."

"Greetings, Fatherest." She hugged him. "Lord, why doesn't this tree grow well in every part of the garden?"

"The roots of all plants take in nutrients from the soil. Different trees require different combinations of nutrients, or they will not thrive. The amount of light and water must also be right. This soil and location are good for the tree of life."

"So, we must learn to create the right conditions to grow the tree in other areas?"

"Yes, and the time grows short before you must leave the garden."

"Eleven years."

"Livi, are you prepared to give birth one more time in the garden?"

She swallowed and looked away. "What if I say I'm not ready yet? Will you be angry?"

"I won't be angry, but another wife and husband will have the joy of nurturing the special souls I intend to knit together in the womb."

Livi lifted her head and made eye contact with the Lord. "Let it be me. I'm willing."

"Very well. One year from today, you will give birth for the final time in the garden, your fourth set of twins."

Garden of Chara, Year 90, Shap, Day 31

A year later, Livi gave one last powerful push.

Solis cried out. "I see a head ... a head and feet?"

"What?"

"The boy is turned the wrong way and is very small. A third the size of his sister. They're holding hands." He held the brown babies with thick, curly black hair, stunned. "They came out at exactly the same time, she headfirst, he feet first."

The brown-eyed girl screamed at the top of her lungs, and the shriveled boy stared silently with piercing black eyes. He barely moved.

"Is our son well?"

"I don't know." Solis placed the babies on their mother's chest and turned away. *What's wrong with this boy?*

Livi said, "See how she touches her brother so gently? And he clutches her hands."

"She shall be called Caressa for her tender touch."

"And what shall be his name?"

"I don't know. I'll wait until they are tested and then name him."

Solis trudged down from Hilltop Castle into the forest's thick gloom, where the branches threatened like spears. He knelt among the nettles and leaves on the forest floor and prayed. "Lord, what's wrong with my son? Help him. How will he survive Erimea? Even paradise will consume him."

The Lord did not answer Solis.

When the children were three days old, Solis planned to repeat his ritual in a calm pool near Heaven Falls. This time, Livi stood in the pool next to Solis. He sat in the water, held each child face down on his forearms, and lowered them into the water. "Do you want to live?"

Caressa kicked her arms and legs, flipped over, and grabbed her father.

Solis raised her up. "You're a strong little girl."

The boy flipped over, but his arms and legs remained pressed to his chest, and he sank in the water with his eyes open.

Solis's shoulders slumped. "Swim, boy, swim."

The boy held his breath, and he stared at his father.

"You're failing your first test."

"Enough." Livi moved to save the boy, but Solis plucked the child from the water and held him.

He glared at his wife. "I wouldn't let the boy drown."

The boy remained silent, but he leaned his head against his father's chest and stared. The boy and Caressa clutched each other's hands.

"This boy is nothing like my other children, so weak and small ... your name shall be called Pitiful, for the Garden will consume you." Solis stomped off into the Garden, holding Caressa and the boy. He called on the name of the Lord.

Livi followed him.

In the middle of the Garden, Solis stopped at the riverbank from which he had been taken, and he gave the two babes to Livi. "Does God know? Is there really a loving God? Am I his son?" He sank to his knees and clutched the ground with his fists. He made a mound of dirt, then gripped the dirt and tossed it in the air as he cried out to the Lord. "Lord God, you must help my son. I demand it. This is wrong. Oh, Lord, help my boy." He continued in this way until he was covered in dirt, exhausted and weeping, but the Lord didn't appear.

Livi went to her husband with the children in one arm and brushed the dirt from his hair. "My dearest, let's go home. The boy will be all right. He's begun eating a little."

"No, I'll wait here on my knees for the Lord." Solis looked around, bared his teeth, and growled into the air. "He's making me wait. He hears, and I ... will ... wait forever, if I have to."

Then, the Lord appeared about four paces in front of Solis and spread his arms wide. "What is it you wish me to do for the boy?"

"May I express myself freely?" Solis stared at the ground.

"You may."

Solis sprang to his feet and charged the Lord, ramming him with his head. They both fell to the ground. Solis pounded his head into the Lord's chest. "What's wrong with the boy? Iam, strengthen my son to be like the other children."

Livi's mouth gaped. She set the children on the ground and tried to pull Solis off the Lord. She screamed, "Stop it. Stop it right now." But she wasn't strong enough to move her husband.

Solis continued beating against the Lord. "Make him well. Bless him to be like my other children. Don't let him be consumed. He needs help."

The Lord grasped Solis's head and held it so Solis could not move. "Listen, my son, the boy is exactly what I want him to be. I have blessed him. He will not be like other children. Accept him as he is. You, Livi, and the other children will give him the help he needs." The Lord released Solis and wrapped his arms around him. Solis trembled, wept, and sought to regain composure. "Do you understand?" He stood, pulling Solis up with him.

"I understand, but I don't understand."

"Will you obey my command?

"Yes, Lord, but ... yes, I will obey. Please forgive my outburst."

"I always want you to express your heart to me. Also, give the boy a suitable name. He shall not be called Pitiful." The Lord departed from their sight.

Solis and Livi sat on the ground with Caressa and the boy. Solis cradled the boy, and Livi held Caressa.

The boy stared at Solis, then at Livi, and then back at Solis.

He stroked the boy's face. "What do you see, my son? What do you see, my small boy?" Solis sighed and wiped away a tear. "With your big black eyes, do you see I was wrong, my darling son? Do you see I'm sorry, my small boy?"

Livi brushed her husband's hair. "My dear, what shall we call him?"

"He sees deeply. He shall be called Seerman. But I will call him Smallo, because he is indeed small. But he is good. His name shall be Seerman Smallo."

Livi nodded, and a smile crept across her face. "Very well. Seerman Smallo."

Chapter Thirty-One

Garden of Chara, Year 90

"In ten short years," the Lord declared to the family, "Solis and Livi will lead you out of the Garden along my way, and you will begin settling Erimea. You must start to prepare in earnest for this great adventure. The time will pass quickly."

Solis, Livi, and their adult children sat on sloping, grassy ground at midday listening to the Lord at Pouchy Cheeks Pond, a favorite spot for family gatherings.

Solis said, "What is your way?"

"It is the way you will show all who follow you on Erimea. The way to God."

Livi said, "Lord, we don't understand. What if we get lost?"

"You'll follow the rivers, and I'll guide you by the sparkles. Solis, you know the patterns in the sky well."

"I contemplate them every night."

"Do not fear. I will be with you. Only be strong and courageous in the face of every difficulty." The Lord disappeared.

Talen said, "Baba, where are we going?"

All eyes focused on Solis for reassurance, and he grew hot with anxiety. "All I know is we must go north to a land of hidden treasure, west to a land by the sea, and southwest to the field of charms."

"I'm all for adventure. I love that part," Talen said, "but this means leaving behind all our children, grandchildren, all our little ones."

Daylig wrapped her arms around Talen as she said, "Mama, how can the Lord expect us to leave behind all that we love and know?" Her blue eyes became wet.

Solis caressed Daylig's fine black hair. "My darling, we want you all to come with us, but the command is for your mother and me to fill and subdue Erimea. We must have children in four regions starting with Chara."

Brilara stood and scanned the faces of her siblings. "Baba, it would be too hard for you two to settle Erimea by yourselves."

"I, ah ... I don't know." Daylig looked at Brilara and turned away. "I'm not sure I can do it."

Livi took a deep breath. "I understand the difficulty, but the Lord has always sustained your father and me."

Mornie said, "Bri is right; we must share this burden."

Damaro said, "Our entire lives, we've heard how Mama and Baba struggled to build Chara. We've heard of hardships faced by God's future people on Earth. We can't expect to be any different. That wouldn't be right."

"I do ... I do agree with that." Talen spoke in a subdued tone. "We have ten years to prepare ourselves and those who'll be left behind."

Daylig's chin trembled. "I pray the Lord gives me strength to endure."

Brilara embraced her parents. "We six will help settle Erimea."

Stron let out a huge breath. "I'm glad that's settled. Where will we go first?"

"Shall we divide up?" Daylig said. "Does each family go to one of the three regions?"

Livi said, "No, we shall stay together."

"Your mother's right," Solis said. "She and I must go to each place and have children. However, you, our children, may stay in the places of your choice along this way we will blaze."

Talen said, "What of the newborns?"

"Your children and grandchildren are all grown." Solis gave Talen a hard stare and spoke in a low, firm tone. "Caressa and Smallo will travel with us."

"They'll still be children. I speak only out of concern for them. Especially for Smallo. The journey may be too hard for him."

"I know your heart, Talen, but we'll take care of Smallo and Caressa." Solis looked around at their small company. "Now, let's focus on the planning."

Damaro said, "What about the healing leaves? We'll need them."

Solis said, "We'll take a supply for daily use and for emergencies. We'll need enough for at least eight years."

"Why?"

"We can't harvest any leaves until the tree is ten years old, or the tree may die. We'll bring seeds and saplings, but it's very difficult to grow the trees from seeds. Only a few survived last time. The saplings, being two or three years old, will have a better chance, and that will reduce the time from planting to the first harvest of the leaves."

Stron said, "How will we carry so many leaves?"

With a gleam in her eye and a grin on her face, Mornie said, "Fear not, big brother. Damaro and I have become experts at building wooden structures. We'll build containers grazers can carry or sledges they can pull along the ground."

Solis said, "Daylig and Talen, can you train grazers to accept heavy loads on their backs?"

Talen said, "I'm sure we can. We now have a herd of more than one hundred grazers, but maybe unstoppables would perform better."

Daylig added, "We've domesticated many grazers and steppers."

"So we'll be able to transport many leaves," Solis said. "We need about four thousand leaves for eight people for ten years. The leaves never dry out."

Daylig's eyes widened. "Baba, how did you determine that number?"

"It's an estimate. A daily bite from a leaf reverses the day's normal aging, and each leaf is good for about seven bites. We could carry almost a year's worth in our own baskets."

"We'll also need many more leaves in case someone is severely injured," Damaro said.

"But the number is manageable, and within eight years, we should have strong trees to provide the needed healing leaves."

"As long as the trees survive and thrive in every place," Stron said.

Solis said, "You and Brilara know all aspects of fire. You will need to prepare all the utensils for making and controlling it to cook vegetables. You have much to teach us. Livi and I will continue studying cultivation of the ground and growing plants."

Livi laughed. "We'll also keep our noses in everyone's business."

She and Solis embraced each other and looked on as their children continued planning and debating priorities. Talen did most of the talking, but the others freely shared their wisdom, and they all enjoyed one another's company.

Solis spoke quietly to Livi. "Remember when Talen and Stron raced around here as toddlers?"

"The time passed so quickly. So much has changed since then. It seems like another life."

"They have all become fine men and women of God. I don't know where we're going or what we'll encounter, but our children will rule throughout Erimea. At some point, you and I will return to the Garden and be at peace."

Dusk arrived and the forest shadows lengthened. A mist fell over the family, and they all saw a vision.

They crept through a field of tall grass and shrubs. Around them stalked strange, sharp-toothed animals. Some family members held spears and cutters. Others held bows and arrows. One of the strange animals attacked a shrub, and a large featherone flew out of hiding to escape the beast. Arrows launched and pierced the featherone, and it fell to the ground. A sharp tooth retrieved the featherone and brought it to the family.

In the vision, Solis cried out. "No, we're the caretakers. We never harm beasts."

The voice of the Lord echoed in the vision. "Solis, the Garden and the rivers are teeming with creatures. They'll soon overrun the environment. Now is the age of the predator, the hunter of animals."

"May it never be."

The vision changed: fur-covered beasts sat around a fire eating meat.

The vision clarified: *humans* covered in animal fur. They even wore animal fur on their feet. The people shivered in the wind and pulled the furs tight around them.

"You are the chief predator," declared the Lord. "You'll need animals for food, coverings, and supplies. From now on, all wild beasts will fear you. Out of fear or hunger, they may attack you."

"No, Lord." Solis cried out and grimaced as if an arrow had pierced him. "Your creatures never attack their rulers, and we don't turn them into goods for consumption. It's wrong. Imagine their fear, and the cruelty. They are kindred spirits, made from the soil, filled with the breath of life."

"Solis, don't resist the will of the Lord. Don't declare wrong what the Lord approves. No featherone or beast of the ground or any always turning of the waters is forgotten before me. I feed them all, but a single human is more valuable than many animals."

The vision ended.

After experiencing the vision, Talen and Stron approached their father. Talen said, "Baba, we may now use animals for food?"

Solis stood and helped Livi from the ground. He crossed his arms. "You've heard the will of the Lord." He stomped off to Hilltop Castle. Livi followed. Everyone else remained at the pond.

Stron said, "He'll calm down. We must make spears, clubs, bows and arrows, and torches to contend with wild animals."

Damaro said, "If we follow the rivers, maybe we can design watercraft."

"What's watercraft?" Stron's eyes widened.

Mornie said, "Stron, you're the visionary among us. You tell us. and we'll build it."

"Solis, wait."

The command in Livi's voice made Solis smile. The sweetest voice in all Erimea. *It guides my conscience and melts my heart.* He turned to face her. "Yes, my darling." The trail had grown dark, but a sliver of glow sliced through leafy branches and illuminated Livi's face as she approached her husband.

"We have known the Lord God for ninety years. I believe he would give his life for us if necessary."

Solis sighed and rolled his eyes. "I know. I feel the same. But why must he always push and test and challenge us? Sometimes in the morning, the face of the sneaking thing appears in my mind, and I see the lifeblood pour out of him. It's my curse to have killed that creature ... I'm no better than Adam."

"And I'm no better than Eve. But you aren't cursed. We have not transgressed God's law, and we must not. For the sake of the children he has blessed us with." Livi spread her arms above her head. "All this is ours to rule and enjoy. But he wants more for us than this. He wants to bless us to be as strong as he is. And that blessing does not come by giving us everything we want."

"Will it come by breaking our hearts?"

"I don't know, but I know we must believe in the Lord God ... Remember what I once said about chiseling, to discover what's hidden inside? Maybe the Lord does that to us, and it hurts."

Solis stretched out his hands to his wife and looked into her eyes. "I promise you and the Lord, I'll always obey him, but I don't have to like it." Then he added with a sad smile. "I'll obey even if it kills me. And you know what?"

"What?"

"You have the shapeliest lips in the whole world." Solis enveloped his wife in his arms.

"Is that right?" Livi smiled and kissed her husband.

Chapter Thirty-Two

Garden of Chara, Year 90, Atta, Day 29

Solis, Livi, and their children and grandchildren sat in the grass in front of Hilltop Castle and talked after the evening meal. The flames from the cooking fire had died down, and smoke swirled from the fire circle. Thick clouds spread across the sky, and darkness grew. Caressa had begun walking and talking, but Smallo barely crawled and rarely made a sound. Livi held Smallo in her arms while Caressa toddled around her siblings, nieces, and nephews.

A long, high-pitched howl brought all conversation to a halt. Another howl sounded, and another, until a chorus of howling rang out from the forest opposite Hilltop Castle.

Solis said, "What's that?"

Caressa ran toward the forest. "Ah ga, Baba. Ah ga, Baba."

Stron scooped up Caressa. "I think she wants to scout out the forest. You're not a mighty woman of valor yet, are you?

"Ya ya." Caressa squirmed in her brother's arms.

Stron handed the baby, who still struggled for freedom, to Livi. "Baba, a new animal has come into the Garden."

Brilara and Daylig lit torches with the remnants of the fire and handed them to their grown children, who stood like guards around the family.

Livi asked, "Do you feel there is some danger?"

"It's the howlies," Brilara said. "I'm not sure they mean us any harm."

"The howlies?"

Daylig explained, "That's what we call them. Before, we'd hear them more in the south. Creatures that massacred a bunch of sneaking things and wicked-looking featherones near Tall Stony in the south. But they've come north."

Talen said, "Mama, Baba, haven't you noticed the dead bodies of small animals lately?"

Solis shook his head. "No."

"Neither have I," Livi said.

Stron said, "Something is killing and eating animals. Some of the animals eaten have been as big as the wild breaths. Remember the vision? It's the age of the predator."

Solis grimaced. "Flesh eating is disgusting. I can't imagine eating flesh. It's full of blood."

Damaro said, "It's true, Baba, something out there likes eating meat."

"Why are your children standing with these torches?" Solis asked as he looked around.

Stron waved his father away from the fire. "Baba, look carefully into the forest right over there." He pointed. "What do you see?"

"Eyes. Yellow eyes glowing in the dark."

"Looks like ten or fifteen animals watching us. Animals are afraid of fire. The torches are to keep any type of killer animal away."

"No animal in the Garden has ever tried to harm me. I need to study them." Solis started toward the forest. "Let's take a look."

Talen, Stron, and Damaro surrounded their father like a tall, brown wall of muscle and restrained him. All three stood taller than their father, Talen, head and shoulders above Solis, with Stron and Damaro a little shorter than Talen. All possessed broad, powerful bodies like Solis.

Talen said, "No, Baba, things are changing. Remember how you taught us to be cautious? Flesh-eating beasts are out there."

Stron said, "Until we know more, it's too dangerous to go out at night." He exchanged a glance with Talen. "We need everyone inside. It's late."

Talen yelled to the group. "Everybody, it's time for all of us to be inside the walls."

When everyone safely returned to Hilltop Castle, Stron and Talen unlashed the main ladder and pulled it up.

Throughout the night, Solis tossed and turned, serenaded by barks, snarls, and periodic choruses of mournful howling. The sounds kept getting closer.

As daylight peeked above the horizon, Caressa woke first and pointed. "Mama, Baba, look."

Solis and Livi sat up in their nest and found themselves surrounded by twenty howlies. The beasts had four thin legs, black and gray coats, long snouts, and ears that pointed up. Small dead animals, many of them pouchy cheeks, hung from the powerful jaws of the beasts. The lifeless bodies dripped blood. The amber-eyed howlies stared silently at the humans, as if waiting for instructions. Their heads reached Solis's waist.

He stood. Veins in his neck bulged, ready to burst. "Don't move."

Livi clutched Smallo and Caressa.

"They're the sharp-toothed beasts from the vision." Solis approached one of the animals.

It crouched and growled.

"Go back. Get off the terrace."

The largest beast, with a brownish-orange coat and bright golden eyes, dropped its prey, turned west, and began a graceful lope down the long, sloping distance of rocks leading from the terrace to the ground. The other howlies followed their leader.

Upon seeing the retreating animals, Daylig said, "What did they do?"

Livi sighed as the howlies departed. "They left these dead animals."

Caressa stroked the fur of a dead creature and picked it up. "From Lorgah."

"They brought us gifts?" Daylig wrinkled her nose. "I suppose we should try eating one. It's been months since the vision, and still we haven't eaten meat."

Solis said, "Gifts from the sharp tooths?"

Talen said, "They're the howlies. I'll ask Stron and Brilara to cook these."

Solis swallowed hard, then scowled. "It's time to eat animal flesh."

That evening, Stron and Brilara skinned the animals. They skewered and roasted them. To everyone's surprise, the roasted animal meat tasted good.

The children of Solis and Livi slaughtered grazers and other animals for food. They discovered animal parts, skin, bones, and fur had other uses. They learned to sew skins together with animal sinew and veins. Small bones served as needles. The Lord taught them to make coverings as garments, but they didn't need to wear them in the Garden.

The morning after the howlies brought the gift of dead animals, three of the creatures returned and dug around in the crevices under Hilltop Castle. Solis and Livi climbed down the main ladder, circled out to the field, and looked back toward Hilltop Castle to investigate.

Livi said, "See there? At the western base of the castle, they each cleared their own space. Small caves."

"Let's get closer."

Livi said, "There are small ones with them now. They're giving birth."

Small black balls of fur tumbled around, seeking their mother's milk.

"Amazing they would choose this place. So close to humans."

Livi pointed. "Five here, three in the middle, and four there."

"More gifts?"

Transfixed, the couple crouched in the grass a few paces from the three mother howlies. One of the beasts let out a high-pitched howl, and the entire pack joined in.

Solis glanced over his shoulder. "We are not alone. I didn't hear their approach. We may be in danger." He and Livi slowly turned. They were surrounded. Each clasped the other's trembling hands. "Don't move."

Solis, Livi, and the beasts remained frozen until the large golden-eyed howlie leader emerged from the pack and trotted past the human pair. After he inspected the twelve pups and the three mothers, Golden Eyes turned and ran back into the forest. The pack followed him.

Livi slumped against her husband's chest. "That was scary. I suppose he was satisfied the mothers and pups were fine."

"Did you see the way the pack stood guard around their sisters and babies? We may be able to use the howlies as sentinels to keep watch over our company during our journey."

Solis asked Daylig and Talen to check on the howlies and attempt to train the pups when they were old enough. For five weeks, the pack of howlies brought food to the three mothers, who rarely left their young. When the pups finished nursing, the mothers regurgitated food for the pups to eat. In the absence of the pack, Daylig and Talen played with the puppies under the watchful eyes of the mothers, who never showed any aggression toward the humans.

Daylig said, "The howlies are very smart. I hope we can train them."

"Maybe they won't be too wild," Talen said. "The babies, anyway."

At six months, the pups were almost as large as the adult howlies, and they traveled with the pack. The three mothers and six of the puppies didn't return to Hilltop Castle, but six did return. These six became the first howlies to live with people. Subsequent generations of howlies that lived with people were called *hounds.* They became pets, hunters, and sentinels that guarded Hilltop Castle. The hounds were tall, about the same height as the howlies, but the hounds grew thicker and more muscular than the wild howlies.

The entire family worked together to prepare for the walk along the Lord's highway. Caressa grew rapidly and spent time with Talen and Daylig working with animals. By the time Caressa reached six years old, she had learned to shoot a bow and arrow and make fire. Like her siblings before her, Caressa was speedy like Livi. Each day, when Caressa returned to Hilltop Castle, she sought the company of Smallo.

Smallo didn't walk until age four, and he didn't speak, but he and Caressa communicated. She always knew what Smallo wanted and how he felt. Solis carried Smallo with him wherever he went, and he tried to teach Smallo everything about the Garden, cultivating plants, and the Lord. Smallo grew very slowly, so he did little work, but he helped Solis with planting seeds.

Solis often said things like, "Smallo, you are my strength. Your peaceful presence gives me peace. You make my every burden lighter and teach me. When you first bowed in wordless adoration before the Lord, you reminded me that even the most intelligent animals don't worship God as humans do."

Smallo responded with gentle hugs and slight smiles, but no words. The boy always carefully observed what was happening, but none of the adults knew how much Smallo understood. Only Caressa knew.

One day, Smallo walked back and forth in front of the mural Livi, Daylig, and others had painted and carved on the back wall of the terrace. The expansive artwork told the story of human history thus far.

Caressa told Livi, "Smallo wants to know what became of the devil inside the sneaking thing."

"How do you know what Smallo wants, Caressa?"

She shrugged. "I just do."

Livi picked up Smallo and gazed into his large, dark eyes. "Why, at five years old, do you want to know such things?"

Caressa grabbed her mother's legs. "Smallo thinks strange things. Hard to understand."

"You know what Smallo thinks?"

"Sometimes I do."

Livi continued. "The Lord said the devil came out of the sneaking thing, but I don't know where he went. Maybe to torment the people of Earth. He hates all of humanity, and he'll never give up trying to hurt us. But don't be afraid of the devil. The Lord is on our side, and he is much stronger than the devil and all his angels."

"Smallo isn't afraid of anything, and neither am I."

Lucido scoffed as he eavesdropped through Ophthalmos. "You foolish children lack the sense to be afraid. You'll learn what fear is when I lead your family to the boiling cauldron and force them to drink from the bitter cup." Through the window, he took note of the sneaking things and how they had changed over time. He plotted how he could use them again.

When the Lord God had declared the age of the predator, he instilled the fear of humans in all wild creatures, but sneaking things inherited both hatred and fear of humans from the first sneaking things. As the human population grew in the Garden, sneaking things grew accustomed to seeing humans in the southern regions of Chara.

Featherones, small animals, and insects enjoyed the scraps of food humans left behind, and sneaking things preyed on the small creatures that feasted on the humans' leftovers. Sneaking things gradually became less fearful of humans, though their hatred remained. They ventured farther north, drawn to the prey they found around Hilltop Castle, but they caught the attention of the howlies as being suitable for food.

The howlies tracked the beasts to their home in the south and attacked. This catastrophic attack of the howlies created a new instinctual fear and hatred within the sneaking things. Most had left Chara many years earlier, but after the howlie atrocity, more left the Garden.

Some retreated to the safety of their nests around Tall Stony. In the years after the births of Smallo and Caressa, generations of sneaking things were born with the added instinctual desire for revenge on howlies and humans, and their bites grew venomous.

A few years before Solis and Livi left the Garden, four sneaking things were born—Gula, Rula, Riga, and Rage. Like all sneaking things, they had thin, black slits for pupils set in yellow eyeballs. Their bodies were yellow or brown with dark bands. These four were intelligent, adventurous, and fearless, and they gained the attention of demonic spirits.

Chapter Thirty-Three

Aetherdon, City of the Air, Year 90

Lucido motioned to Iredin and Vik for a report. "What have your angels learned about Erimea during these ninety years of human existence?"

Vik said, "The Lord's made a marvelous living machine for sustaining and adapting the planet. Millions of interconnected systems and processes. An amazing creation."

Lucido folded his arms across his chest, and his expression turned sour. "How does this God-praise help our cause?"

Iredin hurried to explain. "It's as Vik said, but every process has the potential to destroy human life before it can infect the entire world."

The demons described the deadly mysteries of Erimea's design and how God's own mechanisms for shaping and changing Erimea for good could also destroy the humans. Lucido's spiritual forces had to lead the human band to the right spot at the right time. Death could come from shifting tectonic plates, volcanoes, hurricanes, ground tremors, rivers, lakes, and even the wind.

They especially loved the irony of God's own creation destroying his most prized beings. They chattered on and on about the dangers of the natural world and proposed alterations demons could make to cause the world to be even more deadly.

"Before we alter Erimea, I'll need to make an appearance on the other side of these heavenly realms."

Heaven, Year 90, An appointed day

The angels appeared before the Lord, Lucido among them.

The Lord said to Lucido, "Where do you come from?"

"From roaming about Erimea and walking around on it."

"Have you noticed Solis and Livi and their mighty sons and daughters? They have held fast to my word and are blameless. There are none like them in the entire universe. They and their descendants are my treasured possessions."

Lucido stomped his feet and tramped around before the throne. "Do they serve you for no reason? You protect them and provide for them in every way. The Garden of Chara is too easy, and its land is too productive. Let me curse the ground of Erimea, so it brings forth thorns and thistles, and their labor becomes hard. Let me reshape the path of their impending journey, so straight ways become crooked, smooth ways become rough, and plains become mountains and valleys. Make their way challenging, and they will forget your word and curse you to your face."

"You may not curse the ground so it brings forth thorns and thistles," the Lord said. "However, until their exodus out of the Garden commences, you may alter the terrain of Erimea. You have ten years from now to do your sculpting of the land and then remove your finger to allow natural processes to resume."

Aetherdon, City of the Air, Year 90

Iredin gaped at the vast array of myriad rebels gathered around Ophthalmos. They formed a giant dark funnel spiraling up from the eye of the worlds, all waiting for Lucido, who had commanded them to assemble.

Ophthalmos blinked awake, and the great eye grew ten times larger, and it displayed a grain of sand on a seashore. The grain vibrated and expanded until it was a clear, brilliant gemstone. It rose from the sandy beach and flew through grainfields, forests, and future settlements on the planet until it rose high in the sky where it took the shape of a luminous white cloud. The cloud shimmered and circled around Erimea and poured forth rain and lightning. The cloud left a rainbow in its wake that stretched to the ground and enveloped the planet. Iredin and all the wicked spirits exulted at the sight of Lucido, their great leader, displaying his dominance over Erimea.

The cloud shot higher, and they saw the cloud extend a shining hand with its palm facing them, and the hand waved at them. Then, the hand reached out to them as though it breached the surface of Ophthalmos to embrace them. Iredin, the most intellectual of spirits, tried to restrain himself, but he reached out in hopes of touching Lucido's glorious hand. Iredin saw Vik grasping for their leader with tears in his eyes. The other spirits also stretched toward the hand; none had seen Lucido like this before. The image changed, and the cloud turned fiery red, surrounded by deep space with tiny lights sparkling in the background. A hole opened in space, and the red cloud blasted through and disappeared. Ophthalmos went dark.

Aetherdon shook and *boom boom boom!* drew the spirits' attention upward. The red cloud streaked down past the spirits until it hovered in front of Ophthalmos. The cloud dissolved, and out stepped Lucido, glistening like a diamond. All his angels fell at the glory of his appearance.

"Rise, rise, my brothers," Lucido shouted.

When the spirits regained their senses, they burst with uproarious shouting and applause.

Lucido strolled around Ophthalmos to his throne. "My brothers, we will employ a two-pronged strategy against the humans on Erimea. We will enhance the physical dangers of the planet and attack based on the principle of a thousand psychic bites."

Iredin ran his hands through his thin strands of hair. "What do you mean by psychic bites?"

"Wounds to the personality." Lucido tapped his fingertips together. "Humans aren't the unique individuals we are. They are a single race deeply affected by the sins of their ancestors, so they continually hurt each other and model sinful behaviors."

Vik said, "That's why the fall of the first parents on Earth was so effective."

Lucido said, "Yes, every single earthling has had great violence done to their personalities such that they learn to hide their true selves, thinking it will protect them. Most forget their God-given identities. People hide them beneath a layer of fear, so all their lives they wear a protective mask. They can't be at peace when they are estranged from God and each other."

Iredin shook both of Lucido's hands and bowed. "Hail, Daystar. He will restore us. Brilliant! We can use their fear and drive them into sin. We can show God his design of these creatures is deeply flawed, so he abandons his intentions for them. They cannot be redeemed."

"Presently, the emotional injuries of Erimeans are not severe, so they are still true to themselves and don't naturally attack each other. We will enhance our thought attacks with strategic precision. We will bombard their minds with harmful notions against themselves and one another until the Erimeans make our thoughts their own and retreat under a shell of pretense and self-loathing. We will use the same techniques repeatedly until we have a breakthrough and they violate God's law. Then, the downward spiral will begin on Erimea just as on Earth."

Lucido assigned a team of his angels, the derangers, to each human to stoke fear and discontent continually. "We will pursue this strategy forever," they vowed. "Time is on our side."

Lucido turned to address his angels, who had studied the design of Erimea. "Now, my brothers, is your time to earn your moniker, the engineers of destruction." Lucido erupted with booming laughter as he paced through the demon soldiers. "We have ten years to wreck the foundations of this planet. May your work bring harm to a thousand generations of humankind. Swarm deep and be strong; work from the inside out. Now go. I will watch over you."

The evil spirits ripped into the heart of Erimea and shattered massive plates on which the land rested and displaced them from where they had been anchored. The foundations of the planet became unstable. Super-heated molten material and poisonous gases seeped toward the surface. Great mountain ranges, valleys, and canyons appeared on the surface of the land and in the depths of the seas. Beautiful yet deadly areas formed on the surface, and the demons smoothed out the paths to these places to attract the people to their own destruction.

Lucido himself altered the banks of the river that powered Heaven Falls, so it flooded through Mornie's Mountain Pass. He guided the river's new route until it eventually threatened the safety of Hilltop Castle.

Amid their sculpting of the land, Lucido shifted his focus to upcoming events. "The original pair must never return home. Without their guidance, their offspring will likely fall into sin. If the tree of life doesn't grow as well in other parts of Erimea, perhaps we can make the settlers pine for its healing power. Erimea's dangers may make them desperate. The Charan gardeners we may infect with feelings of insecurity and scarcity, so they're unwilling to share the leaves of life. The settlers of other lands may become dishonest merchants willing to cheat for gain or pirates willing to take what they want by force."

Iredin said, "Soon, the lot of them will forget the meaning of 'love your neighbor as yourself,' and they will plunge into the same murderous conflict that rages on Earth."

"We will expose the Erimeans as players, misers, and thieves. No better than the earthlings."

Iredin said, "Players, misers, and thieves?"

"Yes, all idolaters. Every corner of Erimea has its own joys, wealth, and dangers. Players long for pleasure. Misers love wealth, but fear losing it. And thieves desire pleasure *and* wealth and are willing to steal it. And the Most High God will see the foolishness of all his hopes for his beloved humanity."

Lucido hesitated and turned back to face his two demon lieutenants. "Find out how you can stir up the sneaking things against the caravan. Today's beasts may prove more useful than their forefather."

Chapter Thirty-Four

Garden of Chara, Year 100, Helpe, Day 1

One month before the exodus of Solis and his family, the population of the Garden of Chara had grown to 178. Every adult person and most children had contributed to preparations for the expedition, which Solis named Sojourners' Way.

Damaro designed big bagger, a filling device, and positioned it near their home's main ladder. Big bagger had a funnel at the top and a chute out the side, along with a frame for supporting bags made of sewn animal skins. Livi, Solis, and others emptied food baskets into the funnel, and the chute directed the food into the bags. They had bags for grain, dried fruit, vegetables, and meat. Big bagger had a platform for filled bag storage that would allow the bags to be strapped onto the grazers' backs on departure day.

While working on big bagger, Livi saw rock darters, pouchy cheeks, and rodents scrounging for food around the platform and on the ground. "Shoo. Get away." She stomped her feet. "Get away; that's our food."

The little beasts retreated.

Solis strolled by and waved to Livi. "Let's check the other supplies. We must make sure everything is right." He examined a cutter, a pin-and-plug pounder, and a wood scraper from a sledge platform full of tools. Another sledge contained torches and implements for making fire.

A sledge consisted of two small trees as poles and an angled platform with low sides between the poles. While they traveled, one end of each pole was attached to a grazer's yoke with goods secured on the platform. The other ends of the poles dragged on the ground.

Livi pointed to a sledge with a ten-year supply of the healing leaves. "Will we really need this many leaves?"

"We'll need much more. There's another supply for emergency use."

Livi strode to the next sledge, filled with twelve tree of life saplings. "May these trees provide a bountiful harvest."

"At best, it'll be seven or eight years after planting." Solis contemplated the saplings and ran his hands over several root balls. "These are the most important items we carry. Life."

Livi nodded. "The gift of health and life to future generations throughout Erimea."

"We must protect these little trees at all costs. From a thousand plants that sprouted, only these twelve survived—and countless seeds went into producing each sprout."

Livi's voice rose in pitch. "I hadn't thought of it like that." They moved to another sledge. "I don't like living in these shelters." She pulled up a lightweight tent made of animal skins with eight poles sewn into the skins. "Too small. I need space to breathe."

"I hope to sleep under the sparkles, but we may need shelter from the cold wind. We're used to the Garden's warm, gentle breezes." Solis turned his face to receive the soothing air currents. "But I remember the powerful gale that knocked me off Tall Stony." He frowned at a sledge full of hunting weapons—spears and bows and arrows. "I'll never get used to these killing devices."

"See here. Much good comes from hunting and keeping animals." She examined a supply of wool blankets made from the sheared fur of beasts they called the shaggy steppers. Livi also checked ten sets of skin and fur coverings—one pair for each member of Sojourners' Way. She held up one small skin and another much smaller one.

Solis hung his head and looked away from the children's coverings. "I've been thinking about what Talen said, and it breaks my spirit to think he may be right."

"Right about what?"

"He said this journey will be too much for Smallo."

Livi hugged the garments to her chest. "I couldn't bear to leave my babies behind."

"Caressa may be strong enough, but Smallo—"

"I'll carry Smallo the entire way, if I must." Livi dropped her arms and returned the items to the sledge. "I will not leave him behind."

Solis rubbed his forehead. "We must inquire of the Lord ... Lord, help us to know what to do."

Livi and Solis both fell to their knees and prayed.

The voice of the Lord said, "Smallo and Caressa must not travel with you. I have other purposes for them."

"How can I leave my babies? I'm like so many broken branches," she wailed.

"Broken branches?"

"Wrenched, twisted, stripped." Her voice broke. "For what purpose? To build this world? Is it my fault to have birthed them? Every joy is turned to bitterness."

There is no purpose. Everything is at the whim of an uncaring God. Remember, he gave you the choice. God knew the consequences of your decision.

"It's my fault." Livi fell prone and sobbed. "I should have had them long ago so they would be grown by now."

Solis held Livi as her older children and grandchildren gathered around to comfort her, but she found no consolation.

As might loomed, Solis and Livi beckoned Caressa and Smallo to them. Livi held Smallo.

Caressa stood with her hand on her father's shoulder. "Smallo wants to know why you're so sad today."

Livi cried. "We have just learned you and Smallo won't be part of Sojourners' Way. We have to leave you behind."

Solis squeezed Caressa to himself. "It breaks our hearts to leave you." He bowed his head, and tears streamed onto the terrace floor. "Ah, we're distraught."

Caressa also wept and pounded her father's chest. "Baba, why are you leaving me?"

Solis held Caressa tighter. "Oh, my darling daughter, it's God's command to us."

Caressa screamed. "Why is Lorgah so mean?" She searched the sky. "Iam, please let us go."

Livi took Caressa. "My baby, Iam loves us all very much. He's not being mean. He knows best."

Caressa clung to her mother as her tears fell.

Smallo stood, and the four hugged each other. He spoke for the first time. "Baba, Mama, we'll be all right. I know Lorgah has a purpose for us."

Solis sucked in a quick breath. "You can speak." He picked up the boy and spun him around. "We've been waiting for ten years to hear your voice."

Livi lowered the hand covering her mouth. "I can't believe it. Say something else, baby, please."

Smallo shook his head and jumped into the nest where he and Caressa slept.

Caressa wiped her tears and sniffed. "Smallo doesn't like to talk."

Solis and Livi sat in stunned silence. Profound joy had suddenly been mixed with agonizing frustration.

Livi and Solis sat on the main ladder of Hilltop Castle. Solis's shoulders slumped, and Livi leaned her head against him. "We should be happy. The boy can speak."

"Yes, fourteen words." Solis sighed. "The boy doesn't like to talk."

"At least he spoke words of comfort to us. Smallo loves his family."

"Years and years." Solis put his arm around his wife. "We'll miss so much of their lives. I hate it."

"At least Caressa and Smallo have each other."

"Yes. Somehow, they can communicate. Their nephews and nieces will take care of them."

Livi said, "The Lord will look after them."

"He has other purposes for them. What purposes?"

"Only the Lord knows." She dropped her hands in her lap and let out a sigh. "We need to focus on Sojourners' Way preparations. That's our purpose."

Solis stood on the ladder and extended his hand to her. "Yes. Let's get some rest."

That night, Smallo and Caressa spoke to one another silently, as they often did.

Smallo said, *Baba was sad like this the day we were born. Do you remember?*

No one remembers the day they were born.

I do. I remember everything Mama and Baba said. I saw and heard their words, but I didn't understand for a long time. I made Baba very sad back then.

We make Baba happy. You can't see things people say.

I can. I made Baba so sad he was mad at God. He fought God for me.

He did not. Baba loves God.

I know, but he knocked God down when we were three days old.

Caressa shook her head and sighed. *Why don't you talk more? Mama and Baba would like that.*

I don't like talking. I have a lot to think about. Smallo pressed his hands into his forehead. *There's too much swirling around in my mind. I'm trying to sort it out. The past, the future. It gets confusing sometimes.*

Seerman Smallo. Caressa tapped his head. *What's going on in there?*

Smallo smiled and pushed her hand away. *I'm glad you're not leaving me alone.*

I'll never leave you. You're the other half of me. Time for sleep, my brother.

Chapter Thirty-Five

Gula, Rula, Riga, and Rage departed their nest under Tall Stony and swam upstream in Sweet Water Whirlwind. They rested along the muddy banks near Heaven Falls. The scent of a meal wafted over to them.

Demons Iredin and Vik had appeared to them in the form of sneaking things to persuade them into pursuing easy prey near the home of the humans. A feast of tasty, warm, little blood-filled creatures awaited them, but they would be there only a few more days.

The four beasts crept from the river through the tall grass. They caught a faint scent of the hounds, but the hounds were not nearby. They passed the sledges of supplies, approached the big bagger, and waited for their prey.

First, four small featherones landed and pecked at fallen grain. Then, rock darters crawled onto the platform searching for bits of meat. Big, juicy insects gorged themselves in the grass.

Rula sprang first. Then, Gula, Riga, and Rage pounced on their prey.

Livi wiped her brow in the midday heat and was dumping a bucket of dried berries into big bagger when a commotion broke out under the platform. She jumped to the ground to discover four sneaking things with their victims hanging from their jaws.

Heat exploded in her eyes. "Get out, you evil slime!" She swung her cutter back and forth and moaned with fear and fury.

The surprised predators ran in circles to escape until one beast attacked Livi's heel.

"Ouch. The slimy brute bit me." She swung her cutter and sliced off the critter's head. The other three dashed into the grass and escaped, but not before Livi struck again with her cutter and hacked off another's tail. "Oh, I'll kill all of you." She chased the beasts until she ran into Solis.

He grabbed her. "What are you doing? Why are you limping?"

Livi struggled against him. "Let me go. I'll exterminate all sneaking things. It bit me." She held up her foot.

It had swollen to three times its normal size. Blood poured out of the heel wound.

Solis's eyes bulged. "You're badly injured. Have you eaten the healing leaves?"

"No. Let me go. They're getting away. I'll destroy—" Livi staggered and vomited. "You're blurry ... can't breathe." She lost consciousness.

Solis laid her on the ground. He fumbled with the leaves as he pulled them from his basket and applied them to her wound. He placed one leaf in her mouth. "Wake up. Eat this." He crushed the leaf and pressed the ointment onto her tongue. "Please, be all right." Solis held Livi's immobile form.

Mornie approached her parents, Damaro a step behind her. "What happened?"

"A sneaking thing bit her. It must be deadly."

"Poison." Damaro picked up the severed head and squeezed it. "Look, fangs for injecting the venom."

Livi coughed and pressed her hands to her eyes. "My head hurts. I was chasing the beasts. What happened?"

Solis helped Livi up. "You fainted avenging yourself."

"They're from the evils. Serpents that threaten this mission."

"Or dumb creatures seeking food." Solis's face took on a somber expression. Agents of the devil again? Possibly. "In a bit more time, you might have been dead."

Livi pointed to the severed head. "One day, I may cut off all their heads."

Solis let out a heavy sigh. "Or they may kill you. The leaves wouldn't bring you back from that."

Talen and Daylig arrived with hounds.

Solis said, "Where have you been? We could have used the hounds."

Daylig said, "We've been working with them. We selected these twelve to join Sojourners' Way."

"Your mama was attacked by sneaking things, but she fought them off. Help her to the terrace."

Damaro reached out to give Talen the sneaking thing's head. "Teach the hounds to be alert for this scent."

Talen recoiled from the offering, but reluctantly took the head and let the hounds sniff it. "Mama's a warrior."

Chapter Thirty-Six

Stron said, "Baba, we want to show you something." Stron, Brilara, and Damaro led their father to the end of the long line of sledges. They stopped at an odd formation of layered logs, its crossed sections bound together with rope. "Can you guess what it is?

Solis circled the object and squatted to examine it. "It's some sort of platform."

Stron laughed. "But what is it?"

"I have no idea. What is it?"

"It floats. It's a watercraft. We made three more like it, and we made two smaller crafts, each from a single log."

"We can float down the river on it?"

"If we need to. It's called a raft, and we can bind all four rafts together to make a barge for carrying our goods. Mornie and Damaro built them."

Damaro said, "More than rope holds them together. There are interconnected joints with pins, slots, and plugs. They are sturdy."

"What are the smaller watercraft called?"

"Dugouts. Two or three people can fit into one. Maybe for exploring."

Solis said, "Very nice. When did you have time for this?

Damaro stood tall with his legs spread wide. "We've been working on a river-going vessel off and on for ten years."

"How will you move them overland?"

"Two rafts can be hauled on one sledge, and the two dugouts can fit nicely on a single sledge with room for other supplies."

Solis nodded and smiled at Damaro and Mornie. "Congratulations on this invention and your ingenuity ... All my children surpassed me long ago."

Garden of Chara, Year 100, Helpe, Day 31

The Lord met with the family at Pouchy Cheeks Pond.

Solis said, "Lord God, tomorrow, Sojourners' Way will depart from Chara and leave behind all we know and love. We do this to fulfill your command to fill and subdue Erimea. The eight of us are proud to do your will, but isn't there some other way? I know you want us to change, but—"

It's because you're all lazy and corrupt.

"Why must we change?" Talen said. "Have we fallen short of the mark you established? Have we displeased you in some way?"

"You have not fallen short of the mark, and I hope you never will," the Lord assured them. "You are all completely innocent in my sight. But to be like God, you must be more than innocent; you must be holy and complete."

Solis said, "What does it mean to be holy and complete?"

You'll never be good enough.

"Let me tell you a story. There was a man, God's servant, who lived among the vile and wicked humanity of Earth, yet remained sinless in all his ways. God's servant walked upon the earth and never sinned, yet he was made to suffer at the hands of wicked men and women. That man learned obedience through the things he suffered, and in so doing, he became perfect. So, there is great value in suffering for God's sake. My call to each one of you is to become perfect by doing my will, no matter how hard it may seem. Do you have the faith to accept this purpose?

Solis said, "We do, and we'll ask you no further questions."

All the members of Sojourners' Way agreed.

The Lord departed.

That night, as they strolled back to Hilltop Castle, Damaro spoke privately with Solis. "Baba, this means innocent people will suffer. But in your vision of life on Earth, you said sinful people suffered because of their sins."

"Yes, correct."

"So, sinful people suffer because of their sins, but innocent people suffer to be made perfect? Does the suffering of sinful people make them become perfect?"

Solis squeezed Damaro's arm and laughed. "You think too much. Suffering is not going to help sinful people if they keep sinning. But if it causes them to repent, to change their ways, then I suppose suffering helps them. Still, I think sinful people will still have the consequences of the sins they committed previously. You ask the Lord about that, but I think sinners will have to deal with their prior sins."

"I'm glad we only have to deal with suffering for the Lord and not sinning against him."

"I'm glad God is God and not me."

"In the story the Lord just told all of us, does God's servant live on Earth now?"

"Maybe. Or he could be part of what the Lord calls future history."

Chapter Thirty-Seven

Garden of Chara, Year 100, Marri, Day 1

On departure morning for Sojourners' Way, the entire community helped with the final securing of goods and yokes to the grazers. The people covered all the sledges with animal skins, except the one with the saplings. Each sapling stood about three paces in height, and its roots were in a ball of soil wrapped in skins. Four rows of saplings were arranged three abreast, and wooden slats were pressed against the dirt balls to secure them.

Solis said to his children, "We have ten sledges of materials, each yoked to a grazer. Is that right?"

Damaro said, "Yes, and we have three more grazers with food strapped directly on their backs."

Daylig said, "We have three extra grazers we'll rotate in, so each grazer will get days off with no load."

Solis held his walking stick and looked around at his children. "Are we ready to depart?"

At that moment, the ground shook. Trumpeting, rumbling, and roaring engulfed the crowd, and the people trembled and prepared to scatter.

"What is that noise?"

Fifteen unstoppables with huge, curved tusks raced up Northeast Circle like a massive gray-and-white landslide. Ten more emerged from Unstoppable Forest Trail.

Mornie's face turned ashen. "They're going to trample us." She and the crowd ran toward the terrace ladders; pushing and shoving ensued.

Talen shouted, "It's okay. They're friends."

The animals stopped short of the humans, and four approached him.

Daylig nuzzled the animals. "We've been working with them. Talen and I expected some to join us."

Solis said, "What will they carry? One could easily carry the load of five grazers."

Stron said, "That's what I told Talen and Daylig, but they wouldn't have it."

Talen leaned his head against one creature's long nose and stroked another. "The unstoppables won't carry any load."

Solis said, "Why not?"

Daylig came up to her father. "Baba, unstoppables can't be treated like grazers."

Talen said, "Unstoppables possess great intelligence and sensitive hearts. To force them to carry loads, we would have to break their spirits."

Livi placed her hands on Talen and Daylig. "All right, these giants are your pets. Why will they join Sojourners' Way?"

"Mama, a single unstoppable," Talen explained, "can topple a large tree, roots and all. And they enjoy it. They eat roots, bark, and leaves."

Daylig said, "At some point, we may need to clear a forest."

Talen said, "They're gentle and accept our instructions, but they're still wild."

"Your gentle beasts"—a grin spread across Solis's face as he nodded—"may be useful in clearing the land."

Talen said, "Yes, Baba. These four have volunteered. Their unstoppable family is here to see them off, as ours is."

Solis raised his voice and his arms. "These four unstoppables will join Sojourners' Way. It's time for everyone to say goodbye."

The children of Livi and Solis hugged their children, grandchildren, and all their descendants. Livi and Solis spent a private moment with Smallo and Caressa.

Solis knelt before his children and hugged them. "Your mother and I love you very much. One day, we'll return, and you'll tell us about all the great things you've done for the Lord. By then, you'll have your own children who also have many little ones."

Livi said, "We are so proud of you two. Smallo, you are a mystery, but the Lord has something great in store for you. Caressa, you will become an amazing woman of valor. I see it every time I look at you."

Caressa said, "I'm going to be like you, Mama."

Smallo wrapped his arms around his parents' necks and said, "Love you, Baba. Love you, Mama."

Solis said, "Remember to obey Skyon and Leadra." The married couple, grandchildren of Solis and Livi, had agreed to be guardians for Caressa and Smallo. Then, Solis took his place at the head of the caravan. "It's time for Sojourners' Way to depart."

The entire community both cheered and wept as they followed Northeast Circle to the Neverway Passage. Skyon carried Smallo. When they reached Neverway, Smallo shivered, moaned, and wept.

Solis grabbed Smallo and held him. "My darling boy, what's wrong?"

Livi took the boy as tears welled in her eyes. "What is it, my baby?"

The boy couldn't speak through all his tears.

Caressa said, "The Lord showed Smallo something. Your journey will be exceedingly difficult."

Smallo calmed. His facial features fell, and he gazed into the space between Solis and Livi. A strange voice came out of the boy's mouth, as of an old man. "Put on the armor of God. The battle is not against flesh and blood. Beware the water bubbles." Then, Smallo closed his eyes.

Caressa said, "It's okay. He's sleeping. Smallo is tired."

Livi returned the boy to Skyon. With anxious hearts, she and Solis led Sojourners' Way out of Neverway Passage, and their family members returned to Hilltop Castle.

Solis wiped a tear from Livi's cheek. "How was that for a sendoff?"

"Miserable. The worst."

"Every eddy of flowing water makes bubbles. What did he mean about the bubbles?"

"Who knows?"

After a couple hundred paces, they turned left and followed a winding river flowing north. Solis called it Rapid River.

Sojourners' Way, with eight human souls, headed toward the land of hidden treasure, but they didn't know how far their journey would take them. Talen and Daylig followed their parents, leading the four unstoppables. Then came sixteen grazers—ten pulling sledges, three loaded with food, and three loaded with empty storage containers for items they might acquire en route. Stron, Brilara, Damaro, and Mornie brought up the rear. The twelve hounds patrolled up and down the line of travelers as well as around the group's perimeter, alert for any dangers. The remaining unstoppable herd continued east, away from the Garden.

The familiar river's cascading sounds comforted the travelers, but Solis was perplexed by what Smallo had said about the armor of God. Was every problem caused by the devil? Did the devil cause no problem at all? Solis shook his head. The answer to both questions was no.

If you don't keep everything and everyone in line, this journey is doomed.

With the strange voice, Solis heard noises from the river. He grasped Livi's hand and stopped walking, checking his surroundings before resuming.

Livi said, "What is it?"

"I don't know. I thought I heard clicking and scratching and a splash of water ... Probably nothing but antics of an always turning. And sometimes my own thoughts disturb me. Do you remember the story of Tawal and Sola?"

"The smoke-dragon slayers. The Lord told us of them."

"The Lord told them and us to put on the armor of God."

"They ignored God's armor, but we'll wear it. I can recite my version." Livi put a hand to her forehead. "A truthful heart within and without, intent to behave rightly. Peace that comes from the good news I am always near you. Faith in me. Confidence I will preserve you through any trouble. Heeding the word I speak to you and praying always. Put on these things."

Solis nodded. "We taught these to our children ... but Smallo—"

"What did our baby see? The way his little body trembled." Livi sobbed. "I fear for him."

"He fears for us. What of Caressa? She sees into his mind. Maybe the sneaking thing attack was a message from an evil spirit. Not just the action of hungry beasts."

"They make my skin crawl."

"Yet, they are mere instruments."

"How will the armor protect our family?"

"Only God knows."

Chapter Thirty-Eight

The journey's first ten days were uneventful and surprisingly easy, as if the path along the river had been cleared for Sojourners' Way by a friend—or perhaps a foe. Smallo's warning weighed on Solis and Livi and kept them on edge. They walked from morning until late afternoon, except on the seventh day when they rested. Restday continued to be a time of relaxation and reflection on God and his creation. On all the other days, they walked. Even on those days, they discussed the Lord's teaching, and he often appeared to them.

Solis and Livi grieved the separation from their youngest children and reminisced often, especially early in the journey.

On the first night, Livi looked back at the Charan mountains. "Remember the day they went missing?"

"I thought you were going to die."

"They were just five years old. Thankfully, Talen got them down after he spotted Caressa scaling the highest levels of Hilltop Castle with Smallo strapped to her back."

"I wonder where she got the desire to climb things." Solis gave his wife a silly grin. "I recall being out in the field with Smallo. He stood transfixed in front of a single yellow flower, staring at it, smelling it, feeling the surrounding soil. As though he were searching out the mysteries of Erimea in that little plant."

"Maybe they're both explorers at heart."

By Solis's count, they walked about twenty-six thousand paces each day. The first bit of excitement occurred on the third day, when they discovered a hole in one of the bags containing tree of life seeds. They found the droppings of a small animal.

Damaro wasted no time in sewing up the bag.

Solis stomped around the sledge, jutting a finger at the newly repaired bag. "This loss cannot happen again. After our own lives, the saplings and these seeds are the most critical thing—"

Talen put his hands on his father's shoulders. He lowered his voice. "Baba, we know all—"

Solis pushed Talen away. "Do not interrupt me." His eyes flared at his son. "The tree of life is our promise and gift to all Erimeans who will follow us. The guarantee of life and health."

"Baba, we are all adults," Stron said. "We know the importance."

Solis continued to march and lecture until sweat poured down his face.

Eventually, Livi touched his arm and spoke in a soothing tone. "My dearest, we understand."

Solis finally relented with a sigh, and the caravan continued.

On the eleventh day, they met a thick forest, impassable to the sledges. A clear path continued to the left, away from the river, circling the forest. To the right lay a small, rocky ridge, beyond which flowed Rapid River. Solis led the group around to the left for about two thousand paces until white mist obscured their view.

A gust of wind cleared the mist. Before the caravan sat a series of ponds surrounded by colored soil of blue, green, orange, and yellow. Colored bands overlapped each other and formed sandy fingers reaching out from the ponds. At the center of the first pond, water bubbled up and sent steam into the air. The ponds behind the first also sprayed up white mist, and the light scent of eggs filled the air.

The unstoppables refused to go near the first pool and retreated. The grazers followed. The beasts relocated near the river and munched on the grass and bushes. Only the humans and the hounds remained around the first pond, mesmerized by its beauty.

Talen said, "What is this?" He reached for the pond water.

Solis, remembering Smallo's warning, restrained him. "It may not be safe."

"It's okay, Baba." Talen pulled away, plunged under the water, and disappeared.

He's a reckless fool.

One of the hounds followed Talen into the water.

Livi ran to the water's edge and screamed. "Talen. Talen. Get out!"

The hound bounded out of the water and around to the opposite side of the pond, where it pawed the dirt.

Talen burst above the water. "It's fine. It's warm. I never felt anything like it. A warm bath."

Daylig also jumped in. "Mama, it's warm and refreshing." She backstroked through the water toward the burbling center of the pond. "Feels so good."

Solis wailed, "Get out! Get out. You don't understand the danger. Hurry away from the bubbles."

Slowly, Talen and Daylig got out. Talen spread his arms wide. "Why are you two so upset? It's warm water."

Solis took Talen by the arm. "Son, Smallo warned us about bubbling water. We didn't know what he meant ... look, your skin is turning red. Does it hurt?

Daylig said, "I'm itching and burning."

"Hurry, go rinse in the river." Livi pointed. "We don't know what's in that water. Hurry."

Daylig ran. Brilara, Mornie, and Damaro went with her.

"Come on, Happy," Talen called to his hound. "Come on, girl."

Instead of following the command, she plunged in again and swam through the middle, where the water bubbled furiously. The hound yelped and yelped, but she continued to swim across. Before she reached the pond's edge, the animal let loose an agonizing, mournful howl and sank.

Talen dove back into the water and pulled out the hound. "She's burned. Scalded. Burning up."

Stron snatched up the hound and hustled her to the river. "Come on, brother. To the river to cool."

Talen fell to the ground with his hands on his head. "My poor Happy."

Livi said, "You didn't know. Maybe she can be saved. Go to the river and rinse off."

Talen staggered away.

Solis stared down at the water and reached out. The steam condensed on his hand. "That's what water does when it's heated. Turns to steamy mist. We could cook food that way. This is Hot Killer Springs."

"Look at that." Livi's voice brought Solis out of his thoughts. "I didn't see that before."

Another gust of wind cleared the steam and revealed a green mountain beyond the pond covered with shrubs and wildflowers.

Solis followed his wife's gaze up the mountain. "There's smoke coming out of the top. Let's go take a look."

As they hiked up, Livi took her husband's hand. "That could have been Talen or Daylig, not the hound."

"I know." Solis bent over, hands on his knees. "My firstborn boy and girl. May I never see my children suffer so."

You're an incompetent leader.

Solis snatched his walking stick from among the flowers and leaned on it. "Lord, give us strength."

"My dearest, you are the strength of this family."

The pair reached the upper ridge of the mountain on the eastern side in about two thousand paces and discovered it was the edge of a great mountain range that stretched far into the west. An uneven, ragged ring of black-and-gray rock formed the lip where they stood.

Solis and Livi looked down into a deep crevice. The bottom quivered. A quaking, heaving, smoking solid mass. The surface rippled and belched smoke, and the crevice vomited burning red liquid that quickly cooled to a steamy black rock on the sides of the crevice. Fortunately, the wind blew the smoke and fumes away from them.

Solis hollered over the deafening noise. "The surface rises, then down and back up."

"Like something is trying to break through. Smells horrible."

In that moment, the ground shook. A crack formed on the opposite side of the mountain, and a gray plume of smoke blew out. Lightning flashed inside the plume. Red-hot liquid poured out the western side of the mountain.

Livi said, "Lightning's striking in the smoke."

Solis pointed. "Look, the trees over there are burning."

"Let's get out of here. This is more dangerous than Hot Killer Springs."

The mountain rumbled several more times as they raced down through the trees and brush. Fear that the east side of the mountain might split open drove them down in a hurry.

"This shall be called Tremble Mountain, the way it shakes us."

Chapter Thirty-Nine

Stron and Talen finished digging a shallow grave for Happy as their parents reached the river.

Talen looked at Solis and Livi. "The burns were too bad."

Livi hugged him. "We're sorry, son. There's much we don't know about our own world."

Talen muttered tearfully, "I should have taken better care of her. I should have known."

Solis said, "Only the Lord knows everything. We must live and learn."

Damaro emerged from the darkness of the forest. "It's six thousand paces through this stretch of woods. Lots of small- and medium-sized trees. Lots of brush. Only a few really big trees. We can avoid them if we decide to clear a path through."

Solis said, "I suggest we let the unstoppables rip through these trees. Daylig and Talen, what do you think?"

Talen strode over to his father. "They can do it. We have to show them which trees to take down."

Daylig said, "Talen, let's mark the trees for the easiest route."

Mornie said to Talen and Daylig, "Did you see the little featherones landing on the backs of the grazers?"

"We call them *grapeckers*," Talen said. "They eat insects off the grazers. I don't think these featherones are harmful." The grapeckers possessed sharp claws, gray bodies, red eyes, yellow bills, and an appetite for ticks and maggots.

Daylight stood high in the sky, but Solis said, "We'll camp here for the night. Unyoke the grazers. The unstoppables can work while it's still light and then rest for the night. Stron and Brilara, let's get the fire started." He stopped and sighed. "I suppose the rest of us should hunt for dinner."

Solis, Livi, Damaro, and Mornie retrieved their weapons of choice. Solis preferred a spear for hunting always turnings. They all favored fresh meat over the dried food they'd packed.

Solis said, "Who'll go with me?" He took a few steps up the rocky ridge and planted his spear. "Today, I predict a great haul from the river. I feel it."

The family looked at the confident expression on Solis's face and burst into laughter.

Even Solis joined in. He shrugged. "There's a first time for everything. Who's coming?"

Mornie said, "I'll go with Baba." She grabbed a spear.

Solis and his daughter climbed over the small rocky mound that divided the river from the path.

Mornie put an arm around her father and leaned her head on his shoulder. "I'm afraid, Baba."

"What's wrong?"

"I miss home. Everything here feels unsafe." Tears gathered in her eyes. "Will Damaro and I ever see the Garden again?"

Solis hugged his daughter. "At one time, the Garden felt dangerous to your mother and me. The first time I entered Hilltop Castle, I thought I'd die. Then, it became home. A place of rest and peace. The Lord will do the same for you and Damaro wherever you end up."

When they came to the river, they separated to hunt always turnings.

Stron and Brilara were collecting firewood while their father prepared to hunt in the river. Stron laughed with his wife. "For ten days, he's gone to the river and caught nothing."

"I know, but that's our baba." Brilara giggled. "He never gives up."

Livi and Damaro chuckled.

Livi and Damaro selected bows and arrows for featherones and other small game.

Damaro said, "I'll go with Mama, and we'll take a couple of hounds."

Livi and Damaro took a few steps and scanned for game. "I don't think your father can bring himself to kill anything. He's the gentlest and kindest man in the world."

"I know. He's a great man." Damaro pointed at one of the hounds who stood motionless in front of a bush. "He's spotted something. Be ready, Mama." He motioned to the hound. It attacked the bush, and up flew a great featherone. Livi let fly an arrow, and it struck the animal dead in its breast.

Livi said, "Yes, our supper."

The other hound retrieved the featherone and brought it to Stron.

By late afternoon, Damaro and Livi returned, ready for rest and a meal. Stron and Brilara had already cooked up much of the hunters' game. The trickling of gentle river water and the aroma of good food made for a relaxing gathering.

Solis and Mornie dragged themselves over the ridge of rocks, weary from prowling around in the river.

Stron said, "How was your luck today?"

Mornie raised a haul of four large always turnings. "I had a great day."

Solis remained silent. He returned his spear to its sledge and stood near Livi, warming himself at the fire.

Stron smiled. "The bow-and-arrow hunters also did well. Three fat featherones of different types and a small wild breath. We could lie here and feast for days."

He and Brilara had sliced and skewered the day's catch. Now, they passed out the roasted meat on sharp spits. Roasted vegetables were placed in several large wooden bowls for everyone to enjoy.

Daylig and Talen came out of the forest, and Daylig clapped her hands. "Everybody, we had a great day clearing twenty-two big trees, stumps and all."

Talen said, "Plus a bunch of shrubs and little trees. It's not a straight path, but the grazers and sledges should make it through easily."

Solis said, "Let's thank the Lord for this sumptuous meal and an exciting day." After prayer, he said, "Where are the big brutes?"

Daylig said, "Foraging for their favorite foods. Leaves, roots, bark, and berries. They'll feast for some time, like us. Then probably go for a swim."

Talen took a bite of his food and motioned to his father. "Baba, there is a tree the unstoppables refused to touch. It was buzzing along a large portion of the trunk."

"Buzzing? Could be bees that produce the golden sweet." Solis smacked his lips and rubbed his belly. "So good. You should have seen the sweet, sticky stuff oozing out of the tree."

"No golden sweet in that tree. There's something strange. I want you to take a look in the morning."

Solis said, "I will, but now who wants to tell one of the Lord's stories?"

Brilara spoke up. "I'll tell one of the stories of Earth's future history. May it never happen on Erimea. May we learn its lessons and never live through these things." She unfolded her tall, lean frame and jumped up. Brilara commanded attention with her confident posture and warm, caring eyes. In the declining light, she acted out a man walking alone. Red wavy hair framed her face and striking mismatched eyes. "This is the tale of when the lonely man traveled from Jerusalem to Jericho. He was called a Jewish man. Robbers beat him, stripped him, stole everything he had, and left him for dead."

"Robbers are humans, right?" Daylig wrapped her arms around herself and moaned. "I will never understand how they can harm each other like beastly predators."

Mornie said, "Stripped of what?"

Solis said, "Of his covering. On Earth, it's shameful to be seen without any covering."

"Why, Baba?"

"After Adam and Eve sinned, the first thing they did was to hide themselves because of their shame. So, they made coverings for themselves to hide under."

Livi said, "For us, it's different. If we ever wear animal skins, it will be for protection."

"Dead skins." Solis shook his head and pinched the skin on his arm before patting his chest. "I will always be most comfortable in my own skin."

Livi said, "If we were ever to meet an uncovered earthling, we should immediately avert our eyes, so as not to add to their shame."

Mornie said, “Sounds like earthlings wear coverings to hide who they are or to pretend to be something they aren’t.”

Damaro said, “It’s strange the man didn’t apply the leaves.”

Solis said, “On Earth, they’re cut off from the leaves.”

“How could they live without the healing leaves?”

Brilara sat to regain everyone’s attention and then stood and continued. “One of the man’s friends passed by, but he didn’t help because he had important business to take care of. Then another friend came along, but he also refused to help the poor injured man.”

“These are strange friends,” Mornie said.

Brilara took several marching steps. “Then, a man called a Samaritan, one hated by the Jewish people, came along and helped the Jewish man.”

Solis looked skyward and studied the sparkles. “I’ve often wondered how humanity on Earth will divide the way we’ve heard about in the stories.”

“The Samaritan somehow overcame the division and hatred to be a neighbor to the injured man. He showed the poor man compassion.” Brilara ended her story with a flourish and returned to her seat.

Damaro said, “Earthlings must be fools to destroy each other.”

Livi said, “Careful, they are your cousins. We’re no better. They’ve been deceived.”

Solis said, “The Lord warned us trials will come to challenge Erimea. We must teach our children well, so they are good neighbors to everyone.”

Stron said, “I can see how things could easily go wrong between people.”

“You would never rob me or beat me, brother,” Damaro said.

Talen nodded. “Stron wouldn’t intend to, but some great problem or mistake that causes suffering we haven’t known could occur. If we’re not careful, we could turn on each other.”

Solis said, “Let’s pray that if we suffer, we’ll suffer together and never fall into opposition.”

The family stretched out around the fire and slept. The hounds kept watch and made sure the grazers didn’t wander.

Gula and Riga looked down on Sojourners' Way from the rocks and flicked their tongues to smell the delicious, warm-blooded creatures hidden in the grass near the camp. The two sneaking things did not hunt there, because they feared the fire and the hounds.

Fear felt strange to Gula and Riga. Their bodies ached with homesickness, and with the hopelessness of this adventure. They returned to the river and curled up under a log that jutted out into the water. The two slimy creatures rested uneasily.

Solis dreamed about Tremble Mountain. It transformed into a monstrous living beast with eyes flashing lightning and claws with sharp pincers. The mountain leapt and crashed onto Solis, who lay immobile. The mountain's pincers slowly tightened around his neck.

Tremble Mountain rumbled threats. "Go home. If you continue, I'll consume your family with burning vomit. I will bury Sojourners' Way."

Solis broke free, slammed his fists against the mountain, and curled his lips. "Never. Not as long as Solis lives." In the nightmare, Solis prayed. "Lord, save Sojourners' Way from this haunted mountain." He woke up shaking and coughing. His whole body ached, and he could not rest. An angel of the Lord touched Solis's head and let him sleep.

Chapter Forty

The next morning before anyone else woke up, Talen shook his father. "Baba, let's go."

Solis rolled over and stretched. "What is it, son? Feels like I just got to sleep."

Talen clasped his hands. "Remember the buzzing tree."

"Yes, all right." Solis retrieved two large wooden bowls and a smaller one, careful not to disturb the other sleepers. "Maybe we'll gather some golden sweet ... a breakfast surprise for everyone."

Talen led Solis along the cleared path. Before long, Solis said, "See, son, here is a tree with golden sweet oozing." He reached into the tree with the small bowl and filled the large bowls with golden sweet.

Baba's so confident and so wrong.

Talen bounced from one foot to the other. "Baba, that's not what I wanted to show you."

Solis set the bowls on the ground and followed Talen farther along the trail. The forest woke, and the songs of featherones serenaded them. Small creatures scurried about as they came to another tree with golden sweet.

Talen went a little past the second tree dripping with golden sweet and stopped in front of a medium-size tree with an opening at the bottom as large as a man's head. He leaned against the tree trunk. "Listen."

Solis placed his ear at the base of the tree and raised up to his full height. "A lot of buzzing bees in there. I wonder how high it goes. But no golden sweet."

"No ordinary bees. These are monsters." Sweat beads formed on Talen's forehead, and he wiped them away.

"Monsters?"

"Almost as long as my palm. Three or four times as large as regular bees. They don't make golden sweet. They steal it. The big brute bees murder and rob their little brothers."

"What?"

"They haven't ventured out yet this morning. They have large orange heads with black and yellow bodies. They were out yesterday afternoon. Come over here." Talen led Solis to the river, where the dead body of a short-haired, gray climber the size of a small hound lay.

"Poor beast."

"This climber made the mistake of going after the golden sweet in the tree back there." Talen pointed to the killer bee tree. "Those guys didn't like it. About a hundred swarmed the climber and stung it repeatedly. Its cries horrified me."

"The stings must have been terrible."

"The beast yelped like Happy being boiled alive, only worse. The climber scampered across the log in the water and dove in to escape the brutes. It dragged itself out of the river, swollen to three times its normal size. I found it dead later."

"Look at all the puncture wounds. Poison in the stingers." Solis squatted to examine the creature. He found a stick and used it to roll the animal over. He winced. "Completely covered. Pierced as with a hundred hot needles and swollen around each wound. Poor thing, a horrible way to die."

The two men returned to the hive near the big brute bees' tree.

Solis said, "Looks like nobody's home here."

"That's because the big ones attacked the little bees and bit off their heads. They carried the dead bodies and the golden sweet home where all the big brutes feasted on the golden sweet and the dead bodies of their little brothers."

"Pretty gruesome." Solis shivered.

"I suspect the hive you collected from will be their next target. Good you collected before they got up."

"I'll get no more. Too dangerous."

"Good, we must be careful not to provoke the murder bees."

"I agree, but I'd like to see how they attack the little brother bees."

When Solis and Talen returned, the others were finishing breakfast. Daylig and Livi found a black boulder with a flat face, and they marked the rock with images of Hot Killer Springs and Tremble Mountain.

Solis laid a hand over his heart. "You are skilled artists. You're always drawing. Recording our world beautifully, the good and the bad."

Livi said, "Thank you, my dearest. Where have you two been?"

He held out the bowls of golden sweet. "Gathering a treat ... and studying an amazing little predator."

The family shared and savored the golden sweet treat.

Talen said, "Today, Daylig and I and the unstoppables will finish the pathway, so we'll camp here again tonight."

The next morning, Sojourners' Way was ready to maneuver through the bumpy, holey path the unstoppables had cleared. Stron and Livi had walked the route and noted roots and branches from the felled trees jutted out along the path like skewers waiting to pierce a careless man or beast.

Solis said, "The murder bees have an agonizing and poisonous sting. If they swarm after you, run to the river and take shelter under the tree. Everyone else, wait until the critters clear out."

Talen said, "Baba will stand near the big brutes' nest. Don't disturb them and don't touch the golden sweet dripping from the hive with the baby bees."

"If we don't give them a reason to attack, we'll be fine." Solis leaned on his walking stick near the tree of the murder bees.

Livi led the way. Each person held a healing leaf in one hand. With their free hands, they guided grazers slowly through the twisty pathway.

Stron brought up the rear to guard against mishaps. He smiled at his father and hugged him as he passed the nest of merciless insects. "We've made it past the danger." Stron focused his attention on the ground surrounding the base of the tree with the killer bees. "Look, one scout flew out, and now another."

Both men observed the flight path of the murder brutes to a hungry climber in the tree savoring the sticky goodness.

With alarm, Solis hollered, "Oh no, where did you come from?"

The climber swatted at the bees and crushed one. The second scout returned to the hive, and a swarm like black buzzing smoke poured from the base of the tree. The climber jumped out of the other tree and dashed between Solis and Stron. The beast bashed into Stron's leg and knocked him to the ground. Stron dropped his leaf.

"Run!" Solis cried out.

The climber and the two men flew to the river, with Solis in front of Stron. The first of the bees clamped onto Stron's leg, then another and another until the killers covered both legs. They stung all at once.

You're going to lose everything because of your careless father.

Stron screamed and collapsed at the water's edge. "Ow. Run, Baba. They got me." Poison and pain paralyzed his legs.

Solis turned, threw his walking stick onto the riverbank, and pulled his son into the water. "Plunge under."

Stron pulled with his arms, and Solis stroked with arms and legs until both were underwater. With the whirling, buzzing swarm in furious pursuit, Solis and Stron reached the fallen tree.

Solis said, "Did you eat your leaf?"

"Dropped it." Stron shook his head.

"Hurry and swallow this."

Stron ate the leaf from his father.

The swarm divided. One half attacked the climber's back, exposed on the water's surface. The beast cried and rolled over to wash the bees from its back. They attacked its belly, so it rolled and rolled, attempting to escape.

Stron felt his legs healing, and he tapped the soft underside of the tree. "It's rotten. Clear a space for air."

The other half of the swarm swooped and brought their fury onto the tree while the two men clawed pulp from the tree's underside. They made a narrow space where their heads bobbed above water, but the sides of the tree remained submerged. Thousands of murder bees bombarded the exposed tree trunk, but they didn't go under the water's surface.

Solis clapped his hands over his ears to drown out the deafening buzzing hum. "They're attacking the tree like mad."

"They can't get through. We're safe."

After a little while, they no longer heard the brute bees.

Stron sighed. "They're gone. Let's go."

Solis shouted. "Oh no, they're here. Two sneaking things under the water in front of you." He pulled his son back and moved between him and the sneaking things. Solis slashed the water with his cutter, but he missed the beasts.

"What is it, Baba?"

"The things that bit your mama." Solis scanned the water. "Go home, you stupid servants of the devil. Don't make me kill you. The demons will never stop us." In a rage, Solis sliced his cutter through the water again. "I nicked one creature." A ribbon of blood dispersed in the water.

Stron looked back at the tree. "There they go."

Father and son watched the pathetic sneaking things writhe away along the riverbank.

The rest of Sojourners' Way scrambled over the rocks to the riverbank in search of Stron and Solis.

Mornie saw them first. "Baba. Stron. Are you all right?"

Her father said, "Yes."

Some of the family wept. Others trembled, shaken by all they had heard and seen, but the family gathered around and hauled Solis and Stron from the river. Brilara came sobbing and wrapped her arms around her husband before checking his injuries.

Solis retrieved his walking stick. "Let's get out of here. For these two days, we've been haunted by wicked spirits."

Livi shook her head. "First, let me look at you two." She stooped to examine Stron's wounds and groaned. "Your legs are swollen. Huge ... hundreds of stings. You ate your leaf?

"Yes, Mama."

"Does it still hurt?"

"Yes, but I feel the healing. It's much better."

Livi also stopped Solis and hugged him. She sighed. "You're not hurt?"

"No, my darling. I'm fine."

Brilara said, "Baba, what were you slashing at in the water?"

Solis opened his mouth but paused.

Stron said, "Baba saw two sneaking things."

Livi leaned her head against her husband's chest. "The evils still stalk us ... will they never leave us alone?" Her face turned ashen.

"I cut one of the beasts. Both fled. I had a terrible dream last night. Now I know the devils will never stop, but neither will we." Solis stroked Livi's hair as he told her about his nightmare. "The Lord is our helper."

Brilara moaned. "I hate this place." She wrapped her arms around Stron. "Let's get out of here."

Stron said, "Look at the dead climber floating there." Stron collapsed after a few steps, but he popped up. "That was strange. My legs suddenly became weak."

Solis named the region Pincer Wicked Lands. Sojourners' Way continued north, following Rapid River. After leaving the Pincer Wicked Lands, rugged terrain slowed the progress of Sojourners' Way. The daily distance traveled was cut in half.

Chapter Forty-One

Lucido, Iredin, and Vik gathered again in Aetherdon, the dark realm of wicked spirits.

Iredin growled like an animal. "They're in the grip of anxiety but keep escaping."

Vik smiled. "Every step they take is filled with uncertainty."

"Big Baba and Mama"—Lucido's lips curled in a sneer—"seem determined to reach the land of hidden treasure, but we may be able to shake the resolve of the others."

Iredin said, "I suggest we attack the youngest couple first—Mornie and Damaro—and see what trouble we can stir up within the family."

Vik said, "Good. Mornie is already having doubts about the mission."

"Then we'll go after the others." Lucido snorted with laughter. "Soon, they'll forget about brotherly love."

Iredin said, "When we break the first family, we'll have a template to use with the Gardeners."

Iredin waited for the perfect opportunity. After the fourteenth day of Sojourners' Way, the family bedded down. The demon lieutenant spotted his prey and grinned. He whispered into Damaro's sleeping mind: *Why does your father favor your older brothers over you? You and Mornie do the lowliest of tasks, repairing what the others break. The family doesn't respect your work.*

Damaro replied, "Not so, Baba loves us all. We all labor hard for the sake of Sojourners' Way and the Lord."

You are wiser and better than the others, but you are wrong about this, Damaro. Demon Iredin's grisly face formed a sinister grin as he imagined the discord that might arise. *Watch what happens in the coming days. Blame will fall unfairly on you and your sweet wife. This word is from the Lord.*

Damaro mumbled, "Why would the Lord sow discord between brothers?"

The demon departed.

On day fifteen, Sojourners' Way reached hilly terrain with patches of grass and shrubs growing between jutting rocks and boulders that forced a jarring, zigzagging route. For the first time, everyone tied fur-lined boots over their feet.

By day twenty, the sledges required daily repairs. Each evening, when they set up camp, Damaro and Mornie spent a long time working on the sledges and animal yokes so the equipment would be ready the next morning. The work was difficult, and they ran low on the rope and replacement logs they had cut and formed in the Garden.

One morning, Talen led a grazer over a rock that caught the edge of a sledge. The sledge rose up on the rock and then crashed to the ground.

Damaro hustled to his brother. "Talen, the left pole of your sledge has splintered badly. Soon, it'll have to be replaced. Please avoid the boulders. Stron, you're doing the same thing."

"Surely, you see there are boulders everywhere." Talen raised his arms and let them drop, not looking back at his brother. "If I could avoid the crags, I would."

"You could if you would pay more attention."

Talen looked at Stron and rolled his eyes.

Stron rubbed the back of his neck. "Damaro, we're doing the best we can. The sledges aren't sturdy enough."

"Why don't you complain to Baba?" Talen pointed toward their father. "We're just following him."

"No, see how wide this area is? We follow Baba, but we each choose our own path. Try to avoid the big rocks."

Talen said, "Like Stron said, the sledges are not sturdy enough."

Damaro shook his hands in front of his face. "How could I possibly design sledges for terrain like this? I've never seen anything like it."

Talen made eye contact with Damaro and spoke softly. "Look, we're not blaming you, and we'll help with the repairs as much as we can."

Stron spoke through clenched teeth. "Sure we will, Talen, right after you and Daylig finish tending to all the animals beaten down by this land, and after Brilara and I gather firewood and cook this evening's meal. We'll have plenty of time to help Damaro and Mornie with repairs ... I see no problem at all."

None of them cares about doing a good job.

"Fine," Damaro jerked his head from one brother to the other. "Destroy the equipment. I have nothing more to say."

You have every right to be irritated right now.

Mornie spoke in a clear, soft tone. "My brothers, we're all worn down from these last few days. We've got to work together and not bicker with each other. Maybe we should ask Baba to stop earlier, so we have more time to do chores before dark."

Stron nodded his approval. "Extra time might be good for all of us."

Talen said, "We have to remember to help each other out."

"We really have to," Daylig said. "We're too few for anything else."

Damaro grasped Mornie's hand and leaned toward her. "I guess we'll see what happens."

Brilara sighed. "I'm glad that's over. Maybe we can be happy tonight."

Sojourners' Way did stop early that day, but firewood was scarce, so Brilara and Stron spent extra time scrounging for wood. Talen and Daylig spent a long time searching for the four unstoppables. Daylig also washed the facial wounds of two grazers injured by scrapes against roots of overturned trees. Then, she applied clay to the injured areas. Damaro and Mornie labored long and hard alone on repairs until everyone lay exhausted in the four tents encircling a crackling fire. The hounds and grazers rested nearby.

Brilara looked around at her family. *Everyone is miserable, but they press on.*

You're trapped. You can't escape to the joy of home.

Talen stared at the fire. "All four unstoppables are gone."

"What happened?" Stron asked.

"Probably looking for food. No good trees around here."

Solis suggested, "Maybe they'll return."

Daylig said, "Maybe. They're loyal but have minds of their own."

"This is a beautiful barren land." Livi gazed across the rocky landscape, her face shining. "So different from the Garden."

Mornie said, "This land has a harsh allure. It hides a reward, if we endure."

"I miss home," Brilara said.

Solis said, "Bri, sing us a song of home."

Brilara moaned. "Oh, Baba. That would break all our hearts."

Livi said, "No, please sing."

The others all joined in encouraging Brilara to sing.

She stood, her brown skin and dark auburn hair glowing in the firelight. "All right then. I'll sing 'We Six.'

"Remember looking out from atop Hilltop Castle?
I do. I do.
High up, high up we climbed.
We scaled Hilltop Castle.
We six, my brothers and sisters and me.
Talen and Stron, powerful
As Chara's hills,
Daylig and Bri, resolute
As Mama's will.
Mornie and Damaro, faithful
As Baba's heart.
We gazed, we gazed,
On our garden and its glory.
Heaven Falls roars and flows,
Splashes and crashes to the river below.
Sweet Water Whirlwind twists and turns,
And waters all the garden green,
All the garden green.
The great trees in the middle,
Life and death, honored and feared.
Tall Stony in the south,
Home of golden sweet and sneaks.
Golden sweet and sneaks.
Remember looking out from atop Hilltop Castle?

I do. I do.
We six, my brothers and sisters and me.
We dreamed. We dreamed
Of our garden and its story."

Everyone applauded, and Solis said, "You've always had a lovely voice. But I recall that you six would come to your mother and me with great curiosity about the rest of Erimea."

Livi tossed a twig into the fire and watched it go up in flames. "I remember that, but we couldn't say. We didn't know. I myself once burned to explore this world, but then ..."

Damaro said, "What, Mama?"

"Children, responsibility, grandchildren, and more. More work. More love. More to learn. More to enjoy than I ever imagined, right there at home."

Stron leaned over and patted his mother's hand. "And now everything is different."

Talen said, "I've always been ready to explore. The Lord gave us all of Erimea. I relish this opportunity, though it has hardship and sorrow. I miss my children and the babies."

"We have each other." Mornie shot a fist in the air. "The mighty first family of Erimea. Bri, is there more to the song? Please sing it."

No one understands your need to be free of all this.

Brilara didn't respond at first. She reveled in the memories of the Garden, especially of singing with Stron and their children. "Very well. I've added some since Sojourners' Way departed.

"We looked past the mountains,
Toward Neverway. Toward Neverway.
We dreamt of what was beyond
Our garden and its glory.
Remember? We longed to know.
We six, my brothers and sisters and me.
Talen and Stron, powerful
As Chara's Hills.
Daylig and Bri, resolute
As Mama's will.
Mornie and Damaro, faithful

As Baba's heart.
Now we see a beautiful land,
So strange, so arduous.
Scary. Unknown. New.
We long for what we knew.
Our garden and its glory.
Familiar, easy, true.
Let us see
Joy in mystery.
Let us find
Peace in the unseen.
My brothers and sisters and me."

Daylig said, "Your music is lovely. Thank you."

Solis and Livi stood and went to their tent. "Beautiful, Bri. Goodnight, everyone."

Brilara slipped into the tent she shared with Stron, with her head bowed. Her song had encouraged everyone except herself.

The pain of this journey is too much.

As Sojourners' Way moved north, the nighttime temperature had dropped steadily, so they no longer slept out under sparkles. At night, they wrapped up under the skins and furs.

A few moments later, Stron came in and found Brilara, her head covered in fur, sitting on the makeshift bed. Her lips moved in prayer, but her words were unintelligible moans. A rumble sounded in the distance, and a cold wind blew through the camp.

Brilara looked up at Stron with bloodshot eyes amid a tear-stained face. Her gaze dropped.

Stron knelt before his wife and lifted her chin. "You were wonderful tonight. What's wrong?"

She's going to drain you and hold you back from your dreams.

"Remember when we discovered fire? I felt horrible that day."

He squished his eyebrows together. "Finding fire ... was the most exciting day of our lives."

"But Baba got burned, and I caused it." More tears fell.

"I was to blame also, not just you."

"I can't stand the thought of his agony. Is it a sin to break Baba's heart?"

"What are we—"

"I'm pregnant."

Stron jumped into a squat with his arms raised. "Great, isn't it? We can be the first to have children in the new land."

Brilara stared and shook her head. "I want to give birth at home. This land wants to kill us. We belong in the Garden with our children."

Stron sat beside her, and she buried her head in his chest. He caressed her hair. "Yes, Baba will be deeply saddened if we return. But to sin is to break God's command. We won't be doing that."

"I'm sorry to disappoint you."

"Oh, my wife, my sister. You could never disappoint me. I love you so. I'll tell Baba and Mama in the morning."

Chapter Forty-Two

A crack of thunder roused Solis from his slumber, and a light tapping sound drew him outside.

"Who is it?" He emerged from the tent he and Livi shared. He looked around. Thick, dark clouds hovered above. A fat drop of water splattered across his forehead. "What is it?" Solis held out his hands; water pelted them, and he tasted it. "Cloud water falling?"

Livi emerged from the tent. "What are you doing?"

"Set out every empty container. It's cloud water from above."

"Cloud water falling?" Livi maneuvered in the dark to the sledge where they stored clay dishes and pots in a wooden crate. The downpour increased as she removed the leaves and soft materials that protected the containers. "It's cold." She handed several large bowls to Solis.

He set the bowls on the ground near their tent. "Soon, we'll be able to refill our water bags."

"How is it falling?"

"I don't know. Remember in the Garden how low fog looked like clouds and left water on the grass and leaves?"

"I do, but it came up from the ground."

"This is the same, but from above."

Livi wrapped her arms around herself. "Let's get out of this ... this cloud water?"

"I name this a *cloudburst*."

They returned to their tent. The storm continued late into the day. Solis retrieved the water bowls, lest they be blown away. Then, he and Livi cuddled together. The storm howled, rumbled, and grew in intensity.

With each lightning flash and boom, more of the normally fearless hounds came whimpering to Talen and Daylig's tent until there were too many to fit. Daylig and Talen divided the hounds and brought three or four to each of the other three tents. The sky growled and flared like Tremble Mountain, and a torrent of water erupted.

Talen scanned the rocky hillside and heard mournful bellowing. He strained to see the grazers through the downpour and darkness. "I must check on our broad-chested charges."

Daylig smirked. "Skittish and spoiled babies. You're not going out alone."

She wants to control you. Don't let her.

They each wrapped a skin tight around themselves and went out into the storm, which blew the water like stinging pellets against their faces.

Daylig said, "What is this? Water arrows flung from a windy bow?"

Lowing and the nervous stamping of hooves led the couple. They found all the grazers huddled together near a small tree about a hundred paces from the camp. The grazers' eyes were wide open, their ears up on full alert.

"Good idea," Talen said, "but not much shelter."

The grazers pressed toward their masters and nudged for attention. Talen and Daylig called them each by name and brushed their backs. The beasts calmed down, and lightning flashed. The brief light revealed a large stony outcropping with a rocky overhang.

"Did you see that?" Daylig said.

"Yes, that'll be better." Talen grabbed Big Fig, and Daylig led Smacks to the stony shelter. The other grazers followed.

"At least this will keep them out of the wind." Talen kissed his wife. "I'll stay here. You go back to the tent."

Daylig leaned against her husband's chest. "I don't like leaving you out here alone."

At that moment, the three hounds that had been in their tent came scrambling out through the dark.

"I guess they didn't like being alone either."

"You take Zola and Chip, and I'll keep Stones with me."

Daylig returned to camp with the two hounds, and Talen slept on the ground with the grazers and Stones.

At daylight, Solis stopped by each tent to speak with his children and to distribute dried foods. He told them they wouldn't travel until the cloud water stopped. The deluge covered the hill where they camped, and mountain runoff turned the ground into a raging river threatening to sweep them back the way they came.

Solis took Talen's place with the grazers, so Talen could rest in his tent. Stron and Damaro also took a turn in the outcropping. The downpour continued all morning and soaked through their tents, drenching all the supplies of Sojourners' Way.

While Damaro tended to the grazers, he somberly observed the downpour, shook his arms, and rolled his shoulders. "If this keeps up, we may get a chance to test our watercraft."

Your family will probably wreck another piece of your handiwork.

In the early afternoon, the cloudburst receded and daylight shone. The members of Sojourners' Way questioned one another about the cloud water, for they had never seen it before.

Solis directed the family to spread out all their belongings to dry. Grain and food bags were emptied onto large flat stones so they would not rot. The blankets and tents were also laid out on the ground. Solis and Livi poured the collected water into the water bags. Stron and Brilara couldn't build a fire because water had soaked all their materials. The family rested and guarded the food to make sure wild animals stayed away.

Solis called to Stron, "Let's go scout out what's ahead."

They walked away from the camp and down a path that sloped sharply. In the distance, a deep stone canyon of multicolored rocks and mountain peaks stretched out before them.

Solis noted his son's somber mood. "What's wrong?"

Stron's going to let you down.

Stron gaped. "Did Bri say something?"

"Not with words. This morning, you both seemed troubled. Especially Brilara."

"She doesn't want to hurt you and Mama."

"Tell me." Solis grabbed Stron's arm. "What's wrong?"

Stron took a deep breath. "Baba, we want you to release us from Sojourners' Way."

"Why?" Solis pressed his lips tight into a grimace.

"She's with child, and she wants to give birth in the Garden. This land ... this journey is too much for her."

"A return trip with only two of you will be too dangerous."

Stron set his jaw. "No, we know what to avoid. Give us two hounds, a grazer, and a sledge with food and a few supplies."

"You may face something new. Things constantly change. You're going to endanger your lives and those of Sojourners' Way. We're already too few."

"Bri and I can be back in the Garden in two weeks." Stron pushed back his shoulders. "She's only a couple of months along. We don't know how long it will take us to get to this new land."

"Let me think about it and talk to your mother and pray." The bright light of day turned dim for Solis at the thought of separating from Stron and Brilara. "For now, let's see what's ahead."

"We are your children ... capable, resilient ... free."

He's shirking real life and the Lord's work.

Solis strode ahead, Stron keeping pace.

After about five thousand paces, they came to the edge of a huge canyon. To their left rose a ragged wall, a tall mountain's sheer face. Scruffy plants and jagged rocks protruded from up and down the wall's extreme height. To their right, a cliff. A sharp, stony drop-off to the canyon floor below, where the river cut a crooked route.

A flat rim of dirt and rock formed a pathway between the mountain wall and the cliff. The rim, four paces wide, wound along the mountain wall, but they couldn't see how far the rim stretched.

Solis remained speechless for several moments. "Is this a vision, heavenly splendor? This cannot be real. It's too immense for my imagination, beauty beyond Chara."

"Like from another world. I feel small right now, Baba."

Solis fought back tears. "So strange, a million times greater than Heaven Falls, see the colored layers of the rocks—green, red, and white. Are we inside a massive upside-down mountain? It shall be called Downside Canyon."

Stron pointed. "Look how deep. If we fell, we might fall forever. Fluffy white clouds float below us? And mighty featherones circling under the clouds. How can this be?"

Solis gazed down. "A long way down, blue waters meander like a ribbon over a rocky land. The sweet scent of pine is in the air." Solis raised his hands. "This rim shall be called Glory Ridge, for its glorious view. God has done this." He evaluated the terrain. "We'll have to walk this rim and see if we can take this route. If not, we'll have to climb over this mountain. Your mother will hate either."

"This soil is still wet from the downpour. May be slippery."

The two men stepped over the rocks blocking the rim and set off on their hike. The rim rose and fell along the mountain edge, dropping sharply at times. At one steep midpoint, the rim turned sharply to the left. If they had continued straight, they would have fallen. Solis called the place Devil's Bend. After two thousand paces, they reached the river level.

Solis said, "We can do this. It stays wide enough. Do you agree?"

"Barely wide enough. Keep tight control of the grazers. One false step, and over the edge they'll tumble."

The two men ate and rested by the river before attempting the trek back up the rim.

Solis and Stron returned to camp in the late afternoon. Tents were up, and the family was hard at work. Talen and Daylig loaded the sledge and bags with the dry supplies. Damaro and Mornie returned food to the storage bags using large leaves as scoops and funnels. Livi and Brilara gathered wood for a fire.

Livi took hold of Solis's arm. "We need to talk."

Solis said, "Brilara spoke to you?"

Livi nodded. "She's torn. She wants to return home, but she fears for us."

The couple walked to the river and sat under a tree. The water spiraled in front of them. In a couple thousand paces, the river would crash over a waterfall down into Downside Canyon.

Solis tilted his head and made eye contact with Livi. "Returning is a bad idea, because it'll be treacherous for them and more difficult for Sojourners' Way. I know Stron is determined to go back."

"Did the Lord command them or us?"

Everyone must remain committed, or you will all fail.

"He gave us the command to fill Erimea with our offspring, but we can't succeed alone."

Livi squeezed her husband's hand. "We survived the Garden alone, didn't we?"

"We did."

Livi shook her head, and tears flowed down her face. "Does Sojourners' Way hold our children captive against their will?"

"No, they're free to choose their way." He gazed out at the foamy water kicked up by river rocks. "So, I suppose, we should offer them all the choice to return."

Livi wrapped her arms around her husband. "I fear what they may choose."

"Let's pray." Solis clutched Livi's hand in his. "Lord, help us keep faith with you, with these children of ours, and with future generations whose well-being we hold in our hands. By your authority, we ask it."

"So be it."

The rustle of leaves and the snap of twigs caught their attention. They peered to their right along the riverbank. The Lord pushed aside a tree branch and stood before Solis and Livi, and they bowed and worshipped him.

The Lord said, "Does the Lord God give you freedom to obey or not? To follow the Lord or not?"

Solis said, "Yes, Lord, but not to obey your command is sin. What if one chooses sin?"

"Every choice holds consequences. The consequence of sin is death."

Livi said, "The consequences may be dire, but this is about preferences. Not about sin. Even the Lord gives freedom."

Solis's mouth went dry. "Still, we dread the choices the children may make."

"Never give in to fear, or you will wind up in the devil's arms." The Lord held his hands wide. "Solis and Livi, even if all forsake you, I never will. Be strong and courageous. Overcome every dread and disappointment." He departed from their sight.

Solis nodded wearily. "So be it, Lord. We will face whatever they choose."

Solis and Livi met with Stron and Brilara privately and gave them their blessing to return to the Garden. Solis called a family meeting for that night.

Glow and sparkles illuminated the camp, and a fire cracked, popped, and hissed while Sojourners' Way huddled. Solis and Livi stood together while the rest of the family formed a solemn array around their parents. Daylig, Brilara, and Mornie held hands. Talen and Damaro each rested a hand on Stron's shoulders.

Solis clasped his hands together, paced, and let his hands drop to his sides. "My darling children, in the morning, Sojourners' Way will divide. Stron and Brilara desire to return to the Garden, and though your mother and I don't believe this is the best decision, we send them with our blessing."

Livi said, "Stron and Brilara are free to make the decision they believe is best."

"Your mother and I will proceed north to the land of hidden treasure, but each of you is free to choose the way you will go. Talk among yourselves, get some rest, and let us know your decision by morning. Any questions?"

There were none.

Solis and Livi retired to their tent and listened. Most comments were hushed and inaudible to the parents.

The six siblings gathered around the fire under a clear sky. Glow hung low and illuminated their tear-stained faces.

Brilara stared into the fire. "Ten years ago, I was the one who said we couldn't let Mama and Baba make this journey alone."

You're shallow and unserious.

"Now I'm the first to want to back out."

Talen nodded. "This is true."

"Bri, we all agreed with you then, but things change." Daylig moved over and put her arms around Brilara. "If Talen and I continue, I don't know what I'm going to do without you."

"I hated the thought of leaving our family behind," Talen said, "but now the adventure bug has bitten me."

"After Happy died, I told Baba how unsafe this journey felt." Mornie looked over her shoulder at the way they'd come. "Sometimes it seems this land is angry with us, but still there is something that draws me forward."

Damaro's shoulders sagged. "I thought the six of us would be together forever."

Stron said, "We all did. No matter what, we'll be together forever in spirit."

Talen whispered, "So be it, brother."

Mornie said, "If we all go back, Baba and Mama will be alone."

"Mama and Baba can do anything," Daylig said.

Talen shook his head slowly. "No, babe, they can't. They never give up, but they need help."

"It's getting late." Brilara stood and started clapping. "We six forever. Again."

They all repeated, "We six forever."

The couples went to their separate tents to make their final decisions of whether to proceed or return to the Garden.

Chapter Forty-Three

Solis lay on the tent floor wrapped in a blanket. He stared at the ceiling, and the ground grated against him. "What if they all return? Mornie told me she feels unsafe in this land and misses home. I'm not sure about Daylig."

Livi sat with her head in her hands. "I don't know. I miss Bri and Stron already. If they all go—I don't know. Talen is an adventurer, but if Daylig is unhappy ..." A cold wind sliced through the tent.

"We're already short-handed ... but the Lord promised to be with us."

"I want ... more than the Lord." Livi again buried her face in her hands. "That sounds awful, but I do."

"I know, but with the Lord, we can stand any loss."

With a face devoid of emotion, she asked, "Can we?"

"This will be a long night."

One of the hounds howled outside their tent.

After an uncomfortable night of shifting and turning, Solis and Livi woke and learned only Stron and Brilara were leaving Sojourners' Way.

Solis and Livi embraced and prayed. "Thank you, Lord, for your mercy. Help us trust you more."

The family said their goodbyes. Solis gave Stron his walking stick, a grazer pulling a sledge of food and supplies, and two hounds.

He lifted his head and made eye contact with Stron and Brilara. "God's grace be with you. When you reach the Garden, take charge of Caressa and Smallo. Raise them as your own children."

Brilara said, "We will, Baba."

Stron nodded. "We will. We'll teach our people all you have taught us. Baba, we know you are the son of God. We'll follow your ways."

"And Mama, you're truly God's daughter. My inspiration and example."

Livi hugged and kissed her son and daughter. "Be careful along the way back."

Sojourners' Way then consisted of six people, nine hounds, and fifteen grazers—nine pulling sledges, three loaded with food, and three with no load. Solis decided someone would have to guide each grazer across Glory Ridge to ensure the beasts didn't tumble over the cliff. This meant the humans would have to make three round trips.

Talen and Daylig checked the animals. The clay they'd placed on the facial wounds of the two injured grazers, Big Fig and Smacks, had been washed away. The wounds oozed a little, and Talen wiped away the flow with leaves, then discarded the soiled leaves. He said, "These two should be fine." Daylig and Talen greeted and brushed each of the grazers to help them be calm and content for yoking and the day's work.

Damaro questioned Solis. "How rugged is the rim, and are there any sharp turns?"

Solis said, "The surface is like what we've seen recently. But Devil's Bend is a very sharp turn."

"The sledges can't make sharp turns. They'll hang on the corners and tip up or break apart." Damaro rubbed his forehead. "I'll have to stand at the corner and push the sledges."

Solis said, "All right, son." He turned to Livi. "Come darling, let's go on ahead." Solis and Livi departed toward the canyon while the rest of the family made final preparations. "We'll wait for you at the start of Glory Ridge."

Glory Ridge was five thousand paces from the camp. When Solis and Livi came close to the canyon, a strong, cold blast of air greeted them, yet beads of sweat broke out on Livi's forehead. Her whole body trembled. "I can't do this. I'm dizzy. I'll fall." She crouched and backed away, falling to her knees. "I'm going to be sick." She vomited.

She's weak. Rebuke her. Curse her. She'll put fear into the others.

Solis knelt before his wife and held her arms. "You can do it. I'll be with you every step of the way. Please get up." He helped Livi to her feet. "Breathe, my darling, breathe."

She leaned against her husband's chest. "My legs are shaking ... I'm unworthy. A voice in my head says, 'You're weak and worthless.' Let me die here ... Iam, help me."

"Reject such thoughts." *Lord, help my wife.* "You will not die. You're courageous. You're Livi, my strength." Solis held Livi close, and her heart beat wildly. "When the time comes, you will place your hand on my shoulder and keep your eyes toward the mountain wall. Don't look down into the canyon. You will not have to guide any grazer. You won't be near the edge. All right?"

Livi took a deep breath and nodded. "I'll try ... Iam, help me."

Livi watched as moments later, Talen led Sojourners' Way to the trailhead of Glory Ridge. Damaro and Talen cleared rocks that blocked the rim. Daylight shone, and a chilly wind met them head-on.

Solis sighed and held the collar of Big Fig, who was yoked to the sledge with the twelve precious tree of life saplings. He positioned his grazer on the right, near the center of the path, with the mountain wall on his left.

When they commenced, Solis yelled, "Slow and steady. We'll be fine."

One pace remained between the sledge and the cliff on the right. Livi followed with her hand clenched on Solis's shoulder and her eyes focused on thc mountain wall to the left.

Livi's legs ached with tension. She wanted to whimper with each step, but she forced herself to be silent.

Damaro followed behind Solis and Livi, carrying an oar from the dugouts. He planned to use the oar as a lever to push the sledges around Devil's Bend. How well would his plan to force the sledges around the bend work? Since Damaro and Livi had no grazers, the others would have to make four round trips to get them all across Glory Ridge.

The hounds managed themselves quietly, frequently peering over the edge of the cliff into the canyon's depths.

Talen followed Damaro with a grazer and a sledge filled with the healing leaves. He said, "Nice, cool day. Incredible view."

Daylig said, "I'm too scared to enjoy the view."

"I have to force myself to breathe," Mornie said. "Stay calm and keep our grazers calm."

The trip along Glory Ridge was uneventful until they neared Devil's Bend. A grapecker with a blood-red beak and black wings landed on the stony ground in front of Solis. The featherone's red eyes focused on Big Fig's face.

Solis pointed at the grazer's eye. "You want the ooze from the sore?" He waved his free arm. "Get out of the way."

The grapecker squeaked *tsik ... tsik ... tsik*, as if announcing a warning or excitement over the bloody discharge.

Solis ignored the little beast and kept moving straight ahead while the creature flew in circles nearby. He guided Big Fig to the right, as near to the cliff edge as he could. Then, he pulled the grazer to the left, saying, "Haw, haw."

Damaro positioned the oar between the corner of the mountain and the left post of the sledge and pushed the sledge as Solis continued to lead the grazer around the corner. Damaro groaned instructions. "Slow, slow. It's clearing ... pull forward ... yes, yes, it's clear." He exulted.

Solis, Livi, and Big Fig headed along a downward sweeping curve, but the grapecker returned and dug its talons into Big Fig's head, pecking at the sore near his left eye. Big Fig raised his massive head and swung right and then left, slamming Solis into the mountain wall.

Solis went down, and Livi fell on top of Solis.

With a snort and a kick, Big Fig rumbled along the rim, leaving Livi and Solis on the ground.

Livi hollered. "Big Fig, whoa, whoa." But the beast kept going, with the saplings swaying in the wind. She imagined the grazer diving headlong into the canyon, followed by the trees of life. She looked down at Solis, her unconscious hero, and pounded the rocks with her fist. "Fly bites, fly bites."

She turned back and saw her two sons struggling to get the next sledge around the corner. Livi stood and stared into the canyon. Dizziness pushed her back down, and her mouth went dry, but she forced herself up and trotted after Big Fig.

She yelled. "Whoa, Big Fig, whoa." She picked up speed and sprinted along Glory Ridge with all her might. Big Fig kept crashing into the mountain wall, so Livi had to run along the cliff's edge until she caught the beast and found the featherone still clinging to the grazer's face.

Livi grabbed the tiny beast and screamed, "Die, demon wings. Bully, die." She crushed the life from Big Fig's tormentor with her right hand and pulled Big Fig to a stop with her left. Livi flung the featherone's dead body against the mountain wall.

"Whoa, big boy. Everything's okay." Livi brushed Big Fig's back to calm him down and wrapped her arms around his neck. "It's okay, boy."

Livi froze when she stumbled over a loose pebble, and the stone flew over the edge and disappeared. She moved left and sank with her back against the mountain wall. Her chest heaved, and her fingers trembled against her head. "I can't believe ... how ... what happened?"

Damaro tended to Solis with the leaves, and Talen came up to Livi. "Mama, you were amazing. Are you all right?"

"No, give me a few moments ... I'm still shaking."

As Livi sat gathering herself, Solis regained consciousness. "What happened?"

"Mama saved the day." Talen pointed at the beast and the sledge. "She caught Big Fig before he fell and took the trees over the cliff."

Solis sat by Livi and took her hand. "My darling has overcome." He smacked himself and shook his head. "Putting all the saplings in the same sledge is the stupidest thing I've ever done."

Talen said, "A mistake, Baba. Just a mistake."

Solis turned toward Livi. "We're only halfway across the rim. Are you ready?"

Livi stood and stared out at Downside Canyon. For the first time, she appreciated its beauty. She took a deep breath and looked down into the rocky, dangerous deep. "Yes, let's be going."

Solis also stood and took hold of Big Fig's collar. "Take hold of my shoulder."

"I can walk on my own. I'm no longer dizzy."

Sojourners' Way continued to the river level. Livi followed Solis and Big Fig, but she walked alone. All except Livi made three more round trips across Glory Ridge and brought down all the grazers and their supplies. She hunted with her bow and the hounds.

Vegetation, soft soil, and animal life abounded at the river level, a stark contrast with the sparse, stony ground of the last several days. Solis named the land Bountiful. That evening, the family gathered by the river, in complete exhaustion. Livi had a fire blazing with three fat featherones and a rooter roasting on spits. The sweet aroma encouraged their spirits, so they feasted and rested.

Sojourners' Way lazed around Bountiful for two nights. While there, Solis separated the saplings. He loaded the extra three grazers with two saplings each, so the sledge contained only six of the little trees of life. The journey became much easier. After five more weeks, the family reached their destination.

Chapter Forty-Four

New Paradise Valley, Year 100, Mult, Day 1

The family camped near the bank of the river. Solis said, "This place reminds me of Chara, our beloved garden." So, he named the place New Paradise Valley. Green mountains stood to the north and east. Sojourners' Way camped in the woods on the western bank of the Rapid River. To the west of the woods, grasslands full of flowers and shrubs stretched for a great distance. The area smelled of sweet plant growth: black-eyed yellows, coneflowers, and brightly colored poppies with crumpled petals.

That evening, the family gathered around a fire. The Lord appeared to them. "Well done. You've reached the land of hidden treasure. New Paradise Valley is yours. Rule it well. Be fruitful and multiply. Subdue this land as you did the Garden of Chara." Then, he departed.

The family celebrated the approval of the Lord. Solis picked a place to set the tree of life saplings on the riverbank, where Rapid River bent to the west. The water swirled and busted over rocks.

Talen helped Solis unload the trees and looked around. "How do you know this is the best spot for planting? Won't this massive old tree block the light from these little things?"

Solis scanned the area. "Set them here. Tomorrow, we'll find places most like Chara to plant these little trees. It's too late tonight."

Another downpour occurred that night, and Solis dreamed he was back in the Garden. Stron, Brilara, Caressa, and Smallo carried him in their arms all over the Garden. Somehow, they all floated above the ground. Everything was well.

He said, "I am the caretaker of all things. Soon, I'll return. Until then, carry on, my darling children."

In the dream, Solis walked alone along the riverbank from which he was taken, and he sat on the spot of his creation. "This is like New Paradise Valley in the north." He closed his eyes and stretched out there until cool water crept under his head. A gale blasted his face, and the wind howled. He looked up and saw a great red dragon sitting in Sweet Water Whirlwind, blowing water furiously upon the riverbank.

The dragon grinned, revealing bloody teeth. "You're no caretaker. You fool, this is a floodplain."

With daylight breaking above the horizon, Solis woke to the sounds of rushing water. He sprang up to see a torrent flowing two paces from the tent he and Livi shared. The other tents were farther back, away from the water.

Solis gaped at the water and splashed into the flow. "Where did this come from? What is a floodplain?"

Talen rushed away from his tasks in the forest with the grazers and hounds back to the camp. "Baba, what is it?"

Solis exclaimed. "The trees." He sprinted to the riverbank where they'd left the trees.

Talen followed. The two men splashed through the swift-flowing water where dry ground had been the day before.

Solis stopped when the water was up to his chest. "This is the spot, isn't it? Where are the saplings?"

Talen moaned. "This is the spot. See the great tree standing there? Only now the water is way up the trunk." He pointed downstream, toward the middle of the river. "Look, Baba." Two of the tree of life saplings bobbed in the water. None of the others were visible.

Solis dashed further into the river, hyperventilating. "No, no, no." He returned to shore, the veins in his neck about to burst. "Tell your mother I'm going after them. I will save them." He ran to the watercraft storage. He grabbed a dugout and an oar and dragged them into the river.

Talen raced back to the camp and woke everyone.

Solis paddled furiously, but the raging current swept him around a river bend and over a small waterfall. He lost sight of the trees, and his dugout spun around boulders. He almost lost control of himself when he focused on the surging water. His mind transported him into the past to when he had fought another raging watery monster, Sweet Water Whirlwind. Its one desire: consume Solis. It seemed his insides would erupt, but he gripped the dugout with all his might. He had to save the saplings.

Down the Rapid River.

Everyone crawled out of their tents and dragged their belongings back from the water. Talen explained what had happened.

Damaro shook his head and ran to the other dugout. "Come on. Baba doesn't know how to control these things." Talen and Damaro launched the dugout and went after their father.

The water, though swift, became less rough. Bright burning daylight cast deceptive shadows and made it hard to see the myriad ins and outs of the shoreline and its overgrown vegetation. For the rest of the morning and into the afternoon, Solis floated downstream and scanned the shore on both sides. More than once, he thought he spied a sapling washed up on shore, and he paddled like mad to reach it. Each time, he found a broken branch or a shrub, but no sapling.

He sobbed. "Iam, please help."

When Solis had no more strength for paddling, he dragged the dugout onto a rocky shore at the foot of a mountain.

Mighty Solis has failed.

All your planning is for nothing.

You are incompetent, useless as a big pile of dirt.

Solis climbed the mountain until he found a wide opening, crawled into a cave, and fell into a deep sleep.

Damaro and Talen found Solis's dugout. They called out for their father but could not find him.

Damaro said, "He might have fallen out."

"Don't say that." Talen's nostrils flared.

"We need to return to camp before dark."

"Let's paddle a little farther." The brothers proceeded down the river. Soon, they stopped, and Talen said, "Let's pray."

"Lead us, brother."

"Oh, Lord, please protect Baba. Return him to us. We ask in your great name. May it be so."

"So be it." Damaro wiped his eyes with his forearm. "We need him more than the trees."

"I hope he realizes that."

The brothers pulled their dugout from the water and carried it back to camp on foot.

You don't need him. He acts so superior; remember how he ranted about the lost seeds?

Damaro pressed his palms to his forehead. *Why do I think such wicked thoughts?*

Solis slept all night in the cave. In the morning, he woke with fury in his heart. "I hate cave darkness. Stinking, dank hole. At least it's not tight." He crawled to the cave opening and sucked fresh air bitterly. "I hate daylight. The trees of life ... the future is lost." Solis crawled back into the cave and wept. "Forgive me, Lord. Please take my life." He buried his head in his arms.

The Lord spoke, "Solis, what are you doing in this cave?"

"The trees of life are lost. I've failed you and your people." His head ached. "All is lost. When we die, this land will be a haunt for demons and dismal vermin."

"All is not lost. You have seeds."

He groaned uncontrollably. "Starting from seeds is too hard. Our supply of leaves will run out before we can harvest new leaves. We, your glory, will be gone."

"Will you die without the leaves?"

"Yes, we will die. In one hundred years, my entire life, I've never gone a day without a bite from the healing leaves."

"Is the Lord still with you?"

Solis shrugged. "I don't know."

The Lord commanded, "Solis, open your eyes and answer. Is the Lord still with you?"

He opened his eyes and saw the Lord standing before him. Solis knelt and paid homage to the Lord. "Yes, Lord, you are with me."

"Come out of this cave."

Solis crawled out of the cave and squinted in the bright light. "What am I to do?"

"Eat and drink." A bowl of golden sweet, meat, berries, and water appeared. Solis ate and regained his strength.

The Lord also ate.

Solis smiled. "Eating with the Lord is delightful. But what am I to do?"

"Lead Sojourners' Way. Settle this land. Prepare for the winter cold. It will arrive soon. Populate all four corners of Erimea. Return to the Garden."

"But what about the trees of life?"

"No tree is your source of life. I am your life. You shall live by every word that proceeds from my mouth. Live by faith in me. Do you understand?"

"Yes, Lord." Solis hung his head. "Oh, the grinding ... the grinding. I'm afraid of dying so soon. Death crushes to dirt. Erimea consumes."

"I am with you always. Fear not. Now, return to camp. Your family is worried about you." The Lord disappeared.

Solis climbed out of the cave and walked toward the camp. Livi and their children had been searching for him. As soon as they saw Solis, they dashed to him over a rugged path. Talen and Damaro reached their father first. They hugged and kissed him, and the rest of the family did the same.

Livi said, "My dearest, are you all right?"

"I'm fine." Solis wiped his wet eyes. "But the saplings are lost."

Daylig dropped to her knees. "Oh, Iam, thank you for protecting our baba."

Chapter Forty-Five

Damaro and Talen took a raft downstream twice in hopes that some of the trees had washed up along the riverbank, but they found none. The brothers did find some green rocks, which Damaro wanted to examine, so they loaded them onto the raft.

Damaro pounded the green rocks with other stones. The green rocks were different. "These chunks of material are not ordinary rocks. They don't fracture when I beat them. They yield when force is applied."

Mornie said, "Let me see." She propped a flattened piece of the material against the base of a tree and pressed it in the middle with a wooden spear. "It bends easily. We can form it."

"A thin rock would have shattered. After it's heated, it becomes easier to shape."

"What do you call it?"

"Hmm ... I don't know." Damaro held up the pieces he had been pounding on. "It's hard like rock or stones, but it's malleable like clay. Tougher than clay ... gets shiny and turns orange when polished. Rocks are a mixture of stuff I call ores. This is purer."

Mornie said, "How about pure form ore?"

"I like it. Pure form ore."

"Really? This weird voice in my head said you would hate my idea."

"No way. You're the smartest person I know."

Mornie stared at her husband. "I've had the most critical thoughts since we left the Garden. Beliefs that seem like my own, but always lead me to misery."

"I know that feeling." Damaro took her hands. "Let's remember to reject those thoughts."

Mornie and Damaro developed many tools with the pure form ore and replaced most stone cutter blades with the new material.

Livi used the pure form ore for arrow tips, and even Solis made two large spears tipped with the new material. He still struggled with killing animals, but he committed himself to spear hunting.

The family turned their energy to preparing for the winter cold, though they had no idea how low temperatures would fall. Mornie and Damaro disassembled the sledges and used the wood to construct three small huts with a mud and clay layer to fill gaps between the wood pieces. Sloped roofs of dried woven grasses protected the hut interiors from downpours. A bamboo frame supported bundles of dried grass, which they strapped to the frame. They arranged the huts around a fire pit and hung sheets of the pure form ore over the front of the thatched roofs to minimize fire risk.

Mornie shook her head over the little huts and the heat source. "Most of the heat from the fire is going straight up. We need to capture it."

"How?"

"We've got to think of something. Adults may be able to stand the cold." She patted her belly. "But this time next year, we'll have at least three babies to think about."

Damaro smiled and pulled his wife close. "Three babies in there?"

"You're being silly." Mornie pushed Damaro away. "Me, Mama, and Daylig."

"You three are so fruitful we will soon need bigger places."

"And places that don't lose so much heat."

"I know. That is a serious problem. With no solution yet."

"Yet. All problems have solutions."

You're too insignificant to figure it out.

Livi worked with Solis in everything he did, and after a month of moping, Solis began searching the landscape for fruits and vegetables as well as places to plant the tree of life seeds. She was glad to see Solis was coming out of his shell, but he said little.

Late one afternoon, the couple stood on a small plot of ground cleared for planting. Fruit trees surrounded them, swaying in a brisk autumn wind. Livi threw down a pole she used to poke holes in the ground for seeds. "Have you forgotten you have a wife?"

"What're you talking about? We have work to do."

"I know we have work to do, and I've been doing it alone for the last month while you've been brooding. I let you mourn and sulk for weeks. Now tell me what happened that day and night you were missing?"

"I lost the trees. I don't want to talk about it."

"I know the trees are lost. But why didn't you come home?" Livi grabbed Solis's shoulders and turned him to look in her eyes. "In my hundred years of life, we've not once been apart overnight. I cried all night for you."

How could he forget about you, his helper, so quickly?

"I'm sorry." Solis tried to hug his wife, but she turned away.

"Talen said they found the dugout, but no Baba. My beloved husband was missing. Maybe drowned in the river. Maybe injured, with his life blood draining away. What happened?"

"I tried to correct my mistake, but I couldn't. I struggled in the river until I had no more strength. The river curved around a mountain, so I pulled the dugout to shore and crawled into a mountain cave. I wanted to die because I ... I'm a failure." He sighed.

"You are not a failure. We don't let each other fail. I am your helper. Let me help you." Livi wiped away tears and wrapped her arms around herself. "How could you want to die ... leave me alone with no husband?"

"I never want to leave you, but I was so despairing. I was thinking wrong. The Lord showed me that, but—"

"What did the Lord say?"

Solis held up one of the tree of life seeds. "We're not to trust in this tree for our lives."

Livi's eyes widened. "What? It keeps us alive daily."

"He said, 'You shall live by every word that proceeds from my mouth. Live by faith in me.'"

Livi nodded. "Obey the Lord."

"And complete this mission. He is still with us."

"If we die first?"

Solis said, "Long ago the Lord said, if I fail—"

"Erimea becomes like Earth."

"Where death reigns."

"May it never be."

An icy gale blew in from the river and raised bumps on Solis's arms as he held out a hand to Livi. "Time for a meal. Let's pray we survive our first winter in New Paradise Valley."

That night, the couple looked west as daylight hid below the mountains. Solis said, "My darling, describe for me the sky's colors and all its shades."

"I will, my dearest husband. May we always be together each night to share this pleasure as one."

"So be it."

Mornie and Damaro led the family through weeks of brainstorming about what their preferred dwelling would be, with efficient heating as a vital requirement. The family agreed on a raised-floor home Damaro called the warm stone design. Damaro and Mornie explained the construction process.

"First," Damaro began, "we'll build a brick fire pit, which will be below the floor and outside the living space. Everything will depend on bricks."

Solis said, "What are bricks?"

"Fire-hardened clay soil," Mornie said. "We'll need hundreds or thousands of bricks of three different sizes. We'll need to clear flat land, cover the site with a layer of small stones, and build the fire pit. Then, we'll stack foundation bricks in a series of rows. The stacks will be higher than the top of the fire pit."

Livi frowned. "Smoke will come through the bricks and kill us."

Damaro said, "Not if we do it right. We'll make mortar, a mud mixture, to go between the bricks. Especially the ones that form the floor slab. Smoke will flow through channels under the floor and out the other side of the house. The mortar will prevent smoke from entering the house."

Mornie said, "The hot smoke will heat the floor, which will warm the house. We'll build brick walls and a thatched roof. The bricks should hold heat for a long time."

Damaro said, "A small fire should heat the house all night in the winter, if the floor slab holds heat like we expect."

Solis said, "It's too late for this winter?"

Mama and Baba don't trust your ideas.

Mornie said, "Yes, we need to start next spring making bricks and building."

The temperature dropped steadily day by day. One morning, Solis and Livi surveyed the area around their camp searching for fresh fruit. Most trees stood bare, undressed by the cold.

Solis grabbed a branch of a bush that had once held berries. "Look at how the leaves have withered; many have fallen. Why?"

"It's stripped of its fruit." Livi had a faraway look in her eyes. "That never happened in the Garden. A few weeks ago, featherones swarmed these plants."

"And gobbled up the last of the berries." Solis crossed his arms. "I should have been paying more attention and harvested the fruit earlier."

Livi said, "Not once did it get this cold in the Garden. Even the featherones and other beasts have fled or gone into hiding. Talen and I hunted all day yesterday and spotted only one wild breath, and it got away."

"The creatures know something about winter, and we're just learning."

New Paradise Valley, Year 100, Atta, Day 28

The family was thankful for their large supply of dried food. Wrapping up in skins, furs, and boots became routine. They stored food in their huts and kept a roaring fire going all day and night for warmth and to scare away hungry animals.

The family remained bundled in their huts most of the time. They suffered extreme cold for weeks. One bright and shining morning, Solis and Livi snuggled alone in the camp until the sounds of human shouting and hounds barking pricked their ears.

Solis jumped up. "Sounds like danger." He grabbed two long spears and ran toward the commotion.

Livi picked up her bow and arrows with the deadly sharp, pure form ore edges and followed. "What's happening?"

Solis and Livi ran toward the river, frigid air stinging their cheeks. They stopped at the river's edge, viewing something they'd never seen before. Their children playfully slid and slipped on top of the water.

"Mama," Daylig shouted, "the river has hardened. Cold, hard water. Ice."

Talen swung Daylig. When he released her, she twirled around, laughing and struggling to stay on her feet.

Livi called back, "Is it safe?"

Mornie rubbed a mitten-covered hand on the frozen water and peered through it. "It's thick and rough."

"Sturdy as a stone bridge," Talen said.

Daylight glistened off the river ice. Ice also hung like glittering daggers from the trees on both sides of the river. Solis and Livi scanned the area, trying to make sense of the scene, until Solis spotted upstream, to his right, a huge black-and-gray furry creature along with a smaller one like it. Both pawed through the ice at the river's edge.

Damaro and Mornie skated near the river's center in front of the creatures.

The beast crushed an always turning in its jaws and growled at them.

Solis warned, "Don't run. Back away slowly."

None of the siblings heard their father.

Mornie said, "Run."

They all fled downstream over the ice.

The growler stood and snarled, revealing claws and long sharp teeth. Twice as tall as a man and the bulk of six men. The growler dropped to all fours and lumbered in pursuit of Mornie and Damaro, who struggled for traction on the ice.

Screams came from all four siblings, and the hounds barked and harassed the beast. It swiped at the hounds but continued downstream.

Talen stopped and placed himself between the beast and his siblings. He faced the animal, raising a small cutter in his hand.

Livi screamed, "Stop, you monster." She raised her bow and let fly an arrow as the growler crossed in front of her.

The arrow struck the beast in the left shoulder. It howled and sprawled on the ice.

Solis ran along the riverbank. "Back, back, mama growler. Don't make me slay you."

But the beast rose and continued toward Talen. Then, it stopped and eyed Talen. The growler pawed the ice and looked back at its baby. Without warning, the beast charged Talen.

Talen raised his small cutter and crouched in a battle stance.

Solis heaved one of his spears. It stuck in the growler's side behind its left shoulder.

Livi also struck with a second arrow in a hind leg.

The beast went down again, but this time, it attempted to flee the way it had come.

Solis pursued the growler on the ice. With a guttural roar, he hurled his second spear, and the beast fell dead.

He ran to Talen and embraced him. "Son, what were you thinking?"

Talen held up his cutter. "Cut off its nose or die." He met his father's gaze. "Baba, I must protect the creatives. Damaro, Mornie, and Daylig all make new things to better this world. I'm an explorer. Expendable, like a speck in the wind."

"No, my darling son. You are the leader, the heartbeat among us."

Solis's sons skinned the growler and hung the fur to be prepared as a garment for their father.

That evening, Solis and Livi sat alone in their hut. A fire roared outside, and a cold wind rattled through their dwelling.

Livi said, "You know we had to strike the beast. It was a danger to us."

"Yes, but I'm sorry it didn't stop before my first spearing."

"You had to stop it to save Talen."

His supposed courageousness is a cover for cowardice.

Solis shook his head. "Talen feels he must protect the others ... I wonder if I should have let the growler flee."

"It would have died anyway. The first spear surely punctured both lungs."

"Probably true. But my anger scares me. It's a raging in my heart, a merciless dragon desiring freedom to destroy."

"My dearest husband, nothing can be allowed to stop this family. For our sake and for the Lord's."

"So be it. For the Lord."

Chapter Forty-Six

New Paradise Valley, Year 101

During their first spring in New Paradise Valley, the three women gave birth to five babies. Livi bore one. Daylig and Mornie each brought forth twins.

Through the spring and summer, the family cared for the newborns and made bricks for the warm stone home design. By the time autumn arrived, they had built three warm stone homes with thatched roofs. The dwellings provided greater warmth in winter while burning much less wood.

Not until the third spring did the tree of life seeds produce any saplings. By the tenth year, only one sapling survived. The young tree was still at least two years from producing fruit and being able to provide a steady supply of leaves.

Solis and Livi, their three young children born in New Paradise Valley, their first children, and twelve grandchildren stood outside their homes and consumed the last of their original supply of the tree of life leaves. Despite Solis's attempt to mask his concern, his face held a somber expression. "My darling family, the Lord has provided a sweet life for us here in New Paradise Valley. Let us all enjoy each moment and always walk with him. Now, you young ones may go play."

The children scattered, giggling as they played together.

The adults huddled around their parents, and Talen said, "Baba, what are you fearing?"

"The grinding ... grinding of our bodies to dust. I don't know how long we can survive without the healing leaves. They almost magically sustain us and cure every hurt and—"

"The magic's gone," Damaro finished.

Daylig said, "But the Lord isn't. Our mission isn't complete, so he will sustain us now."

Each day for the next week, Solis and Livi wondered if it would be their last, but Daylig was right—the Lord sustained the family, although they began to age.

For two years, time wore on their bodies, but they didn't notice the difference. During the twelfth year in their new land, they again enjoyed the fruit of the tree of life, taking bites from its leaves daily.

The society of New Paradise Valley grew, and the people discovered new types of pure form ores. They named them bronze and iron to distinguish them from the original ore they called copper. The forging of pure form ores led to stronger and tougher materials and great advances in cutters and tools for construction and hunting.

Livi had a small sword and a knife made of iron. "With these, I can clear a field or cut up wild prey, or perhaps battle a growler." She named the sword Hearty and the knife Piercer.

Minerals and jewels were found in the land, and people found methods for enhancing food production.

Solis and Livi led their family north to the land of hidden treasure in the year 100. Solis remembered the Lord's instructions to reconstitute Sojourners' Way in the year 150 and journey west to the land by the sea. In the year 148, Solis appointed Talen to lead an expedition to explore the way west and return with a report. After ten months, the expedition returned, and Talen reported to a gathering of adults. The population of New Paradise Valley had grown to forty-eight men, women, and children.

Talen said, "The journey will require four months because of the distance, but someone has prepared and marked the way for us."

Solis said, "It could be demon tricks to lure us into dangers like Hot Killer Springs."

"We encountered many dangers along the way and many forks in the road, which we explored carefully. Some traps led to injuries, but thankfully we all survived. But not without help."

Livi said, "What kind of help?

"We found four trees of life growing along the way."

Solis said, "How could that be?"

Talen shrugged. "At numerous points, there were two or more ways to go. Many times, we explored all the options. Time after time, we found a mark that turned out to be the best and safest route through every danger."

Livi said, "What mark?"

Talen spoke to Damaro. "Help me with this, brother." The two brothers held up a piece of a large branch about two paces long. "We found marks like this carved into trees or drawn on boulders all along the route."

Livi gasped at the familiar marking.

Talen said, "Yes, Mama, it's like your scar."

Living in the north land required wearing garments for comfort and protection, so most people had never seen the scars the first parents bore.

Solis said, "It must be the Lord."

"I don't know. We saw no other evidence of a person, but we certainly have a friend who has gone before us. Maybe long before."

"Remember," Livi said, "long ago the Lord told us the image would help our children choose the correct path."

Chapter Forty-Seven

Mid Seacoast, Year 150, Helpe, Day 10

Solis and Livi led a new Sojourners' Way west to the land by the sea. Talen and Daylig joined, but Damaro and Mornie stayed behind. The married inventors loved New Paradise Valley and made it their permanent home.

The reconstituted Sojourners' Way of six married couples arrived at the white sandy beaches of a great blue sea. The land by the sea consisted of grassy coastal plains bounded by the sea on the west, with rolling hills and multi-colored mountains of gray, white, brown, and green to the east.

The land was full of evergreen trees that stretched straight up sixty or seventy paces, with tops among the clouds. Cypress trees, berry vines, and an assortment of plants also grew there, along with a tree of life. The plentiful animal life included unstoppables, steppers, and wind striders. Taming and riding wind striders became common practice.

Talen loved the new land, and the massive sea fascinated him. Early one morning, he and Daylig watched the sea from a high hill. The whitecaps and waves breaking against the shore captivated them. Suddenly, the sea foamed, and the waves became like churning river currents. Then the water shrank away, and the white sand beach expanded, stretching and revealing debris previously underwater. A few moments later, a speeding wave two paces in height came back, and water went farther up the beach before retreating. The receding wave swept away the debris.

When a monstrous second wave returned, Talen said, "Look at this. It's towering ten paces in the air and roaring." The wave violently pushed water all the way up to where Talen and Daylig stood before rushing away again. After less than a quarter day, the sea calmed, and the waves returned to normal.

"The sea is amazing and beautiful," Talen said. "Tremendous power is there. I long to sail it and feel its might beneath me."

Solis called the region Mid Seacoast, and the people built wooden homes and populated the land. Talen made his living catching always turnings and other sea creatures. Livi gave birth to four children at Mid Seacoast. Daylig bore six babies, and the other four women of Sojourners' Way gave birth to many children. The population swelled, and from that time siblings no longer married each other. Instead, they married their cousins.

Aalto, a son of Solis and Livi, born in Mid Seacoast, married his cousin, Merike. Talen and Daylig trained Aalto and Merike to care for animals. Talen ran his hand along a grazer's side to its flank. "Feel right here." Talen guided Aalto's hand to just before the animal's hip. "In a healthy animal, this area should be full and rounded; if it's sunken, you probably have an underfed beast." Merike also felt the flank.

Daylig said, "You need to spend time observing the animals' normal behavior and take action when there's a change in behavior or appetite." Daylig went to another grazer and pointed to its front leg. "This animal began moving differently, and we noticed this joint was swollen. So we rubbed the joint with a liniment." Daylig explained how to make the liniment.

Merike rubbed the grazer behind its ears. "What other changes should we be concerned about?"

Talen examined the grazer's face. "Discharge from the eyes or nose; sometimes they get a fever, and we wash them with water and rub them. We wish we had more medicines, but we'll show you the plants we use to treat sick animals."

Mid Seacoast, Year 195

One evening as daylight colored the clouds, Livi sat in her home, watching the Great Blue Sea with her hands folded in her lap. The home of Solis and Livi sat on massive pillars that rose high above the beach, where warm breaths of wind from the temperate climate blew in from the water.

Solis also gazed at the waves crashing on the beach as great-great-grandchildren scampered around the room.

Livi said, "This has been our home for almost forty-five years. The most luxurious we've ever had."

Solis said, "Yes, soft-cushioned seating, paneled walls. Lovely artwork. Plentiful food at hand."

"A home full of life and laughter ... but in a few years, we will leave it all behind and start over again. I'm tired of moving."

"That's our mission."

"Talen and Daylig say they're going to stay here ... I want to keep the gifts I've been given."

"Then we'd miss what's next. We live by faith."

"What's happening in New Paradise Valley and Chara? My children, my home, every treasure is stripped from me." Her words cut with a hard edge. "I'm going for a walk."

Livi marched down to the beach and kicked the sand every few paces. Daylight disappeared, and glow and sparkles illuminated her way. The whoosh of the waves and the warm, salty sea air comforted Livi. She looked back at their home and saw lanterns hanging across the balcony. "Lovely, like the terrace at Hilltop Castle."

She sat in the sand and gazed at the water, black and glistening. "Wine-dark sea, that's what Talen calls you. Can you give wisdom and understanding? Talen, my sailing son, says you hold power and mysteries for us to unlock." The sea breeze picked up force, and mist stung her face. "Is it true? Do you have something to say?"

A voice screeched on the wind, "Sea secrets can be yours ... if you fall down and worship me."

"What was that?" Livi's muscles tightened, and she prepared to flee. "Evils shall not beguile me again." She forced herself to relax. "Leave me. I'm not afraid."

With her arms shaking, Livi scooped sand in her hands and let it flow through her fingers. She did this several times, and then she prayed. "Iam, help me. What good is it to have all these things when I cannot keep them? Soon, someone else will enjoy all this. I don't mean to be ungrateful, but what is the point?" She leaned back, rested on her elbows, and studied the blanket of bright, sparkling lights in the dark sky.

The Lord appeared on the beach in front of Livi. "Greetings, daughter." He strolled toward her.

Livi jumped up and fell on her face, breathless, and worshipped the Lord. "Greetings, my dear Fatherest, Lord God."

The Lord lifted Livi and hugged her. "Sit here with me." They sat on the beach, and he wrapped an arm around her shoulders. "I heard your prayer."

Livi leaned against the Lord and felt the warmth of his body. "I remember when you first carried me into the Garden." She basked in her memories of the early days with the Lord. "Lord, you have given me everything I could desire, but—"

"Do you love the blessings more than you love me?"

"No, Lord, no. But I ... please forgive me. Help me always to put you first and to be grateful." Livi closed her eyes and covered her face with her hands as tears leaked out. "I have always been ... so unworthy of this way. Forgive me."

"Teach all your children, this great people, so they know my ways. Daughter, do you love me?"

"Yes, Lord."

"When the time comes, lead these people with your husband to the field of charms. Livi, do you love me more than every gift you've received from my hand?"

"Yes, Lord. You know all things. You know that I do."

"Yes, daughter, I do."

"Thank you, Lord."

"Daughter, there was a man on Earth, a great king. I blessed him with tremendous power, wealth, and every luxury for pleasure and entertainment. I gave him not only material wealth, but intelligence and wisdom beyond that of any other man. This great king possessed a curious mind. He delighted in the study of all aspects of the natural world and human nature, so his understanding was very great. Yet, this king despaired of life itself, because he knew his time upon the Earth was short, and one day, someone else would enjoy all he had worked to achieve."

Livi stared at her knees and let out a heavy sigh. "I understand that man. It's bitter. What am I to do?"

"Enjoy this life, but most of all delight yourself in my service and my ways. My calling will always end in joy and satisfaction, not bitterness." The Lord disappeared from Livi's sight.

She stared after the Lord with loving eyes and then stood and walked back up the beach with her hands clasped behind her back. "Yes, Lord, so be it."

New Paradise Valley, Year 199

The first warm stone homes had grown into a complex of dwellings painted a variety of colors for the extended family. The entire population of New Paradise Valley—four hundred people—lived in similar groupings of homes.

Damaro sat behind his home sorting through a load of copper ore.

Rohee, a big man and a great-grandson of Damaro, arrived like a slow-moving mountain. He led a grazer pulling a sledge of wool. "Forebaba Maro, you know the latest thing is to dig pits for ores and bust them out with fire and quenching water."

"I know, I prefer to gather copper above ground. Those pits can be dangerous." Damaro looked at the wool load. "You're thinking of going into mining?"

Rohee laughed. "Oh no, I've had cousins get hurt mining. I just like keeping up with the latest technology. My flock's grown to two hundred shaggy steppers. They keep me fully occupied ... You got time to come with me to the Trove? I could use some help to unload."

"Sure, I'll help you out."

The two men walked toward Rapid River until they reached the Trove, a bustling place where tables and stalls were set up for trading goods. The Trove resounded with voices and laughter like at a family reunion and smelled like fresh produce, spices, and baked goods.

Rohee found a man who produced wool blankets and clothing. "Sil, I have a large load of fine wool for you today."

Sil, a tall man with muscular limbs like light-brown corded rope, jumped up and inspected the product. "I expect nothing but the best from you." He held some to his nose, rubbed it between his fingers, and stretched the wool. "I'll take this. What do I have that looks good to you?"

Rohee shook his head. "No woolen goods today. I need grain and meat."

Sil marked numbers on two smooth stones and handed them to Rohee. "Take these tokens and get what you need over there."

"Thank you, brother." Rohee and Damaro unloaded the wool.

Rohee took the tokens to the stalls of those offering meat and grain and obtained what he needed. "I love coming to the Trove. Brothers and sisters helping each other." Rohee hesitated as if weighing his words. "Forebaba, sometimes I get the notion that people are against me. Makes me ashamed, because I know it's not true."

Damaro patted Rohee's shoulder. "I often forget it, but the devil sows seeds of distrust in our hearts. Don't beat yourself up, but root out such lies."

At day's end, all the merchants gathered, returned the tokens based on identifying marks, and exchanged goods. They made sure the day's exchanges were fair and everyone had all they needed and more.

At the Trove that day, Damaro observed a potter spinning a platform with a stick until the platform spun rapidly. The potter set the stick aside, and the platform continued spinning while the potter shaped wet clay into a dish. "That is fascinating." Damaro watched as the potter made a variety of pieces.

Damaro told Mornie about the potter, and together they designed a round solid disc called a wheel that could be mounted on a pole they called an axle. Soon, carts with two axles and four wheels were being pulled everywhere by grazers. A great improvement over dragging sledges.

Chapter Forty-Eight

Balsam, Year 200, Awak, Day 19

Solis and Livi led nine other couples, including Aalto and Merike, on a three-month journey from Mid Seacoast southeast to the field of charms. Solis named the region Balsam because the trees and shrubs produced an aromatic fragrance. In Balsam, Aalto and Merike became animal doctors. They taught themselves new techniques to treat sick and injured creatures.

In the new land, Sojourners' Way celebrated the discovery of a tree of life thriving in the forest. It appeared to be older than any tree of life found outside the Garden.

Livi gave birth to five more children in Balsam.

In every place he lived, Solis studied how to identify and care for the different types of plants. Late one morning, after they had lived in Balsam for two years, Solis and Aalto ambled along a trail near a swift-flowing stream, examining what grew there.

Aalto bent over a plant and plucked it up. "The Lord God speaks to us when he's present with us, but he also speaks to us through the plants he created."

Solis said, "Why would he do that?

"So we have the enjoyment of figuring out complex puzzles. God employs the land to tell a story."

"What are you talking about?"

"The Lord tells us some things directly, others he hides completely, but sometimes he provides clues for us to figure out the meaning."

Solis focused on his son with rapt attention. "The plants tell you their secrets?"

"Yes, in a sense. Balsam supports a tremendous number of diverse habitats, so it has many more types of plants and animals than Mid Seacoast and New Paradise Valley combined. Leaves, fruit, or roots often resemble a part of an animal's body, and sometimes that part of the plant alleviates an injury or ailment pertaining to the corresponding animal part. It gives Merike and me a place to begin our testing."

Solis said, "Give me an example of how you have become more effective at animal care."

"Grazers wear a yoke, and they get wounds all the time. We have always wrapped the wounds in a mud liniment. But mud mixed with herbs and oils from plants found only in Balsam allows wounds to heal more quickly. Here's another example: striders get stomach pain. We've found a plant that clears it up."

Solis smiled and shook his head. "My children have surpassed me in every area."

"Baba, we learned it from the way you always study things. Mama's artistry taught us to draw, so we can record our findings with pictures."

Solis tapped Aalto's shoulder. "But the plants never spoke to me." Solis grinned. "What will the neighbors think?"

"That Merike and I are crazy?"

"Or geniuses."

Aalto and Merike became more effective in treating animals than any other doctors, and people from around the region brought their creatures to the couple.

Balsam, Year 205, Unio, Day 5

Solis and Livi dwelt with their family in Balsam in a warm stone home located in a forest community. The region was cold for only a couple of months each winter, so they rarely lit a fire for heating. The Lord appeared to Solis and Livi while they sat outside their home as their adult children prepared the evening meal. Torches hung from surrounding tree branches, a fire crackled, and children played in a nearby field.

The Lord said, "At the conclusion of this year, there will begin a time of testing for all Erimea. For a certain time, you will no longer see me or hear my voice."

Solis jumped up. "May it never be, Lord."

Livi said, "No, Lord. We can't survive without hearing your voice and seeing your face. You're our life."

"I'll be with you every step of the way. I'll see and hear your every word and respond as appropriate. But you will not see my face or hear my voice for a time. You must live according to all I have commanded you thus far. Live by faith. Do not fear."

Solis said, "For how long?"

"That's not for you to know. Every man, woman, and child of age to understand has received this same message from me." The Lord paused. "My great servants, Solis and Livi, in the year 250, you must follow the Balsam River for three months and return to the Garden of Chara on the first day of Marri. Meet with your descendants at midday at a place called Lookout Station and guide them in the way of righteousness. It will be a day of decision affecting all of Erimea."

Livi moaned and paced. "Where is Lookout Station? What decision? Lord, will you have resumed speaking to us by then? How will we know what to say?"

"Remember all I have taught you. You already have the wisdom you will need then. Travel northeast along the Balsam River to where it divides from Sweet Water Whirlwind east of the Garden. At the midpoint of your journey, you will see a massive black stone."

Solis said, "Yes, Lord. We will follow the Balsam until we see Chara. May we still pray to you, and you will hear?"

"Yes, pray at all times."

Solis hugged the Lord. "Living without you will be worse than living without the healing leaves."

"I will be with you. Do not fear. Overcome every obstacle." The Lord disappeared from their sight.

For the next five months, the Lord interacted with the Erimeans regularly, as he always had.

When the year ended, the testing began.

Few noticed any change until days later when they called upon the Lord, and he did not appear. The people grieved, but they remembered the word of the Lord and continued to teach their children the ways of God.

Four years into the time of testing, the trees of life outside the Garden began to fail. After five years, all the trees were dead, except for those in the Garden of Chara.

The four regions of Erimea remained isolated from each other because the routes were still undeveloped. Travel was hard and dangerous for all but the most experienced explorers. Erimeans outside the Garden learned to live without the healing leaves. The people aged slowly. Human death was a rare occurrence, and many people forgot all about the healing leaves.

Concerned leaders in New Paradise Valley resolved to send a secret delegation to acquire the healing leaves from the Garden of Chara. When the delegation returned, the leaders stored the leaves in an undisclosed location in case of an emergency, and they didn't inform their citizens.

Likewise, the leaders of Mid Seacoast sent an expedition to the Garden to collect a supply of leaves. The leaves were kept in secure storage and used only for the most grievous injuries.

In Balsam, the population was initially too small to send people to the Garden, so injured people were treated by Aalto and Merike. The expertise the couple gained in working with animals assisted them in providing care to people.

Chapter Forty-Nine

Aetherdon, City of the Air, Year 206, Shap, Day 1

Lucido, Vik, and Iredin gathered, and their souls still reverberated with excitement over the most recent havoc they had wreaked on Earth. They wondered at times about the life they had abandoned when they rebelled against God, but they reveled in their demonic activity. At times, Lucido pondered the idea of repentance, but it remained a concept beyond his imagination.

Lucido crossed his arms and sneered. "Now is the opportune time to begin in earnest to plant the seeds of Erimea's downfall." He rubbed his hands together. "Yes, this marks the beginning of a happy new year."

Vik said, "Why now? Erimeans all still remember the Lord's teaching."

Iredin responded with a quick snort. "Sow seeds of doubt and fear now."

"And, by the year 250, reap a harvest of blood." A wicked smile crossed Lucido's face. "There will be more people born in the Garden who have never seen or heard the Lord for themselves than now exist in the entire population of Erimea, and our dear angels, the derangers, will continue to deform their personalities. A crop ripe for destruction."

Iredin said, "They multiply like vermin."

"Like a disease," Vik sneered. "Where shall we begin?

"The Garden is mine." Lucido laughed. "You two choose between the northern and the western lands. We will expose this race as faithless frauds."

Iredin said, "I'll take New Paradise Valley."

"Leaves Mid Seacoast for me." Vik rubbed his hands together in delight.

"Appeal to their basest self-interests," Lucido said. "Help them forget they all sprang from the original pair. Rip away their innocent veneer. Appeal to their love of pleasure, wealth, and power. Convince your humans their concerns are not selfish but for the good of their region. Practical and reasonable."

Vik said, "What about Balsam?"

“Ah, Balsam, the new home of the first pair.” Lucido clenched his jaw and ground his teeth. “I’ll torment them last of all, but their choice won’t matter. By then, our machinations will be grinding their purpose to dust.”

Iredin strolled to Ophthalmos and viewed Earth and then Erimea. “I wonder if the growing use of garments in the three regions may be useful to us.”

Lucido’s eyes brightened. “Explain how that might be.”

“On Earth, they cover up with clothing, and yet to many earthlings, the human body is merged with sexuality, especially the nude body. They have corrupt attitudes and intentions, so they continually lust after one another’s bodies.”

“But on Erimea,” Lucido pondered Iredin’s observation, “the unclothed body is completely separate from sexuality. Like animals, they’re innocent in that regard. Let’s do some research and find a way to use these new coverings to our advantage.”

Outside the Garden of Chara, wearing garments became a common tradition because of the weather. The Gardeners, who had no need for clothing, usually only wore a bag or basket of healing leaves with perhaps a belt to hold a small cutter or other tools. Gardeners also wore shells and stones as bracelets and necklaces and decorated their belts in various ways, but they viewed those who wore clothes with suspicion.

Gardeners would say to one another, “What are they hiding?” or “What are they ashamed of?”

Lucido was a constant invisible influence in the Garden of Chara. The great demon whispered into the hearts of many people. Garden residents appointed a council of five citizens as their representatives to meet monthly to make decisions regarding the Garden. Lucido attended each council meeting invisibly.

Garden of Chara, Year 215

Chairman Geog sat waiting for the other council members to arrive at Lookout Station, between Mount Mercy and Neverway Passage, for the morning meeting. Lookout Station was so named because everyone hoped to be at the site when Solis and Livi returned whenever that happened.

His good friend Maris arrived. "Good morning, Geog," she greeted. "Were you at the Restday reading of God's word by the Students last night?"

"Good morning. Yes, I love the stories of our history. But I long for the time when Restday was more refreshing, just relaxing all day in the company of Iam and family."

"Me too. Though the Students added some formality, they're still a blessing. I'm studying, so one day I can read it for myself."

Geog nodded. "I wish I could read. Maybe one day. Do you remember our great father and mother?"

"No. I was there when Sojourners' Way departed, but I was too young to remember."

"Same here, but my parents told me stories"—Geog pointed at the bloody stick at the crest of Mount Mercy—"of how they battled the dragon on our behalf."

"I love that story. May we be here when they return. Even more so, I want to see the Lord again."

Together, Geog and Maris repeated a common refrain: "May we see his face soon."

The other council members, Coura, Anthros, and Delmar, arrived and everyone sat on the ground around a large stone table.

Geog started the meeting with a prayer. "Dear Lord, please be with us in this meeting. Bless our decisions and our families. May we see your face soon."

Everyone said, "So be it."

Geog pressed his lips together in a slight frown. "We're here to discuss the future well-being and security of our growing population. The team of stonemasons has departed in search of massive stones for the gate project. It'll require years to complete."

Maris patted Geog's hand. "It's the right thing to do."

"What if the gate's closed when the great ones return?"

"It's a precaution," Coura said in her calm tone. "It will probably never be closed."

"I hope not," Delmar said. "But soon, we may be hard-pressed to take care of our own people."

Geog sighed. "That's true. At present, we have a Garden population of eight thousand two hundred people. By 250, we project over sixty-five thousand."

Anthros said, "It's not just the tree of life fruit and leaves. We must plan how to feed and house all our Garden citizens."

"That's why we're here." Geog smiled.

"We had a delegation visit recently from New Paradise Valley. They had iron blades for harvesting fruit and healing leaves." Delmar shook his head. "Never saw anything cut so effectively."

Anthros said, "Could easily be turned into weapons."

"Calm down, Anthros." Maris raked her hand through her crimson hair. "They're our brothers."

"Yes, but what if they demand more than we want to share?"

No one had an answer to Anthros's question. The council turned to other business, and the meeting ended before midday.

As they left, Maris said to Geog, "Last week, one of my grandsons, Denis, said to me, 'Mama Maris, look how the baby climbers eat from the tree of knowledge. They don't die. Maybe that's why I can't catch them.' When I asked what he meant, he said, 'I guess they got smarter than us. Maybe we should eat too.'"

Geog shuddered. "Remind the boy that God's commands are for humans, not animals."

"I worry about the coming generations. I'm going to encourage Denis to join the Students."

"One of my young adult neighbors said a member of a party from Mid Seacoast told him he heard people in a new settlement called Balsam had begun talking to plants and trees. Even praying to them and asking for healing."

"That's ridiculous," Maris said. "What did your neighbor think?"

"She said maybe we should try praying to the tree of life for wisdom. She complained it's been so long since the Lord spoke to her, he doesn't seem real. She's given up hope of seeing him again."

Lucido laughed at the council's concerns. The seeds of fear were sprouting wonderfully. He couldn't ask for more. The people lapped up his lies and rumors like sweet treats. "Yet, the Students concern me." Lucido instructed his demons, "They love the God of the word; turn them, and they'll love the word as their god."

Chapter Fifty

New Paradise Valley, Year 226, Unio, Day 30

Commander Grittier shrugged off his cloak and breathed a sigh of relief. He had just returned from leading a year-long expedition through the regions of Erimea. "I'd forgotten about the feast this week. Navigating these alleys is as challenging as the wilds of Erimea, so many people and their animals." Grittier reclined against a table with two other men.

Alaric, a region leader, chuckled. "I doubt that. You should have been here last year for the Feast of Sojourn celebration. It was even more crowded. Events of every sort were held to honor God. Speeches, banquets, concerts, and contests: spear throwing, climbing, water races, and my favorite, sampling savory treats."

Eero, another leader, said, "It's hard to believe it's been one hundred twenty-six years since the great ones arrived."

Grittier nodded. "A long time ago, I was in Chara for the Salvation Day celebration, and that was very special. One day, maybe all Erimeans will share in that party."

Alaric said, "Enough of that. Commander, please proceed with your report."

Grittier said, "A massive stone gate has been installed in the Garden of Chara's Neverway Passage. We learned the gate was installed five years ago but has never been closed."

Alaric said, "For what reason was the gate installed?"

"Unknown, sir."

"They fear us." Alaric pounded his fist on the table. "They know we need more of the healing leaves. But we would never take them by force."

Eero said, "I wouldn't be so sure about that. What else, Commander?"

"Mid Seacoast has developed tremendous shipbuilding capacity. They've begun to explore unknown parts of Erimea. That region has the straightest, heaviest trees I've ever seen. Perfect for a battering ram, sir."

Alaric swallowed hard and covered his mouth. "May it never be. Anything else?"

"A new settlement called Balsam has doctors with expertise in treating human injuries when the leaves are not available. We've returned with a supply of medicines from Balsam. I suggest forming an alliance with Mid Seacoast and Balsam."

Alaric said, "Commander, give us a brief update on the special project we asked you to undertake."

Grittier sat up and smiled. "Yes, sir. The history of human death. Human death is quite rare, but once it occurs, it doesn't release its victim. Human death has occurred in all known regions. The first recorded death occurred in the Garden of Chara in 102, not long after the commencement of the famous sojourn. The numbers, though small, have increased steadily as the population has grown."

Eero's mouth fell open. "I hadn't realized it started so early. The leaves were plentiful then."

"Yes, sir. The first death was of a child who fell from a tree."

Alaric said, "Were the leaves not available? Was the child alone?"

"Leaves were present, and so was the family. Witnesses state the parents immediately applied the leaves. Apparently, the trauma to the head caused death on impact."

Eero said, "What did they do with the body?"

"In those days, people disbelieved in the reality of death, so they took the body home and treated it like an injury. They applied ointment from the leaves to the wounds, squeezed the juice into the victim's mouth, and waited. We still do this."

Alaric said, "How long did they wait?

"After two, maybe three days, decay and death were obvious. The body was then buried after a ceremony of remembrance."

Eero said, "Can't we tell the living from the dead?"

The commander said, "Not always. Some witnesses report being unable to detect breathing, but when they applied the leaves, the victim revived. That instituted the tradition of always employing the leaves and fruit no matter how severe the injuries appeared."

Alaric said, "What other conditions resulted in death?"

"Extreme blood loss. This is very rare and typically occurred when the victim was alone in a remote area and separated from the leaves. Drowning is another cause of death. Victims become disabled by ingestion of water. Aid must be rendered almost immediately to save drowning victims."

"Some of our industries are prone to falls and head trauma." Alaric stood and paced. "We need to develop safety training and equipment to protect our people."

"Mining of pure form ores comes to mind as a high-risk operation." Eero rocked back and forth with a faraway gaze. "If death becomes more common, we might have a revolt on our hands."

Alaric said, "Commander, please dictate the rest of your report to the secretary. Be sure to record the number of deaths by year and region, the nature of the trauma, and remedies attempted. Thank you for gathering the data."

"My pleasure, sir."

Eero said, "Thank you, Commander Grittier."

The commander left the two leaders.

Alaric said, "I long for the days when the Lord walked with us."

"You're not alone. But he promised to hear our prayers and be with us. We need to learn how to grow the trees of life again. Our people are aging."

Alaric said, "We need to send farmer-scientists to study the Garden soil and techniques."

"We must send them at once."

Balsam, Year 250, Brea, Day 1

Solis and Livi reassembled Sojourners' Way and departed at dawn for the Garden of Chara after one hundred fifty years away. This time, the first parents would be the only couple staying in the group. Their five adult children born in Balsam would travel with them half the journey and then return to their birthplace. Two skin-covered, grazer-pulled carts with wheels carried food and supplies. Two wind striders and four hounds were included among the hunting animals joining the travelers.

Prior to departure, Solis spoke to Livi. "Years ago, the Lord revealed the journey home should take three months."

"So, we'll arrive a month early?"

"Yes, I want to be sure we're in the Garden well before the Lord's deadline of Marri 1."

"It will be good to be home again. I wonder what has become of Caressa and Smallo."

"The Lord had a special purpose for them."

"Their childhood will be long past ... the only ones we missed."

"I'm sorry we missed it, but we also had a purpose to fulfill, and we're almost done." Solis took his wife's hand. "You've sustained me through all these travels. My darling, your brown eyes are the loveliest I've ever seen. I love you very much."

"You sweet man." Livi pulled him close, breathed in his pleasing fragrance, and kissed him. "I love you too. Your love is the sweetest thing in my life. More than that, you're the greatest man in the world. That's why God made you the firstborn of creation, the son of God. You show us the way."

Lucido eavesdropped on the first couple with a mixture of disgust and envy. They worshipped each other. He spoke into their hearts: *Your mission will fail. You and your kind are worthless, selfish, fearful idolaters.*

Mid Seacoast, Year 250, Awak, Day 16

By midmorning, Talen and Daylig completed a meeting with the shipbuilders and were walking to their home on the beach—the same home their parents had lived in. The couple had contracted the construction of a new water vessel for the business they operated together. More than a hundred people were on the beach that morning, mostly carpenters building seagoing vessels.

Talen said, "How this area has grown ... it's amazing. We're fulfilling the Lord's command to fill the planet. We've gone from twelve people to seven hundred sixty-eight."

"Are we also achieving the command to subdue Erimea?"

Talen looked out at whitecaps churning above the dark blue water. "The sea alone is so powerful. We harvest its bounty, but will any generation subdue it? Can we even control ourselves enough to love one another?"

"What do you mean?"

"A month ago, a contingent left for the Garden of Chara. The alliance with New Paradise Valley was invoked. Trouble is brewing."

"Over the tree of life?"

"Yes. They say Neverway Passage is closed."

"Closed? But we're of one blood. They'll open for us."

"May it be as you say." Talen looked again at the sea, but the water changed and became foamy with river-like swirling. At that moment, the sea receded from the shore. "That's strange."

Hounds, steppers, unstoppables, and other animals ran for the hills.

Alarm seized Talen's chest. He remembered a similar scene from fifty years earlier. "Take cover! A giant wave is coming."

The workers all stopped and stared as the water fell away and uncovered debris on the beach.

Talen raced out of the house, screaming, "Run! Get off the beach. A giant wave is coming. Head for shelter."

The people responded immediately.

A deafening roar thundered out of the deep like a thousand unstoppables trumpeting. Talen was still running along the beach, warning the workers, when the giant wave rose and struck. The wave slammed him to the ground and washed him inland, along with tree trunks and lumber. Debris battered Talen's head, legs, and body. The mad, frothing wave dragged him out to sea, finally slinging him, unconscious, up on the beach.

Of the hundred people on the beach that morning, Talen had saved seventy-eight from injury. The giant wave swept away four souls. Eight died on the beach, and ten others were left severely injured. Talen was among the injured, with fractures to his head and limbs. The Mid Seacoasters cried for the healing leaves, but they had none.

The people recovered the injured and brought Talen home to Daylig. He remained in a semiconscious state, more lucid at some times than at others. Daylig and all Mid Seacoast prayed for Talen's recovery.

Another group set out from Mid Seacoast to join those already heading to the Garden. They cried, "Open Neverway, that we may live."

A quarter day earlier and two million paces away in the Great Blue Sea, Vik gleefully watched as the floor of the sea dropped in response to sudden and violent underwater shaking of Erimea, causing a mammoth piece of underwater mountain to plunge into the depths.

The force drew away the seawater from the beaches of Mid Seacoast. Moments later, a massive underwater wave barreled toward the shore like a hidden hammer. For a quarter day, Vik screamed exultations and chased the wave like an usher of death, anticipating the destruction to come upon the unsuspecting beach workers.

The death and devastation pleased Vik, and he spoke into the minds of the heartbroken Mid Seacoasters: *Be inconsolable in your anguish and unrelenting in your demands, for you are in the right.*

New Paradise Valley, Year 250, Nam, Day 28

Efforts to regrow new trees of life yielded few seedlings. Even the plants that survived required more than ten years before producing fruit or leaves that were ready to harvest. The population of the region had grown to over three thousand one hundred people.

Alaric, now governor of the region, stood before a group of twenty other public representatives. "It's been confirmed. Neverway is routinely kept closed."

One representative jumped up and shouted, "What are we going to do? Deaths among our people are rising."

"We have no choice." Alaric scanned the faces around the table. "We must send the reapers to the Garden of Chara."

"What about the gate?"

"We must breach the gate. The reapers have been instructed to harm no one and take only the fruit and seeds we need to stem the tide of death for ten years."

Lieutenant Governor Eero said, "Our messengers to Mid Seacoast should have arrived three months ago to inform them we must activate the alliance. They should already be on the move with the equipment to bash the gate to bits by the time our reapers are in position."

Alaric nodded. "The road builders have completed the mountain highway. Now, our reapers should be able to make the journey in thirty days."

Another representative rubbed the back of her neck. "When will the reapers depart?"

"The sickles and scythes are ready." Alaric's face held a grave expression, and he turned his gaze downward. "The blades are sharpened. The reapers set out tomorrow at dawn."

"Governor, the Gardeners are our brothers and sisters. What if they resist?"

Alaric hesitated. He spoke without emotion. "Our alliance with Mid Seacoast states, 'It is self-evident all Erimeans are equal heirs of the great first parents, Solis and Livi. Therefore, we all have equal rights to the tree of life. This vital resource must be shared equitably for all time. No single region may restrain free access to the trees of life.' This means the reapers are legally and morally authorized to take the fruit and leaves by force."

"When did the Gardeners agree to that statement?"

Eero said, "The statement is right and reasonable. There is nothing more to discuss."

Iredin reinforced all their fears and spoke to their minds: *Right is right. You are in the right. Fight for the lives of your people. If the Gardeners resist, force them to do right by your people.* Iredin rejoiced at the bloodshed he expected. Those people were no better than brute beasts.

Chapter Fifty-One

Mid Seacoast, Year 250, Awak, Day 17

Destry and Epona, two daughters of the first couple, set out from Mid Seacoast to inform their parents of Talen's injuries. When they arrived in Balsam, they told Aalto and Merike the news and continued their trek to reach Solis and Livi. Aalto and Merike departed for Mid Seacoast in hopes of helping Talen.

Six weeks after Sojourners' Way departed from Balsam, Solis and Livi's five children born in Balsam who had accompanied their parents separated from them and returned to their homes in Balsam. They left one cart and two wind striders with their parents. Cloudbursts caused miserably slow progress. The couple slogged over rugged terrain and got stuck in the mud.

One warm evening, Livi and Solis rested by their campfire under a stand of trees near the Balsam River. Solis had eight rows of seven pebbles, each laid out on the ground near a huge black boulder that rose out of the river like an ominous sentinel. He touched the stones and muttered to himself.

Livi said, "What are you doing?"

"Counting the weeks and days since we left Balsam. I used to be able to track things in my mind." Solis shook his head. "My memory isn't perfect anymore, but with aids like these pebbles, I can still recall each day. We're late."

Livi's eyebrows drew together as she peered down at the pebbles. "How late? How do you know?"

"The Lord said this rock is halfway to Chara. It's been two months. We should have been here two weeks ago."

"Can we still make it?"

"We'll have to go faster."

"We should ride the striders." Livi brushed her husband's thick hair with her hand and looked at her own beautiful braids that hung well past her shoulders. In both, gray strands glinted amid the black. "Hmm ... I hadn't noticed before, but we *are* changing. I wonder why."

In the morning, the couple transferred as many supplies as they could from the cart to packs they could strap to the two wind striders. As she released the grazer, Livi brushed the big beast's back. "Tiny, you have been a faithful friend. Do you want to go back to Balsam?"

Tiny looked at Livi with big, round eyes, wiggled his ears, and breathed out a mournful lowing sound.

Livi turned Tiny in the direction of Balsam. "Get up." She gave Tiny a swat on the rump.

The beast ambled a few steps before stopping for a grassy snack.

Solis and Livi mounted the striders and continued the journey to the Garden. By midday, they reached a fork in the path. To the left, the trail looked bright and clear. On the right, the path ran closer to the river with thick tree branches and plant growth forming a dark, shrouded tunnel.

Livi pointed left. "This way looks easier."

"Remember, the path to Hot Killer Springs looked easy."

"The evils haven't struck in a while. Do they still stalk us?"

"Let's stay close to the river," Solis said.

The couple dismounted and held their breath as Solis led them and their animals through the dark opening. In the overhead branches, creatures scurried away as if making way for these intruders. Through the gloom, Livi spied hairy eight-legged creatures the size of her hand to the left and right. She grasped Piercer, ready to slash any beast that decided to be unfriendly. After about a hundred paces, the path opened again. The couple mounted the striders and resumed trotting.

When they reached a field of tall grass, a white streak appeared against the blue sky. Bright as lightning, it circled above the trees before coming down in a swirling vortex ahead of them.

Solis and Livi dismounted and crouched in the grass. Livi whispered. "What is it?"

"I don't know. Reminds me of when the Lord brought you down from the heavens."

A strange, shimmering, winged creature emerged from the trees. The being said, "Greetings, my friends. Do not be afraid. I'm a messenger sent by the Lord, your God and my God."

The creature's beauty struck Solis and Livi speechless. With their mouths gaping, they slowly rose from their hiding place. The creature had the shape of a man of great height with bronze skin, and he wore a white robe with a golden sash. White hair flowed from his head, and his eyes flashed blazing red like fire, then black, and finally white.

Solis stepped forward, trembling, and bowed low. "Greetings. What sort of being are you?"

"I am an archangel. Day and night, I stand in the presence of the Most High God. I bring you a message from the Lord God. Your son Talen is dying. If you go to him, I've been given the authority to save his life. If not, Talen will surely die."

Solis said, "Why didn't the Lord come and tell us himself?"

"Remember, the Lord said you would not see him for a time. That's why he sent me with this warning."

Livi said, "How can this be? The Lord commanded us to go to the Garden."

"True, but things change. The Neverway Passage is now blocked by a great stone gate. The Lord knows you cannot enter the Garden, so salvage your mission by saving Talen's life."

Solis summoned his courage. "You're lying. Talen isn't dying, and Neverway is not closed. We would never close off the Garden of Chara."

"Very well," the being snarled. "You will answer to the Lord. You have rebelled against his will." He vanished.

Livi sat on the ground. "What if Talen is dying? How can we fulfill our mission if Neverway is closed?"

Solis sat by his wife and put his arms around her. "My darling, it cannot be true. That was a lying angel. The Lord commanded us to go to Chara."

Livi pushed Solis away, fell on her face, and prayed. "Oh Lord, let us know the truth and guide us."

At that moment, Solis and Livi heard the beating of hooves. Destry and Epona crested a hill and rode up to their parents, exhausted from their long ride with little rest.

Solis's voice trembled. "What is it? Why are you here?"

Destry and Epona climbed down from their striders, staggered for a moment, and caught their breath. Destry said, "Baba, Mama, Talen has been severely injured."

Livi flew to her feet and grabbed Destry. "What happened? Is he going to live?"

Epona said, "Talen saved others from a giant sea wave, but it caught him and beat him against the sand and debris."

Destry said, "You must come back to Mid Seacoast with us. There may be war in the Garden. They've closed Neverway. Our men are marching, prepared to breach the gate by force to get the leaves from the tree of life."

Livi stared at her husband. "The angel spoke the truth. He must be from God."

"My firstborn son." Solis bent over, his head in his hands. "Long ago, I promised him I would always come for him." He fell to his knees and clawed his fingers into the hard-packed soil. "Lord God, please come tell us what to do."

Livi shrieked at her husband, "I know what to do. Go to Talen. Right now! If we do, the angel said Talen will live."

Solis shook his head and raised his voice to match Livi's. "Not without a word from the Lord. He commanded us to go to the Garden of Chara. We *must* go to the Garden."

The bright, shining angel appeared again.

Destry and Epona shielded their eyes and fell to the ground.

"Do you see?" he said. "I spoke the Lord's truth. Do you believe me now? You must turn back and go to Mid Seacoast, and Talen will live."

Solis said, "No, I don't believe you. You contradict the Lord." He pointed in the angel's face. "Your eyes betray you. I've seen them before in the Garden. In the sneaking thing."

The angel turned to Livi. "Dear woman, your husband is mad. If you return, I may still be able to save Talen."

She stared at her husband, and then at the angel. "Let's go, girls. Back to Mid Seacoast." Livi mounted her strider and turned back.

Destry and Epona kissed their father and followed their mother.

Solis stood with outstretched arms. Speechless.

The strange angel laughed and disappeared.

Livi rode so hard that Epona and Destry couldn't keep up, and a distance opened between them and their mother. Livi bowed her head and cried out. "Oh Lord, my heart is torn. I'm truly broken branches ... Am I nothing more to you than a delivery vessel for your will?" Livi shook her head. "Forgive me, Lord, I know better than that."

The trio continued northwest toward Mid Seacoast, and Livi admired the sky's beautiful hues as daylight sank.

Chapter Fifty-Two

Solis wept as he rode toward the Garden. The loneliness that dissipated so long ago came roaring back, tearing at his soul. Livi's expression of anguish as she left was etched in his mind. He prayed. "Iam, please forgive my beloved. The angel deceived her. Mother's love drives her. Protect her, save Talen, and give me strength to complete this way ... your way."

The journey wore on Solis's spirit and body. His lower back and arms ached, and their protests grew. His body threatened to betray him as he rode. "Lord, I can do all things with Livi by my side, but somehow ... I've failed her ... I've failed Talen. Let me not fail you."

As he watched Solis's despair, the angel Alexander wailed to the Lord, "Oh God, his vigor is dissipating fast. Shall I strengthen the man?"

"No," the Lord replied. "Hold back your hand from aiding him, kind guardian. Watch and learn about humanity."

The lush greenery along the Balsam River grew ominous, and clouds blocked glow and the sparkles. The river took on a stagnant stench of death, and the water became quiet, as if even the river itself had refused to flow. Solis dismounted and moved toward the riverbank. Twigs cracked with each step, and he stumbled over tangled undergrowth.

A vision flashed through his mind in which he took one step too many and tumbled into the river. The vision disappeared.

Solis froze. He reached through the gloom and felt the rough bark of a large tree. Holding onto the tree, he scooted around it. His foot slid across a slimy rock and splashed into the river.

The water's edge. He drew back and sat with his back against the tree. A fire would have been nice, but he was too exhausted to build it. He dozed.

In the middle of the night, the clip-clop of hooves broke the silence. He thought he was dreaming until the sound grew louder, and he concluded it might be real. He croaked out a greeting. "Livi, is that you?" He realized he had hardly spoken above a whisper, so he cried out again, louder. "Livi, I'm here." The beat of the hooves faded as the rider passed by, and Solis returned to slumbering.

At dawn, when daylight peeked above the horizon, he saw a solitary figure walking toward him. Livi. Before Solis could rise, she threw herself upon him. "Are you all right?"

"You came back." Solis embraced his wife as if she had been gone for years.

"I'm sorry."

"What made you return?"

Livi looked away from her husband. "Our purpose ... and ... wanting to not fail you or be separated from you. I'd rather die than do that. I couldn't stand thinking of the hurt on your face when I left."

"How did you find me?"

"I thought I heard something when I passed last night, but I wasn't sure where. I returned and searched until I heard the whinny of your strider."

Solis reached for his pack. "You've been up all night? Eat and rest here for a little while."

Livi hesitated. "You're sure the angel was an imposter?"

He nodded. "His eyes changed, like in the garden. And he opposed the Lord's word, like in the Garden."

That very day, Solis felt physical pain in his heart as if he had been stabbed with a knife. At the same time, Livi grabbed her chest and winced for just a moment. Solis didn't ask what she had felt. He feared what it might mean.

Mid Seacoast, Year 250, Nam, Day 2

After two weeks of drifting in and out of consciousness, Talen awoke and became alert. He saw Daylig and six of his children standing around him, along with their grandchildren.

Talen spoke in a whisper. "My beautiful wife. My dear ones, I love you all very much. How did the workers fare?"

Daylig brushed away a tear. "You saved a great many of them. You're a hero to us and all Mid Seacoast. Are you feeling better?"

"I feel wonderful." He looked up and saw angels standing with his family. "Look, there are men standing here with us. Their clothes are white, shining bright as lightning. You all look puzzled. See the dazzling light?"

One of the angels said, "Talen, man of God and man of adventure, the Lord has called you home. Arise."

A smile spread across his face. "The time of my departure has come. The Lord has called me away. May God bless you all." Talen breathed his last, and the angels carried his soul to paradise.

Daylig and the family mourned for Talen, and they buried his body in the hills overlooking the sea.

Garden of Chara, Year 250, Helpe, Day 31

Solis and Livi rode from dawn until dark every day for weeks until they reached the Garden of Chara. Sweet Water Whirlwind River became shallow as it flowed south out of the Garden under Tall Stony. Then, it dropped through a series of small falls and again became a swirling, deep river. Sweet Water Whirlwind curved and split into four channels east of Neverway: Two of the channels were the Balsam River flowing southwest past the Garden on the south side and Rapid River flowing north. Tree-covered mountains surrounded the Garden of Chara with gray and red stony outcroppings, with moss-covered boulders spread throughout.

In the late afternoon light, Livi looked up at the south side of Tall Stony and then down at the rough frothing of the river flowing underneath. "How do you plan to get into the garden?"

"I can't believe Neverway is closed," Solis said. "I want to see that first."

The pair continued northeast around the garden until they could look back to the west and see the massive stone gate.

Solis shook his head. "What are our children thinking? What do they fear? Are we not one family?"

"What's your plan?" They stood in the darkness of the gate as shadows lengthened.

"We're one day early. We get in. Learn what's going on and attend the meeting tomorrow on the first of Marri."

"Your plan to get in?"

Solis said, "There must be watchmen. Surely, they will open for Solis and Livi." He marched up to the gate and bellowed, "We are Solis and Livi, your first parents. Open up."

After several moments, a reply came from the top of the gate. "Sorry, stranger. We cannot open for another night at least, by order of the Council of Nine."

"We are not strangers. We are Solis and Livi."

The guard laughed. "My aunt and uncle are Livi and Solis." Other voices joined in the laughter. "Everyone has someone named after the legends."

A young female voice said, "You know, some say they're not real, just myths. We can't let down the rope."

"They doubt our existence?" Solis leaned against the wall and looked at Livi. "Let's climb to the top of Heaven Falls and enter through Mornie's Mountain Pass. Remember where Talen got stuck?"

Livi crossed her arms. "I remember, but I'm not climbing Heaven Falls."

"What do you suggest?"

"Pass through the waters under Tall Stony. There's clearance above the water."

"I don't want to pass through the water. It may still be home to a nest of sneaking things."

"I know." Livi took a deep breath. "I'll light a torch. That will keep them away. If not, I'll slice their heads off." She put her hand on her blade, Hearty.

"Your plan is terrible." Solis swept his arms through the air. "Deadly venom. A single bite, and you could die in short order."

"You go through the mountain pass first, get the leaves, and wait for me on the other side of Tall Stony. If I get bitten, the leaves will heal me."

Solis took Livi into his arms. "You must wait well into the night to give me enough time. You have the supplies for the torch?"

Livi said, "Yes, but hurry. You must get through the pass before it gets too dark."

"I'll light a torch as well."

The couple embraced for several moments, kissed, and went their separate ways.

Chapter Fifty-Three

Light faded as Solis circled the north side of the Garden, climbed past shrubs and trees, and over rocks adorning the mountains that held Heaven Falls and his first home, Hilltop Castle. The sting of rejection at the gate faded with the satisfaction of being back at his beloved Chara.

He breathed in the sweet aroma of the Garden. The higher he climbed, the steeper the slope became, and Solis pulled on roots, bushes, or trees—whatever he could grab—while his feet dug into the soil, and his legs strained to propel him up.

Solis dragged himself to the crest of a ridge and rested his muscles, which screamed with burning pain. To his left, part of the mountain rose further, although he was near the peak. In front, the black waters of Sweet Water Whirlwind River swept like a shimmering whirlpool as it prepared to descend Heaven Falls. To the right stretched the rest of the ridge that formed the riverbank. Solis scanned the rocky wall to his left for a crevice, the opening at the beginning of Mornie's Mountain Pass, but he found nothing.

He searched his memory. As little boys, Stron and Talen had explored the passage from inside the Garden to this side, and Stron had described a marker they saw when they had emerged from the pass. Two hundred forty years ago. So long.

Solis stared at the mountainside as he walked backward along the ridge. A warm wind blew, the clouds cleared, and glow illuminated the top of a large stone. A man's head, that's what Stron had said. The stone protruded above the water. Behind it, Solis saw the dark outline of the top of a crevice. Flooded. Most of Mornie's Mountain Pass was underwater, the river flowing through the passage.

"Let it not be." He held his head, squeezed his eyes shut, and moaned. "Not water." *Lord, will this never pass?*

Solis had to swim in the swirling water to get to the passage. The water writhed like a beast ready to dash him against the rocks or consume him, ensuring he was never seen again. He rocked back and forth and slapped his hands against his thighs. He jumped out and plunged beneath the surface. So cold. He bobbed up and stroked frantically with his arms once, twice, five times, before grabbing the large rock. Solis swallowed river water, choked, and spat it out.

He pushed off from the rock, made another stroke, and reached the edge of the opening. His feet touched the bottom of the passage. He rested a moment with the river beating against his back. "Lord, help me."

After Solis headed north, Livi mounted her wind strider and rode to the south side of the Garden outside Tall Stony. She was in no hurry, since she had to wait until midnight to be sure Solis would be waiting for her when she emerged from under Tall Stony. She chose a large stone in a grassy spot as her preparation area. She unsheathed Hearty and Piercer and inspected her trusty weapons. She laid out her torch and other fire-starting items.

Livi pulled out of her pack two narrow bones and set them on the stone. She wrapped her long braided hair into a bun and inserted the two bones through the arrangement.

The water surged higher than she realized: above the foot of Tall Stony, which would create a problem if there was no space for keeping the torch lit and for breathing. Livi took a closer look before it got dark.

She grabbed Piercer from the stone and crept up to Tall Stony on the right side of the river. Then, she waded across as the dark water's rapid flow almost knocked her off balance.

No clearance.

Livi crossed to the left side and found a narrow slot, where she could peer under Tall Stony. The space opened so she could squeeze through the slot, and then crouch or crawl along the bank all the way through. In the worst-case scenario, she would have to wade in the water. Either way, she would be able to keep her head and the torch above water.

She returned to the stone, placed Piercer next to Hearty, and sat in the grass. She ate and drank and thought of all her encounters with the sneaking things. Her skin crawled. Every meeting was awful. Nasty beasts. In cahoots with the evils. She spat.

Livi closed her eyes and tried to relax. Soon, she fell asleep and dreamed she was under Tall Stony. Sneaking things surrounded her. Livi flew up and spun above the beasts with Hearty and Piercer in her hands. She lowered the blades and cut off their slimy heads while they cried out, "This is our home. Why are you killing us?"

She exulted and said, "Because you oppose us. This is ours. You don't deserve life."

The slaughter continued until the river ran red with the beasts' blood. In the dream, Livi saw herself, satisfaction on her face, her garment dripping with blood, and severed body parts clinging to her hair. She looked down in horror and found there were no sneaking things below her. Instead, floating in the dark waters, were the swollen, rotting bodies of executed human children. The stench choked Livi.

She shot awake, sweaty and trembling, and she gagged at the thought of what she had done in the dream. "Never. I would never do that. No one would ever do that." Then she recalled the long-ago vision she had had of Earth, and she feared what the dream might mean.

With his head tipped back, Solis could keep his mouth above the water. The current pushed him against the passage's sharp, rugged walls. *Too tight. Too dark. Can't breathe.* The walls closed in.

"Oh, no. I'm stuck." Caught at the chest. He couldn't move. "Help me. Help me." No one could hear him. He pressed against the rock, with arms and chest aching. Finally, he budged, slid back, and pressed above the pinch point. He was free.

A glint of glow lit part of the passage, and the space opened, so Solis was able to float and propel himself through by pushing off the walls until he reached the part where several passages converged. He braced himself with his hands and feet, and he searched his surroundings to determine which passage to take.

Then, he remembered. The sixth one. A sudden rush of water pushed him down the passage opposite him and to his left. He no longer had any control. The water beat him against rocky walls and shot him down and out of the passage and over the falls.

Glow shone on Livi. It was about midnight. Time to enter the garden under Tall Stony. She composed herself, sheathed Piercer, cinched up her garment, and lit the torch.

"Lord, make me worthy of this way."

With Hearty in one hand and the blazing torch in the other, she crossed the river and went to the slot in the rock face. Livi stuck the torch in the slot and looked around. She saw nothing but the riverbank and the quick-flowing dark water.

She squeezed through the opening and crouched, flashing the torch around. On both sides of the river and in the crevices above her head were hundreds, maybe thousands, of sneaking things.

Many splashed into the river and swam to the opposite riverbank, some dug into the dirt, others hid under rocks, and some stared at the intruder.

Livi recoiled back into the slot, retched, and looked away, trying not to make eye contact with the creatures. She forced herself forward, sweeping the torch in front and above her to clear any remaining creatures and motioning with Hearty. She stared back at them. For the first time in her life, she felt their fear and pitied them. "You don't hurt me, and I won't hurt you. I promise."

She continued along the left riverbank for a hundred paces, crouching all the way, until she saw glow illuminating the exit from under Tall Stony.

A chilling hiss greeted her. In the water to her right, a large green-and-yellow sneaking thing rose up and opened its jaws, revealing fangs dripping with black water like blood.

"Lord, help me." Livi drew Hearty back across her body, ready to slice the creature's throat with a strong backhand stroke. "Don't make me." They stood in a motionless standoff for what seemed like an eternity until the beast sank into the murky flow and swam away.

Livi scrambled the last few steps from under Tall Stony, but she didn't stop until she climbed up the slope and was well clear of the nest. She lay on her back, gasping and looking back down from where she had come. Then, she looked up. "Thank you, Lord." She fought to catch her breath. "Probably should have gone north with my husband."

She rolled over, staggered to her feet, and scanned the area. No Solis. Not anyone. Livi paced and clutched herself as sobs burst out. "My dearest husband." Livi sprinted north toward Heaven Falls, following Sweet Water Whirlwind River. "Bright shines this love of mine. Bring back my love to me."

An astounded Gardener watched a body somersault out of Heaven Falls. It flipped forward several times, head over heels, and crash-landed flat on its back. A man floated unconscious, face up, in a deep basin of water. The current turned him and sent him downstream, headfirst. She grabbed hold of his garment and pulled him from the water.

Chapter Fifty-Four

Solis opened his eyes and met the kind gazes of a man and woman who knelt beside him beneath torchlight. The pair had oval faces and golden-brown skin. A band adorned with shells held the woman's braided hair.

The man said, "My wife saved you from the water. You were hurt."

The woman smiled and held up the fruit and leaves from the tree of life. "You're going to be all right."

"My name is Hoshea, and my wife is Aminta."

Solis began to feel better, and he sat up. "Thank you, Aminta, for saving my life."

"You're welcome, stranger." Aminta clasped her hands to her chest and looked at her husband. "He could be him. The Students said he would fall here with the water."

"The Students said there would be a couple."

Aminta said, "Stranger, what is your name?"

"My name is Solis. I was once caretaker and ruler of this garden."

Aminta's face brightened as if a fire had been lit in her cheeks. "It's him! It's him!" She laughed, clapped, and danced. "We've been waiting for you."

"No, it can't be," Hoshea said. "This is a poor outsider. No doubt seeking the leaves and fruit. Don't be afraid. We'll share freely."

Aminta glanced from Hoshea to Solis. "Solis, where is your wife, and what is her name?"

Solis jumped up as if he'd been struck by lightning. "What am I doing? My wife entered from the south under Tall Stony. She's in danger."

Hoshea scoffed. "No one enters that way. It's full of poisonous, slithering—"

"I must go." Solis took five bounding steps.

Almost immediately, he ran into another person in the darkness.

They both yelled in alarm and tumbled to the ground. He shook himself and crawled over to the person. "Livi."

His wife rubbed her head, where they had collided, healing leaves scattered about her.

Solis reached out to his wife. "My darling, are you all right?"

Livi gave a startled cry. "Solis, beloved. I'm all right. What happened to you?"

Aminta said, "He was hurt, and you are too."

Solis caressed Livi's hand. "You burst into the light like the fiercest hunter. Yet, you are a feast for my anxious eyes. Thank God you overcame the beasts."

Aminta knelt by Livi, squeezed some of the leaves, and rubbed the ointment into a cut on Livi's head, sustained in the collision with Solis. "May I ask what your name is?"

"I'm Livi. Mother of all the living."

Aminta burst with excitement. She flew to her husband and swung herself around him. "Thank you, Lord! I knew it. I knew it."

Hoshea said, "You must come to the meeting tomorrow. The council will know what to make of it."

Solis said, "Aminta, is it your normal practice to be out here in the middle of the night?"

"No, sir. But these are not normal times. The Students said, 'When Neverway is closed, look for the return of the first parents.'"

"Why are there no others with you?"

Aminta shrugged. "Some forget. Some don't trust everything that's written. None could imagine how you could come with the water of the falls. I'm amazed. I'm shocked. You'll help us, won't you?"

Solis gasped. "Now I remember ... I saw you in a vision long ago. The Lord called you one of his most godly ones. We will help if we can. Please tell us what to expect."

"Who are the Students?" Livi said.

Hoshea said, "The Students are our beloved teachers. They tell us the meaning of the writings, God's word and our history."

Solis said, "Have they taught of our children, Stron, Brilara, Smallo, and Caressa?"

Hoshea motioned for Solis and Livi to follow him. "Come to our home." He led them to an orchard aisle with a long row of homes on each side. "We don't know much." He lit a lamp.

Their small hut had only two rooms. Brown wooden planks fitted neatly together served as the floor, which was covered with colorful soft rugs. The walls were also planks painted white and decorated with multiple strings of yellow, pink, and red ornaments of stones and shells, along with woven tapestries of garden flowers and trees. The aroma of baked bread filled the house.

Hoshea invited their guests to sit. "Please recline at the table."

Solis and Livi sat on feather-filled floor cushions, and their hosts set before them plates of bread, roasted meats, fresh vegetables, and bowls of fruit, as well as clay jars of a purple drink.

Hoshea and Aminta joined them at the table.

A pained expression crossed Aminta's face as she took Livi's hand. "Great mother, Stron and Brilara are here with us, but we don't know about the fourth twins, that's what we call Seerman Smallo and Caressa. Others say they left Chara long ago and served God mightily, but we don't know where they are now. Those at the School of the Prophets may know."

Solis said, "Take us to the school. Who are the prophets?"

Hoshea said, "It's not in Chara. We don't know where it is. The prophets invented the alphabet. They wrote our history on stones and scrolls."

Aminta said, "They wrote God's story ... and your story from the beginning."

"We don't understand." Solis rubbed his forehead. "Scrolls? What is alphabet? What does 'wrote' mean?"

Aminta nodded. "It's hard to explain. We can't read or write either."

Hoshea said, "It's like symbols ... images that represent the words we say. Your story thrills our hearts. The Students read to us and make copies of the writings. The writings are our most treasured possession in the Garden."

"Everyone knew the stories, but now they're recorded."

"Pictures tell a story. But we don't understand write or alpha—" Livi pinched her lips together. She shook her head. "Tell us about the meeting tomorrow. Why is Neverway closed?"

Hoshea shrugged and turned his palms upward. "Others know more than we do. Some are afraid there are too many people to share the leaves. Some in our age group have many doubts and fears about the Lord."

Solis said, "What doubts and fears?"

"We were born after the testing began, so we never saw the Lord." Hoshea glanced at Aminta. "My wife and I trust the Lord and believe the witness of our parents and others. We know he hears and sees all things, but most of us have never seen the Lord."

Aminta said, "We all long to see the Lord. Why won't the Lord speak to us? Are we cursed like Earth? Are the great parents real? Some wonder about other sources of wisdom. We've heard, in other parts of the world, people talk to plants ... maybe worship them."

"No one worships plants." Solis grimaced. "Only worship the Lord. To study the natural world, to draw meaning from the appearance and structure of plants, and to learn from created things is not to worship them."

Livi said, "You shared generously with us. Don't you have fears also?"

"We trust the Lord." Hoshea spoke without hesitation. "We share because we know he will provide."

Aminta said, "Yes, many are like us. Others worry. But there are also many wiser than we are who know more about the world." Her voice trailed off, and she looked at her guests. "I've prayed for your return. Please come to the meeting tomorrow and help us. These are confusing times."

"Daughter, that's why we've come." Livi pulled Aminta to her chest and held her. "Fear is a terrible master. I've seen visions of the devastation unbridled fear has wreaked on Earth. Sometimes, I'm aghast at my own fear."

Aminta rested in Livi's arms and spoke dreamily. "When we were little, boys and girls raced up and down these orchard aisles shouting, 'Fly like Livi.' Or we'd climb rocks and cry out, 'I'm Solis.' 'I'm a rock darter like father Solis.' The children still do this."

"We'd laugh as we recalled Solis at Heaven Falls," Hoshea smiled and patted Solis on the shoulder. "When you roared so loudly, you frightened a hundred demons."

Aminta said, "No one could ever be as kind and generous as Solis or as beautiful and determined as Livi. We have races from Tall Stony to the tree of life and back to reenact how you saved our great father from death." Aminta felt Livi's braids against her face. "Great mother, your braids are beautiful. May I take them down and oil your hair?

"Yes, daughter, if you like."

Aminta began to work on Livi's hair. "Where did you find the silver to weave in? I love the way it shimmers."

Livi smiled. "That's the way it grows now. Every strand is mine."

"It's lovely. I'll plait your hair in my favorite style. A halo like a crown."

All emotion left Hoshea's face, and he let out a heavy sigh. "Solis and Livi are heroes in our eyes. Highly honored and beloved. We have longed for their return."

"Yes," Aminta said. "Great mother, how many children do you have?"

Livi's face brightened, then turned dark. "My children are spread across this world. I gave birth to eight babies in the garden, three in the north, four by the sea, and five in Balsam."

"Twenty. I hope to have as many."

Hoshea said, "The meeting starts at midday. Everyone will be there. After various leaders have spoken, the council chairwoman will invite others to speak. At that time, you may rise and address the council." Hoshea stood and reached his hand out to Aminta. "We should let our guests rest." The two hosts brought out bedding for Solis and Livi and retreated into the other room.

In the quiet of the night, Solis and Livi overheard the soft whispers of their benefactors.

"They are the great father and mother, aren't they?"

"They don't look the part. No tears, my sweet girl. The Lord will provide."

Chapter Fifty-Five

Garden of Chara, Year 250, Marri, Day 1

Livi woke first and crept out into the eerie darkness that smelled faintly of smoke. Night retreated, and six tiny houses emerged like ghosts from the dark, each shrouded with creeping vines. The homes were nestled in the orchard aisle around a grassy circle, which held a gray wooden table with a blood-red box mounted on top. Livi sat on the ground near the table and fiddled with the lid of the box. The box had two carvings, one on each side, that resembled the scars she and Solis bore. The box was empty.

She scanned one direction hoping to see Pleasant Meadow and in the other direction for Heaven Falls, but the dwellings blocked the view of these symbols of her love. More houses than she'd ever seen jammed the entire orchard aisle's length. Was this the Garden of Chara? So strange, it hurt her heart. The quiet *clip-clop* of hooves grew.

Livi had dreamed of being back in the Garden for one hundred fifty years, but the dream always included her children. Where were they? What were they doing? How were they doing? They had all obeyed the Lord and served him. Yet emptiness filled her, not joy. Livi bowed her head and wept.

"Excuse me, sister." A man's deep voice shattered her solitude.

She jumped.

"I'm sorry; don't be afraid. We still share with strangers. I saw you looking for the healing leaves." He held out a few thick green leaves. "My name is Horis. These are for you." The man led a grazer with a cart full of leaves.

She took the leaves. "Thank you, Horis. I'm Livi."

"Yes, Livi, named after the great mother. Are you all right?"

"I was just ... feeling out of place. How did you know?

"Your garb—that's unusual here. Some people would hold it against you, but not me, you understand. As they say, 'We're one blood.' Right?" He filled the red box with leaves and patted the box. "These are for the folks here." He motioned toward the surrounding homes.

"There's a process for handing out the leaves?"

"Of course, we can't have just anyone harvesting and dispensing such a precious gift."

"I suppose not." Livi took a bite of a leaf.

"Do you see these houses hold not just plants, but also food baskets for you."

"For me?" Livi turned and discovered brightly colored containers hung from the facades.

"We all provide for our neighbors. My work takes me all over Chara, but I never carry food with me, because something sumptuous is always nearby. Soon, hearths will fire up, and there will be savory hot foods for all. We share whatever we have, even crafts and artwork." He handed her a necklace set with small painted stones like the ones she often made. "You know the saying, 'We are their children'?"

Livi said, "I've never heard that. Whose children?"

Horis looked away and back at Livi. "How could you not know that? Our great father and mother had a feast every day and night at Hilltop Castle. They shared everything they had and taught us to do the same. We are *their* children."

A grin took over Livi's face. "What is the meaning of the carving on this red box?"

After an impatient huff, he said, "Every Erimean child knows the symbol of our salvation from when the great parents defeated the dragon and saved us from Earth's fate. Have you never been to a Salvation Day celebration?"

"I haven't."

Horis shook his head. "I must be going. May we see his face soon." He waited for Livi's response.

"I pray for that every day."

"Not what I was expecting you to say, but that is a worthy prayer." Horis departed.

Are these my children? Livi wondered. *These* are *my children. How wonderful. Thank you, Iam.*

Chapter Fifty-Six

Garden of Chara, Year 250, Marri, Day 1

Maris was now chairwoman of the council, which had grown to nine people. After a prayer, she brought the meeting to order. Lookout Station amphitheater consisted of a circular platform. The council sat at the front behind a white stone semicircular table. Grassy ground sloped up around the platform. Thousands of people sat behind the council members in tiered semicircular rows that curved in front of the platform.

Solis and Livi followed Hoshea and Aminta into the gathering and took seats on the ground near the back. Residents immediately recognized Solis and Livi as outsiders and treated them kindly, but with suspicion, because of their clothing.

Maris said, "My fellow citizens of Chara, we are here today to discuss matters regarding the gate of Neverway Passage and the distribution of the bounty from the trees of life. Matters of great import that affect not just those of us dwelling in the Garden of Chara, but the entire population of Erimea as well. Our responsibility is tremendous. After our scheduled set of speakers, you will be given an opportunity to briefly address the council. After the public meeting, the council will meet to make final decisions concerning these things. We ask you to be attentive and respectful of each speaker."

Geog, vice chairman of the council, controlled the meeting agenda. "Our first speakers are Stron and his wife Brilara, the first-generation children of our great father and mother. Welcome."

Stron and Brilara climbed several stone steps, took their positions behind a gray slab lectern perched on four stone pillars in the center of the platform, and faced the council members and Gardeners in attendance. Stron leaned forward and placed his hands on the lectern. "Thank you, Geog, Maris, and members of the council, for the opportunity to speak. We all know from the history of the Garden of Chara that one hundred fifty years ago, my father and mother, Solis and Livi, led Sojourners' Way out of the garden at the command of the Lord God to fulfill God's will that humanity multiply upon the face of this planet and subdue Erimea. My wife and I were part of that group, but we missed the Garden so much we returned to raise our family here. Yet, our siblings continued across this planet in obedience to the Lord."

Brilara stood beside her husband at the lectern. "In leaving Chara and filling Erimea, our siblings and our baba and mama did not give up their right to the blessings of the tree of life. They sacrificed a comfortable life for the Lord's will and for all of us. They blazed a path for us so that one day, we might also visit other parts of the world, find family, and receive a warm welcome. We should remember the children of Solis and Livi born in other parts of this world are not aliens. They are without question our family. We are of one blood. The closing of Neverway speaks a lie that claims they are other. A different people. If Neverway Passage remains closed, we are killing ourselves. My husband and I urge the council to order Neverway opened, never to close again."

Geog said, "Thank you, Stron and Brilara. Our next speaker is former councilman Anthros. Anthros, welcome."

Anthros took the lectern. "Thank you, Geog and council members. No one is disputing we are all descendants of the great mother and father. My concern is the cultural practices and belief systems that developed in different parts of the planet have made us different peoples and can be dangerous to us Gardeners. People this council has sworn to protect. We have heard some regions worship plants, animals, and even the sea and the sparkles. That terrible way of life has intrigued some of our young people. People in the north wield iron blades. We have heard they only understand power and will take what they want by force if we let them. In addition, whether we like it or not, the trees of life are in limited supply. We have the responsibility to manage that resource for the good of all Gardeners. I respectfully ask the council to let Neverway remain closed."

Five more leaders of various factions addressed the council until Maris said, "We have heard from all the scheduled speakers. Does anyone else wish to speak?"

Solis raised his hand. "Yes, Madam Chairwoman." He and Livi pushed through the crowd and ascended the podium. "My wife and I would like to speak."

Maris said, "Very well, please identify yourself."

"I am Solis, and this is my wife, Livi. We are your first parents."

The crowd began to murmur their disapproval. Some laughed.

Voices began to protest, "Impostors."

"Dismiss them, Maris."

"I stood near them, and they smelled funny."

Maris said, "Order, please. Order. Sir, from your animal skins, I see you are from the regions. How did you get into the Garden?"

"I came over Heaven Falls by way of Mornie's—"

"Ridiculous! Impossible," someone shouted.

The crowd grew more rambunctious.

Maris shook her head.

Livi yelled, "It's true. I came through from under Tall Stony." She pressed her palms on the lectern and leaned toward the crowd. "We came at God's command to save you from your fears. Listen to my husband."

Many in the crowd scoffed. "Under Tall Stony? Foolishness."

"Away with them."

"Let's go home."

Hoshea stood and hollered, "My friends. The prophecy said the great ones would come when Neverway is closed. I implore you, listen to them and then decide."

Maris said, "Quiet down, everyone. Go home if you wish, but this council will hear the strangers."

Geog said, "You heard Chairwoman Maris." He stood on the podium between Solis and Livi. "Order, please. We will respect the visitors and hear what they say."

Maris said, "Please proceed, sir."

Solis stood next to Livi at the lectern, with his head bowed. He rubbed his tired eyes. They had both aged after almost forty years without the healing leaves. The effort expended over the last two weeks had sapped his strength. Weariness came over him all at once. Solis lifted his head and looked at the crowd of thousands of strangers, more people than he had ever seen or imagined. His heart raced, and his hands trembled.

Livi wrapped her arms around her husband. "My dearest, are you all right?"

Solis glanced at his wife. "I'm overwhelmed with fatigue."

At that moment, Solis and Livi felt the loving arms of their children around them. Stron whispered, "Baba and Mama, we know it's you."

"You've come to help us just in time." Brilara spoke through tears. "Please speak to the people, Baba. Your children."

Solis nodded and breathed deeply. Not strangers. He spoke in a deep, resounding voice. "Maris, thank you for allowing us to address this council. I am Solis. I was once the caretaker of this garden, its ruler, its king. This is my wife, Livi. She is indeed the mother of all the living, my queen. But none of that matters now. We are like you, servants of the Lord. I ask you to listen to our son and daughter, Stron and Brilara, and open Neverway.

"My dear children—for you are all my children—one day soon, your population will grow beyond the capacity of the mountain walls of Chara, and many of you will journey into the rest of Erimea. God has commanded humanity to fill the planet. Won't you still deserve access to the tree of life? Living beyond these mountain walls doesn't change our right to the blessings of the Lord. At this moment, delegations are marching from Mid Seacoast and New Paradise Valley. Please open Neverway and receive them as brothers, sisters, and true neighbors."

Anthros rose from the crowd and dashed to the podium. "We shouldn't believe these imposters. They're not the great father and mother. Why are you wearing those filthy rags? What are you hiding?"

The crowd resumed complaining.

"Anthros is right."

"They don't look like any of the drawings of the real Solis and Livi."

"Where is your crown of gleaming black hair?"

"Show yourselves. What are you hiding?"

"We're not ashamed." Solis stripped off his garments, and Livi did the same.

"Look, she's armed with a belt of iron blades." Anthros backed away and interposed himself between Livi and the council. "An assassin. A threat to the council."

Livi raised her voice. "We're as innocent as all of you. Garments are commonly worn on the outside. This sword and knife are for slaying animals for food and self-defense against any mad beast. They've never been used against human beings."

"How do we know you're telling the truth? You're spies."

Aminta ran up onto the platform. "Look, everyone. She has the scar of the bloody stick on her chest, and he has the same scar on his back." She squealed and danced. "It is the great father and mother! I knew it. I knew it."

Many in the crowd began praising God. Some ran up on the stage and embraced Solis and Livi, exclaiming, "It's true. It's true," or, "We must listen to the great ones."

Stron said, "I tell you all, this is my father and mother."

Joy swept through the hearts of the council members, and they wept with delight, for they had all hoped to see the return of Solis and Livi, the first parents of Erimea.

Chapter Fifty-Seven

Chairwoman Maris celebrated and shouted, "This meeting is adj—"

"God's word is ..." rose the chant.

A chorus of voices responded, "a tree of life."

The Gardener crowd parted, and a group of thirty men and women marched up the platform steps and hugged Solis and Livi. They had no leaf baskets; instead, they wore woven, multi-colored bands around their heads, arms, and torso. Small boxes dangled from the bands, and tree of life leaves with markings were tucked into the bands.

The crowded rejoiced. "Hurray, for the Students. They will lead us."

A tall, bright-eyed man with wavy black hair led the Students and sang again, "God's word is ..."

The Students raised their fists and led the people in crying out, "A tree of life." The Students and the people chanted this repeatedly.

Maris pounded her gavel and yelled, "Efsevis, Efsevis, bring your people to order if you wish to address the council."

Efsevis waved his arms to silence the crowd. "Chairwoman Maris, with all due respect, I'm surprised your council failed to consult the Students before you submitted this question to novices in God's word."

Maris's face turned red. "The Gardeners chose this council to lead them. But please present your concerns to us."

Efsevis's lips curled into a half-smirk. "I meant no disrespect." He turned and bowed to Solis and Livi. "The Students are thrilled for the return of the great father and mother, but even they cannot know the consequences of opening the gate. Since the testing commenced, our work has grown in significance. The written word of God has eternal importance. The tree of life leaves impact this life only. The prophets entrusted their writings into the hands of the Students. We study the writings, practice the commands, make copies, and teach our people God's word. For some writings, there are currently no copies, only originals. We have no secure place to ensure the writings are protected and preserved for future Erimeans."

Solis narrowed his eyes. "Are you saying your brothers and sisters are a threat to your precious writings?"

"How can we be sure the outsiders will respect the word of God? We've heard all kinds of things about them as false worshippers, capable of great destruction."

Livi pointed at Efsevis. "My husband and I have walked with God longer than all your prophets. We are your first teachers."

"Yet, you've been gone a long time. You have no idea what God has revealed to the prophets." Efsevis pounded his chest. "*We* are the protectors of the word of God and the history of Erimea. We are the scribes who make God's ways known to all Gardeners."

Solis said, "It's been almost fifty years since the Lord has spoken to any of us. Why haven't you spread the word to the other regions? Why are you hoarding the word to yourselves?"

Efsevis groaned. "Making copies and teaching takes time. Travel is nearly impossible. Chairwoman Maris, how do we know these untaught citizens of other regions will respect the writings? We must have a plan in place to protect the writings. The great father and mother cannot understand the importance of God's word for those of us who have never heard or seen the Lord."

Solis turned and faced the council. "At this moment, delegations from Mid Seacoast and New Paradise Valley are on the march here. Why not welcome them with the words of life and the leaves of life?" Solis stared at Efsevis. "Stop being led by fear. Devils have bewitched your minds. You must resist the invisible forces of wickedness. Be generous with your outside family, and they will respond with gratitude and honor."

A woman stepped out from among the Students. "My name is Chari. Efsevis, maybe we were wrong. Standing in front of us are the son and daughter of God, flesh and blood, not stone tablets. Maybe we have failed to understand the application of some of the writings. Remember the most ancient sayings include, 'Do not fear.' and 'Love God and love your neighbor as yourself.' Shall we protect the writings and not practice what they say?"

Livi said, "Efsevis, if the Lord returns today, which will you esteem higher, the Lord or the writings?"

Another man stepped out from among the Students. "Madam Chairwoman, my name is Denis." Denis smiled lovingly at Maris. "What if the outsiders really are unlearned and wicked?

"Exactly," Efsevis said.

Livi shouted, "Wicked?"

Denis shook his head. "I mean, remember why we became Students. The writings about Earth's future history teach enemies may be converted if we go the extra mile. We should risk it."

"I have nothing more to say. You may avoid war and still betray the future." Efsevis glared at the council and wagged a finger. "The Students will hold you accountable if, by your decision, you put the word of God at risk." Then he strode away, leading most of his group with him.

Maris sighed and adjourned the public meeting, and the council moved to a private meeting space, but they requested Solis and Livi to wait outside.

Maris studied the other members of the council and exhaled. "What a day. The return of the great mother and father. I'm still quivering. And my grandson, Denis, made me so proud."

"Denis is a good man," Geog said. "I thought our decision concerned whether to share the healing leaves. But the Students raise a valid fear for the writings."

"If there is war, everything is at risk," Coura said.

Geog said, "If we open and they regard us as enemies to conquer, we lose without a fight. Their technology is superior, but our numbers are far greater."

Maris said, "Let's bring in the great parents."

After Solis and Livi were seated, Maris continued, "The council is still weighing our decision. We don't know the people from other regions. As you know, travel is treacherous."

Livi said, "We have taught our children from infancy to love God and to love others, and they have taught their children and grandchildren. That is the way of Erimeans."

Solis said, "The Lord calls us to be brave. Don't be led by fear. Being afraid is to be a puppet of the devil. My wife and I have withstood endless physical hardships and demonic attacks, and we have learned God designed humans to persevere with courage and kindness. That is the true nature of humanity, not the fear I've seen today."

The entire council stared at Solis in silence for several moments.

Maris said, "If we are to act with courage and compassion, the decision is easy for me. I say open Neverway."

The decision for some of the council members was not so easy. The vote was five to four. The Council of Nine ordered Neverway Passage opened. They met with the delegations and negotiated an agreement for sharing the fruit and leaves of the trees of life, and a research collaboration aimed at growing and caring for the trees in other regions of Erimea.

One month later, Solis and Livi strolled along Unstoppable Forest Trail, as they once loved to do.

The Lord God appeared. "Greetings, children."

They worshipped him. Solis sprang from the ground and threw his arms around the Lord. "Lord, it's wonderful to see your face again and to hear your voice."

"Praise you, Lord," added Livi.

"Solis and Livi, you have done well over these two hundred fifty years you have walked upon Erimea. You have advised your descendants, and they have chosen well. I will once again walk among the people, as I did formerly. Life on Erimea has only just begun. There is a long future yet to be fulfilled. Lucido and his angels have not given up. You all must remain vigilant to walk in my ways."

"We will, Lord. Tell us ... what has become of ... Talen"—Solis's voice broke—"Caressa, and Smallo."

The Lord took Solis and Livi into his arms. They leaned into their God and felt the warmth of his beating heart. "I've already revealed to you what has become of Talen. You both felt it in your hearts as though Piercer had struck you. As for Smallo and Caressa, they served you and me by planting the tree of life seeds throughout Erimea long before you came to Mid Seacoast. You will learn more of their story at the proper time."

Livi said, "What's all the fuss about writings and prophets? Now that we have you again, Lord, we don't need any of that."

"My child, you don't understand. In the distant future, Erimeans will no longer need to see me to walk with me. They will be filled with the Holy Spirit, and they will accomplish amazing things. The writings will be a tool of the Holy Spirit. In those days, I will no longer appear visibly to your children."

"May it never be," Solis said. "Not seeing you breaks our hearts."

"Don't be afraid. That time is thousands of years in the future, when Erimeans have grown mature. It will be a wonderful future, though not without great challenges."

Chapter Fifty-Eight

Garden of Chara, Year 260, Shap, Day 7

One afternoon, Solis found Livi working alone on the mural she had begun two hundred sixty years earlier, when they first made Hilltop Castle their home. "What are you working on, my darling?"

Livi said, "I've been thinking back over our lives and all the Lord has done for us. But I wish I had done one thing differently."

Solis became completely still. "That's amazing. I was thinking about one regret I have too. We've grown so much alike."

"We've had a wonderful life. What is your regret?"

"First, tell me what you would have done differently."

Livi smiled. "Let me finish what I'm working on, and then I'll show you."

"Then, I'll also tell you my one regret."

Two days later, Solis climbed the main steps of Hilltop Castle, carrying a new walking stick.

Livi called Solis over to the mural. "Come, I'm finished. Let me show you. What do you see?"

"I see the Lord carrying a figure. It must be you, because I see the scar above your heart. You have something in your hand. You've painted a large blue circle above, and the Lord is carrying you to it."

"Yes, my dearest. This circle is the Earth, and I'm holding the bloody stick. A long time ago, the Lord showed me a vision of Earth. He called on me to take up the bloody stick and go help my twin sister, Eve, but I was afraid I would fail, and I was afraid to leave you behind. I begged the Lord not to make me go, and the Lord relented. I'll always love you, but now—"

"Look." Solis held up the walking stick, stained with red blood. At the top was a carving in the shape of sneaking thing. "We both had the same vision, and we were both afraid." Solis hugged his wife and wiped a tear from his eye. "I'm still afraid, but finally I have the courage to leave even you behind and do the Lord's will."

"Yes, my dearest. After all we've been through, we found the strength we needed."

"May the Lord send us to Earth together. Maybe it's not too late to help." They knelt and prayed.

The Lord appeared to them. "I have heard all you have said, and I'm very pleased with you. But you have already learned the lesson of what it means to be like God, and you have achieved that goal. There is no need for you to take on new burdens. I will send another to help Earth. That man will be a son of Adam. Be at peace. There is still hope for the children of Adam and Eve."

Solis said, "Lord, I was full of fear, but part of me wanted to embrace Earth's people. Will we never see it?"

"You will not see Earth in this life, but I promise you, many generations from now, the descendants of Solis and Livi will develop the technology to travel between the sparkles through interstellar space and one day reach Earth. If your descendants cling to my ways, they will walk on the Earth with the descendants of Adam and Eve."

Livi said, "Thank you, Lord. We're satisfied."

Chapter Fifty-Nine

Garden of Chara, Year 365, Shap, Day 5

Solis and Livi's dream of helping people on Earth eventually became a worldwide aspiration in Erimean hearts, celebrated with an annual holiday called Interstellar Mission Day.

Early in the morning, Solis and Livi sat on the terrace of Hilltop Castle. Solis pointed toward the sky. "Once, I wanted to touch the sparkles, but now I know the struggle of merely crossing a portion of Erimea." He crossed his arms and leaned back. "Now, these children dream of space travel. Seems like an impossible dream."

The Lord spoke to Solis. "My son, all things are possible with God. But soon you will see wonders beyond the sparkles and all things of this world. You have completed your course. The time of your departure has come. Tonight your soul will be filled with joy and longing, but I will satisfy your hearts. Tomorrow morning, assemble your family and meet me at Neverway Passage."

Livi gazed into the sky with her hands raised. "Lord, will you take my husband and leave me behind?"

"Your time has not yet come."

Livi fell on her face and implored the Lord. "If I've been found worthy in your sight, please take me when you take my beloved husband."

"You are worthy."

The next morning, all the residents of Chara gathered at Neverway Passage. They wept and said goodbye to Solis and Livi. Animals converged as they had when God created the man. The ground shook as a herd of unstoppables came rumbling and trumpeting for the occasion.

Before the Lord appeared, he spoke to the Father and the Holy Spirit. "Shall I show them our glory?"

"Show them a portion."

Lord God, adorned in majesty and dignity and clothed in glory and splendor, appeared.

Every creature, human and beast, became weak and fell to the ground because of the brightness of his appearance.

"These two shall enter our imperishable paradise," the Lord declared, "the first of many Erimeans whose bodies will not see corruption." One day, he would strip off the glory of godhood to bring all the children home. The time of his suffering would come, but now was a time for celebration.

"Arise." The Lord strengthened every creature, so they were able to stand in the glory of his presence. "None of you will walk upon Erimea forever. At the proper time, all who are faithful will be gathered to be with me eternally. Today, your great father and mother depart Erimea never to return. Honor their memory."

Solis and Livi stood by the Lord, one on the left and the other on the right. He took their hands, and all three rose into the air until the clouds hid them. The people cheered and praised God as they watched in amazement.

As Solis, Livi, and the Lord rose into the clouds, Solis said, "Tell us the stories of our children. Talen and Daylig and the Great Blue Sea. How the inventions of Damaro and Mornie changed the world, and how Smallo and Caressa have blessed Erimea. Tell us of the future. Will we destroy the tree of death? When will your Holy Spirit come upon the children? When will the people of the twin planets walk together? When will you gather all people to yourself?"

"Your questions are endless." The Lord laughed. "Did I not make you myself? Where shall I begin?"

"We missed so much," Livi said with her head bowed. She looked up, and her eyes beamed. "But you have kept every promise. Tell us what we missed from the day Sojourners' Way departed Chara. Every detail."

Chapter Sixty

Lucido settled into his throne in Aetherdon with Vik seated on his right and Iredin on his left. The three demons gazed through Ophthalmos and saw Earth. "Take heart, brothers, our domination of Earth is complete. Every soul born there falls into sin and becomes useless for God's intended purpose, and there is no one to redeem them. I will never understand why God thought so highly of these flesh and blood creatures, but we have proven our point. The Holy Spirit will never dwell in them, for they are unworthy of such a blessing.

Iredin spoke gloomily. "What of Erimea?" The scene in the eye on the worlds flashed to the second twin planet.

Lucido said, "It's just a matter of time. With one more vote on the council, we could now be enjoying the beginning of war on Erimea. Our approach with the Students almost worked. We will continue our efforts so that the greatest Erimeans will separate from the least of their number. So the wise glory in their wisdom, the mighty glory in their might, and the rich glory in their riches while forgetting the love of God and the kindness and justice due their neighbors. Humanity is still young in the universe. Their true nature will become evident in time, even to God Almighty. Until then, we have profitable work to do."

Vik said, "I suggest we continue to give special attention to the fourth twins of the first family, Smallo and Caressa."

"Agreed."

THE END

Author's Note

Thank you for reading *Paradise Unfallen*. Please take a moment to sign up for my monthly email newsletter at www.ChuckRichardsonStories.com You'll be the first to know about my new book releases. The newsletter includes articles about spiritual matters and various Bible-related topics. Please be sure to leave a review on Amazon.

Download the *Paradise Unfallen* short story prequel for free:

"The Birth of Rebellion": https://dl.bookfunnel.com/qy6vs4kxdy

Another novel by Chuck Richardson:

True Status (available on Amazon: https://www.amazon.com/True-Status-Chuck-Richardson-ebook/dp/B0CCT3S538/ref)

Follow me on:

Instagram: https://www.instagram.com/chuckrichardsonwriter/

Facebook: https://www.facebook.com/Chuck-Richardson-Stories-102476425056471

Pinterest: https://www.pinterest.com/rcrichardson2222/

Acknowledgements

Thank you to my wife, Ruby, for your constant love and support. I love you. I'm thankful we get to go through this life together.

Thanks to Larry Sanders, my friend and church elder. Thank you for the way you lead the flock under your care. Thanks for being my beta reader and for always encouraging my writing.

To Esther LoPresto, my editor, thank you for your expertise, kind guidance, and diligence in working through this manuscript. You challenged me to be a better writer and storyteller.

Thank you to the brothers and sisters at Newburg Church of Christ. You have been a tremendous support and encouragement to me in both my teaching and writing endeavors.

Don't miss out!

Visit the website below and you can sign up to receive emails whenever Chuck Richardson publishes a new book. There's no charge and no obligation.

https://books2read.com/r/B-A-IKHOE-QZFMH

BOOKS 2 READ

Connecting independent readers to independent writers.

About the Author

Chuck Richardson writes speculative fiction with a Christian worldview for people who question everything and seek truth, and he blogs about the Bible. Chuck is a former engineer, technical writer and freelance newspaper writer.

Chuck's debut novel, *True Status* (2023), was a 2024 Next Generation Indie Book Award finalist. Chuck believes the most important thing for everyone to learn is what God thinks about them. His writing explores questions about sin, redemption, sanctification, and the battle between good and evil. Chuck's second novel, *Paradise Unfallen*, imagines a world where the first parents did not sin.

Chuck was born and raised in Rome, New York. He always loved reading and writing and even considered majoring in English in college, but practicality won out and he earned a BS in Mechanical Engineering and a Master of Education degree. Over the years, Chuck pursued his interest in writing as a freelance writer for a Black community newspaper and a local business newspaper, editing newsletters for a Friends of the Library group and for a professional association. Chuck considers himself to be an educator, so after fifteen years as an engineer for two large manufacturing companies, he changed careers to work as a quality management consultant and trainer in which he endeavored for eighteen years.

Chuck now lives in Louisville, Kentucky with Ruby, his wife of over thirty-eight years. They have two adult daughters, Brittany and Jillian. Chuck was a Curriculum Developer for a company that produces e-learning technical training materials in Southern Indiana until he retired in March 2023. Chuck's position combined technical writing and being a subject matter expert.

Chuck has served as an elder, deacon, and teacher in the churches of Christ for more than thirty-five years. He is a passionate believer in Jesus Christ. Chuck enjoys teaching adult Bible classes and especially likes helping teachers become better teachers.

Chuck enjoys doing yard work, and before he began spending most of his free time reading and writing, he tried to complete one or two woodworking projects each year. He ran track and cross-country in high school and is still interested in sports, watching college and professional basketball and football games now and then.

Read more at https://chuckrichardsonstories.com/.

www.ingramcontent.com/pod-product-compliance
Lightning Source LLC
LaVergne TN
LVHW090554110826
845146LV00001B/124
* 9 7 9 8 9 9 2 7 2 5 8 1 0 *